Praise for Annelise Ryan and *Working Stiff*

"Sassy, sexy, and suspenseful, Annelise Ryan knocks 'em dead in her wry and original *Working Stiff.*"
—Carolyn Hart, author of *Dare to Die*

"Move over, Stephanie Plum. Make way for Mattie Winston, the funniest deputy coroner to cut up a corpse since, well, ever. I loved every minute I spent with her in this sharp and sassy debut mystery."
—Laura Levine, author of *Killer Cruise*

"Mattie Winston, RN, wasn't looking for excitement when she became a morgue assistant—quite the contrary—but she got plenty and so will readers who won't be able to put this book down."
—Leslie Meier, author of *Mother's Day Murder*

"*Working Stiff* has it all: suspense, laughter, a spicy dash of romance—and a heroine who's guaranteed to walk off with your heart. Mattie Winston is an unforgettable character who has me begging for a sequel. Annelise Ryan, are you listening?"
—Tess Gerritsen, *New York Times* bestselling author of *The Keepsake*

"Matty is klutzy and endearing, and there are plenty of laugh-out-loud moments . . . her foibles are still fun and entertaining."
—*Romantic Times*

"Ryan, the pseudonym of a Wisconsin emergency nurse, brings her professional expertise to her crisp debut . . . Mattie wisecracks her way through an increasingly complex plot."
—*Publishers Weekly*

Books by Annelise Ryan

SCARED STIFF

WORKING STIFF

Published by Kensington Publishing Corp.

Working Stiff

Annelise Ryan

A Mattie Winston Mystery

KENSINGTON BOOKS
http://www.kensingtonbooks.com

KENSINGTON BOOKS are published by

Kensington Publishing Corp.
119 West 40th Street
New York, NY 10018

All Kensington titles, imprints, and distributed lines are available at special quantity discounts for bulk purchases for sales promotion, premiums, fund-raising, educational, or institutional use.

Special book excerpts or customized printings can also be created to fit specific needs. For details, write or phone the office of the Kensington Special Sales Manager: Attn. Special Sales Department. Kensington Publishing Corp., 119 West 40th Street, New York, NY 10018. Phone: 1-800-221-2647.

ISBN-13: 978-0-7582-3453-7
ISBN-10: 0-7582-3453-8

First Kensington Books Trade Hardcover Printing: September 2009
First Kensington Books Mass-Market Paperback Printing: August 2010

10 9 8 7 6 5 4 3 2 1

Printed in the United States of America

This one is for Ryan Douglas, my best production ever.

Acknowledgments

Warm thanks go to Jamie Brenner, my agent, and Peter Senftleben, my editor, for believing in me and making this happen. You guys rock my world. Thanks, too, to Doug Clegg, for keeping my flagging spirits up and pushing for Mattie every time I was ready to give up on her. To my family, thanks for all your loving support and faith in me, for understanding why I sometimes become a social recluse so I can write, and for being my best promoters.

And finally, a hearty thanks to all the family, friends, coworkers, and miscellaneous acquaintances in my life who ever made me laugh, especially those of you who share my warped and occasionally dark sense of humor. Laughter truly is the best medicine and this book is my small way of trying to return the favor.

Chapter 1

I'm surprised by how much the inside of a dead body smells like the inside of a live one. I expected something a little more tainted, like the difference between freshly ground hamburger and that gray, one-day-away-from-the-Dumpster stuff you get in the discount section at the grocery store. Of course, all I've seen so far is the freshly dead, not the deadly dead. Apparently the deadly dead can invade your nostrils with molecules of nasty-smelling stuff that clings and burns and threatens to make you vomit for days afterward.

Or so says Izzy, and he should know since cutting up dead people is what he does for a living. And now, so do I. It's only my second day at it, but I can already tell it's going to be a real conversation stopper at cocktail parties.

At the moment, we are standing on opposite sides of an autopsy table with a woman's body laid out between us, her torso looking as if it's just been filleted. I'm sure we create a strange tableau, and not just because of the open corpse. Izzy and I are the yin and yang of body types—the Munchkin and the Amazon. The only thing we have in common is a tendency to put on the pounds: Izzy is nearly as wide as he is tall, and I'm cursed—or blessed, depending on your perspective and what century you were born in—with the perfect metabolism for surviving long periods of hunger. My body is a model of energy efficiency, burning calories the way a miser on a pension burns candles.

But that's where our commonalities end. Izzy is barely five feet tall, while I hit the six-foot mark at the age of sixteen (though I tell anyone who asks that I'm five-foot-twelve). Izzy has a dark, Mediterranean look while I'm very fair: white-blond hair, blue eyes, and a pale complexion, though not nearly as pale as the woman on our table.

Izzy reaches over, hands me the woman's liver, and asks, "So, what do you think so far?" He sounds a little concerned, which isn't surprising. This job takes a bit more getting used to than most.

"Think? I'm trying not to think." I place the liver on the scale beside me and record the result on my clipboard.

"Aw, come on. When you get right down to it, is this really all that different from what you were doing before?"

"Uh, yeah," I answer in my best *duh!* tone.

"How so? You used to cut people open. You handled their insides. You saw blood and guts. It's pretty much the same, no?"

Hardly. Though it's been a mere two months since I traded in the starched white lab coat from Mercy Hospital that had my name, MATTIE WINSTON, RN, embroidered across the pocket, at the moment it feels like an eternity ago. This is nothing like my work in the OR. There, the patients' bodies were always hidden behind sterile drapes and waterproof shields, the field of focus nothing more than an iodine-bronzed square of skin and whatever lay directly beneath it. Most of the time I never even saw a face. But this . . . not just a face but the entire body, naked, ugly, and dead. And there's no poor-man's tan here. These people are the color of death from head to toe. It's a bit of a mental adjustment. After twelve years of working to save people's lives, I now remove their innards after they're dead and weigh them on a scale like fruit. Not exactly a move *up* the career ladder.

"Well, for one thing," I tell Izzy, "my clientele used to be alive."

"Live, schmive," he says, handing me a spleen. "With all that anesthesia, they might as well have been dead. They didn't talk to you, did they?"

"Well, no, but—"

"So it's really no different, is it? Here, hold this back." He directs my hand toward a pile of lower intestine and sets about severing the last few connections. "I don't think it's this job that's bothering you. I think you miss Dr. Wonderful."

Dr. Wonderful is Dr. David Winston, who is not only chief of surgery at Mercy Hospital but also my husband, at least until I get the divorce papers filed.

"You do miss him, don't you?" Izzy persists.

"No, I don't."

"Not even the sex?"

"There's more to life than sex." I utter this with great nonchalance despite the fact that Izzy has hit a sore spot. During the last few months of my marriage, sex ranked just below plucking my eyebrows and cleaning out the toilet bowl on my list of things to do. Now that I no longer have the option—unless I want to don some stilettos and a tube top and cruise the streets—my libido seems to be growing by leaps and bounds.

Izzy shakes his head in wonder as he hands me a kidney. "See, that's the difference between men and women. Men, we always miss the sex."

"Good," I say bitterly. "I hope David is missing it like crazy."

"It doesn't look like he's missing it at all."

My heart does a funny beat, almost as if it's echoing the *uh-oh* that I'm thinking. I look over at Izzy but he's studiously avoiding any eye contact. "What the hell is that supposed to mean?"

He sighs and shakes his head.

"Do you know something, Izzy? If you do, spit it out."

"You mean you haven't seen the woman who's been coming over to your . . . to David's house the past few nights?"

His quick correction stings, but not as much as his information does. I've been consoling myself ever since the split-up with an image of David pining away for me . . . regretful, sad, and lonely. The only communication we've had since I left is one long rambling, remorseful note, in which David apologized exactly nine times and swore his undying devotion to me. Izzy's suggestion that my side of the marital bed had barely grown cold before someone else moved in to heat it up—and I have a pretty good idea who that someone else is—brings tears to my eyes.

"No, I haven't seen any woman," I tell him, struggling for a tone of casual indifference. "But that's because I haven't looked. It doesn't matter anymore. I don't care what . . . or who David does anymore."

"Oh, okay."

I can tell from Izzy's tone that he isn't buying it, but I'm determined not to ask him what I'm dying to know. We begin taking sections from the organs we've removed, Izzy doing the slicing and dicing, me placing the carved pieces into specimen bottles as an awkward silence stretches between us. As soon as we are finished with each organ, I place it back inside the body cavity. After several minutes of this I finally cave in.

"All right, you win. Tell me. Was it her?"

He shrugs. "I've never met her. What does she look like?"

His question hurls me back some two months in time and the memory, as always, triggers a flush of humiliation. Back then, David and I both worked in the OR at the local hospital. Despite working in the same place, we rarely did cases together, agreeing that it was wise to try to separate our professional lives from our private ones so the dynamics of one wouldn't interfere with the intimacy of the other. That's the story I bought into, anyway, though since then I've wondered if David's motivation was something else entirely.

Things came to a head on a day when David had a heavy

load of regular surgeries coupled with several emergency cases. He called late in the evening to say he still had one more case to do and that he planned to crash at the hospital for the night. It was something he'd done before—usually because he had an unstable patient he was worried about—so it didn't raise any alarms with me.

Knowing how much he hated hospital food, I threw together a goody basket for him: some munchies for later that night and some fruit and muffins for in the morning. I didn't call to tell him I was coming because I figured he'd already be in the middle of his surgery. Besides, I wanted to surprise him.

He was surprised, all right, but not half as much as I was when I found the surgical area dark, quiet, and apparently deserted except for a dim light emanating from a small operating room at the end of the hall. Inside the room I found David with Karen Owenby, one of the other surgery nurses. David was leaning back against an OR table, his scrub pants down around his ankles, a look of ecstasy stamped on his face. Karen was kneeling in front of him, wholeheartedly vying for the title of head nurse.

As the image sears its way across my brain for the millionth time, I squeeze my eyes closed in anger.

"Is she really *that* ugly?" Izzy asks, glancing at the expression on my face.

"Uglier," I tell him. "She has horns growing out of her head and snakes for hair."

Izzy chuckles. "You know what you need?"

"For Richard Gere to fall madly in love with me and be my gigolo?"

"No, you need some excitement."

Apparently catching my husband taking his oral exam in the OR isn't excitement enough.

"Yep," Izzy says with a decisive nod. "You just need a little excitement. After all, isn't that what drew you to medicine? The life-and-death pace, the high emotional stakes, the drama?"

We are done with our sampling and the woman's organs are all back in her body, though not in any kind of order. I stare at them a moment, thinking they vaguely resemble that package of stuff you find hidden behind the ass flap on a turkey. It's a definite offense to my surgical sensibilities and I have to remind myself that it doesn't matter—the woman is dead.

"I think I've had quite enough drama for one lifetime," I tell him.

"No way. You're an adrenaline junkie. You thrive on excitement. That's why you liked working at the hospital." He steps down from the stool he has to use in order to reach the table, kicks it toward the woman's head, and climbs up again. Then he positions his scalpel just above her right ear.

"There's really not *that* much adrenaline in the OR," I argue. "In fact, it's one of the tamer areas of medicine, orderly and controlled."

"True, but you were never happy in the OR. The place where you were happy was the ER. You should have stayed there."

"I liked the OR just fine," I argue.

He responds with a look that tells me the alarm on his bullshit detector is screeching. And I have to admit, he's right. The OR was okay, but I *loved* working the ER. I loved the surprise of never knowing what might come through the door next. I loved working as part of a synchronized team, rushing against the clock in an effort to save a life that hung on the brink. I loved the people, the pace, and even the occasional messiness of it all. The only reason I'd left it for the OR was so I could be closer to David.

Well, that and the infamous nipple incident.

"Okay," I concede. "Maybe I am a bit of an adrenaline junkie."

"And like any junkie, if you don't get a fix from time to time, you get edgy and irritable."

"I'm pretty sure that's PMS, Izzy."

"So I have an idea," he says, ignoring my brilliant rejoinder. Having sliced across the top of the woman's head from one ear to the other, he now grabs the front edge of this incision and pulls the entire scalp forward, exposing the skull. It is shiny and white except for a large clot of blood that clings to the right temporal lobe. From the X-rays we did earlier, I know that beneath that clot we'll find pieces of broken bone and an indentation in the skull that's roughly the same size and shape as a hammer—the weapon her drunken, jealous husband used to kill her.

Izzy pauses to snap a few pictures with the digital camera, and then says, "Part of my job is determining the cause and manner of any suspicious deaths in the county, and only part of that is gleaned from the autopsy. There's also investigative work that needs to be done at the scene of the death and afterward."

He sets the camera aside and folds his arms over his chest. "You know, your position here can go one of two ways. You can keep working as a morgue assistant, which is basically what you're doing now, or you can function as a deputy coroner, which combines the morgue duties with investigative work. My last assistant had no training in forensics and no interest in learning it. He simply wanted to do his job and get out of here."

"I can't imagine why," I mutter, eyeing the body before us.

"But you have an analytical mind and a strong curiosity. With a little training, you'd make a great investigator. And frankly, I could use the help. I think you should give it a try, go out with me a time or two and see what it's like."

"You make it sound like a date."

He scoffs. "Yeah, like you would know."

I scowl at him. "Give me a break. It's only been two months."

"And you've spent every minute of it hibernating in your cave."

"I'm healing."

"You're wallowing."

"I am not."

"No? Then tell me how many pints of Ben & Jerry's you've polished off in the past two weeks."

"Oh sure, make me measure in pints so the number will sound worse than it is."

"Okay," he says, arching one eyebrow at me. "Have it your way. Tell me how many *gallons* of Ben & Jerry's you've polished off in the past two weeks."

"Bite me, Itsy."

There's one other thing Izzy and I have in common—a fondness for nicknames. Izzy's real name is Izthak Rybarceski, a mouthful of syllables that even the most nimble linguists tend to stumble over. Hence the nickname, though even that gives him trouble at times. Because of his size there are some who insist on pronouncing it as Itsy, something that drives him up the wall.

For me the problem is just a general loathing of my real name. I don't know what the hell my mother was thinking when she chose it and even she has never used it. All my life I've been Mattie—the only place where my real name can be found is on my birth certificate—and that's fine by me. Outside of my family, there are only a handful of people who know my real name, Izzy being one of them. So I have to be careful. If I pick on his name too much, he might turn the tables on me.

"I don't think I'd make a very good investigator," I tell him, hoping to divert his attention away from my insult.

"Sure you would. You're a natural. You're nosy as hell."

Now there's a bullet item I can't wait to put on my résumé.

"At least give it a try," he says with a sigh.

"But I don't know the first thing about crime scene investigation. Hell, I've only been doing this for two days."

"You'll learn. Just like you're learning here. Just like you learned when you started working in the OR. I'll send you to some seminars and training programs. You'll catch on."

I think about what he's suggesting. We live in Sorenson, a

small town in Wisconsin where the crime rate is low, longevity is high, and the obits frequently tell of octogenarians who die "unexpectedly." Even with what might come in from the surrounding areas, which is mostly villages and farmland, I can't imagine us getting *that* much business. After all, this is Wisconsin, the land of cheese, brown-eyed cows, apple-cheeked people, and old-fashioned values. The only reason we have a medical examiner in Sorenson is because Izzy happens to live here and we are the biggest city within a hundred-mile radius, which isn't saying much, given that our population is only eleven thousand. So how often is a "suspicious" death going to occur? Still . . .

I'm about to argue the point one more time when Izzy says, "Please? Will you just give it a try? For me?"

Damn. His pleading face reminds me of what a good friend he's been to me, especially lately. I owe him.

"Okay, you win. I'll give it a shot."

"Excellent!" he says. "Though perhaps a bad choice of words for our line of business." He wiggles his eyebrows at me and I have to stifle a laugh, though not at his corny joke. At fifty-something, Izzy suffers from that wooly caterpillar thing that strikes so many men as they age. The hairs in his eyebrows are longer than many of those on his head, though there are a few in his ears and nose that look like they might catch up.

Moments later, my humor is forgotten as I place Ingrid Swenson's brain on my scale.

Chapter 2

I'm sitting in the small cottage I call home, reflecting on day number two of my new job. Invariably, my thoughts drift to David and I wonder if Karen Owenby is the woman Izzy saw visiting him. The mere mention of her name fills my mind with murderous thoughts, yet as bitter as my feelings toward Karen are, they're nothing compared to what I feel toward David. His betrayal devastated me.

After catching him in the act on that fateful night, I drove home, threw together some clothes, and fled the house so I wouldn't have to face him again. But I didn't know where to go. I briefly considered heading to my mother's house, but realized that would be a big mistake. My mother is a lifelong prognosticator of gloom and doom, a modern-day Nostradamus. Five minutes with her can induce a severe case of depression in me even when I go into it on the highest of highs. And on the night in question, I was already as low as I cared to go.

In addition to her role as the Great Depressor, Mom is also a professional hypochondriac. She's a full-fledged, card-carrying, many-times-honored member of the Disease of the Month Club and revels in sharing her various aches, pains, and possible terminal diseases with David and me. She has a collection of medical reference books at home that the Harvard Medical School would envy, and getting a doctor into the family has been the pinnacle of her existence. I knew she'd never forgive me for letting David go. Nope, Mom was definitely out of the question.

I then considered my sister, Desiree, who, after a childhood of sibling rivalry and creative tortures, has become my best friend. But Desi thinks of marriage as a sacred, inviolable institution. I feared she would try to convince me that mine was worth saving no matter how grim it had become and that I just might cave under the pressure. Or worse, I might say something about *her* marriage that I'd later regret. Not that her marriage is in trouble—as far as I know, it's doing just fine. But I can't stand Desi's husband, Lucien. He's a lawyer, a good thing I think, since he's a walking, talking sexual harassment suit waiting to happen. Half the words coming out of his mouth sound like dialogue from a bad porn movie and he's been known to pop a chubbie over anything that has, as he so indelicately puts it, "two pairs of lips."

Then there's the matter of Desi's two kids, Ethan and Erika, who sometimes seem like the perfect poster children for birth control. Erika is twelve, and if she isn't actually the devil's spawn, she does a damned good imitation. She's weathering the hormonal storm of adolescence and is as emotionally stable as a crack addict quitting cold turkey. Desi doesn't seem bothered by the wild outbursts, the sullen attitude, the constantly dyed hair, or the nose piercing. She says it's just a phase, though personally, I think Erika is a by-product of the curse crazy old Mrs. Wilding cast on Desi back when we were kids and Desi peed in the old woman's flower garden.

Ethan on the other hand, could be a sweet kid—*is* a sweet kid, I suppose. He's nine and still at an age where he's willing to hug and doesn't think he knows everything. But I can't get used to this fascination he has with bugs. Real ones. *Live* ones. When he sees a bug he gets this wide-eyed, eager expression—almost like a hunger—and within seconds, he's on it. Every time I see the kid he's got some kind of multilegged crawly thing with him—often as not, *on* him. Desi thinks it's cute. I just think it's creepy.

Having ruled out my family as safe havens, I turned to Izzy. We've been friends for more than a decade and I knew I could trust him to be horridly honest but nonjudgmental—exactly what I needed. Plus, he and his partner, Dom, love to dish dirt and I had two candidates who were ripe for the picking.

Dom, who is twelve years younger than Izzy and several inches taller, is auburn-haired, lily white, and slender. His eyes—an unusually deep shade of blue rimmed with long, thick lashes that any woman would envy—are his most distinctive feature. He's a born actor and, prior to meeting Izzy, he tried his luck in both New York and Hollywood before giving up and heading back home to Wisconsin. Nowadays, he keeps house for Izzy and limits his acting forays to a local thespian group.

Since Dom and Izzy are not only my friends but also my neighbors, it took me all of two minutes to throw my suitcases into my car and drive to their place—twice as long as it would have taken me to walk over. Dom answered the door, took one look at my tearstained face, and ushered me into the kitchen. He shoved a box of tissues in front of me, hollered for Izzy, and then busied himself making tea.

Izzy walked into the room, looked at me, and said, "Uh-oh. What's the jerk done?"

"The worst possible thing," I sobbed.

Dom turned around from the stove, slapped a hand to his cheek, and looked aghast. "Oh, no! You mean he wore plaid with stripes again?"

I laughed despite my misery. "No, it's much worse than that. He had sex with someone else."

"That bastard!" said Dom.

"Are you sure?" said Izzy.

"Oh, yes," I said, wincing. "I'm quite sure. I caught him in the act."

"What a fool," Izzy said, and for a brief moment I was flattered by the thought that Izzy considered me enough of a catch that David had to be an idiot to look elsewhere. But then he added, "How stupid is it to do it right in your own house?"

"It wasn't in the house," I said, pausing to inhale some steam from the tea Dom set in front of me. "It was at the hospital. In one of the operating rooms."

"Eeeewwwww," Dom said, making a face. "Aren't those rooms supposed to be sterile?"

"Supposed to be," said Izzy. "But you'd be surprised what goes on there. A few years ago I heard about a doc who was caught trying to use a suction machine to—"

"Hey, guys," I interrupted. "Can we get back to the subject at hand please?"

Dom jumped in with "It was a hand job?"

"No," I said, giggling. "It was a blow job."

"Oh, well that changes everything," Izzy said. "Blow jobs haven't been considered sex since the Clinton administration."

For the next hour and a half, I sat at their kitchen table alternately sobbing, laughing, whining, and listening as Izzy and Dom called David any number of nasty names and cast a host of colorful curses on his wandering, one-eyed trouser snake. By the time they got around to declaring Karen a whoring bitch and me a selfless heroine horribly wronged, it began to feel like one of those religious revival sessions. Several times I was tempted to holler "Amen!" at the end of a particularly rousing criticism or curse.

The fun didn't last long, though. The hard reality of my situation kept creeping back into the forefront of my thoughts—that and the ominous silence of Izzy's phone. In my mind, I kept imagining David frantic with worry once he realized I wasn't home. I felt certain he'd be desperate to find me, to try to explain himself, or maybe even apologize. And I figured it wouldn't take him long to figure out where I was. He knew Izzy and I were close friends, so I was pretty certain that once he determined I wasn't with my mother or my sister, he'd check Izzy's place.

But he didn't. There was no knock on the door, no ringing of the phone, and when I finally gave in and called my mother to tell her not to worry, I discovered David hadn't called there either. Curious, I called home, and when David answered I quickly hung up, stung by the truth of my situation. He was there, he knew I was gone, and yet he'd done nothing to try to find me or talk to me. That hurt almost worse than his infidelity. Everything I had come to believe about my relationship with him, about my life and my marriage, was a lie.

And I still had no place to go.

That's when Izzy came to the rescue. There was a cottage behind his house that he'd had built a few years ago for his mother, Sylvie. At the age of eighty-something, Sylvie's health had taken a turn and Izzy didn't want her living alone. But she was none too keen on living with her son as long as Dom was around. While Sylvie is well aware of Izzy's lifestyle, she isn't particularly happy about it. The mere sight of Dom always makes her clutch at her chest and let forth with a melodramatic *"Oy!" Living* with Dom would probably trigger a rapid battery of *oy*s that would either kill Sylvie or make Izzy want to.

So Izzy compromised by building the cottage and hiring home nurses. After a year there, Sylvie's health improved and she moved into a retirement village where she's still *oy*ing strong. I'm sure she'll die "unexpectedly" at the age of a hundred and something.

Sylvie's defection meant the cottage was empty, furnished, and available. Given my circumstances, it would have been foolish of me to refuse Izzy's offer to let me stay there. Of course, the tiny detail that the cottage is a mere stone's throw from my own house is something I chose to ignore. Besides, it isn't as if I'm *right* next door. We live in a swanky neighborhood where most of the houses sell for half a mil or more and the wooded lots are big enough to erect a good-sized parking lot. All I can see of my house from the cottage is a small section of the roof.

The cottage was meant to be a temporary way station, though so far, "temporary" had lasted a little over two months: sixty-seven days of hiding away and wallowing on my pity pot. And despite what Izzy thinks, I have a very good reason for hiding. Small towns aren't particularly conducive to privacy. Fart with your windows open and the news will likely make it across town faster than the wind can carry the smell. Sorenson is no exception, and given that several people witnessed my hysterical flight from the OR with David chasing after me as he struggled to do up his pants, I have little doubt that most of the townsfolk know every sordid detail.

I finally surfaced from my self-imposed exile a few days ago, and that was because I had to. I'm broke. The pitiful severance pay I had the hospital mail to Izzy's address—four weeks of accrued vacation time that I used as notice so I wouldn't have to show my face at work again—is almost gone. I've spent the bulk of it on essential food items like chocolate and cheesecake, though a few bucks (as Izzy well knows) have gone toward counseling from my two favorite therapists: Ben & Jerry. And another month of rent is due soon—not that Izzy would toss me out if I didn't pay—hell, he's willing to let me stay in the cottage indefinitely for free. But pride is about the only thing I have left at this point and, warped as it is, setting up house in a Frigidaire box seems preferable to taking a handout.

I'm just as determined to avoid asking David for help. Our checking account is a joint one and the checkbook is in David's desk at home. All of the credit cards are in his name, too, and while I don't think David is mean enough to freeze all the accounts, I can't be certain. And I sure as hell don't want to risk further humiliation by going to the bank to find out. Besides, trying to sneak a few measly bucks here and there isn't my style. I want to earn my money fair and square and with my pride intact—by nailing David's ass to the wall in a highly messy divorce proceeding.

Once again it was Izzy who saved the day, this time by offering me the job as his assistant. While the actual work it entailed did give me pause, I knew I couldn't afford to be picky. When I tried to think about nonmedical jobs I had enough training for, the only thing I came up with was prostitution. And then I realized that, in one way, the clientele at this new job were perfect: they were probably the only people in town who didn't know the sordid saga of David and me.

So thanks to Izzy I have a new job and a new home. I have a chance to start over and leave a painful past behind. And as I sit here looking out the window at the distant flash of headlights from a car pulling into David's driveway, I tell myself I don't really give a rat's ass who might be visiting.

But I do. It's perverse and stupid and destined to cause me pain, but I have to know.

Which means there is at least one other job I qualify for: that of the village idiot.

Chapter 3

I'm not sure what haute couture dictates for night spying, but it really doesn't matter since my choices are severely limited. In my hasty flight from the house two months ago, I shoved what I could into a couple of suitcases. Several times I've thought about going back to retrieve more stuff—I still have my key, so it would be simple enough to get in, assuming David hasn't done something drastic like change the locks. But I'm afraid. Not of David, but of myself and the strength of my convictions. Loneliness is a powerful motivator.

Fortunately, the meager clothing I do have includes a pair of black slacks and a black turtleneck. Worried that my blond hair will shine like a beacon in the night, I'm delighted I also have a brown scarf among my absconded treasures. I dress, tie the scarf around my head, and then give myself a quick perusal in the mirror. I look like the bastard love child of Mrs. Peele and Zorro but it will have to do.

It's early October and the night air has a bracing bite to it. Halfway through the woods my nose starts to run and I swipe at it with my sleeve, leaving a shimmering slug trail that glistens in the light of the full moon. Soon I am standing behind a tree at the edge of Izzy's property, gazing across a wide expanse of yard at a lit window in what used to be my home. The blinds are drawn, but unless David or his new hussy has seen fit to replace them, I know there is a small gap on one side. David may be good at fixing people, but when it comes to household projects he is sadly inept. When he installed the brackets for the blinds—a project he insisted on doing himself so he wouldn't have to pay someone else—he got one of the brackets half an inch higher than the other. As a result, the blinds hang at an angle, leaving a narrow gap on one side of the windowsill.

I glance over at the driveway and see a gray BMW parked next to David's Porsche; Karen Owenby drives a gray BMW.

I make my way across the yard knowing the house is set far enough back from the road that no one driving by can see me. When I reach the window, the bottom of it looms tauntingly a foot above my head, and after trying a couple of jumps I realize I'll never get high enough long enough to see anything. Frustrated but determined, I skirt around the house and find a wheelbarrow in the backyard with a small pile of pine bark mulch in it. I steer it around front, park it beneath the window, climb atop the mulch, and peer through the glass.

David is sprawled on the couch in front of the gas fireplace, his legs extended in front of him, the amber light from the sterile flame dancing across his face and making his blond hair shimmer. I can tell he is restless; one foot keeps time to some imaginary beat and his face bears an expression of tired impatience. A shadow falls over him as a dark-haired figure steps up to the couch: Karen Owenby.

She doesn't look very happy—in fact, it looks as if she and David are having one hell of a row—and I try to find some solace in that even as I feel the last tenuous threads of my heart give way. Karen is pacing back and forth in front of the couch, pausing occasionally to wag a finger in David's direction. The house is too well built for me to hear what she is saying, but the shrill tone of her words is unmistakable.

She pauses a moment, hands on her hips, torso bent forward, her jaw flapping a mile a minute. And I see David's expression change; his brow draws down in anger, his eyes narrow to an icy glint. He pushes off the couch suddenly, making Karen backpedal so fast she nearly falls. David grabs her by the shoulders, and at first I think he is trying to keep her from toppling over. Then I realize he isn't steadying her, he's shaking her.

Karen's hand whips up and slaps his cheek so hard I can hear the *thwack* of skin against skin from outside. As David's face darkens, Karen spins away from him, grabs her coat from the chair, and hurries toward the front door. I spend a few seconds relishing the quickly reddening handprint on David's face before it dawns on me that Karen is leaving and that I'll be in plain sight from the front porch should she happen to glance in my direction.

What's more, David is right behind her.

Panicking, I step back to climb out of the wheelbarrow, misjudge the distance, and hit the edge of it instead, tipping it over. My legs straddle the bed like a saddle and I come down hard on the edge, sending a lightning bolt of pain from my crotch all the way up to my teeth. For several agonizing seconds I am frozen, my teeth clenched tighter than a patient with lockjaw. I am unable to move, unable to breathe, and my ankle, which is half mangled in the metal framework beneath the bed of the wheelbarrow, throbs with a growing tempo. I bite back a scream that's trying to box its way out of my lungs and hold perfectly still, praying I won't be seen.

Above the ringing in my ears, I hear Karen yell, "You'll be sorry, David. Don't do it or you'll be sorry." David's only response is to slam the door. I watch Karen march down the driveway and climb into her car, and as soon as the engine turns over, I disentangle my foot and slide off the wheelbarrow into a heap on the ground.

The pain is incredible and I make a quick deal with God, promising to cut off my right arm if she'll just toss down a syringe full of morphine. Then I quickly amend that to my left arm, realizing I will need the right one to administer the shot. But either God has better things to do or the fact that I haven't been to church in twenty years has her feeling less than generous.

After a few minutes of quiet agony, I struggle to my feet and lurch home. I briefly consider running a bath and soaking for an hour or so to ease the aches, but it sounds like too much work. Besides, my injuries go beyond the mere physical; my emotions feel as raw and abused as my crotch.

Sleep beckons and I figure a night of rest will not only get me through the worst of the physical pain, it will allow me to bury my emotions inside a cloud of oblivion. I limp into the bedroom, strip my slacks and underwear off in one fell swoop, gingerly kick them away, and then ease myself into bed still wearing my shirt and bra. As my head hits the pillow, I feel something hard poke me. I reach up, pull a chunk of mulch from my hair, and toss it onto the floor. I'm about to turn out the light when it hits me.

I sit up and pat my head, even though I already know what I'll find . . . or rather what I *won't* find. Frantic, I look around the bedroom, but there is no sign of the scarf anywhere. Grunting with pain, I crawl out of bed and retrace my steps to the front door, peering through the window at the porch. Nothing.

Shit.

I pray the scarf dropped in the woods somewhere and isn't lying beneath the window next to the wheelbarrow. *Oh, God. The wheelbarrow!*

I groan and briefly consider going back to eliminate the evidence of my visit but the pain between my legs wins out. Morning will be soon enough, I decide. Instead, I gimp my way to the bathroom, swallow a handful of aspirin, and head back to bed.

I'm asleep in ten minutes flat; humiliation is very exhausting.

Chapter 4

The shrill chirp of a beeper brings me instantly awake. I sit bolt upright in the bed and reach over to turn on the light. Years of pulling on-call duty in the OR have trained me well, but for a second or two I'm confused. Part of my mind is telling me to get dressed and drive to the hospital, but another part reminds me that I don't work there anymore. Still another part wonders why it feels like I'm about to give birth to a bowling ball. Wincing against the pain, I hang my legs over the edge of the bed and grab the beeper.

It's Izzy. I know that without looking at the readout since he's the one who gave me the damned thing in the first place, in case he got a call. I mumble a curse, first at him, then at myself for being dumb enough to give in to his stupid idea.

Glancing at the clock I see that it's just past three in the morning—an inhuman hour by anyone's standards—and decide to ignore the page. I can't call Izzy anyway; I never bothered to have the phone turned on since my original plan was to stay in the cottage for no more than a few days. And I figure if I don't show up, Izzy will just go on without me. So I might as well go back to sleep. Pleased with my decision, I ease back into bed and pull the covers up. The next thing I know, Izzy is standing over me, shaking my shoulder.

"Come on, Mattie. Get up. We have a call. A homicide."

"I don't want a call," I whine, throwing off his hand and burrowing deeper under the covers. "And I sure as hell don't want a homicide."

"Yes, you do."

"No, Izzy. I assure you, I don't."

"Get up."

"It's three in the morning. Can't these criminals honor banker's hours?"

"Come on. Dom's making coffee, if that will help. It won't be so bad once we're there. You know how it is. Once you're up and moving, it's a piece of cake."

Easy for him to say. He doesn't have a hematoma the size of Texas in his crotch.

"Just go on without me," I tell him. "I'll catch the next one." He steps closer and starts to make a grab for my covers but I stop him cold by saying, "I'm naked from the waist down."

He backs up like I pulled a gun on him, his hands held out in front of him. "Fine, if you want to play hardball, I will too. If you don't get up, I'll start telling people your real name."

Moaning, I roll over, give him a dirty look, and sit up, feeling a million muscles scream in agony. My right leg, the one with the mangled ankle, is numb clear to the thigh.

He bends over, picks my pants up from the floor, and tosses them at me. "Put these on and let's go."

I stare at the pants a minute, my bleary mind still struggling to come fully awake. "How'd you get in here?" I ask.

"I have a key, remember? But that's beside the point since you didn't bother to lock the door." He eyes me warily a moment, then asks, "What the hell is that in your hair?"

I reach up and pull out several small pieces of mulch. Tossing them on the floor, I say, "New hair treatment. This herbal stuff is all the rage now, you know."

He stares at me, then shakes his head and turns away. "I'll be waiting in the living room. Hurry please."

I'm feeling cranky so I give a petulant stomp of my foot once for good measure, then swallow down a shriek of pain when I discover that my injured ankle isn't nearly as numb as I thought. Once the stars go out, I start pulling on my slacks and have my bad leg in before I realize I've forgotten my panties. I look around on the floor, don't see them, and figure they must be under the bed. Getting them will mean kneeling down, and I'm not too keen on that idea. As stiff as my body feels, I'm afraid I won't be able to get back up again, and the thought of having to call to Izzy for help while I'm on the floor with my naked ass in the air isn't very appealing. The dresser is across the room and I eye it for a second before deciding to go commando. At least I won't have to worry about unsightly panty lines.

Five minutes later I've plucked the rest of the mulch from my hair and we are on our way, Izzy behind the wheel. His car, a 1963 Chevy Impala, fully restored, has a bench front seat. In order to reach the pedals, Izzy has the seat up as far as it will go, which leaves me scrunched like a pretzel, my knees just under my chin. One good bump and I'll have teeth coming out my nose.

"What have we got?" I ask, finally awake enough to remember that my job now entails messing with dead bodies.

"A residential break-in, possibly a robbery. There's one victim—a woman."

I nod thoughtfully, as if such a scenario is a part of everyday business, but the truth is, Izzy's words strike fear in my heart. Things like this aren't supposed to happen in small-town America. I console myself with the thought that it probably happened in a bad section of town, the result of bad people doing bad things, like a drug deal gone wrong. But then Izzy pulls up in front of a house at the end of a cul-de-sac in an upper-middle-class neighborhood. Several police cars, an ambulance, and four or five other cars are parked willy-nilly out front, the darkened, quiet light bars on the official vehicles serving as a grim testament to the situation inside. On a nearby lawn, a small cluster of neighbors congregate, whispering and gawking.

After I climb out of the car, Izzy reaches over, opens the glove box, and removes a small, plastic wallet. He hands it to me and says, "Keep this with you at all times. You never know when it might come in handy."

I flip the wallet open and see an ID card with my picture on it—the same picture that is on my driver's license, I note. It identifies me as a deputy coroner for the county but lest there be any doubt, there is also a shiny, brass-colored badge in the wallet with DEPUTY CORONER written across the top in bright blue. Izzy obviously didn't waste any time once I agreed to go out on a call with him, and I'm tempted to act annoyed at his presumptuousness. But the badge is kind of cool looking and, in an odd way, it makes me feel important. So I hook the wallet in the waist of my pants with the badge showing and follow Izzy toward the house.

Normally, my long-legged stride puts me yards ahead of his stubby-legged one, but tonight it is all I can do to keep up. I think my bowling ball may be crowning and the numbness in my right leg is rapidly receding—something I'm not at all sure is a good thing. Izzy pauses on the porch, reaches into the black suitcase he is carrying, and hands me a pair of latex gloves.

"Put these on," he says. "Then stick your hands in your pockets and keep them there unless I ask you to do something. Don't touch anything."

I do what he says, thrusting my hands into my pants' pockets and trying to look like I know what I'm doing. A uniformed police officer meets us at the door, nods at Izzy, and then waves us into the house. Two steps later I catch my first whiff of death—a smell I've come to know during my years working the ER. It's a distinctly unpleasant scent, a mix of blood and other bodily excretes that are released when sphincters relax.

The house is a nice one, tastefully decorated in a contemporary fashion with thick carpet that cushions my aching feet. As we pass through a formal living room into a family room, I feel something odd near my injured ankle where the nerve endings are now rapidly coming to life. I glance down to see the bottom eight inches of my pant leg bulging on one side, as if my calf is sporting a woody. Only, this woody is composed of white cotton edged in elastic, a small portion of which is peeking out just above my shoe.

I've found my missing underwear.

After a quick glance around to be sure no one is watching, I do a little Riverdance maneuver and the panties slide the rest of the way out, settling on the floor between my foot and a nearby chair. I am about to snatch them up when I hear a voice say, "Hey, Izzy!" and sense someone approaching.

With one quick flick of my foot I kick the panties under the chair, and then look up to see who's coming. My eyes lock in on a tall man with a craggy but handsome face and a head of thick, black hair. He steps up to Izzy and briefly shakes his hand, then turns his gaze toward me. As I take in blue eyes, black lashes, and a stature of at least six-four, my heart rate speeds up a notch or two.

"This is Mattie Winston, my new deputy coroner," Izzy says, making the introductions. "Mattie, this is Detective Steve Hurley. He's with Homicide."

Kill me now.

"Pleasure to meet you," I say, extending a gloved hand over Izzy's shoulder and praying I won't drool. Hurley grabs my hand and gives it a brief squeeze. My face flushes hot, then the heat spreads. I wonder if Detective Hurley has ever investigated a case of spontaneous combustion before, or if I'm about to become his first.

"Have you ever processed a homicide scene before?" Hurley asks.

"No, I—"

"She's a nurse," Izzy says. "Worked at Mercy up until a couple of months ago."

I can't figure out if this is a good thing or not, or even what relevance it has. Apparently, neither can Hurley. His brows draw down in puzzlement for a second, but then he shrugs and says, "Whatever. Just be careful what you touch." With that, he turns away and heads toward a group of people huddled together in the middle of the room.

I steal a glance toward the floor, relieved to see that my panties are well out of sight, and then follow Izzy into the room as I wonder how I'm going to get the panties back. A second later, the huddle of people opens up to let Izzy through and all thoughts of my underwear flee my mind.

Lying on the floor in front of me with a bullet hole in her chest is Karen Owenby.

Chapter 5

I gasp, and everyone in the room turns to stare at me. Detective Hurley gives me a scathing look, which he then turns on Izzy. "Don't tell me she's never seen a dead body before."

"I've seen dead bodies before," I snap, like this is a good thing. "But I know this one. I mean, I knew her. That's Karen Owenby."

Hurley's eyes narrow.

Izzy looks at the dead woman, then at me, then back at her. "Are you sure?" he says, leaning close and whispering into my left breast. "I don't see any snakes coming out of her head."

I give him a shut-up nudge with my elbow and follow it up with the death-ray look I learned from my mother, which zips by harmlessly a good six inches above his head.

Hurley's eyes narrow even more, tiny slits with their own death rays emanating from them, straight in my direction. "How do you know her?" he asks.

"I worked with her at the hospital. She's a sl—a nurse in the operating room there."

Hurley turns and looks at one of the uniformed officers in the group, who nods at him.

Izzy grabs my elbow and steers me a few feet away. "This really is her?" he says in a low whisper.

I nod, too numb to speak. In my mind's eye I can see David shaking Karen by the shoulders only hours before, an expression of dark fury on his face.

"Look, if you'd rather wait outside, I'll understand. I didn't know . . ."

I swallow hard and consider his offer. But all my mind can focus on is the scene I witnessed earlier. Finally I shake my head. "I'll stay," I manage.

Izzy eyes me worriedly. "You sure?"

I nod again, this time with conviction. "Yes, I'm sure."

"Okay, then. Here's what we do."

Izzy first asks Hurley to walk us through what has happened so far. One of the uniformed officers, a guy named Larry whom I know from my days working the ER, explains that a frantic 911 call came in from this address, made by a woman named Susan McNally, the victim's roommate. Apparently Susan came home from a date and found the victim dead on the floor.

Larry then explains how he and another officer were the first to arrive and he tells Izzy everything they did to determine the victim's situation and secure the scene.

"This information is critical," Izzy informs me as he scribbles notes in a small pad, "in establishing what led up to the victim's death. Plus, we need to know everyone who might have had contact with the body. If we find any trace evidence that isn't from the victim, we need to be able to determine its source and its significance."

Izzy walks me through the process of identifying and establishing a perimeter around the body, which includes blood splatters that spread well beyond the immediate area. Someone, most likely the roommate, has already walked through one small pool of blood, tracking it through part of the house before the police arrived. Izzy carefully photographs the blood splatters, the footprints, and finally, the body itself. In addition to the pictures, he draws a sketch of the area in his notebook, showing the general layout of the room, what pieces of furniture are where, and the position and location of the body.

When this is finished, he removes a package from his suitcase that contains a folded, white, paper sheet, which, when opened to its full size, is some ten feet square. We lay it out alongside Karen's body so that when we turn her over onto it, any trace evidence that might be clinging to her body will be captured on the sheet, which will then stay with the body until it reaches the morgue.

Using rubber bands, we secure brown paper bags over Karen's hands, labeling them with the date and our initials. Izzy explains that this is to preserve any trace evidence that might be found on the hands or beneath the nails, and that paper bags are used rather than plastic ones to prevent moisture buildup, which can damage certain types of evidence.

As we work, Izzy points out certain details that will help us determine how long Karen has been dead. There is a flattening and clouding of her corneas, and while her skin feels cool to the touch, it still feels warmer than the ambient temperature in the room. Izzy shows me how to assess the degree of rigor mortis that has developed, which in this case, only involves the muscles of the face and jaw. We then turn Karen over onto the sheet and check her back, arms, and legs for livor mortis—a discoloration of the skin caused by blood pooling. This is complicated by the vast amount of congealing blood clinging to Karen's back. The bullet's exit wound is here too—a jagged hole three times the size of the entry wound.

After assessing all these factors, Izzy makes the pronouncement that Karen has been dead for at least two hours, but probably not more than four.

I get caught up in the technicalities and science of what we're doing, forgetting at times that this is the dead body of someone I knew and worked with for more than six years.

But every so often the realization that this cooling, empty shell of flesh is Karen Owenby hits me like a cold wave breaking over my back. It is impossible not to identify with her . . . to wonder if her death was instantaneous, or if she lay there a while knowing she was dying, unable to get help, hoping someone would find her.

I wonder who hated Karen enough to want her dead. A family member? An acquaintance? The roommate, perhaps?

David?

While we work, the people around us go about their own tasks, dusting surfaces for fingerprints, drawing sketches of the scene, taking photographs, and examining every square inch of the place. When we're finished with our examination, Izzy and I wrap the white sheet around Karen's body and slide her into a body bag. Two guys from the Johnson Funeral Home have been standing by, waiting for us to finish, and once we have the body bag loaded and closed, they hoist it onto their stretcher so they can carry it to the morgue. They've just started wheeling the stretcher toward the door when Hurley hollers out, "Hold it."

I turn to look along with everyone else and am horrified to see Hurley on his hands and knees in front of the chair that is hiding my underwear. With his gloved hand, he pulls the panties out and holds them gingerly between two fingers, looking at them as if they are some sort of toxic nuclear waste.

As my brain starts scrambling to figure out a way to either fess up to, or dismiss the significance of the underwear, Hurley places a finger inside each end of the elastic waistband and pulls it taut, holding the panties out for all to see. "Look at the *size* of these bloomers," he mutters, and from the look on his face, you'd think he was holding up the combined sails for the *Nina,* the *Pinta,* and the *Santa Maria.* A couple of the cops in the room snigger.

"I don't think they belong to the victim," Hurley continues, his brow wrinkling in puzzlement. "She's smaller than this and the lingerie I found in her dresser is all fancy stuff. Like from Victoria's Secret. These are kind of plain."

Maybe that's what drew David to Karen, I think. She had better underwear. I hear more sniggers from the bleacher section and suddenly fear everyone in the room can read my mind.

"And look how worn the elastic is," Hurley goes on. He tugs the waistband a few times to show just how far it can stretch. "Izzy, did you see any evidence that the victim was sexually molested?"

"Nothing obvious," Izzy says. "But I'll let you know for sure when I've completed her post." He hands me a paper sack and says, "Go bag those."

I am only too happy to oblige. I walk over to Hurley and grab the panties from his hand, stuffing them into the bag.

"Hey, careful with those," Hurley says. "They're evidence."

Yeah, evidence that I need to start a serious diet. I fold the top of the bag closed while I wonder what the penalty is for tampering with crime scene evidence. No way am I going to admit now that those panties are mine. And if I can figure out how to get away with it, this evidence is going to disappear.

I'm pondering my dilemma and following the funeral home stretcher out the door when Hurley grabs me by the arm. He holds me a moment, giving me a quick scan from head to toe. "There's something you're not telling me," he grumbles.

Shit. He figured it out. Took a gander at the broad beam of my ass and made the connection.

"What else do you know about Karen Owenby?" he asks, eyeing me suspiciously.

Oh, *that.* Well, there's the fact that she's a husband-stealing, skin-flute playing, two-timing slut, but I figure I probably shouldn't speak so unkindly of the dead. Frankly, I'm reluctant to speak at all, the scene I witnessed earlier between David and Karen still fresh in my mind. I've seen enough episodes of *Murder She Wrote* to know things aren't looking particularly good for David right now. And while I currently consider him a lower life form than pond scum, I don't think he's capable of murder. I need some time to sort things out.

Of course, all Hurley has to do is ask questions at the hospital and he'll know everything anyway. Gossip spreads through that place at warp speed, and by now it's likely even the dishwashers in the cafeteria know all the gory details, right down to the size and shape of the birthmark on David's Mr. Winkie.

"Well?" Hurley prompts.

"I think she's seeing my ex-husband," I offer as nonchalantly as I can.

Hurley's eyes narrow. "Ex-husband? You're divorced?"

"Might as well be. It's not final yet, but the papers have been filed. Well, sort of."

"Sort of?"

"I haven't actually filed them yet. But I'm going to."

Hurley scrutinizes my face for a moment and my ears start to feel really hot. "And you *think* this Owenby woman was seeing your husband?" he asks.

Oh, she's seen him all right. "I'm pretty sure they had a . . . relationship," I mumble.

"His name?"

"Whose?"

Hurley's eyes fire tiny arrows at me. Man, he's *good.*

"Winston," I tell him. "Dr. David Winston. He's a surgeon."

I see Hurley's mental wheels spinning and can practically smell the burning rubber. "How long you two been split up?" he asks.

"Couple of months."

"And how long has he been seeing this Owenby woman?"

"I'm not sure," I say. This answer is an honest one. I have no idea how long, or even if, David was seeing Karen before that fateful night in the OR.

Hurley cocks his head and gives me a funny look. It dawns on me that he might consider *me* a suspect—the woman scorned and all that—and I am about to act insulted when I remember that a murderous thought or two has crossed my mind in the past couple of months. One of the side perks of having a career where you're saving lives all the time is that it gives you an endless source of ideas on how to end them. I'd mentally exercised some of my more devious ones on Karen countless times.

Hurley whips a pen out of his shirt pocket and a little notepad out of his jeans pocket—mighty nice fitting jeans, I note—and scribbles something down. "What's your phone number?"

"I don't have a phone." The look he gives me suggests that I better not be lying.

"Do you have an address? Or do you live in a refrigerator box?"

I almost laugh at that one, but something tells me Hurley might take it the wrong way. So I give him my address—Izzy's address, actually, since the little guest cottage doesn't have one of its own. Then he asks for David's address. When I give him that, his eyebrows shoot up.

"You live next door to your ex?" he asks, askance.

"Sort of."

"That's a bit masochistic, don't you think?"

"Are you a detective or a shrink?"

"A little of both, actually," he says, flashing me a crooked grin.

I'm about to come back with another witty retort but I'm rendered temporarily speechless when my mind conjures up a vision of a psychiatrist's office with me stretched out on a couch and Hurley standing beside me. He bends down, his face moving closer to mine. . . .

"Anything else, Detective?" I ask, clearing my throat and putting my mental mini movie on pause. I'll store it for now and play the rest of it out later.

"Yeah. Given your, uh, proximity to this case, I think it would be best if you weren't involved with the autopsy."

"Understood." And fine with me. The thought of doing an autopsy on someone I know is discomfiting, to say the least. I may hate the woman, but that doesn't mean I want to see her dressed like some hunter's ten-point kill. Besides, I have places to go and things to do. At the top of the list is getting my underwear back.

Chapter 6

The sun is coming up as we leave Karen Owenby's house. Izzy says he'll drop me off at the cottage on his way to the morgue and suggests I come into work around ten, giving him plenty of time to finish the autopsy on Karen.

I take advantage of the ride home to quiz him about my latest interest. "So what do you know about this Steve Hurley guy?"

"Not much. He moved here a few months ago from Chicago for reasons no one quite knows. He was a homicide cop there, too, and rumor has it he pissed off someone higher up in his department and got blackballed out of the place."

"Pissed them off how?"

"Who knows? I'm not even sure that's the truth. It may just be speculation."

"Is he good? I mean, does he know what he's doing?"

"He seems quite good, actually," Izzy says with a tone of respect. "I imagine he has a lot more experience than most of the other cops here given that he spent fifteen years on the force in Chicago, four of those as a homicide detective."

"So why here? Why Sorenson of all places?"

"I have no idea. Maybe he got tired of the big city and wanted a taste of small-town life."

"Does he have a family?"

Izzy shoots me an amused look. "Quit being so damned cagey, Mattie. I could tell you were practically drooling over the guy. Why don't you just come out and ask if he's married or dating? That's what you really want to know, isn't it?"

"No," I say, indignant. "I was just trying to make polite conversation. Excuse the hell out of me."

"Oh, okay."

"And I wasn't drooling."

When we reach the house I unfold myself, climb out of the car, and spend a minute leaning on my door, shifting from one foot to the other as I wait for the feeling to return to my legs. Stalling. Hoping. But Izzy can always outlast me, damn him.

"Fine," I say eventually. "Give it up. Tell me what you know."

Izzy smirks. "He's single."

"Is he seeing anyone that you know of?"

"I haven't heard anything definite, but word has it Alison Miller's been sniffing around."

Like me, Alison is a Sorenson lifer. We went to school together. Now she does double duty as a reporter and photographer for the local paper, which comes out twice a week on Monday and Thursday mornings. I don't consider her interest in Hurley as any real threat.

"If I know Alison, she's most likely just using Hurley," I tell Izzy. "Hoping to get an inside scoop. Besides, I happen to know she has a thing for bald men."

I send Izzy on his way and, once inside the cottage, I waddle into the bathroom, turn on the water in the tub, and strip. I hesitate before climbing in, aware of the painful throb I can still feel between my legs. My nurse's training tells me I should apply ice for a while to try to minimize the swelling, but the thought of sticking an ice pack down there gives a whole new meaning to the term *frigid.* In the end I give in to the soothing warmth of the tub.

After half an hour of luxurious soaking, I climb out, dry

off, wrap myself in a towel, and down another handful of aspirin. Then I collapse onto the couch and start digesting everything that's happened.

I wonder if anyone has told David about Karen yet. Glancing at my watch, I realize he should be in the OR soon if he has surgeries scheduled for the day. I figure if I pop over to the hospital, I can catch him before he starts and be the one to break the news. That way I'll have a chance to see the expression on his face when he hears about Karen's murder.

But first I have to take care of the evidence from my nocturnal spy mission.

I dress and head off through the woods, searching for my scarf along the way. When I near the clearing I freeze and mutter a curse under my breath. David's car is gone, as I hoped, but another one is parked in its place. And beneath the same window where I was last night is Detective Hurley, standing beside the wheelbarrow, my scarf in his hand.

I hide behind a tree watching his ponderous expression and trying to decide how the hell I'm going to lie my way out of this one. As soon as Hurley wanders around to the far side of the house, I tiptoe back through the woods, hop in my car, and lead-foot it out of there.

I'm not too crazy about the idea of showing my face at the hospital, but I hope that if the Fates are with me, I'll be able to slip in, do what I need, and slip back out again. Unfortunately, the OR is a limited-access area, and because I no longer work at the hospital, I won't be able to get in there on my own. And I'm not sure I want to go in there alone anyway; some of my ex-coworkers will undoubtedly consider my presence as an open invitation to ask painful, probing questions under the guise of social duty. I need an escort who can not only get me in, but also effectively deter any attempts at chitchat. And I know the perfect person for the job: Nancy Molinaro, the director of nursing.

Unfortunately, my plan goes awry as soon as I set foot in the hospital lobby. There, off to one side being interviewed by a news crew from one of the local network TV stations, is Gina Carrigan, wife of Sidney Carrigan, one of the surgeons at Mercy Hospital. Gina is a tiny, pretty woman with huge blue eyes, short blond hair, and the sort of camera-loving aura that drives paparazzi wild. She is well-known, well liked, and highly respected in Sorenson, in part because her husband, Sidney, comes from money—lots of it. The Carrigan family have been big shots in Sorenson for several generations.

Sidney and Gina live in the family home, a beautiful old house that sits on a gazillion acres of land just outside of town. I've been there several times for parties and have often admired the understated but obvious wealth. Even with my limited knowledge of the art world, I know that the paintings they have hanging in one room alone are worth about ten times my yearly salary.

Despite all that wealth, or perhaps because of it, Sidney is very generous. He's a great philanthropist, donating money to several worthy causes within the community. Gina gives too, but of her time more than her money, leaving the checkbook in Sidney's hands. She volunteers for all sorts of community projects, regularly heads up task forces designed to promote some worthy cause or another, and can always be counted on to take an active stance on any issue that affects Sorenson and its citizenry. Her efforts, combined with her movie star looks, have made her a media darling locally and have even segued into the national news a time or two. Wherever Gina goes, a newspaper reporter or TV camera often follows. The woman gets the sort of ink and airtime any politician would envy.

Consequently, running into her now is like my worst nightmare. I lower my head and hurry across the lobby, hoping I can sneak by without being noticed. But Gina sees me and immediately hails me down, right in the middle of her on-camera speech.

"Mattie! Yoo-hoo! Over here."

I see the camera swoop in my direction and want to duck

my head and run. But I know the cameraman already has me in his sights and that my best bet at this point is to try to turn the moment into nothing more than a hideously boring social encounter.

So I paste on my best smile and walk over. "Gina! How good to see you," I say, giving her a hug. I hate hugging tiny women. It always makes me feel like some sort of genetic accident. "You look great as always," I tell her. And it's true. Gina always looks stunning no matter where she is or what she's doing.

"You look pretty good yourself," Gina lies. "What brings you to the hospital today? Are you coming back to work?"

"No," I answer with a nervous laugh, keenly aware the camera is still running. "Not today anyway." I turn to give the film guy a dirty look and he finally lowers the camera, though I notice he hasn't bothered to turn it off.

"I hope you're not here because of any health problems," Gina says, looking prettily stricken.

"No, nothing so dramatic. I'm just here to . . . um . . . visit a friend. What are you up to?" I add quickly, eager to change the subject.

"Well, it *is* breast cancer month, you know. So we're doing a public service spot to remind women about the importance of regular self-exams and mammograms. You know the drill."

"Of course."

"Say," Gina says, her eyes widening with excitement, "want to be on TV? We need to film someone having a mammogram. Would you be willing to volunteer?"

Oh, yeah, that's my idea of stardom. Getting my boobs squished between two plastic plates on network TV. "As fun as that sounds, Gina, I'm afraid I'll have to pass. I'm in a bit of a rush."

"Okay," she says with a pretty pout. "Another time then. It sure is great to see you, Mattie. Don't be such a stranger. And take care of yourself."

"Thanks. You, too." I make a hasty departure and manage to get to the nursing office without any further delays.

When I enter the outer office, Celia Watson, the main secretary and Nancy Molinaro's personal guard dog, is sitting behind her desk, typing at a stunning ten-word-a-minute rate. Celia is about as suited for her secretarial job as elephants are for flight. I once asked her to type up a memo for the OR that was to go to a public health department. The memo was less than a page long, yet it had taken Celia an entire eight-hour shift to type it. Then the thing had seven errors in it, including the phrase, "in the interests of *pubic* health," something I would later discover Karen Owenby had a special interest in. We all figured the only way Celia had managed to keep her job for the past five years was that she had some sort of dirt on Molinaro.

"Morning, Celia," I say.

"Mattie!" Celia's face breaks into a beaming smile. "Never thought I'd see you around these parts again."

That made two of us. "Molinaro in?"

"She is, but she's on the phone. Is this an emergency? 'Cause if it's an emergency, I can stick my head in there."

Part of Celia's perceived job description is the spreading of whatever rumors might be circulating, embellishing whatever and whenever she can. The hotter the gossip, the more excited she gets, and I can tell she is bursting at the seams to deliver the news of my arrival. For Celia, the sight of me is like the scent of a fresh kill to a hyena.

I've never really liked Celia so I decide to be spiteful just for the hell of it. "I'm in no hurry," I lie, easing myself into one of the molded plastic chairs that line the wall. "I'll just wait."

I grab a nursing magazine that's four years out of date and start flipping through the pages as Celia watches me. After thirty seconds, she starts fidgeting in her chair, a tentative expression on her face. Beads of sweat pop out on her forehead and run into her eyes, dampening the twenty pounds of mascara she has on her lashes. Three blinks later she has a trail of tiny black dots below her lower lids, as if a bug has run through an inkwell and then across her face. After three minutes of her continuous squirming, I come to the realization that I've grossly underestimated my ability to be spiteful. She's driving me crazy.

"What is it, Celia?" I say finally, lowering the magazine and letting out a weight-of-the-world sigh. "I can tell you have something you want to say. Spit it out."

She giggles like a schoolgirl and says, "Sorry, but I just have to know. Is it true David has a heart-shaped birthmark on his whatsit?"

I give her the evil eye but it's a wasted effort. People like Celia are born with a force field in place.

"'Cause if he does," she sniggers, "then you could say he walks around with a heart-on all the time." She slaps her thigh and barks out a laugh, obviously pleased with herself.

"Shouldn't you be typing something?" I ask.

She dismisses my question with a wave of her hand. "Nothing urgent. I can bang it out in no time."

I roll my eyes and bite my tongue.

"Hey, Nancy just hung up. Let me tell her you're here." She picks up the phone and buzzes the intercom. "You'll never guess who's here to see you," she says. Then she giggles. "Nope, it's Mattie Winston." A pause, then, "No kidding!" followed by "Okay." She hangs up the phone. "Go on in," she says, rubbing her hands together with glee. She follows close on my heels as I head for Nancy's office and I know she'll be parked outside the door as soon as I close it, her ear to the wood.

As are many directors of nursing, Nancy Molinaro is often referred to as the DON. The term derives from the initials in the title but it's used on Molinaro for a totally different reason. Rumor has it she's a former mob boss who underwent a botched sex change operation before entering the witness protection program. She has a broad stocky build and unusually long sideburns. The dark hair on her head is both shorter and thinner than that on her arms and legs. Bleach does little to hide the push broom on her upper lip and a broken jaw that never healed properly gives her a whispering lisp. There are those who swear that a horse's head is her favorite bed-time companion.

People she doesn't like or who cross her in any way have an odd habit of disappearing. Though no one has actually seen it, everyone knows she maintains a hit list, which is some-times called the shit list, but more often referred to as the Molinaro Fecal Roster. Anyone who makes it onto the list will eventually get a Friday afternoon summons to the nurs-ing office, then never be heard from again. Some think the Friday timing is so administration will have an entire week-end to find a replacement. Personally, I think it's so Molinaro will have an entire weekend to hide the body.

"Hello, Mattie." She greets me with a phony-looking smile and a suspicious gleam in her eye. "What a nice surprise. To what do I owe the pleasure?"

"Actually, I'm here to see David, but I figure they won't let me into the OR on my own. I want to talk to him about Karen Owenby."

"Karen Owenby?" Molinaro sits up straighter, her tone as wary as her expression. "What business do you have with Karen?" She probably thinks I'm here to exact some sort of revenge. Apparently she doesn't know someone beat me to it.

"None. I need to see David."

"Karen's not here today, anyway," she adds quickly. "She took a few personal days."

More than a few, I think. "I guess you haven't heard yet. Karen's dead. Someone broke into her house last night and shot her."

Molinaro's reaction surprises me. There isn't one. Finally she says, "You're serious?"

"Dead serious," I answer, an admittedly bad choice of words.

"How do *you* know about it already?" Molinaro asks, her eyes narrowing.

"I was there."

Molinaro's right hand drops off the desk toward her lap. I imagine she is fingering the revolver she keeps strapped to her leg, trying to get it loose without snagging any hairs.

"I was there officially," I explain. "I work in the ME's office now." I pull out my badge and flash it at her.

She weighs the facts a moment and apparently finds something amusing in them, because a hint of a smile curls her mustache.

"Anyway, I need to talk to David."

"Why?"

I don't think telling her I need to rule him out as the killer will open many doors for me, so I opt for evasiveness. "Official business. Part of my new job and all. You know."

Molinaro stares at me for the longest time and I find myself feeling relieved it isn't a Friday. "He's not in the OR," she says finally. "He's down in the ER. We had a multicar pileup this morning and there are several surgical candidates in the aftermath."

There is an undeniable tone of glee in Molinaro's voice. No doubt she hears the *ka-ching* of dollar signs adding up. Multiple trauma on young patients with insurance is good business for a hospital, especially if they end up in the OR, where the rooms are rented by the minute and the average markup on items is somewhere around 2,000 percent. For the price of one OR Band-Aid you can buy ten cases of the suckers at Wal-Mart.

"Come on," Molinaro says, rising from her chair. "I'll take you down there."

Walking into the hustle and bustle of the ER is like a ride in a time machine. Izzy was right, damn it. I hadn't merely liked working in the ER, I'd loved it. The sounds and smells of the place bring back a delicious feeling of anticipation.

As I follow Molinaro toward the main desk, the curtain

on one of the cubicles we pass is flung aside and Phyllis Malone steps out. "Mets!" she hollers when she sees me. "Good to see you again."

"You, too, Syph."

Syph is short for syphilis. Nurses in the ER have a tendency to refer to patients by their disease or diagnosis rather than their name. Instead of Mr. Jones or Mrs. Smith, it's "the Leg Fracture in Bed Two" or "the Kidney Stone in Bed Six." Back when I worked in the ER, we sat around one night discussing this habit, then decided to pick out nicknames for ourselves that were both a disease and somewhat close to our real names. It took a while but eventually everyone had a nickname and, over time, they stuck. The best we came up with for Mattie was Mets—short for metastases, the term used for the spread of cancer. It isn't great—not nearly as good as Ricky's Rickets or Lucy's Lupus—but at least I fared better than Phyllis.

"We're looking for Dr. Winston," Molinaro announces in her haughty, lisping tone.

Syph says, "I think he's in Bed One with the Blunt Abdominal Trauma, Probable Ruptured Spleen."

"Thanks," says Molinaro. "Do you have an empty room anywhere?"

"I don't think anyone is in the ENT room," Syph says, her gaze bouncing back and forth between me and Molinaro.

I hear the sliding doors to the ambulance bay open, look over, and see Hurley stroll in. I quickly step to one side, hoping to hide behind Molinaro, but it's like trying to hide a redwood behind a rose bush.

David chooses that moment to appear from behind curtain number one like the booby prize in *Let's Make A Deal.* He sees me right away and freezes to the spot. He blinks and stares at me for several long seconds, then says, "Mattie?"

With that, Hurley turns and sees me, too, the expression on his face reminding me of the one my nephew Ethan gets when he sees a bug on the wall. “What are you doing here?” Hurley asks.

“I used to work here,” I tell him with as much indignation as I can muster, hoping it will disguise the fact that I am more or less avoiding the question.

Hurley studies me, his eyes giving me a head-to-toe perusal that leaves me confused about whether I want to run and hide, or wrap my legs around his waist and ride him home. He turns to David. “You are Dr. Winston?”

“I am.”

“I’d like to speak with you please. If you have a moment.” Hurley flips his detective badge out like it’s an invitation.

“Sure. But make it quick. I have a patient I need to get up to the OR.”

“In private,” Hurley says.

I realize Hurley is going to haul David away, which means I won’t be able to see David’s reaction when he finds out about Karen. Then Molinaro, of all people, saves the day. “Is this about Karen Owenby’s murder?” she asks.

Hurley shoots me a look that makes my toes curl up like the witch under the house in *The Wizard of Oz*. He is clearly pissed. He doesn’t stare at me for long though, because David lets out a “What?” that sounds like the yelp of a wounded dog. All the blood drains from his face and he staggers back as if he’s been hit.

Syph, who is standing across the room, looks up at the sound of David’s outburst and studies the faces in our group for a second. Then she approaches and says, “Let me guess. You told them about that nipple incident, didn’t you?”

Chapter 7

Hurley hauls David off, just as I feared he would. I try to tag along but Hurley shoots me another one of his looks and says, "Stay put. Your turn is coming."

I take that as my cue to leave. Molinaro is in a huddle with several of the ER nurses as I make my exit through the doors to the ambulance bay, planning to walk around the outside of the building so I can avoid another encounter with Gina and her TV crew.

I head for work, where I find Izzy in his office. Sitting next to him is a man about my age with long brown hair pulled back into a ponytail. He's wearing glasses so thick they make his eyes look bigger than his head.

"Ah, Mattie," Izzy says. "We were just talking about you. I want you to meet Arnie Toffer."

Arnie stands and gives my hand a hearty shake. He's about six inches taller than Izzy, which still leaves him a good half-foot shy of me. I'm starting to feel like Snow White.

"Arnie just got back from a seminar on fiber analysis," Izzy explains. "He's an evidence technician and someone you'll need to work closely with. His job involves processing fingerprints, tire tracks, fibers, tox screens . . . that sort of stuff. Snagged him from LA. He's one of the best."

I instantly make the connection that, as an evidence technician, Arnie is the person most likely to be in possession of my underwear, which means he is about to become my new best friend. And despite what the cliché says, I know that the quickest way to a man's heart isn't through his stomach, it's through his penis. So I shift into light flirt mode, hoping that Arnie isn't gay and likes to read comic books about women from the planet Amazon.

"You sound like a pretty versatile guy," I tell him, making and holding eye contact. "You must be very smart to know how to analyze all those different types of evidence."

"Well, I *have* had a lot of experience," he says, puffing his chest out a bit.

"I'll bet you have," I say, flavoring my tone with the barest hint of innuendo. "And since I need to learn how to do some of this stuff, I'd love to be able to watch what you do. To see you in action."

Arnie's smile broadens into something uncomfortably close to a leer. He stares at me a moment and then officially completes our little mating dance by ogling me from head to toe and winking. "I'd love to show you some action," he says with a crooked, half grin.

Damn, *Animal World* would be proud.

"Good idea," Izzy says, seemingly oblivious to all the innuendo zipping through the air. "We don't have any autopsies pending so why don't you take Mattie up to your office, Arnie, and show her a few ropes."

The mention of me and ropes in the same sentence makes Arnie's eyes grow wide. "Sounds good to me," he says, licking his lips and making me wonder if I've taken the flirting thing a bit too far.

"When you're done with Arnie you can take the afternoon off if you like, Mattie. Make up for the time we spent out in the field last night."

"Thanks. I could use a nap."

"One other thing," Izzy says, opening his desk drawer. "I want you to have this so I can reach you more easily." He hands me a cell phone along with a battery charger, and I realize my days of ignoring pages are over. Then he hands me a piece of paper. Typed on it is the number for my phone and instructions for its use. At the bottom, written in Izzy's hand, are instructions for paging his beeper.

Fully wired for communication, I leave Izzy's office and follow Arnie down the hallway, studying a bald spot that is starting to appear on the crown of his head. He stops by a locked door that marks a flight of stairs, sliding a card into a panel on the wall. I hear a faint *click* and he pulls the door open.

"Only one flight up," he says.

"A key card?" I say with a sinking feeling. Without access to the area where the evidence is kept, it's going to be much harder than I thought to steal back my underwear.

"Didn't Izzy give you one yet?"

I shake my head.

"He should have. Ask him about it. He probably just forgot. All the employees have one. It's one of the security measures we use to assure the integrity of any evidence we keep here."

I make a mental note to ask Izzy about the key card as soon as possible. Arnie waves me through the door, insisting I go up the stairs first. I sense his eyes on me as I climb and try to clench my ass cheeks together so they won't jiggle too much. But this makes me feel like Herman Munster when I walk so I give up, letting my jiggly parts jiggle and letting Arnie watch. I consider it a fair trade. After all, I *did* gawk at his bald spot.

Arnie's office is nothing more than a desk parked in one corner of a laboratory. Lining the walls are various machines, several of which are humming, whirring, or making other odd mechanical noises. A gooseneck lamp sits on the desk—the only significant source of light in the room at the moment, though I notice there are fluorescent fixtures in the ceiling.

"This is the true brain of forensics work," Arnie says proudly as we enter the room. "Sometimes the cause of death is as obvious as the nose on my face and then there are times when the cause isn't obvious at all. That's when you have to get down to the microscopic level to find the real answers."

He pauses and gives the room a wary once-over, as if he expects to see someone lurking in the shadows. When he looks back at me his eyes are drawn down to a steely glint. "Even when the cause of death seems obvious, it may not be," he says, his voice a few decibels lower. "There are things . . . people . . . ways. . . . You know what I mean?"

I don't and start to wonder if Arnie might be a slice or two shy of a full loaf.

"You married?" he asks me.

"Not exactly," I answer, taken aback by the sudden change of topic.

"Last time I checked, the law says you either are or you aren't."

"What are you, the marriage police?" I sneer, wishing an instant later that I could take it back. I need Arnie to like me.

He chuckles. "Divorced, eh? I figured as much when I saw the band on your finger."

"I'm not divorced yet. But I will be soon," I add quickly. "And what band?" I examine my hand, curious. I'd removed my wedding ring the day after I moved out of the house and haven't worn it since.

"That white band of skin at the base of your left ring finger," Arnie says. "Shows you were wearing a wedding band until recently. That, combined with your bitchy attitude when I asked about marriage, suggests divorce."

"Oh," I say, seeing that there is indeed a small band of skin at the base of my finger that looks like the underbelly on a fish. "I'm sorry. I didn't mean to snap at you. It's just that it's still a sore subject." I settle into a nearby chair, grimacing as I hit the seat a little harder than planned, reminding myself of another sore subject in the most literal sense. "Didn't Izzy tell you about my situation?"

Arnie shook his head. "Izzy doesn't talk much about personal stuff. He values his own privacy a lot so he's pretty good at respecting others'. If you have a secret you don't want to get out, it'll be safe with him. Discretion is an important part of his job. And his life."

I know that what Arnie says is true. In a small town like this where old-fashioned values still prevail and dirty secrets don't stay secret for long, having an openly gay government official is a bit unusual. While the position of coroner is a state-elected office, a county board can opt to appoint a medical examiner for an unlimited term instead of, or in addition to, electing a coroner. In counties with populations over five hundred thousand, a medical examiner is mandated, but in our county, the presence of a trained forensic pathologist who was interested in the job was all it took.

Izzy does his job and does it well and that results in a lack of flack from the citizenry. And while Izzy doesn't try to hide the fact that he's gay, he and Dom always exercise great discretion when it comes to their relationship. They live together and that alone is enough to raise an eyebrow or two. Whenever they appear in public together, they are models of just-friends behavior.

"Though really," Arnie goes on, "in today's society privacy is nothing but an illusion. The government knows everywhere you go, everything you do. You know those little magnetic strips on the back of your credit cards and bank cards?"

I nod.

"Tracking devices. They're encoded with all kinds of information about you. Every time you use one of those cards, a bunch of information gets recorded in some secret computer the government has hidden away. They put trackers on money, too. Little wires embedded right into the fabric of the bills. And those UPC codes they use to scan purchases? That's the government's way of keeping track of everything you buy. They know what you like to eat, what you like to wear, your favorite color, even your favorite TV shows. Cable works both ways, you know. While you're watching it, someone else is watching you. And do you know why it seems as if the homeless problem in this country has become so rampant?"

I don't answer, which is just as well since Arnie doesn't stop long enough for me to get a word in edgewise.

"Because half of those people aren't really homeless, that's why. They're spies . . . government spies. The government learned long ago that it's the perfect cover. No one is as invisible as a homeless bum on the street."

He pauses to breathe and I guess my skepticism is showing because then he says, "What? You don't believe me?"

"Well . . ." I eye him warily, unsure if I should try to humor him and slowly back out of the room, or if it's safe to go ahead and tell him I think he's nuttier than my Aunt Gertrude's pecan pie. "Maybe some of that stuff is possible," I venture, "but I don't think the government uses it much. I mean why would they care about what I eat or what TV shows I watch?"

"Because, while our free society is just an illusion, it's an important illusion. It's what keeps us happy and content. It keeps us from rising up against the government. It keeps us placid. But the truth is, our government is far from a democracy. A few key people have all the power and pull all the strings. The rest of them are merely for show."

"Come on," I argue. "Don't you think that's a bit far-fetched?"

"You can believe that if you want, but I know the truth. They're out there. Hell, do you have any idea how many man-made satellites are now in orbit around the earth? More than eight thousand. *Eight thousand!* Why do we need eight thousand satellites? For cell phones and TV signals? Not hardly. Of course, the official line is that only about six hundred of those satellites are actually working." He scoffs so hard and fast it sounds like a gunshot.

"Like we're gonna believe that!" he says, his voice dripping with sarcasm. "And even if it is true, we only need a handful of well-placed satellites to handle all the communications and legitimate research needs we have in the world. Know what all those other satellites up there are for?"

I have no idea but I'm beginning to hope one of them is aimed at Arnie. And that it has a death ray of some sort, though I'll settle for stun mode.

"To watch us. That's what they're for. They can remote control a satellite right now and aim it at your house. They have special cameras that can see right through your roof and walls, watch you in your bedroom, watch you in your *bathroom,* for Christ's sake!"

My face flushes hot as I think about some super-duper eye-in-the-sky watching me in my bathroom. The very idea gives me the heebie-jeebies.

Arnie sucks in a deep breath and looks around the room with a startled expression on his face, as if surprised to find himself here. "Sorry," he says. "I sometimes get a little emotional about this stuff."

The man is a master of understatement.

"So, anyway—he makes a broad sweep with his hand—"this is where I work."

"It's . . . um . . . very nice. Are you happy here?" I can hear how dumb it sounds even as I say it, but I'm still a bit rattled by Arnie's rant and it's all I can think of at the moment.

"Yeah, I love it," Arnie says. "Izzy is great to work with. He's got a great mind. And I'm often on my own here. I work better that way."

That isn't too hard to believe, I think.

"My primary function is to review, examine, process, and interpret the evidence we collect, everything from fibers and dust particles to bloodstained clothing."

"So, walk me through a case from start to finish," I say, glad to have him finally focusing on the topic I want to discuss. "Tell me what evidence was collected and what you did or intend to do with it. For instance, that case that came in this morning, the woman who was shot to death. What have you done with the evidence related to her case?"

I purposely don't mention Karen's name, striving for a tone of reasonable curiosity peppered with indifference. I don't know if Arnie knows of my connection to the case, but if he doesn't, I want to get as much out of him as I can before he finds out. Hurley told me to stay away from Karen's autopsy, but he didn't say anything about learning what the evidence might reveal. Besides, if I'm going to be investigating cases, I need to know all this stuff.

Arnie leans back against the countertop and wags a finger at me. "See, now that's where you'll go wrong every time. Lesson number one: Why do you think she was shot to death?"

I blink at him in confusion. "I was there at the scene. I saw her."

"What did you see?"

"A woman with a bullet hole in her chest and lots of blood all around."

"How do you know it was a bullet hole?"

I think about that. "Because the cops said it was."

"Don't believe what you hear. Only believe what you know to be true based on your own observations and research. Are you absolutely certain the hole in her chest couldn't have been made by something else?"

"No," I admit.

"For the sake of argument, let's assume it *was* a bullet hole. How do you know the bullet killed her?"

"Well, she was dead. And I do know dead," I assure him. It's amazing the things I can take pride in.

"But how do you know she was shot while she was still alive? How do you know she wasn't killed by some other means and then shot to cover up the real method?"

I think Arnie is getting a bit farfetched now, but I'm starting to get into it. Besides, he has a point. The clues have to be carefully and scientifically evaluated. I'm beginning to see how jumping to conclusions can be dangerous.

"Well, there was a lot of blood," I tell him. "If she was already dead when she was shot, her heart wouldn't have been pumping and there wouldn't have been so much blood. Plus, there were some sprays of blood, from arterial pressure. If she'd been dead already, she wouldn't have had any arterial pressure."

Arnie gives me a look of surprised pleasure. "Very good," he says. "That's the type of observational skills that will serve you well around here."

I beam at him, feeling like a character in an Agatha Christie novel.

"Now, let's look at the other evidence we have on that case." He turns toward the countertop and picks up a clipboard.

"We have lots of trace evidence," he says, scanning what appears to be a checklist on the clipboard. "We have the bullet that killed her—it's from a .357 Magnum and we can match it to a specific gun if we find one. We also have some trace evidence Izzy found on the body that doesn't appear to have come from the location where the victim was found: two blond hairs, each one about an inch or so in length, and three wool fibers in a teal blue color, most likely from a carpet."

I feel my skin grow cold. David's hair is blond and the carpet in our living room is teal-colored wool.

"Then there's this," Arnie says, showing me a picture. It's the back of a shoulder, the white skin marred by three, oval-shaped bruises. In my mind I replay the scene where David leapt from the couch and grabbed Karen by her shoulders, shaking her. Somehow I know his fingers will fit those bruises perfectly.

I must look as shaken as I feel because Arnie is staring at me kind of funny and asks, "Are you all right?"

I nod.

"You weren't there during the autopsy this morning, were you?"

I shake my head but offer no explanation.

"Why not?"

There is a long silence while I stare at the walls and Arnie stares at me. Then I have a brainstorm. "I'm sorta kinda too close to the case," I tell him. "I know the victim." I hope this will be explanation enough. At the hospital, it was always understood that no one would work on anyone they were related to if it could be avoided. I feel certain the same principles apply here.

"Know her how?" Arnie persists.

I let out a perturbed sigh, realizing that Arnie won't give up until he knows it all. "I think I might be a suspect," I admit.

"A suspect?" I expect Arnie to throw me out of his lab immediately. Instead he says, "Wait, let me guess. Your almost ex was dipping his wick in the victim."

"Yeah," I say, surprised and impressed by Arnie's ability to ferret out the truth. Later I'd learn the dink had known the whole story all along and had, in fact, assisted Izzy on the autopsy in my absence.

"So did you do it?" Arnie asks.

"No! Of course not."

"Bet you would have liked to though, huh?"

I start to utter another protest but quickly realize Arnie will see right through it. "The thought might have crossed my mind a time or two," I admit sheepishly.

"Good."

"Good? I admit to contemplating the homicide of a woman who is now dead and you say *good?*"

"Absolutely. One of the most important things you'll learn in this job is who you can trust. Had you told me you'd never thought about killing the woman who stole your husband, I'd know you were lying to me. It's perfectly natural to hate the other woman, to wish all kinds of pestilence on her, and to dream up at least six miserable ways for her to die, preferably with you as the executioner." He stops and gives me another long look. "Though I gotta say, if your husband was baking his cake in someone else's oven when he had you at home, he must be a total idiot."

I'm flattered. And more impressed with Arnie each passing minute. "Thanks," I say, bestowing him with my best smile.

"So do you think your old man might have offed her?"

My mood does an immediate nosedive. I don't know what has me more upset, the thought that David might have killed Karen or the fact that I even care.

"I don't know. I don't think he did it. But I saw—"

I stop, realizing I'm about to tell Arnie about the argument I witnessed. Until I have a chance to evaluate things a little more I don't want that information to get out. But Arnold Paranoianegger zeroes in right away. "What? What did you see?" he pushes. I know in my heart he'll never let it go and I resign myself to spilling the beans. But then the phone rings and I realize that for once, the Fates are on my side. My salvation proves painfully short-lived, however.

"Yeah, she *was* here," Arnie says into the phone, widening his eyes at me. "But she just this second left. Want me to see if I can catch her?" He listens, says, "Hold on," and then hits a button that sends the caller to Hold Hell. "It's Detective Hurley," he tells me. "You know him?"

"Oh, yeah." I roll my eyes and lick my lips. Talk about conflicted!

"He wants to talk to you. Should I tell him I wasn't able to catch you? There's a back stairway to your left that will take you straight out to the parking lot. Go right now and by the time Hurley figures it out you'll be long gone."

"You'd do that for me? How do you know you can trust me, that I'm not a killer?"

"Because you didn't lie to me. And because Izzy says so and his word's good enough for me. Besides, I consider myself to be a good judge of character and I can tell you're not the killing type."

I can't help myself. I sandwich his face between my hands and plant a big kiss on his forehead. "Thanks, Arnie. I owe you one."

As I dash toward the stairs, I hear him say, "Hot damn! Can't wait to collect on *that* one!"

Chapter 8

Thirty seconds later I'm in the parking lot sliding into the front seat of my car. I know Hurley is going to be pissed but frankly I don't much care. I'm not ready to talk to him yet and still haven't thought up a reasonable, face-saving excuse for my scarf being below David's window. And unless Steve Hurley is the densest brick in the building, it won't take him long to put two and two together. In fact, I'm pretty sure he already has except he's come up with five and doesn't know it.

I'm not sure where to go. Once Hurley figures out I'm not at the office he'll probably check the cottage, so going home is out of the question. I consider hiding out at Izzy's house—it's only two in the afternoon and Izzy won't be home for several hours yet. That's a good thing, because while I'm not sure I can count on Izzy to compromise himself by hiding me from the police just because I don't feel like talking to them yet, I know Dom will do it. Dom hates cops, for reasons I've never been able to ferret out. Still, if I go to Izzy's it won't be hard for Hurley to find me there—it's a little too close to home for comfort.

I want to talk to David, but I know he'll be tied up at the hospital for hours. The lack of sleep is catching up to me, so I make a short-term decision on where to go by pulling into a Quik-E-Mart for a cup of the sludge they try to pass off as coffee. I park on the far side of the store, away from the street and next to the garbage bins, just in case Hurley is cruising the streets looking for my car. As I climb out and shut the door, I hear something rustling around inside one of the Dumpsters. For an insane moment I seriously consider walking over to look inside but then a vision of John Hurt with a crab-legged alien stuck to his face wises me up and I hurry into the store instead.

The girl behind the counter looks to be about fifteen years old though I know she has to be at least eighteen to work here and sell cigarettes. She is tall—damn near as tall as me—and built like a pole, straight up and down, not a curve anywhere, her pants threatening to slide off her boyish hips. She is dressed head to toe in black and has dyed her hair to match. The heavy eyeliner around her eyes gives her a sort of punk Cleopatra look, though I doubt Cleopatra ever had tiny hoops pierced through her lip and each nostril. There are multiple hoops in each ear, too, plus two in each of her eyebrows and one in the web between her thumb and forefinger on each hand. Her belly button also has two hoops in it—one silver and one gold—and through the tight fit of her short black T-shirt I can see that she has a hoop through each nipple as well. Rounding out the piercings I can see is a barbell-shaped stud in her tongue that clicks on her teeth when she talks. I shudder as I think about the piercings that I can't see and wonder if this is what my niece Erika will look like in a few years.

I pay for my sludge, the price of which is relayed to me in clicking grunts, and head back to my car. Again I hear the odd rustling sound coming from the Dumpster and again I decide to ignore it, figuring it's probably a rat. But then I hear a tiny, plaintive cry that freezes me to the spot. A second later, I hear it again—a pitiful cry that tugs hard at my heartstrings.

I set my coffee on the car roof and against my better judgment, close in on the Dumpster, the smell of rotting food growing stronger with each step. The top of it is closed but there is a smaller door high up in the front that is hanging open several inches. Standing back as far as I can, I reach for it and pull. After waiting a few seconds to make sure nothing is going to leap out and get me, I cautiously poke my head inside.

About two feet below the hole, between an empty beer bottle and a large potato chip bag, two blue eyes gaze up at me, tiny but lively. At first I think it's a baby, one of those hidden pregnancy dumps that teenagers seem so fond of these days. Then I comprehend the fur, whiskers, and pointy ears that go with the eyes. It's a baby, all right, but not a human one. And not John Hurt's alien either. It's a kitten: longhaired, gray and white, barely as big as my hand.

It squalls and mewls, its eyes beseeching me. I reach in to scoop it out and its claws immediately dig into my sleeve and hand. I coddle and shush and murmur, stroking its fur and trying to gently pry its claws from my skin. It quiets finally, but those claws aren't budging. I realize there will be no escape without blood being drawn, so I do the only logical thing left—I get in my car and drive one-handed to my mother's house, cursing as I watch my forgotten coffee cup spew its contents all over my back window.

My pale coloring and Scandinavian features come from my mother, though her hair long ago turned from pale blond to pure white. She hasn't seen more than five minutes of sunlight in the last decade for fear of developing melanoma and has had every mole that had the audacity to appear on her body promptly removed. Consequently, her skin is so white it's almost translucent, a detail she uses to great advantage whenever pallor is a symptom of her disease du jour.

Despite her paranoia and a deep conviction that she must be harboring some dreaded illness, my mother is the picture of health—physical health anyway. She takes a handful of vitamins and herbs every day, eats balanced meals, and hasn't an ounce of fat on her body anywhere—a trait I apparently did not inherit. My mother treats her body like a temple, albeit a temple she expects to crumble any minute. That's not likely, however. No self-respecting germ or disease would dare to set up shop in my mother's body. I fully expect her to live to be 130 or more.

Unfortunately, her wonderful physical condition is offset by her mental health, or lack thereof. In addition to her hypochondria, or perhaps as a result of it, she has a mild case of OCD—obsessive-compulsive disorder. While the disease can manifest itself in any number of quirky little habits or traits, in my mother it is limited to an obsession with germs. No germs are allowed. They are wiped, sprayed, disinfected, and otherwise obliterated from every surface imaginable. You really can eat off my mother's floors. In fact, never being one to let good food go to waste, I have done so many times in the past.

Though my mother is generally happy to see me, today the living fur muff I have wrapped around my wrist tempers her delight.

"What? Are you crazy?" she screeches, throwing her hands up in disgust and backing away from me. I half expect her to make the sign of the cross with her fingers and hold them out in front of her to ward me off. "Do you know what kinds of diseases cats carry?" She begins to shake. "And . . . and . . . that cat-scratch fever thing, that's nothing to sneeze at, you know. Not to mention that pulmonary disease you can get from cleaning out their litter box."

"That's only a problem if you're immuno-suppressed and vulnerable to opportunistic diseases, Mom. Which I'm not." One nice thing about having a mother who's a professional hypochondriac is that she knows almost as much medicine as I do. I don't have to talk lay lingo with her like I do with most people.

I head for the kitchen, grab a saucer from the cabinet, pour a little milk into it, and put it down on the floor. The kitten sniffs the air a second and finally withdraws its claws. I set it down next to the saucer and watch as it steps into the middle of the milk, shakes its foot once for good measure, and begins to drink. Mom draws in a hiss of disgust and I know she will throw the dish away after I leave.

"Well, what about me?" she says, staring at the kitten, her lip curled in disgust. "You know my aunt Beatrice had lupus and that affects your immune system. What if I have a genetic tendency for something like that?" Her hand reaches up to her neck and she digs her fingers in near her carotid, checking her pulse.

If my mother can be believed, she has had more aunts, uncles, cousins, and grand-whatevers than anyone else I know, though I've yet to see any proof that most of them ever existed. Every last one of these relatives supposedly succumbed to some awful disease—generally something rare, highly obscure, and genetically linked. And if someone in the lengthy family roster fails to fit an awful-disease bill, my mother always knows a friend, a neighbor, or a friend-of-so-and-so's who will fit. She claims to have seen more cases of rare and unusual diseases than most long-term medical professionals.

When I was little she regaled me with horror stories about all the bizarre maladies that befell people, first highlighting symptoms that were always vague and general, and then telling me how she'd had just such a symptom herself. I spent the better part of my childhood thinking my mother would take to her deathbed any day. As I got older, I came to realize that Mom was actually quite healthy—she just didn't have all her oars in the water. By the time I started nursing school, her little eccentricity turned out to be a benefit. Listening as Mom described all those diseases and disorders over the years imbued me with a good bit of knowledge, giving me an unexpected edge in the classroom.

"Sit down, Mom. We need to talk."

She does as I instruct but continues to count her pulse, her lips moving slightly as she ticks off each number. I refill the saucer and accidentally pour some milk on the kitten's head. It keeps on drinking with nary a pause.

"Mom, there's something I need to tell you about David."

The hand at my mother's neck falls to the table with a pronounced *thunk* and she gapes at me, her mouth hanging open. "What now? Isn't it enough that you're divorcing him? I still can't believe you're doing that. He's a doctor. You don't divorce a doctor."

That is #4 in Mother's Rules for Wives. It weighs in with only slightly less importance than Rule #3: marrying someone taller and heavier than you (easy for her to say since she's thin and only five foot six) and Rule #2: never allowing your husband (or any man, for that matter) to witness, or even become aware of, certain bodily functions. There are seven more rules—like the Ten Commandments of Marriage—and Mother swears that if you follow them all religiously you'll have a happy marriage. Whenever I remind her that her own track record of four divorces isn't much of a reference, she'll dismiss my objection by mumbling something about lessons learned.

My response to my mother's raising of Rule #4 today is the same one I've been giving her for the past two months. "He screwed around on me, Mom."

She pish-paws that with a wave of her hand. "That kind of stuff happens. You know how men are." She narrows her eyes at me and says in her best Nostradamus voice, "You didn't hold out on him, did you? Because I told you what happens if you don't give them whoopee whenever they want it, didn't I?"

She'd told me, countless times. It's Rule #5.

"Get counseling or something," she says. "It's not worth throwing away a good marriage over."

"We don't have a good marriage, Mom. In fact, we don't have any marriage at all at the moment, except on paper." I suck in a breath and then drop the bomb. "And the woman David was seeing has been murdered. David is a suspect."

Mom turns horribly pale—which for her means turning damned near invisible—and I think she might actually get her lifelong wish to become deathly ill. "You don't seriously think he killed someone, do you?" she whispers. Despite her color drain, the look on her face suggests that she finds the idea kind of intriguing.

"No, Mom. I don't. At least I don't think I do. But I know that he saw the woman only hours before she was killed and that they had a horrible argument."

"How do you know that?"

Oops. "It's not important how I know. Just believe that I do."

"Have you talked to David about it?"

I shake my head and open my mouth to drop my next bomb—that I, too, might be a suspect—but stop when the kitten makes its presence known by leaping onto my leg and sinking its claws into my skin like a rock climber hammering home his pitons. Hissing through my teeth, I reach down and pry the creature loose, only to have it do this amazing wriggle-flip thing that transfers the pitons to my sleeve with lightning speed. It hangs on for dear life, looking panicked and mewling pitifully. I pull it off my sleeve, wincing as I hear claws rip loose of the fabric, and settle it in my lap on its back with its legs in the air where they will do less harm. With one finger I rub its stomach. It relaxes immediately and starts to purr.

"Well, lookie here," I say, squinting between its back legs at two furry little bumps, each one about the size of my prom night pimple. "You're a boy."

My mother clucks her disapproval.

"I need to think up a name for him," I muse.

"You're actually going to keep that creature?" my mother says, aghast.

"Sure. Why not?"

"I already told you why. Cats carry diseases. And those litter boxes are so . . ." Her eyes grow wide suddenly. "Do you even have a litter box?"

I shake my head. "Not yet."

"Well, what . . . how . . . if . . . oh, my." She sputters for a few seconds as she considers the possibilities. I can almost see the images in her head—a montage of slasher-movie scenes where everything that would normally be covered with blood is covered with cat shit instead.

"Don't worry, Mom," I say, watching her turn apoplectic. "I'm leaving. Your house is safe." I pluck the kitten from my lap, stand, and head for the door, my mother close on my heels.

"You really should get rid of that thing," she says. "Are you going to see David?"

"As soon as I can."

"Well, please give him my regards and let him know I'm not responsible for the insanity that has obviously overtaken you. That comes from your father's side of the family."

Next to obsessing about her health, my mother's other favorite hobby is trashing my father and his family. My parents divorced when I was in kindergarten and my only memories of my father are vague and misty. They bear such an unreal quality that I often wonder if they're real memories or something I conjured up during my lonelier hours.

My mother has remarried three times and divorced three times since my father—she's not an easy woman to live with. And while I have no idea where my "real" father is and haven't seen or heard from him in thirty years, I have a trio of delightful stepfathers, two of whom still live nearby.

"Your father's family has Gypsy blood in the line. You know that, don't you?"

"How could I not, Mother? You remind me of it several times a year."

"Yep, Gypsies," she goes on. "A bunch of expert con artists, stricken with wanderlust. The whole lot of them." Then, as she realizes I'm leaving, she hits me with a last-minute wave of maternal concern. "Are you doing okay, Mattie? Do you need anything?"

"No, I'm fine, Mom. Thanks."

"Be sure and wash those cat scratches well with some strong antiseptic. You don't know where that cat's been."

"Sure I do. I found him in a Dumpster."

My mother clutches at her chest and I think she might pass out. But she rallies, as she always does. "How are you set for money?" she asks.

"Great," I lie. "I've got a job now."

"Really? That's wonderful." This is said with a forced tone of fake delight since my mother's idea of a perfect life is to marry a wealthy doctor or lawyer (though the doctor is imminently better) and never work again. She never understood my desire to continue working after I married David. "What kind of job is it?" she asks.

"I've gone to work with Izzy, as his assistant."

Her expression turns to puzzlement. "Izzy? But isn't he a coroner or something like that?"

"Yes, he's the medical examiner."

"But that means he works with dead bodies, doesn't it?"

"Yes, he does, Mom. So do I now."

Mom's shoulders sink and she looks at me with a woeful expression. This news is irrefutable proof that I have fallen about as low as I can go on her ladder of success. "Oh, Mattie," she says with a tone of sadness I might expect if I'd told her I was living on skid row. "Has it really come to this?"

"It's a good job, Mom. I like it. Granted, it's not for everyone, but it suits me just fine right now." Then I think of something that might sway her opinion. "Plus, I'll get to see all kinds of interesting diseases and disorders. I'll be able to see how they affect the body in a way I never could when I was nursing."

I see a gleam in her eye. "You'd tell me if you saw something . . . worrisome, right?" she asks. Coming from anyone else, I might think the question reflected a fear that some pestilence or plague of community-wide, if not global, proportions might pop up one day. But in my mother, it's merely a sign of her excitement over finding a new source for symptom and disease information she can use to expand her repertoire.

"Of course I would, Mom," I assure her, winning a smile of approval.

"Do you have a phone yet? You need to have a way to keep me informed." She hesitates a second and seems to realize her comment needs something more. "Informed about how you're doing," she adds.

I flash on the cell phone Izzy gave me earlier. It's in my purse, along with the slip of paper that has the number on it. But frankly, the past two months without a phone have been rather enjoyable, the only downside to it all being that I have to drive to get my takeout rather than having it delivered. I know that if I give my mother the number, she'll be calling me several times a day to share her latest crop of symptoms.

"Not yet, Mom. But when I get one, you'll be the first to know." And in saying that, I am abiding by Relationship Rule #9: Try to Avoid the Truth when You Know It will Hurt.

One hour later I pull up in front of the cottage, my car laden with $136 worth of cat supplies. I have four kinds of cat food, a cat bed, a dozen cat toys, cat vitamins, cat grooming supplies and a cat collar big enough for four kittens. I also have three large containers of cat litter: one that is guaranteed to clump for easy cleaning, one that's a bunch of blue and white crystals, and the other the ordinary clay kind. I've gone all out on the litter box, getting one of those huge, elaborate gizmos that looks like a feline apartment building. It has a top on it and a door so the kitten can do his business in private. The pimply-faced kid at the pet store assured me it's the cream of the litter box crop.

I set it up, put down some food and water, and give the

kitten—whom I've decided to name Rubbish in honor of where I found him—the run of the place. I toss twenty dollars' worth of cat toys down in front of him, but after a few curious sniffs, he sticks up both his nose and his tail at them. Hungry, I head for the kitchen and nuke a can of chicken noodle soup. I'm standing by the sink eating it when I hear an odd thumping noise, like a screen door banging in the wind. *Thump-ump.* And again. *Thump-ump.*

Curious, I set my soup down and head out to the living room to look around. I wait for the sound to come again and am about to give up when I hear it—*thump-ump*—coming from the bathroom. I walk in and see Rubbish pawing at the door to the cabinet beneath the sink. He opens it an inch or so but lacks the strength and coordination to squeeze through to the inside. Instead, he keeps bashing his head against the door just as it closes. *Thump-ump.*

As soon as Rubbish sees me, he sits down and meows. I walk over and open the cabinet door, then laugh as he bounds inside. "You think this is something special, eh?" I say to him. He ignores me and starts sniffing around like he's looking for something. Did I have a mouse in there, perhaps?

I kneel down in front of the cabinet and look inside. There is a bottle of toilet bowl cleaner, a bar of soap, a couple rolls of toilet paper, and a box of forty tampons. I push everything around to make sure there are no critters hiding in there, then shrug and stand back up. Rubbish continues to sniff, then zeroes in on the box of tampons. I'd torn the top off the box for easy access and the outside wrappers on the individual tampons are made out of some kind of crinkly paper that rattles when Rubbish swats at it. He seems to like this and does it again.

I head back to the kitchen to finish my soup and by the time I'm ready to leave, Rubbish has fished one of the tampons out of the box and is batting it around the bathroom floor in a game of kitten soccer. I spend twenty dollars on cat toys and all the little beast wants to play with is a twenty-five-cent tampon.

Watching the kitten is entertaining, but I have places to go and things to do. Before Hurley shows up and has a chance to question me, I want to talk to David. Because one way or the other, I have to find out if my husband is a killer.

Chapter 9

David's office is located next to the hospital in a building that serves as home to several physicians' offices. There is a small parking lot in back intended for staff and a much larger one out front for patients. I pull into the back lot; I still have a key that opens the back door to David's office and I don't want to announce my presence by stepping into the front waiting room. Besides, David's receptionist, Glenda, considers herself David's gatekeeper and it's a job she takes very seriously. Getting by Glenda is like trying to sneak past a pack of hungry dogs wearing an outfit made out of raw beefsteaks.

The first person I meet is Colleen, David's nurse. As office nurses go, Colleen is perfect in my eyes. She's smart, capable, and easy to get along with. At the age of sixty-something, she shows no signs of slowing down, much less retiring.

Colleen doesn't so much as arch a brow at the sight of me even though she knows exactly what the situation is between David and me—or at least what it was before we both became suspects in a murder case. Colleen has always liked me and I'm counting on that to work in my favor. But I know I have to tread carefully, for if Colleen is forced to choose between me and David, I feel certain her loyalties will fall on the side of her employer.

"Hello, Mattie," she says. She has one hand on an exam room door, a patient's chart in the other.

"Hi, Colleen. Is David in with a patient?"

"Actually, he's not here at the moment. He was called over to the hospital for an emergency consult. But he's due back any second. Why don't you wait in his office?"

I nod and breathe a sigh of relief. Access to David's office is exactly what I want. I thank Colleen and turn to enter the inner sanctum.

The room is nicely furnished, befitting a surgeon of some skill and reputation. The desk is mahogany and massive, though piles of patient charts obscure most of its surface. The chair is tufted leather in a rich burgundy color and behind it is a credenza, also mahogany and also covered with charts. A few feet in front of the desk are two more burgundy leather chairs that are comfortable enough but much more austere than David's. The walls are painted a cream color that is safely neutral without being cold and two bookcases and a trio of healthy-looking potted plants give the room a certain professional warmth.

My eyes linger at the top of one of the bookcases where I can see a framed photo of David and me at our wedding. A fine patina of dust covers it like a death shroud and I wonder if it is there due to some conscious effort on David's part or if it's so much a part of the background that he's totally unaware of its presence.

I move toward David's chair and settle into it, hearing the leather creak comfortably. David's skinny little ass has carved a slight depression in the seat in the shape of his cheeks. My derriere, being somewhat . . . fuller, shifts uncomfortably trying to find a fit. A smell, one that I have come to associate with David, wafts up to me: a mix of old leather, Ivory soap, and a tinge of pipe tobacco.

The pipe is David's one and only vice . . . if you don't count his penchant for playing hide the snake with someone other than his wife. He keeps a pipe along with a small pouch of tobacco at the back of his middle desk drawer and sometimes at night, after everyone has gone home, he'll take it out, light it up, and indulge himself. I've been allowed the privilege of being in his presence during this little ceremony on a few occasions. I smile at the memory and feel an aching tug of nostalgia for what we once had, for the dreams and hopes that now seem gone forever.

I open the middle drawer as far as it will go, reach toward the back of it, feel the pipe and the little leather pouch, and grab them both. I've always loved the smell of a pipe. In fact, it is one of the things that drew me to David. When I first caught the scent of it on him I found it both oddly familiar and surprisingly comforting, though I had no idea why at the time. Later, my mother told me that my father had smoked a pipe.

After tossing the pipe back in the drawer, I unroll the pouch to get a better whiff and a business card falls out of it onto my lap. It's for a Mike Halverson, owner and manager of Halverson Medical Supply. I've heard of the place before; it's one of a handful of local supply companies that provide stuff to both the hospital and the doctors' offices. For David to have the card is not unusual, but finding it wrapped up inside his tobacco pouch strikes me as a bit odd.

I hear the squeak of the back door opening and quickly roll the tobacco pouch back up, tossing it in the drawer next to the pipe. I ease the drawer closed and then throw my legs up on David's desk, leaning back to stare at the ceiling, trying to look nonchalant. When I realize I'm still holding the business card, I slip it into my slacks pocket.

David walks in a second later and stops short when he sees me.

"Mattie."

"In the flesh," I say. "Not that you would remember what my flesh looks like."

It's a low blow, one I didn't intend to make, and the effect on David is instant. He winces as if I've slapped him.

"I suppose I deserve that," he says.

"I suppose you do."

He sighs heavily; it's a gesture I know well and it irritates me. "Sorry to bother you," I say with a hint of sarcasm, "but I need to talk to you about Karen Owenby."

His face flushes red and he looks away, over toward the bookcase with the wedding picture. "It's terrible. A terrible thing."

"Yes, it is. What do you know about it?"

He looks at me then, his expression a mix of sadness and suspicion. "What do *I* know about it? Not much. Just what the cops told me."

"Which was . . ."

"That someone killed her. Shot her. In her own home."

"Did you tell the cops that you're sleeping with her?"

"I'm not sleeping with her."

"That's right, you were wide-awake and standing up as I recall."

David has the good grace to look embarrassed and his gaze shifts to his shoes. "I told the detective about that one incident," he says sheepishly. He raises his head and looks at me in earnest. "Which is the last time anything happened between me and Karen, Mattie. I broke it off with her that night. After seeing the look on your face, I knew I'd made a terrible mistake. I wanted to take it all back, to make it go away. I never meant for it to happen. I never meant to hurt you."

I'm ready to hit him with another one of my snappy comebacks, but he sounds so sincere and looks so pathetic that I lose my enthusiasm for the kill. He's rolling over and showing me his vulnerable underbelly, and a part of me wants to get up and go to him, to try to regain what we once had. Another part of me wants to take advantage of his foolish acquiescence and disembowel him. I do neither.

"What else did you tell the cops?" I ask him.

He shrugs. "Wasn't much to tell."

"Really? Did you tell them that you and Karen had a heated argument at your house just hours before she was killed? A fight that had her so angry she slapped your face?"

"No," David says, his expression turning worried. "I didn't think—" He stops and looks at me, a dawning awareness replacing the concern on his face. "How do you know about that?"

"I saw it. I looked through the front window and saw the whole thing."

"You looked through the window," he repeats, sounding momentarily dazed. Then the significance of it registers and his voice grows angrier. "The front window? Wait a minute, you were spying on me?"

"I didn't mean to," I lie. "I needed to get some things from the house and when I saw another car parked in the driveway, I thought it might be prudent to find out who was there before I went in. So I looked in through the window. And I saw the whole thing."

David turns away; his jaw clenches, his eyes narrow, and the muscles in his cheeks jump and twitch. I watch him, trying to guess what is going on in his mind. I realize then that I am putting one hell of a lot of trust in my own judgment, banking on David's innocence despite what I've seen. But what if I'm wrong? What if the man I've been married to all these years is a sociopath?

"Did you tell the cops what you saw?" David asks.

I debate my answer for a second, wondering if I should lie for the sake of insurance. But my gut still says David could not have done this. I want to believe that. For some reason, I *need* to believe that.

"No, but only because they haven't really questioned me yet. I saw Detective Hurley snooping around outside the house this morning and he found the wheelbarrow I was standing in still parked beneath the window. I think he might have guessed that I was there."

"So, lie. Don't tell him you were there. Or if you want to

tell him you were there, don't tell him what you saw. Make something up."

"Make something up? Why? What are you hiding, David?"

He looks me straight in the eye then. "Do you actually think I could have killed Karen?"

I stare back at him, back at those eyes that can change from gray to blue in the flash of a second. And in them I see the blank page that is my future and the emptiness that is now our past.

"No, I don't," I say finally. "But I do think you know something. Something you're not telling me."

"Nothing important," he says. "Believe me, if I thought I knew something that could shed some light on this tragedy, I'd say so."

"What were you and Karen arguing about that night?"

He looks at me for a long second, then turns away. I know him well enough to know I've just been weighed, considered, and found lacking.

"It was nothing really. She was just upset that I didn't want to pursue a relationship with her."

He's lying. I'm certain of it. But all those years of being married to him taught me that stubbornness is one of his strongest suits. I know I'll never get him to budge.

"Fine," I say, feeling cross, hurt, and once again betrayed. I push out of his chair and head for the door, but he grabs my arm as I pass by.

"Wait, Mattie. Tell me what you're going to say to the police."

I gaze straight into his face, straight into his eyes. I see worry there—not surprising since I have proof he has lied to the police—but no malice.

"I don't know," I tell him honestly. "I guess I'll figure it out when the time comes."

Chapter 10

As I pull into my driveway, I realize the time is here. Hurley is parked outside the cottage. I consider turning my car around and making an escape, but I know I'll only be stalling the inevitable. So I park instead and watch as Hurley gets out of his car, trying to get a read on his face. It is utterly placid, giving away nothing, so I shift my gaze to his butt instead, watching as he leans back into the car to grab a cell phone from the front seat.

I finally get out of my own car and walk over to greet him, flashing him my best smile. "Good to see you again, Detective."

"We need to talk." So much for the niceties.

"Sure," I say with a shrug, hoping he won't see how badly my hands are shaking. "Come on in."

I lead the way into the cottage, and as I step inside Hurley says, "Don't you lock your door?"

"At night I do," I tell him, ignoring the fact that I'd forgotten to do so last night. "But I leave it open during the day. Izzy's partner, Dom, is usually around to keep an eye on things, and besides, it's not like I have a whole lot here that anyone would want."

"Did Karen Owenby have something that someone would want?"

Good point. "Jewels?" I offer weakly.

He shakes his head.

"Stocks, bonds, securities?"

Another shake.

"Drugs?"

His eyebrows rise at that. "Why did you mention drugs?"

"She's a nurse. She works in a hospital where she has access to lots of narcotics. It happens."

A strangled mewling sound emanates from the vicinity of the bedroom and Hurley spins around. "What the hell is that?" he asks.

"A kitten. I rescued him from a garbage Dumpster this afternoon."

"I don't like cats," Hurley says, curling his lip in a way that makes me want to bite it.

"He's not a cat, he's a kitten. Tiny. Harmless. Helpless. You know, the sort of thing those big, brave firemen rescue from trees." I say this last part with just a hint of breathlessness and am amused to see Hurley straighten up and puff out his chest. Men are so easy.

Hurley turns back to face me. "You told me earlier that your husband was seeing this Karen Owenby, yet he tells me he broke it off a couple of months ago, right after the . . . um . . . indiscretion you apparently witnessed."

Indiscretion? Is that the going term for it these days?

"He's my *ex*-husband," I say, feeling churlish.

"I thought you said the divorce isn't final."

"Fine. Be picky. It's not technically final. But it will be." I whirl away from him and head for the bedroom. Rubbish is sitting on the floor near the edge of the bed and beside him are the mangled remains of a tampon, sans wrapper. I scoop Rubbish up with one hand and grab the tampon with the other, stuffing the latter into my pocket. Holding the kitten close to my chest, I stroke him until he starts to purr.

Hurley has followed me, and when I turn and see him standing in the doorway to my bedroom—tall, straight, blue-eyed, and one fine specimen of testosterone-ridden flesh—my face flushes hot.

"See?" I say, swallowing hard and grasping at conversational straws. I thrust the kitten toward him. "Not real ferocious."

"Just wait until it grows up," Hurley says, backing up a step and frowning. "Cats are like the devil reincarnated."

I can see his fear is real, and find it both endearing and amusing. A smile teases my lips at the thought of this big burly guy being frightened by a tiny one-pound ball of vibrating fur.

"So why did you tell me your husband . . . *ex*-husband . . . was still seeing Karen Owenby?" he asks, finally taking his eyes off the kitten and focusing them on me instead. "What made you think that?"

"I assumed they were still seeing each other. Maybe I was wrong." I enunciate each word carefully, keeping my tone neutral. I am keenly aware of the fact that we are standing in my bedroom with my unmade bed right behind me, and my hormones are flaring like a sunspot. I sense that Hurley is very aware of it as well. For a long second we share one of those innuendo-laden moments that has the lifespan of an eye blink, though at the time it seems to last forever.

"I'm curious about something," Hurley says. "This place . . ." He gestures about the room. "How did you come to be here?"

"Izzy is a good friend of mine. He had the place, no one was staying here, so he let me move in. Why?"

"It seems a bit, oh, I don't know . . . masochistic. I mean, being this close to a beautiful home you once called your own, a husband I assume you once loved. Why so close?" He's fishing. I know it, and I suspect he knows I know it.

I give him a shrug. "It's comfortable. It suits me. And since a lot of my stuff is still in the old house, I consider it conveniently located."

He reaches into his back pocket and pulls out my brown scarf. "Does this look familiar to you?"

He is watching me very closely. I bend over to set the kitten on the floor, momentarily hiding my face in case my surprise at seeing the scarf shows. I pet Rubbish a few times, stalling so I can collect myself. When I feel certain my expression is sufficiently neutral, I straighten, walk over to him, and take the scarf in hand. My brain whirrs, clanks, clangs, and steams, weighing the consequences. *Lie . . . truth . . . lie . . . truth. What to do, what to do.*

Finally, I look up at him with what I hope is angelic innocence.

"It looks like one of mine," I say, handing the scarf back to him. "Though I can't be sure. Where'd you get it?"

"Over in front of your hus—*ex*-husband's house. Found it on the ground beneath a window, beside a wheelbarrow with some mulch in it." He gives me a questioning arch of his brow. I come back at him with my best "Is there a point to this?" look and say nothing. For several seconds we stare at one another in silence, but there is no unspoken innuendo this time. It's a pure contest of wills, one I sense I am about to lose. I know I'm not going to be able to gaze into the incredible blue of those eyes for very long before I start to either pant or drool . . . maybe both. Fortunately, Hurley gives way first, glancing down nervously at the kitten, which has chosen this moment to saunter over near his feet.

Good kitty! I make myself a mental note to give Rubbish a treat as soon as Hurley leaves.

"About this, uh, wheelbarrow," Hurley goes on, doing a two-step away from the kitten. "It looks like it was placed beneath the window so someone could stand in it and look inside the house. I noticed there's a small space at the bottom of the blinds where someone could look in."

I continue to stare at him, smiling and wearing the same cautiously bemused expression I used years ago on Ethan when he showed me his first collected bug.

"If one so chose," he adds pointedly.

Look. Smile. Say nothing. Don't react.

"And it looks as if the wheelbarrow might have tipped over, because it was on its side with most of the mulch spilled out of it." His gaze remains fixed on the floor, watching warily as the kitten flops, jumps, and pretends to attack something. When I see Hurley's eyes widen, I look down myself, sucking in a breath of panic when I realize what the kitten is playing with—a piece of pine bark mulch.

"Well, now. What do we have here?" Hurley bends over and makes a half-assed attempt to shoo the kitten away. But Rubbish thinks Hurley's hand is a fun new toy and he leaps toward it, giving it a smack with one of his paws. Hurley snatches his hand back and moves away. I seize the moment by giving the mulch a quick flick with my foot, sending it under the bed.

"Just some stuff I tracked in," I say quickly. "All those leaves outside tend to stick to your shoes."

"Damn it, Mattie. That was no leaf," Hurley grumbles. He watches the kitten chase its tail for a few seconds and then says, "Pick that thing up, would you?"

I do so, letting forth with a hefty sigh of annoyance to let him know how put out I am by his request. Then I watch as he drops to his hands and knees next to my bed, exposing the long V-shaped line of his muscular back to me.

Giddy-up.

Two seconds later he rises to his feet, the piece of mulch in his hand. With it are two others, each one a pine-scented nail in my coffin.

Hurley sniffs his findings. "Hmm . . . looks and smells like pine bark mulch. The same stuff that I found in and around that tipped wheelbarrow I was talking about. I wonder how it could have gotten in *here.* In *your* bedroom. Under *your* bed."

I know the jig is up. "Fine," I say. "You got me. I used the wheelbarrow to climb up and look in the window."

"Last night?"

"Yes, last night."

"And?"

"And what?"

He shoots me a look that suggests he might shove bamboo shoots under my nails if I continue to dodge his questions.

"And I saw David." I hesitate, hoping I might be able to stop at a partial truth, but Hurley's eyes narrow down to icy slits that make me feel oddly heated. "With Karen Owenby. They were talking and then she left. That's it."

"What time was this?"

"Between nine and ten, I think."

"And did David leave the house after Ms. Owenby did?"

"I wouldn't know."

"Why not?"

"I'm not stalking him, or running a stakeout," I tell him, offended. "I've never done it before and I certainly won't do it again. I heard that a woman was visiting him and I wanted to know who it was. That's all."

Surprisingly, Hurley's expression softens. He stares at me until I feel compelled to turn away.

"He really hurt you, didn't he?" he says gently.

Tears burn behind my eyes. Hurley's brief moment of tenderness leaves me feeling dumb, labile, and dangerously hormone-ridden. Crying is a solitary, private thing for me. I hate doing it in front of anyone and I'll be damned if I'm going do it in front of this man. So I use Rubbish as a stalling tactic once again, bending down slowly and setting him on the floor, hiding my water-rimmed eyes as I try to collect myself. I scramble for an image of something utterly distracting, something that will reverse my emotional poles, and a second later, the kitten—bless his wicked little claws—gives it to me. With one Herculean leap he launches himself upward and sinks his claws deep into Hurley's jeans, landing mere inches from the Hurley family jewels.

Hurley freezes, his baby blues bugging out of his head.

"Get this . . . *thing* off me," he hisses, barely moving his lips. He looks utterly ridiculous standing there with a pound or so of fur hanging between his legs and an expression of utter terror on his face. I am consumed by an overwhelming urge to laugh, but I manage to swallow it down. Instead, I walk over and kneel in front of Hurley.

"Easy! Eeeaaaassssy!" he hisses as I wrap one hand around Rubbish. All the color has drained from Hurley's face and I wonder if he might pass out . . . and if he does, what it would be like to give him mouth-to-mouth. I think of his lips and briefly imagine my own pressed against them.

I give the kitten a few gentle tugs and, when that doesn't work, I start prying his claws loose one at a time. When I am finished, I look up and see that Hurley now has some color back, most of it a brilliant, blazing red.

I rise, a sly smile on my face. "You okay?" I ask, holding Rubbish close to my chest.

Hurley clears his throat nervously. His hand hovers in front of his crotch, where an unmistakable bulge is beginning to strain the denim. "Fine," he mutters. "I'm fine. I just . . . I don't like cats."

"So you say, but isn't that a cat toy in your pocket? Or are you just happy to see me?"

Hurley scowls and the red grows deeper. "It's an automatic response to a physical stimulus," he grumbles. "To that . . . that . . . creature."

"Rubbish."

"It is not," he snarls. "It's a simple physical reaction. It means nothing. You should know that if you're a nurse."

"No, I mean the cat's name is Rubbish. He's not 'that creature.' His name is Rubbish." I grin stupidly at him, relishing my upper hand. But my glee is short-lived. Hurley knows how to sober up a conversation real fast.

"Your husband lied to me about seeing Karen Owenby the night she was killed. Any idea why?"

"Maybe he doesn't think it's that important."

"You don't think being with a murder victim mere hours before she's killed is important?"

"I didn't say *I* don't think it's important. I said *he* doesn't. *Maybe* he doesn't. Oh, hell, I don't know. But regardless, I don't think he killed her."

"You seem awfully defensive," Hurley says. "You still got feelings for this creep?"

"I *was* married to him for seven years, you know. And he isn't a creep," I say angrily.

Hurley holds his hands up to ward me off. "Sorry. Didn't mean to hit a nerve. Just sounds to me like you're not being totally objective here."

"Of course I'm not. I know things about the man that you couldn't possibly know. I've watched him hold a sick child in his arms. I've seen him cry over the death of a ninety-eight-year-old man. I've lain at his side when he dragged his weary ass out of bed at three in the morning to go perform emergency surgery after spending a twelve-hour day in the OR. I'm sorry, but it's hard for me to reconcile that man with one who's a cold-blooded killer."

Hurley looks momentarily stricken, but he recovers quickly enough. "Would your opinion change any if I told you that we have an eyewitness who saw your ex-husband leave Karen Owenby's house around the time she was killed?"

"An eyewitness?" I echo. If Hurley is hoping to catch me off guard, he has succeeded admirably. He nods; his eyes look cold. "Well," I say, turning away from the intensity of his gaze and feeling horribly depressed all of a sudden. "That does put things in a different perspective. I guess I better hurry up and get those divorce papers filed."

Chapter 11

Izzy and Dom invite me over for dinner and I gladly accept. For one thing, I'm not too keen on being alone. My thoughts are a tangled mess and I need someone to help me sort through all the strings. I also want to find out from Izzy if the autopsy on Karen turned up anything of interest. But the main reason I accept the dinner invite is because Dom is an outstanding cook. And while my personal relationship with food is downright cozy, my personal relationship with a kitchen is totally adversarial. Despite an odd fetish for kitchen gadgets, which has the drawers, cupboards, and countertops in my old home overflowing with such items, whenever I try my hand at cooking, the potential for disaster is even odds.

One of the things Dom does best is Italian and tonight he has made one of my favorites—lasagna, layered with crumbled Italian sausage, tons of rich ricotta, and a mouthwatering combination of herbs and spices that is to die for. Every time I eat it I swear to show restraint but I always fail, leaving the table sated, stuffed, and feeling like a great white whale.

Tonight is no exception, but my glowing sense of satiety turns to a stomach-curdling anxiety when Izzy fills me in on some of the findings from Karen Owenby's autopsy. He's been hinting all through dinner that he has some news, but he waits until Dom clears the table and disappears into the kitchen to tell me what it is. Then he just spits it out, as if it's a piece of gristle.

"Karen Owenby was pregnant."

My jaw drops. "Pregnant? How pregnant?"

"Around twelve weeks."

I quickly do the math in my head; it doesn't take me long. "Shit. You don't suppose—"

"That it's David's?" He shrugs. "No way to know for sure unless we do DNA testing and we send that to Madison. So even if David is willing to volunteer a blood sample, it will take at least a week to get the results back. And that's if I put a rush on it. Normally it's more like three weeks."

"Shit."

"There's something else," Izzy says, leaning back in his chair and looking smug. "Karen Owenby isn't really Karen Owenby."

I stare at him, confused. "Come again?"

"I said that Karen Owenby isn't really Karen Owenby. The fingerprints of the woman in the morgue don't match those on the nursing license application for Karen Owenby. What's more, Arnie did a computer search and turned up a ten-year-old death certificate for one Karen Owenby, an RN in Kentucky. She died of massive head trauma following a car accident."

My mind struggles to wrap itself around this information, but it is boggled beyond belief. "Are you telling me that the woman we know as Karen Owenby was some sort of impostor?"

"That's exactly what I'm telling you. The woman who took her state boards and applied for a nursing license under the name Karen Owenby is not the same woman I autopsied this morning."

"Wow." I sit back and try to digest Izzy's revelations while my stomach struggles to digest a couple of pounds of mozzarella, ricotta, sausage, and pasta. "Does the hospital know this yet?"

"I doubt it. I haven't released the results. At least not officially."

"Unofficially?"

"Unofficially I filled Steve Hurley in on what I found out."

"Including the pregnancy?"

Izzy nods.

"When? When did you fill him in?"

"I don't know. It was toward the end of the day but I'm not sure of the exact time. Why?"

"I just wonder if he knew all this when we talked earlier. If he did, he didn't let on."

"You're too new for Hurley to trust you yet. And while *I'm* confident you didn't kill Karen Owenby, or at least the woman we thought was Karen Owenby, Hurley's not so sure. So don't expect him to be too forthcoming with any information."

I smile, but on the inside I'm seething. Not at Izzy, but at David . . . and at Hurley and his suspicious mind . . . and at myself for caring a fig about either one of them.

"I consider myself a pretty good judge of character," Izzy goes on. "And you're not the killing type, at least not in reality. What you conjure up in your mind is another matter all together."

He knows me too well. And his unwavering faith strikes a chord of guilt. I am afraid his trust in me will have the life span of an orgasm once I finish sharing the revelations I now feel inclined to get off my chest.

"There's something I should probably tell you, Izzy. I haven't said anything to anybody about this yet, but I need to tell someone, to make sure I'm handling things the right way." I then tell him about my nocturnal spy mission and the fight I witnessed between David and Karen.

"You haven't told Hurley this?" he says when I'm finished.

"Not exactly," I confess, giving him a sheepish look. "I admitted to spying on David and seeing him with Karen, but I sort of implied that all they were doing was talking."

Izzy shakes his head. "Mattie, you have to tell Hurley what you saw. Jesus, you could be protecting a killer. Do you realize that?"

"I can't believe David is a killer."

"Can't or don't want to?"

"Come on, Izzy. Is David a total bastard for sleeping with Karen? Absolutely. But a killer? No." I punctuate my declaration by folding my arms firmly over my chest, thereby indicating the matter is closed to discussion as far as I'm concerned.

Izzy leans toward me, concern marking his face. "Think about this, Mattie. Are you sure enough about your faith in David to stake your life on it? Because that's exactly what you're doing."

His words hit right where he intends and I can't deny that I have some doubt. Not much, but enough. "Damn," I mutter.

"Promise me you'll tell Hurley that Karen and David were fighting."

I nod, trying to look properly chastised while I secretly hope Izzy isn't going to attach a time limit to the promise. A quick change of subject is called for.

"Um, there is something else I need to tell you. Something about the murder scene and the evidence we collected there."

Izzy sighs. "What now?" He looks at me in a way he never has before, as if he is only now seeing a side of me he didn't know existed.

"Do you remember the underwear Hurley found under the chair in Karen's living room?"

He nods.

"They're mine."

His eyebrows shoot up, two wooly caterpillars racing toward the peak of his bald head. "Yours?"

"Um, yeah. Do you remember rousting me out of bed that night?"

"How could I forget? The memory of it is burned into my

brain, catalogued right beside my other all-time horrid memories, like the time I saw my grandmother naked."

"Gee, thanks. Well, if you hadn't been so damned determined to drag me out of the sack in a big hurry, I might have had time to realize that my underwear was stuck inside the leg of my pants."

Izzy stares at me a minute, his expression puzzled. Then light dawns and his face splits into an ear-to-ear grin. "You're kidding me, right?"

"No."

He laughs and I lean back in my chair, scowling. "What's so damned funny?"

"This is," he cackles. "Hey, Dom! Come here. You're not going to believe this one."

"Noooo," I whine. But it is too late. Dom breezes into the room, a dishtowel draped over one arm, his eyes bright, his face eager.

"What?" he says, eyeing Izzy and breaking into a huge grin. "Oh, it's a good one, isn't it?"

"It is that."

Dom claps his hands with glee and sidles into his chair. "Dish it. And hurry up. The suspense is killing me."

"You're not going to believe what Nancy Drew here did during her first on-site investigation of a homicide."

Dom leans forward eagerly, his elbows on the table. His eyes dart back and forth, from my miserable, angry face to Izzy's bemused one.

"She contaminated the scene with a pair of her own underwear," Izzy tells him while I silently wish him tortured, castrated, drawn and quartered. "Had them stuck inside her pant leg and didn't know it until they fell out at the scene."

"Oh, no," Dom giggles.

"Wait, it gets better." Izzy is crying now, he's laughing so hard. "Hurley got a hold of them and had them bagged as evidence."

Dom looks at me, his mouth hanging open with wonderment for a second before he, too, bursts into laughter. "Oh . . . my . . . God, girlfriend." He snorts. "Were they clean at least? And were they good ones? Lacy and frilly and sexy? Or were they the cotton white ones with the worn elastic?"

I pout and scowl and otherwise try to shut Izzy and Dom down with scathing looks, but it only makes them laugh that much harder, leaving me to wonder how Dom knows so damned much about the state of my underwear.

"It's not funny, guys."

"Aw, hon," Izzy says as he tries to catch his breath. "It is on our side of the equation."

"Fine," I say with feigned indifference. "Have a ball. Laugh all you want. I'm going home." With that, I head out the door and back to the cottage. Once inside, I head straight for the freezer, grab a carton of Cherry Garcia, and settle on the couch with it and a spoon. It doesn't matter that I'm already stuffed to the gills from dinner, I can always find room for ice cream.

One pint later, I toss the carton, rinse the spoon, and head to bed. As I undress, I take care to fold my clothes neatly, not wishing to repeat my prior sartorial disaster. As I fold my slacks, a white rectangle and a clump with a string attached fall out of one of the pockets. I pick up the clump first, recognizing the remains of a tampon. I toss it in the garbage, then pick up the rectangle; it's the business card I found inside David's tobacco pouch. I study the card a moment, still pondering the significance of it, if any. But my brain refuses to work, probably because all the blood and oxygen in my body is centered on my stomach, where it is busily trying to process enough food to feed a small, impoverished nation for a week.

I set the card on my dresser, figuring I'll look at it again later. Then I drop into bed, falling asleep almost instantly and dreaming that I am five-foot-five, thin, and a gorgeous redhead.

Chapter 12

I report to work the next morning feeling bloated and cranky. Since there are no autopsies pending, Izzy gives me some forensics textbooks to read and settles me in a small library that is part of the office complex. I spend the morning being alternately fascinated and disturbed by the many ways there are to die, learning all about gunshots, stab wounds, hangings, drownings, explosions, and suffocations.

It's easy for me to grasp the physiological stuff; I've seen all sorts of physical damage to the human body in my work as a nurse. But I am overwhelmed by the total science of death, which incorporates physics, chemistry, biology, and even entomology. Ethan would be in seventh heaven.

After a couple of hours of reading I need a break, so I wander upstairs using the new key card Izzy finally gave me. I find Arnie bent over a microscope in his lab, intently studying whatever he has beneath the lens. He appears totally focused and engrossed, so I'm surprised when he says, "Hello, Mattie," without looking up.

"How'd you know it was me?"

"By the sound of your footsteps, the way you walk. Also the smell."

"What smell?" I ask, fearing his answer will be a cross between garlic and Cherry Garcia ice cream.

"None."

I shake my head. "I'm confused."

"You don't have a smell." He pulls away from the microscope, takes off his glasses, and massages the bridge of his nose. Then he puts his glasses back on again, blinks several times, and looks at me as if I'm some sort of apparition. "That's the key, you see," he says. "You don't have any smell. Izzy has a smell, some aftershave he wears. And Cass has certain perfumes she wears."

"Cass? Who's Cass?"

"Cass Zigler."

I shrug and shake my head, letting him know I have no clue who Cass is.

"The secretary-slash-file-clerk-slash-receptionist?"

"We have a receptionist?" The idea seems rather silly to me when I consider that the bulk of our visitors are DOA.

"Cass only works part-time. She files our reports, answers the phone, types up dictation . . . that kind of stuff. I take it you haven't met her yet."

"Nope."

"Boy, are you in for a treat. And speaking of treats, I have one for you."

He rises from his chair, walks over to a counter, picks up a brown paper bag, and hands it to me. I open it and peer inside; at the bottom is my underwear. My face flushes red and I quickly close the bag back up. "Thanks. I think."

Arnie grins. "Izzy told me what happened. Pretty funny."

"So it seems."

"Why didn't you just fess up when Hurley first found them?"

"I don't know," I say, turning away. I'm not sure what is worse—having everyone know the underwear are mine or having them know I was too embarrassed by their size and condition to lay claim to them. "First-night jitters, I guess," I tell him. "I wanted to make a good impression, and having my underwear fall out of my pants at the scene of a homicide didn't seem like the best way to do that."

Arnie snickers. "No, I don't suppose so."

A thought hits me. "Does Hurley know about them?"

Arnie nods and I start ticking through a mental list of other cities where I can live. Big cities. Where anonymity reigns.

"I had to tell him," Arnie explains. "They were logged in as evidence. And all evidence has to be carefully tagged and tracked with a solid chain of possession. Otherwise, it becomes tainted and any decent lawyer will get it discounted. But I got news for you," he adds, his grin widening. "It doesn't matter that I told Hurley because he already knew."

"What!"

"He knew the panties were yours and how they got there. He saw it when it happened. He just took advantage of the situation to mess with you a little bit. Sort of a hazing, I think."

"A hazing," I repeat, feeling my anger—and my humiliation—build. "What a cheap shot."

"Aw, come on," Arnie chuckles. "You have to admit, it's kind of funny."

"I have to admit no such thing." I switch my mental list from cities where I can hide to some of the more heinous methods of dying I've learned about, trying to decide which one I'd most like to use on Hurley.

Arnie eyes me warily and says, "Uh-oh, I don't like that look on your face. Right about now I'm really glad I'm not Hurley."

"As well you should be. Because somehow, some way, he's gonna pay." When it comes to paybacks, I have a very long memory.

"Forget about Hurley a minute and look at this," Arnie says, tapping his microscope. He slides over to make room for me. "This is a slice of Karen Owenby's liver. Take a look."

I put my eyes to the microscope and peer in at a reddish purple smear that looks like the aerial view of an odd-shaped swimming pool. "Is this something unusual?" I ask, clueless.

"Very. It's a liver cyst caused by polycystic kidney disease, a rare, congenital disorder."

"Karen had polycystic kidney disease? Doesn't that usually manifest itself in infancy?"

"Usually. But there is one type that is inherited in an autosomal dominant pattern which doesn't generally make itself known until middle age."

"And that's the type Karen had?"

"Yep. She was apparently asymptomatic, although there are indications she might have had some problems with high blood pressure."

"Interesting," I say, stepping away from the microscope. "That woman is just one surprise after another."

"Ah, so I gather Izzy filled you in on the identification issues."

"He did. Any leads as to who she really is?"

"Not yet. Her prints don't match anything on file anywhere, so it may take a while. Hurley's working on it."

Hurley. The mere mention of his name makes my stomach tighten. It makes a few other muscles tighten as well.

"If anyone can figure it out, Hurley will," Arnie says. "The guy's as tenacious as a pit bull when he's on a case. He has an amazing record."

"How do you know that? Izzy told me Hurley was new here, that he moved up from Chicago a few months ago."

"That's true, but I have connections in Chicago," Arnie says cryptically. "And those connections told me that Hurley is something of a loose cannon. He'll pester and annoy people until he gets what he wants from them. He has little respect for authority, doesn't care whose toes he steps on, and is indefatigable when he's investigating a case. Apparently he can also be difficult to work with. Down in Chicago he went through partners faster than a legal firm full of hundred-year-old lawyers."

"Do you know why he left?"

"Yep. He harassed some rich, influential muckety-muck

one too many times because he was convinced the guy was a murderer. When he wouldn't leave the guy alone, he was told he could either quit or be fired."

"And?"

"And he quit. One month later the muckety-muck was arrested for a double homicide but it came about too late to do Hurley any good. I imagine it must have been a blow to his ego. The guy takes his cases very seriously and he's competitive as hell. It's like a game with him. He needs to solve the puzzles, finger the criminals, and get everything tidied up before anyone else can."

I digest this bit of info and see Phase I of my payback plan falling into place. If Hurley is that competitive, then the task before me is obvious. I need to beat him at his own game by solving Karen's murder before he can. And I'm highly motivated. Not only do I have a professional interest and a personal stake in the case, I figure besting Hurley will definitely make him sit up and take notice of me.

I thank Arnie for all his tidbits and head back down to the library, where I read up on serial killers and criminal profiling. Izzy comes to get me sometime after one.

"Hungry?" he asks.

"Have you ever known me not to be?"

"Point taken. Anything in particular you want to eat?"

"Not really. Though I think I've had my quota of garlic for the week."

"But that's one of the perks of this job. The clientele aren't particularly bothered by garlic breath. How does Chinese sound?"

It sounds great and ten minutes later we are seated across from one another in a cracked red leather booth at the Peking House. After perusing menus that are encrusted with dried samples of nearly every item, we order: pork chow mein and a side of fried dumplings for Izzy, sweet and sour chicken and an egg roll for me.

After the waitress leaves our table, I say, "I'm kind of weirded out by this whole Karen Owenby thing. I mean, I worked with her for over six years and never once suspected her of being anything other than what she said she was." This isn't altogether true since Karen never said she was a slut, but I figure now is no time to be nitpicky.

"The hospital can't be too pleased," Izzy surmises. "It opens them up to all sorts of liability issues. It's very possible the woman wasn't even a nurse."

I think about that. "But her skills were excellent," I tell him. "I find it hard to believe she could've been that good if she wasn't a nurse."

"Hard to believe, perhaps," Izzy says. "But not impossible. There are a number of documented cases where impostors with some sort of minimal medical training have successfully posed as nurses, or even doctors. In fact, in one case I remember, everyone was upset when it was discovered that an ICU nurse was an impostor. And they weren't upset because he was a fake, but rather because he was the best nurse in the ICU and they didn't want to lose him."

"That must have made the rest of the nurses feel good."

"Speaking of which, did any of the nurses at the hospital have problems with Karen? Other than you, I mean."

I shoot him a look. "Not that I'm aware of. She could be a bit short at times, but that's true of anyone, especially when the stress starts to mount. As far as I know, she got along with everyone pretty well." I let out a little laugh. "She got along with some a little *too* well."

Izzy smiles, but it's a smile of sympathy and understanding, not humor. "Think David was the only one?" he asks me.

The question throws me. The idea that Karen might have slept with some of the other surgeons is one I hadn't considered before, though given what I know about a few of them, it wouldn't surprise me.

"I don't know, Izzy. She *was* a bit cozier with some docs than others, but it seemed like friendly cozy, not intimate cozy."

"Did you ever see her act intimate cozy with David?"

"Point taken," I say with a grimace. "Damn, I almost wish I still worked there so I could poke around a bit among the docs and see what shakes out."

Izzy stares at me a second, a thoughtful expression on his face. "Well, there is an alternative," he says. "The hospital is having a public dedication ceremony tomorrow evening to mark the opening of their new wing. They have this big reception planned and afterward they're having a special invitation-only dinner for the hoity-toity crowd." He pauses and gives me a "get-it?" smile.

"Yeah? So?"

"So," he says, rolling his eyes, "it just so happens that I'm considered one of the hoity-toities. I have an invitation."

"That's nice. I don't."

"Ah, but I can bring a guest. And Dom can't come. Won't come, I should say. So why don't you come with me?"

"I don't know," I say, shaking my head. "David will probably be there. And so will everyone else who knows what happened: Molinaro and all the other surgeons and . . ."

"Okay," Izzy says with a shrug. "If you don't think you can hack it, then stay home. I just thought it might be a good opportunity for you to renew some old acquaintances and fish around a little to see what you can find out about Karen."

I have to admit the idea is appealing, particularly if there is a chance of digging up something that can give me a jump on Hurley. But it also means showing my face to a group of people who have probably been laughing behind my back for the better part of two months.

Izzy must have sensed my hesitation because he leans over, takes my hand, and launches into one of his pep talks. "Mattie, it's not as if you have anything to be ashamed of. *You* weren't the one playing dock the submarine in the OR after hours. Remember, living well is the best revenge. So buy a killer dress, get yourself all dolled up, and show those idiots what you're really made of."

He makes me smile. But reality kicks in fast. "I can't afford a new dress. Money is a bit . . . tight right now."

"I can solve that easily enough. I'll give you an advance on your paycheck. Enough for a dress and to get something done with your hair."

"What's wrong with my hair?"

"For one thing, it's shaggy looking. You need a trim at the very least, although a whole new do wouldn't hurt. And you need color, too. Your roots are showing. *Really* showing."

That's one of the things I love about gay men. Ask them for an honest opinion about your appearance and they'll give it to you. With both barrels. And then they'll reload in case you're still standing after the initial barrage.

"It's not my fault," I whine. "My regular hairdresser moved a year ago and I haven't found a new one I like yet. The last one I went to tried to talk me into a pink rinse and corn rows."

"I know someone who would be perfect."

I eye his balding head with skepticism.

"Really. She's very good. And very reasonably priced."

"Fine. Give me her number."

"I'll do better than that. I'll drop you there after lunch. Things are quiet in the office. Take the afternoon off."

"I can't take the afternoon off, Izzy. It's not right *and* I need the money. Besides, won't I need an appointment? It's never good to just drop in on these hair salons."

"First off," Izzy says, "you're a salaried employee so you'll be paid for the whole day. Trust me, it will all work out in the end. There will be plenty of days when you put in way more than eight hours without getting a cent of overtime.

"Secondly, don't worry about needing an appointment. Barbara loves drop-ins. In fact, all of her customers are drop-ins of a sort. Let me make a quick phone call."

Two minutes later he's back. "You're all set. Barbara is

expecting you around two-thirty. Which should give us just enough time to finish eating. I'll drop you off on the way."

"Wow. I'm impressed."

"I have connections," Izzy says cryptically, wiggling those wooly caterpillars.

Chapter 13

Forty minutes later I am stuffed with Chinese food and wedged into the front seat of Izzy's car on my way to Barbara. Despite being in the perfect position for floating in amniotic fluid, I'm feeling pretty chipper. The prospect of both a new dress and a new hairdo has me jazzed until Izzy pulls up in front of the Keller Funeral Home.

"You'll find Barbara inside," he says. "Probably in the basement. That's where she does most of her work."

"Izzy, this is a funeral home."

"I know."

I swivel my chin on my knees and look at him. "Barbara works in a funeral home?"

"Yeah, she does hair and makeup. I've seen her work. It's very good. She's really quite talented."

"But this is a *funeral home*," I persist. I feel like I'm in one of those episodes of *The Twilight Zone* where I'm the only person who gets it.

"Well, yeah. Didn't I mention that?"

I give him a dirty look. "You know damn well you didn't."

"That's why there's no waiting. Her regular clients aren't in any hurry."

"Very funny. Dead humor." I roll my eyes and want to

kick him. But I can't move my legs. "You expect me to get my hair done by a woman who's a beautician for corpses?"

"Give her a try. I'm telling you, she's good. She went to beauty school and all that, although she had to drop out before she finished. That's why she's working here. But she didn't drop out because of a lack of talent. Trust me, Mattie. Give it a shot." He eyes my hair and shudders. "I mean, what have you got to lose?"

There ya go. Both barrels. With my ego blown to bits, I pry myself out of the car and stand on the sidewalk shifting from one foot to the other in a futile effort to get some feeling back in my legs. I know that if I try to walk now I'll have that Herman Munster gait again, something the funeral home folks may think a bit rude.

I open my mouth to protest one last time, but Izzy says, "I'll be back in about an hour and a half. Have fun!" And with that he guns the gas and peels off down the street, leaving me standing there alone in front of Keller's. I turn and eye the building a moment before figuring *what the hell* and heading inside.

The main entrance leads into a large open foyer with several doors lining either side. It is eerily quiet, the thick carpet and acoustic walls absorbing every sound. I suppose that is so the wails and sobs of the bereaved won't travel too far, but that doesn't make it any less creepy. I've never liked funeral homes. There's something so tiptoey awkward about them, as if the dead might be offended if someone were to stomp their feet, or yell, or laugh.

No way am I heading to the basement by myself so, instead, I head for a door marked OFFICE, where I find an elderly woman sitting behind a desk. Her face looks like one of those dried-apple dolls: all wrinkled and shriveled and brown. She has tissue-paper skin covered with liver spots and bruises, and her knuckles are gnarled and deformed from arthritis. Her shoulders are rounded by a dowager's hump, making it difficult for her to look straight ahead.

Upon seeing me, she flashes a sympathetic smile, and then pushes herself out of the chair. I hear a loud creak and wonder if it's coming from her joints or the furniture. Once on her feet, she stands a second, wavering like a reed in the wind before beginning a slow shuffle around the desk. Somehow she manages to shift a box of tissues closer to me as she moves.

"Hello," she says softly. "Can I help you?"

Her help *me*? She looks to be at least a hundred and, if my nursing eye still works, she's about one pill away from multi-system failure.

"It's okay," I say, holding up a hand to stop her. Her slow progression is too painful to watch. "I'm not here for a funeral or anything." Although, the more I look at her . . .

She stops, frowns, and then glances up at my hair. "Oh, yes," she says, flashing me a smile of relief. "You're here for Barbara, aren't you? And not a second too soon either, I might add." She studies me a moment longer, then shakes her head, though I'm not sure if the movement is a judgment or a palsy of some sort. "That color is all wrong for your skin. You're so pale. It makes you look washed-out," she says.

This from a woman who looks like she is made out of onionskin paper.

"I'm fair, not pale," I protest. "My hair got darker as I got older. This"—I finger the dyed ends of my hair—"happens to be the color I was born with."

She scoffs at that. "You were also born with creases in your thighs and a misshapen head. Do you want those back, too?"

I glare at her and ask, "Is Barbara here?"

"She's downstairs. Go back out to the foyer and through the door all the way in the back on the right. Down the stairs and ring the buzzer. We keep it locked, you know. Wouldn't do to have families wandering around down there and coming across all the bodies."

She seems rather glib for a woman who is frighteningly

close to being a body herself. I thank her and hurry back out to the foyer, wanting to escape before she starts her journey back to the chair.

As I move toward the door she indicated, I glance into the rooms on either side of me. In one of them an open coffin is set up on a stand at the front of the room. There are several rows of chairs lined up, but except for the resident of the coffin, the room is empty. I look around, see no one, and venture inside.

Despite the fact that I've seen plenty of dead bodies in my work at the hospital and am likely to see plenty more now that I work with Izzy, I've never been to a funeral with an open casket. I've heard comments from others about how "lifelike" the bodies look and always figured some kind of miracle occurred between the time when I saw them freshly dead and the bereaved saw them at a funeral. But this is the first prepared dead body I've ever seen with my own eyes and it's one I've seen before.

Laid out before me is Ingrid Swenson, the woman with the bashed-in head, my first official autopsy. The difference in her appearance between then and now is nothing short of startling, so much so that I almost don't recognize her. I mean she is dead—that is obvious—there is a certain lifeless quality to her that no makeup or hair style can hide. But her skin looks soft and dewy, her eyes are perfectly shaded, and her cheeks bear an ironically rosy glow. There is nary a hint of the discoloration, swelling, and bruising I saw in her face when Izzy and I autopsied her.

The crowning glory, however, is her hair. At the autopsy it was stained with blood—dirty, dingy, and as lifeless as the rest of her. But now it is lustrously blonde, gleaming with ironic health and streaked with subtle high- and lowlights. It is straight near her scalp—the incision Izzy made totally invisible—and curled at the ends, the soft curves laying about her face and shoulders in a perfect frame. It strikes me as incredibly sad to waste such a good-hair day on being dead.

"So what do you think?" says a voice behind me. I whirl around, startled, and no doubt looking guilty. Behind me stands a short, thin woman with hugely round, blue eyes. Her skin is deathly pale and contrasts sharply with her black hair, which she wears short and spiked, a look that is surprisingly flattering on her. She is wearing stretch slacks, some sort of open smock, and beneath the smock, a tight-fitting tank top with a low-cut neckline that showcases some *very* healthy cleavage—she could hide Jimmy Hoffa in there. And just in case that isn't enough to draw one's eyes to her chest, she has a tattoo of a horse along the crest of one breast, galloping over those rounded hills.

"You must be Mattie," she says, eyeing the top of my head with a pitiful expression. Her voice is low, sultry, and slightly hoarse. She comes forward and extends her hand, which is cold. The question of whether she sleeps in a coffin flits through my mind. "I'm Barbara. Nice to meet you."

"Nice to meet you, too," I say, wishing I had one of my chopsticks from lunch so I could use it as a wooden stake, just in case.

"What do you think of Ingrid here?" Barbara asks, nodding toward the coffin. "Doesn't she look great?"

"She does," I admit. "Your work?"

Barbara nods proudly. "It is."

"I'm impressed."

"Thanks. Come on downstairs and let's see what I can do for you." Her tone suggests she expects to find me every bit as challenging as any dead woman.

I follow her down to the basement into an area that looks a lot like the autopsy suite at work. Two steel tables with gutters around the edges stand in the middle of the room and a network of tubes and bottles hang overhead. At one end of each table is a sink, at the other, a drain in the floor. Cabinets line the walls and a faint but noxious chemical odor lingers in the air.

I assume this room is where the embalming is done and

I'm relieved when Barbara leads me beyond it to a smaller room where a single, wheeled stretcher stands near a wall-mounted sink. Barbara opens a cupboard and pulls out a rolled up pad, which she proceeds to lay out on the stretcher.

"Hop up," she says, patting the pad.

"Huh?"

"Climb onto the stretcher and lay down with your head at the end by the sink so I can shampoo your hair."

"I washed it this morning. You don't need to do it again."

She glances at my head. "You use hair spray?"

I nod.

"Then I need to shampoo to get the hair spray out. Otherwise your hair won't work right."

"Don't you have a chair or something I can sit in?"

"Nope, just the stretcher. Most of my clients don't sit too well."

I chew my lip as she turns away and starts sorting through the cupboard, removing several bottles that contain God knows what. "So you put dead people on that stretcher when you work on them?"

"Yep."

I contemplate the stretcher again, my mind scrambling. "How about if I just bend over the sink and you wash my hair like that?"

"I need you to lay down."

"I don't think I want to lay on a stretcher for dead people," I say finally. "It's kind of . . . creepy."

She turns and gives me an exasperated look. "Don't tell me you're going to be one of those silly squeamish women. I figured you for a strong one, given that you work with Izzy and all."

"I'm plenty strong, thank you. I just don't want to use that stretcher."

She shrugs. "Well, then, I can't help you." She turns back to the cabinet and starts putting away the supplies.

"What do you mean, you can't help me?"

"Just that," she says over her shoulder.

"Just because I won't get on the stretcher?"

"That's right." She sighs heavily. "Look, I've spent too many years working on clients who are in a reclining position. It's what I'm used to. It's how I visualize the hair and makeup. I can and will sit you up when I cut the back of your hair but I've tried to do the rest of it when people are upright and it never comes out right. Sorry, but that's how it is."

I blow out a breath of exasperation and tap my foot as I weigh my options. My hair does need a touch-up—okay, more than a touch-up. It needs a major overhaul. And Izzy has generously given me the time off and vouched for Barbara's results.

Barbara glances at her watch and raises her eyebrows at me. "I have a body coming in at four o'clock that I need to fix up for a viewing tonight. The clock is ticking. What's it gonna be?"

The thought of laying on the stretcher is one thing. The thought of laying there while a corpse waits in the next room prompts me to action. "Okay, let's get this over with." I climb up and lay down, my hands folded over my lap in perfect repose. Oddly enough, it feels kind of natural.

Barbara walks over and stares at me for a minute, then her face splits into a smile. "You won't be sorry," she says, beaming. "I can see it in my mind's eye already. I'm gonna do great things for you, Mattie Winston."

Chapter 14

An hour and a half later, Barbara and I have planned out my entire funeral, including the music, my dress, who will be invited, and which coffin I'll be buried in. I take Barbara's advice and opt for the mahogany box with the blue satin lining. At first I think it makes me look too cold, but once Barbara finishes my makeup and lets me look in a mirror with the blue satin beneath my head, I have to admit it looks quite stunning.

And speaking of stunning, Izzy was right—Barbara truly is a whiz at her work. My hair is the color of sun-baked wheat with subtle highlights of golden flax. The conditioner she uses has left it feeling incredibly silky, yet she's managed to give it more body than it's had since the time Teddy Laver's bratty little brother got cotton candy in my hair when we were riding in Teddy's convertible with the top down.

Even more amazing is my makeup. Barbara introduced me to a whole new color scheme based on brown and russet tones that I likely wouldn't have experimented with on the bravest of days. And I've done some experimenting. In the hall closet of my old house is a box filled to the brim with makeup orphans I've bought and tried over the years: foundations, eye shadows, blushes, lipsticks, concealers, powders . . . you name it.

I would have sworn the colors Barbara used on me are all wrong for my complexion and yet she's managed to turn me from a pale ice queen into a warm vibrant woman—and all without making me look like a hooker. After providing lengthy instructions on the techniques she uses to apply the stuff, she gives me some samples and a list of the brand names and colors so I can go out and buy some for myself.

By the time I rise from my stretcher like Elsa Lanchester in *The Bride of Frankenstein*, I know I'm looking better than I have in a decade or more. I am a woman transformed—perfectly willing to have my hair done for the rest of my life on an embalmer's table.

And despite her rather droll appearance, Barbara is a lively and entertaining conversationalist. During the course of her ministrations, we discuss everything from men and clothing to local politics and world peace. It is a life-changing experience for me—I've finally found a hairstylist I can keep, right through to eternity.

And that gets me to thinking about Karen Owenby. I know Deborah Martin, Karen's hairdresser, because I went to Deborah myself once on Karen's recommendation. I never went back, but not because Deborah's haircut was the worst I'd ever had; that credit went to a Vietnamese woman named Mi at a place called Hairy Kari. Mi's understanding of English was poor at best and after several attempts to communicate what I wanted, I resorted to making chopping motions to the side of my head while I said, "Layer it." Mi's enthusiastic nod led me to believe she understood. During the subsequent translations by the owner, which were triggered by the scream I let out when I looked in the mirror, I found out that Mi thought I was saying "Razor it."

No, the reason I never went back to Deborah Martin is because she wears a ton of perfume—and not particularly good perfume either. It's a noxious, floral scent that, after my one visit with her, had my sinuses messed up for a week. Though I must confess, when I consider that my current hairdresser smells like formaldehyde, Deborah's perfume seems like a minor transgression.

I know that Karen saw Deborah regularly and, with most women, that's the next best thing to a shrink. Women tend to treat their hairdressers as confidantes, the intimacy of what they do promoting a sense of trust and revelation. If Karen Owenby followed true to form, then Deborah Martin might have some insight into what was going on in Karen's life right before she died.

Izzy is waiting for me outside and the look on his face confirms what I already know. "Damn," he says, followed by a low whistle. "She really is good."

On the way back to the office, I share my thoughts about Karen Owenby's hairdresser and Izzy agrees it is worth a shot. I debate making an appointment and approaching Deborah that way, but at the last minute I decide it will be better to use the same "official" approach I used on Molinaro. After calling the salon where Deborah works and discovering that she will be there until seven that evening, I tell her what I want and arrange to meet her at the end of her shift.

I spend another hour or so in the library studying up on my new profession and then wander upstairs to see what Arnie is up to. I find him in his office but he isn't alone. In the middle of the room stands a giant of a man with a surprisingly baby face. His crew-cut hair nearly brushes the ceiling, his feet are the size of a Sasquatch, and his neck looks as big around as a tree trunk. I figure he weighs at least 350, maybe more, although he doesn't look fat so much as he simply looks huge.

When Arnie sees me, he lets forth with a low whistle. "Wow," he says. "You look fantastic."

"Thanks," I say, glowing. He continues to stare at me longer than is comfortable and I realize the big man is gawking at me as well. I make a self-conscious swipe at my nose, suddenly worried I might have a booger hanging there or something.

Arnie finally breaks the tension by introducing me to his visitor. "Joey Dewhurst, this is Mattie Winston, Izzy's new assistant."

Joey thrusts a paw as big as my head at me and says, "Hi. Nice to meet you." I brace myself as I place my hand in his, fearing a bone-crushing grip or, at the least, to have my arm shaken out of its socket. But he surprises me. His shake is firm but gentle, with very little motion. The smile he gives me is dazzling.

"Nice to meet you, too, Joey."

"Joey works as a field technician for a local computer company," Arnie explains. "He goes out and troubleshoots whenever clients have a problem. He's been doing it for . . . what's it been now, Joey? About ten years?"

"Eleven," Joey says proudly. He continues to stare at me with that unblinking gaze for several seconds, then says, "Wow. You're big for a girl."

"Pardon me?" My smile dissolves, as does the glow I was feeling on the heels of Arnie's whistling praise.

Joey's face morphs into a horrified expression. "Oh, geez . . . I'm sorry," he stammers. "I didn't mean anything bad. It's just that most girls make my neck hurt when I try to look at them. I'm pretty big, you know," he says, totally deadpan.

He's big, all right. Huge. And intimidating. Yet despite his size, there is something sweet about him, a bumbling innocence that charms me. "No offense taken," I say. "You're right. I am big for a girl."

The smile he flashes at me is so brilliant it's almost blinding. "It's hard to be big," he says. "My clothes don't fit good, cars are too small, and sometimes I scare little kids, even though I don't mean to."

"Can't say I've scared any kids, but I can relate to the rest of it," I tell him.

He cocks his head to the side. "I'd love to have a girlfriend as big as you," he says wistfully.

I smile, not sure if I should feel flattered or insulted.

Arnie clears his throat. "Joey, you don't want to be late for your next appointment."

"Oh." Joey glances at his watch. "Yeah, okay. I should get going." He flashes his megawatt smile again and blushes sweetly. "It was very nice meeting you, Mattie."

"Nice to meet you, too, Joey."

"Bye, Arnie."

"See ya later, Joey."

He moves with amazing grace considering his size. As I watch him leave, I notice a wide rectangular piece of red material hanging from beneath his shirt, the end reaching halfway to his knees. It's odd-looking to say the least and as soon as he is out of sight, I look over at Arnie, my eyebrows raised in question.

"Don't worry, he's harmless," he says. "Sweetest guy you'll ever meet. He suffered some sort of brain damage at birth and as a result he's mildly retarded and has a few odd quirks."

"Like a total lack of sartorial sense?" I ask.

Arnie looks puzzled.

"I'm referring to that huge piece of red material that was hanging out from under his shirt."

Arnie smiles. "Oh, that. That was his cape. You see, Joey is an idiot savant. Despite his overall mental limitations, he has this incredible ability when it comes to computers. He can take them apart, put 'em back together, or even build them from scratch. He can write programs and troubleshoot existing ones. And his hacking abilities are absolutely amazing. He's quite proud of what he does and thinks of himself as a kind of superhero. He has this little red outfit he wears under his everyday clothes that's part of his alter ego. He's Hacker Man. He even has a big yellow letter *H* on the front of his outfit."

"You're kidding."

"Nope. He can get into any computer anywhere anytime," Arnie says, misunderstanding the genesis of my sarcasm. "He's dug up stuff that will blow your mind."

"Like what?"

"Like the two dozen or so people that Clinton had contact with who turned up dead under the most mysterious of circumstances. Or the fact that our government routinely runs tests on the populace without our knowledge. Or the CIA document that talks about remote viewing and mind control. That kind of stuff."

I don't know what to say. I like Arnie, but his conspiracy theory mentality is starting to wear a bit thin.

"I think he has a crush on you," he says then.

"What?" I blurt out, startled by the quick change of subject. "Who? Joey?"

"No, Clinton," Arnie says, rolling his eyes. "Of course, I mean Joey. Didn't you see the way he was looking at you? And the way he blushed?"

"Don't be ridiculous," I say, but my voice lacks conviction.

"You'll see," Arnie says. "I'm pretty sure Joey's got it bad for you. Something tells me you'll be seeing a lot more of him in the days to come."

Arnie is right. I do see more of Joey. In fact, I see him later that same night as I am getting out of my car at Shear Indulgence, the hair salon where Deborah works. The place is fairly crowded when I arrive and one of the customers just happens to be Joey, who is paying for his haircut and preparing to leave. Deborah is finishing up with a customer and says she'll be with me in a minute, so I have no reasonable excuse for escaping Joey's doe-eyed stare and blushing cheeks.

"Hey, Joey," I say when he sees me. "Fancy meeting you again."

"Hi, Mattie. You're not getting your hair done, are you, because you don't need to. It's very pretty already." His face takes on an "Aw, shucks" expression and he drops his gaze to the floor, where he starts drawing imaginary lines with the toe of his shoe.

"Thank you. But I'm just here to meet someone."

He peers at me from beneath lowered lids and as soon as he sees that I'm watching him, his gaze falls again. "You are very pretty, Mattie," he says in a low whisper. "Do you have a boyfriend?"

"No, I don't. But I don't want one right now," I add quickly, lest Joey get the wrong idea. "I'm going through a divorce."

"Oh. Okay," he says. "Well . . . I gotta go. Bye."

He turns and ducks as he goes through the door to keep from hitting his head. I note that the red cape is no longer showing and wonder if he's taken it off or if it's merely tucked away inside his outer clothing. As soon as he's outside he begins to whistle and then he starts skipping. The incongruity of that huge hulk of human flesh skipping along like a child makes me smile.

"You ready?" asks a voice behind me. I turn and find Deborah standing there with her jacket on, her purse slung over one shoulder. I follow her through the salon to a back door, the stench of her perfume wafting along behind her, mixing with the acrid scent of permanent solution and hair bleach. By the time we reach the alley behind the store, my eyes are burning and I have an instant, throbbing headache.

"So you work for the medical examiner now, huh?" Deborah asks me once the door closes behind us.

"I do." I show her my badge and she glances at it, clearly unimpressed.

"Interesting change of jobs. What made you decide to switch?" She is rummaging around in her purse and finally extracts a bent pack of cigarettes.

"You don't want to know," I tell her, knowing full well she does. "When was the last time you saw Karen Owenby?"

"Two weeks ago." She pauses, shakes out a cigarette, and lights it. As she sucks in that first drag, she assumes a momentary expression of ecstasy. Then she starts talking with the exhale, adding smoke to the assault on my sinuses. "She came in for a color touch-up and trim. She was always good about that. Regular as clockwork. Never let her hair get shaggy or let her roots show to any degree."

Chalk up another point for Karen.

"Did you know Karen was a natural blonde?" Deborah asks, sucking down another drag. "It's rare for a blonde to want to go dark. Seems everyone wants to be blonde these days. Especially around here."

I know what she means. The original settlers to this part of the country, assuming you ignored the Indians who had been here all along, were Scandinavian. Consequently, the ratio of blond-haired, blue-eyed, rosy-cheeked people is high. I wonder if Karen's dye job was part of her disguise.

"Did Karen talk much when she was here?" I ask. "Did she ever mention anything about work?"

"Sometimes. I know she was pretty excited about some sort of investment scheme she had going on at work with some of the surgeons." She shrugs. "Mixing business with pleasure, I guess."

"What do you mean?"

"Well, I'm pretty sure she was sleeping with at least one of the doctors, because she told me. And I kind of think there may have been others."

"Did she mention any names?"

Deborah drops her cigarette and grinds it into oblivion with her shoe. Then she gives me a long, assessing look. "Your husband is a doctor, isn't he?"

"He was. I mean, he is. A doctor, that is. He won't be my husband much longer."

Deborah nods. "I see," she says pointedly. She gives her watch a meaningful glance and says, "Anything else? I need to be somewhere by seven-thirty."

I shake my head and thank her for her candor.

"I hope you catch the bastard who did this, Mattie," she says. "Karen was a really good tipper."

As I watch Deborah leave, I conjure up an image of a gravestone with SHE WAS A REALLY GOOD TIPPER engraved on the surface.

I walk around front to my car and am about to start it when I hear an odd chirping sound. I have no idea what it is at first, but after tilting my head this way and that, I finally determine the sound is coming from my purse and guess that it's probably my new cell phone. I dig around until I find it, then fumble with it for several seconds in the dark as I try to figure out which button to push to answer it.

"Hello?" I say finally.

"Hey, Mattie." It's Izzy. "Where are you?"

I tell him. "I'm just getting ready to head home now. Why? Do we have a call?"

"No. But you need to call your sister right away."

"Why? What's wrong? Is she okay? Did something happen to the kids?"

"Don't panic. Desi's fine and so are the kids. But I'm not sure David is doing too well. Steve Hurley hauled him down to the station for questioning this afternoon and he's still there. It must be serious because David called for Lucien. He says he needs a defense attorney right away."

Chapter 15

A quick call to Desi gets me some details. She tells me that Hurley showed up at David's house with a search warrant in hand and, after going through the place, he then invited David downtown for some questioning. David went along willingly and when Hurley asked for a blood sample, David went along with that, too.

"Lucien called just a bit ago with an update," Desi tells me. "Among the stuff they seized during the search warrant were some hairs from David's brush and some fibers from the living room carpet. Apparently they hope to match those up with stuff that was found on the dead woman's body."

I grimace, remembering my own thoughts about the trace evidence.

"It's not looking very good for David right now," Desi goes on. "Apparently when the detective asked him whether or not he'd seen or been with the victim on the night of the murder, David said no. But it turns out that the detective has evidence to the contrary."

I wince.

"Lucien says he doesn't think they have enough to hit David with a homicide charge yet, but if they want to play hardball, they could toss him in jail for a while on an obstruction-of-justice charge or something like that. He says the detective on the case is something of a hard ass."

"So I've heard," I tell her, thinking that the term "firm" fits Hurley's ass better than "hard."

"Are you going to go down there?" Desi asks.

"I don't know. I guess so."

"Why? What are you going to do?"

I haven't a clue and say as much before hanging up. Five minutes later I'm standing in the foyer of the police station. At the front desk, sitting behind a protective Plexiglas barrier, is Heidi Cronen, who has been the evening dispatcher for nigh onto twenty years. I know Heidi well, not only from my contact with the cops during my days working the ER, but also because Heidi has had several surgeries over the past four years in an effort to diagnose and treat her infertility.

Heidi's face lights up when she sees me. "Mattie!" She hits the buzzer beneath her desk and waves me in through the door that leads to the inner sanctum. Once I'm inside, she stands and gives me a hug. "It's been a long time," she says, stepping back and smiling. "You look great!"

"Thanks. How're things?"

She wags a hand back and forth. "Same old, same old. How are *you* doing? I was so sorry to hear about you and David."

"I'm doing okay. It's been rough at times, but I'm hanging in there." Not wanting to dwell on the subject, I quickly change it. "I have a new job. I'm working at the ME's office now, with Izzy." I pull out my badge and flash it at her.

"Wow," she says, looking suitably impressed. "Do you like it?"

"So far."

"More power to you. I couldn't do it." She shivers and wraps her arms about herself. "All those dead people. Too creepy for me."

"You get used to it," I say, wondering if I ever will. "Plus, I think the investigative side of it will be fun. It gives me an excuse to poke my nose into things."

"And are you here tonight to poke your nose into what's going on with David?"

I nod.

"In your new official capacity or just a personal one?"

"I don't know," I tell her honestly, still unsure just why I am here or what I hope to accomplish. "I guess I should start by talking to Lucien. Is he here?"

"He is. He's been with David and Detective Hurley in the interrogation room for the past hour or so."

I almost smile at the term "interrogation room." Given our city's budget limitations, we are lucky to have a police station. Consequently, the interrogation room does double duty as a conference room. Instead of the scarred wooden table, hard chairs, and concrete floors you see in TV interrogation rooms, this one is furnished with a polished conference table, padded chairs, and wall-to-wall carpeting. There is nothing in the least intimidating about the room, although it's been rumored that the Wal-Mart art on the walls has occasionally been used as a torture device.

"Desi said that Lucien told her they might hit David with an obstruction-of-justice charge. Have you heard anything?" I ask Heidi.

"Only that David apparently lied to Detective Hurley about both his level of involvement with that Owenby woman who was killed and his whereabouts on the night of the murder." She pauses, gives me a sad look, and says, "Is she the one who—"

"Yes," I answer quickly, knowing what she wants to ask and not wanting to hear it.

Heidi glances over her shoulder, then beckons me closer with a crook of her finger. "This is just hearsay," she says in a low whisper, "but rumor has it that Hurley thinks David is the one who killed that woman and that a homicide charge isn't far behind."

I pull back, feeling something uncomfortable squirm in my gut. "I was afraid of that," I mutter.

"Do you think David killed her?" Heidi says, her eyes as big as saucers.

"No. Maybe. Hell, I don't know," I say rapid-fire, ending with a tired sigh. "I don't think so, but then I've been surprised by David's behavior a bit too often lately."

"I'm so sorry, Mattie."

I'm saved from any more of Heidi's pity when I hear a door open behind us and recognize my brother-in-law's booming voice as it echoes down the hall. "I mean it, Hurley. No questions until I get back from the john." I turn and prepare myself for Lucien—never an easy task.

Technically speaking, Lucien is a handsome man. He has blue eyes, clear skin, nice features, and a well-proportioned build. But he always looks rumpled and worn, as if he's slept in whatever he's wearing, and he slicks back his strawberry-blond hair with enough grease to deep-fry a moose. Plus, once you get a glimpse of Lucien's mind or, worse yet, hear the stuff that comes out of his mouth, any hint of attractiveness disappears faster than you can say sleazeball.

Despite his many shortcomings, or perhaps because of them, he's a very successful defense lawyer. His wheeling and dealing skills are legendary and the vast majority of his clients' cases are either reduced to a lesser charge or dismissed altogether. I suspect part of his success stems from his opponents' willingness to give in to his demands so he'll shut up and go away.

Most of his cases are low-profile crimes such as drunken driving, assault and battery, and the occasional car theft. I think there might have been a manslaughter charge or two over the years, but outright cold-blooded murder is a definite rarity. It doesn't seem to be slowing Lucien down any, however. In fact, judging from the extra spring I can see in his step, he's revved up and raring to go.

"Mattie!" He grabs me and gives me a full-body hug, allowing himself to get a few cheap thrills through bodily contact. After I squirm loose, he steps back and gives me a head-to-toe perusal that makes me feel like I need a shower.

"And may I say, doll face, you are looking *mighty* fine tonight." He smacks his lips a couple of times, then squints at me. "You've done something different, haven't you? New haircut? Is that it, honeybuns? Well, whatever it is, it makes you look sexy as hell. Too bad I'm married to your sister 'cause otherwise, you and I could play a little game of Where's Willie Wanker." Lest I have any doubts as to the meaning of his joke, he thrusts his hips a little with the pronunciation of each word in his made-up game.

"Down, Lucien," I say. "Save it for someone who gives a rip." I hear Heidi snort behind me.

"Ooh, you just love playing hard to get, don't you, Mattie baby?"

"Impossible to get, is more like it, Lucien. And I'm not your baby," I say, wondering why I am bothering to correct his crass behavior because I know from past experience that it never works. "How's David doing?"

"Fine, considering. They don't have enough to pin him with anything too serious yet, though it was damned foolish of him to lie like he did. Just makes him look guilty."

"Is this obstruction-of-justice charge anything serious? Will he have to go to jail?"

"Maybe, but it won't be for long. I can't let my own brother-in-law rot away in jail, now can I?"

I consider reminding him that David won't be his brother-in-law much longer, but decide to let it pass for now. It seems a petty detail in the overall scheme of things and besides, knowing the way Lucien's mind works, he'll think I'm flirting with him.

"Can I see him?"

Lucien clucks his tongue and shakes his head. "Might not be best just now," he says. "I think he's a bit ticked with you since he figures you were the one who squealed to the cops about the vic being at his house that night. Technically you did him a favor, since her being there helps to explain the hair and fiber evidence they have. But I don't think David is seeing it that way right now."

"All I did was tell the truth," I whine, feeling a heavy flush of guilt. I look around and lower my voice. "And then only when I was cornered. I didn't have a choice, Lucien."

"Hey, sweet cheeks, I understand. Really I do. But David's not in a spot to be real understanding just now. You can appreciate that, can't you?"

No, I can't. And it pisses me off that every time David does something bad or stupid, I somehow end up being the one who feels guilty.

"Look," Lucien says, "much as I'd love to bend your ear"—he pauses, giving my chest an ogle-eye—"or several other parts of your body, for that matter, I have to whiz something fierce and get back into that interrogation room. But I do want to talk to you about all this. The sooner the better. Is there a time when I can drop by?"

The last thing I want is for Lucien to drop by. "I'll get in touch with you in the next day or so," I tell him, lying like a rug.

"Promise?"

"Cross my heart." I do the accompanying gesture out of habit, before I can stop myself. Not surprisingly, Lucien watches my fingers with a smiling leer before disappearing into the men's room. Seconds later, the sound of a huge fart rips through the air like a sonic boom.

I look at Heidi and roll my eyes.

"He's a piece of work, isn't he?" she says.

"Something like that."

"Any idea what your sister sees in him?"

"Not a clue. I can only assume it's the result of some aberrant gene she inherited from her father."

Heidi chuckles.

"Who's on duty tonight?" I ask. "I need to get some information for Izzy from the file on Karen Owenby."

Heidi picks up a clipboard and starts reading names. "Tommy Mazur, John Quam, Larry Johnson. And, of course, Detective Hurley is in the interrogation room if—"

"No! Not Hurley," I say, trying to block out the image of a sexually laden interrogation fantasy that has just popped into my head. "I don't want to interrupt him. Larry will do. In fact, he's perfect since he was one of the officers on the scene the night of the murder. Any chance he's here?"

"Not at the moment, but I can call him and have him here in five minutes."

"Would you? Thanks. Mind if I wait in the squad room?"

"Not at all."

Like the conference/interrogation room, the squad room does double duty as a kitchenette and break room. I've been here before. Prior to marrying David, I dated a couple of the guys on the force and during my years in the ER I built up more than a passing acquaintance with several others. Nurses and cops always seem to be drawn together—a camaraderie of the trenches kind of thing. Both have jobs that entail odd hours, lots of stress, and dealing with people when they are at their very worst. And at four o'clock in the morning in a town the size of Sorenson, there isn't much to do. Consequently, the cops often showed up at the ER to share a cup of coffee or two and chat away the quiet hours of the night. Our conversations were often ribald, sometimes personal, always lively. The odd hour and the stresses we had in common fostered a level of intimacy that made it easy to talk about things you wouldn't discuss with anyone else. I got to know some of the guys really well during those coffee chats.

That was when I became good friends with Larry, who was going through a bitter separation and divorce at the time. At some point I realized Larry had a crush on me but, unfortunately, I didn't feel the same about him. He's a sweet, nice-looking man with broad shoulders, a trim build, warm brown eyes, and a thick head of dark hair. But I never felt even the smallest spark of sexual tension between us. I adored him; I just didn't want to sleep with him.

Despite our disparate feelings for one another, we have remained good friends over the years. In fact, our bond is tighter than ever, in part because I was the nurse on duty a few months ago when Larry came in for some surgery. There's nothing like getting up-close and personal with someone's hemorrhoids for fostering a true sense of intimacy.

Heidi's predicted five-minute arrival time for Larry turns out to be closer to ten and I'm feeling a little hungry. So I kill time by rummaging around in the station refrigerator, where I find several canned sodas, a brown bag covered with grease spots, a moldy orange, half a dozen containers from the local Chinese restaurant, and a partially used tube of Preparation H.

Larry arrives as I'm sniffing the congealed mass in one of the Chinese containers. "I wouldn't eat that if I were you," he warns. I toss it back in the fridge and greet him with a hug. "You look great," he says, holding me at arm's length. "How have you been?"

"Been good. Up and down."

"I'm very sorry about you and David. It's never easy when a marriage hits the rocks and I guess it's even harder when you find out your husband's a murder suspect, huh?"

That's Larry: blunt and to the point. Back in high school he was chosen Most Likely to Not Go Into Public Relations or Politics. His honesty is a trait that annoyed his wife to no end, a factor that contributed heavily to the divorce. But it is one of the things about Larry I happen to like best. I never have to worry about whether he is holding something back or saying one thing and thinking another. In Sorenson, where most people thrive on gossiped half-truths and vague innuendo, Larry's candor is refreshing.

"It hasn't been easy," I admit. "But I'm holding my own."

"I bet you are," he says with a smile. "You're a survivor."

"Thanks, Lar. Listen, I could use a favor."

"Name it."

"I need some info from the file on the Owenby case." I see him wince and quickly add, "It's for Izzy, for our investigation."

"You should really talk to Hurley," Larry says, shaking his head. "It's his case and he tends to be a bit, uh, territorial about such things."

"Okay," I say, thinking fast. "How about if I just ask you a few questions and see if I can get what I need that way?"

He considers this a moment, then says, "Okay. Fire away."

"What can you tell me about Karen Owenby's roommate?"

"Not a whole lot. Her name is Susan McNally and she works as a teller at Community Bank."

"She's the one who found Karen, right?"

Larry nods. "She was out on a date and returned to find Karen already dead on the living room floor. She was pretty hysterical. We had the paramedics take her over to the ER."

"Did anyone question her first?"

"A little, but she didn't know much. Frankly, she was in too much shock to be of much use to us. I understand Hurley interviewed her later on."

I'd love to know what Hurley found out, but judging from what I've seen of him so far, I suspect he won't be too willing to share. I make a mental note to track down Susan McNally and talk with her myself.

"About the only thing worthwhile we got out of the roomy," Larry goes on, "is that she and Karen were both pretty fanatical about locking their doors. Given that there was no sign of a forced entry, it's certainly possible, maybe even likely that Karen knew her killer."

Another nail in David's coffin. "One other thing, Larry. Hurley told me there is an eyewitness who saw David leaving Karen's house on the night of the murder around the time she was killed. Was it the roommate?"

"Actually, we don't know who the eyewitness is."

"What?"

"Hurley isn't being totally up-front with you. We're not sure there even is an eyewitness. All we have is an anonymous woman who called to say she saw a man leaving Karen's house between eleven and twelve that night. She identified him as David, said she was a patient of his and that's how she recognized him. But she didn't leave her name and the call was placed from a public phone, so we have no way of knowing who she is."

I'm beginning to see what a master manipulator Hurley is. "Thanks, Larry. You've been a huge help."

"Glad to be of assistance. Anything, anytime. You know that."

"You're too sweet."

He blushes and his eyes sparkle. "Hey, listen. Why don't we get together some night for dinner or something? Catch up on old times."

The invitation sounds innocent enough, but given my history with Larry, I figure it's better to play it safe. "I'm not much for socializing just yet, Larry. It's too soon. I've got too much going on, too much to digest."

He stares at me and I can see the disappointment in his eyes. "Please tell me you're not seriously thinking about getting back with David," he says.

"I don't know what I'm thinking."

"You know that Owenby woman was pregnant, don't you?" The pain I feel at his words must show on my face because he immediately slaps himself on the side of the head. "Oh, Christ, Mattie. I'm sorry."

"It's okay."

"No, it's not. I'm such a jerk. I didn't mean to throw it in your face like that. Besides, it was a stupid question. Of course you know. You work at the ME's office."

"Yes, we know about the pregnancy," I tell him. "But we don't know who the father is yet. It's possible that Karen was sleeping with more than one person." My defense of David sounds feeble, even to my own highly subjective ears. Why am I trying so hard to hang on, grasping at so many straws? Why can't I just let David go?

"Well," Larry says, chucking a finger under my chin, "I can see you're pretty ambivalent about all this. I just hope everything turns out the way you want it to, Mattie."

"Thanks." I lean over and kiss his cheek, then give him a wan smile. "Now, if I can just figure out what it is that I want, everything will be right with the world."

Larry laughs. "If only it were that simple."

Chapter 16

The next morning, I call Lucien first thing and learn that David spent the night in jail and is, in fact, still there, pending his bail hearing, which is scheduled for ten o'clock. The charge, as Lucien predicted, is obstruction of justice. But he suspects the cops will later drop that charge so they can pursue a bigger one, like first-degree murder.

When I get to work, Izzy and I spend half an hour at the conference table sipping coffee and speculating about both Karen Owenby's identity and David's degree of guilt. Then we tackle our one autopsy of the day: a forty-eight-year-old man killed in a head-on collision with a semi. The police think the dead man might have been drunk because witnesses said his car weaved across two lanes of traffic before hitting the truck.

The impact of the collision broke nearly every bone in the man's body, leaving him oddly deformed, his shape compressed by the tons of steel that closed in on him. I take some comfort in the idea that his death was most likely instantaneous and hope he *was* drunk, at least enough to have numbed him to the horror of his impending doom. But that hope is dashed when the man's blood alcohol level comes back as zero.

Then Izzy discovers evidence of a massive coronary thrombosis and a lack of blood in many areas of the body, which means the guy had a massive heart attack and was most likely dead before he ever hit the truck.

It is a little after eleven and we are just finishing up the autopsy when a woman pokes her head into the room. She looks like a flower child right out of the sixties: straight black hair, big floppy hat, calf-length peasant dress, sandals, and a string of love beads that hang to her navel. "Hi there!" she says. "You must be Mattie."

"I am."

"I'm Cass. I work here part-time. Answer phones, file, that sort of thing."

"Nice to meet you, Cass."

"I have a message for you. Lucien called and said to tell you that your husband is out on bail."

"Good. I think. Thank you."

"You're welcome. And Arnie said he'd like both of you to come up to his office when you're done here. He has some information for you."

"Will do, Cass," says Izzy. "Thanks."

"Well, that wasn't so bad," I say once Cass is gone. "Arnie made it sound as if meeting Cass would be a strange experience."

Izzy chuckles. "It is, but you'll get used to it."

"What's to get used to? She seems just fine to me."

"Wait until the next time you meet her. Then you'll understand."

We clean up and head for Arnie's office. I can tell from the look on Arnie's face that he is excited about something.

"I have a tentative ID for the Owenby woman," he says. "I tracked down a hospital in Kentucky where the real Karen Owenby used to work. Seems there was an operating room assistant named Sharon Carver who worked at the same hospital and who gave notice a few days after Owenby's death. Then Carver just disappeared from the face of the earth.

There's no further work history, no bank accounts, no nothing.

"However, someone claiming to be Karen Owenby and using her nursing license was hired as an OR nurse in a Chicago hospital two months after the real Owenby's death. According to personnel records at the Chicago hospital, the work history that the fake Owenby provided conveniently excluded any employment during the period that the real Owenby worked at the Kentucky hospital. During an interview, the applicant apparently explained the gap in employment by saying that she took some time off to help a sick family member."

"Good work, Arnie," Izzy says.

"Thanks."

"How did you figure it out?" I ask him.

"I just assumed that the person who stole Karen Owenby's identity had to be both someone who knew her and someone who had a working knowledge of an OR. I backtracked from the reference information the hospital here had on file for Owenby and noticed a gap of several years. Using the information from the death certificate for the real Karen Owenby, which listed her place of death as Ashland, Kentucky, I started calling area hospitals. Sure enough, I found one where she'd worked.

"So I asked the hospital if they had any employees who quit or were fired around the time of Owenby's death and they came up with two names: a man and a woman. The woman was Sharon Carver and she worked as an aide in the OR, which also happened to be where Karen Owenby worked. So I had the hospital scan and e-mail me a picture of the Carver woman from her personnel file. Had them send one of Owenby, too. Check it out."

He turns to his computer and pulls up two photos side by side. I look over Izzy's shoulder and sure enough, the woman labeled as Sharon Carver looks exactly like the woman we knew as Karen Owenby but with lighter hair. The real Karen Owenby was quite pretty, I note, her features delicate and refined looking.

"How soon before we can verify?" Izzy asks.

"Sharon Carver has no prints on file," Arnie explains. "And I haven't found any family yet. She listed parents as the next of kin on her job application at the hospital in Kentucky, but apparently the names, address, and phone number she gave for them were fake. No one at the hospital seems to know much about her. Apparently she only worked there for a few months. I've got some inquiries out to dentists in the area to see if we can find anyone she might have gone to. Other than that, I'm not sure where to go."

Izzy says, "The application Carver filled out at the Kentucky hospital. They still have it?"

Arnie nods.

"Give this information to Hurley and see if he can get that application and check it for finger or palm prints. If we can match one up with the woman in our morgue, it won't be proof positive, but it certainly adds to the slate."

"Will do," Arnie says.

"The thing I don't get is why," I say. "Why did this woman impersonate a nurse and take over her identity?"

Arnie shrugs.

Izzy says, "Drugs maybe?" He looks at me. "Do you know if there were any incidents of drug diversion at Mercy during the past few years? Maybe she was copping and selling on the street."

"I know there was a problem back about four years ago, but they caught the nurse who was behind that one and fired her. Sent her away for rehab, I think. And she wasn't selling, just using." I shake my head as I think. "I really doubt that Karen was involved in anything like that. She worked there for six years. If she was diverting drugs, someone would have tapped her by now."

"You're probably right," Arnie says. "But just to be on the

safe side, I'll have Hurley check and see if there were any suspected drug problems at the Kentucky hospital around the time Carver was working there."

"Another possibility," Izzy says, "is money. After all, Carver was only an aide and they don't pull down much of a salary. So maybe she just wanted the higher pay that an RN gets. She paid attention while working as an aide in the OR, picking up tips, lingo, and techniques. Then, when the opportunity arose, she passed herself off as an RN by using the dead woman's name, license, and work history."

"How'd she come about a work history if she didn't use the Kentucky hospital?" I ask.

Arnie says, "Simple enough if you think about it. Mentions of prior places could have come out in conversation. Plus, there might have been info in the obituary. Or Carver could have attended the funeral and subtly pumped family or friends for information about past jobs. Once you get a hospital name, it's simple enough to call the personnel department and say you're checking a reference. Most places won't tell you much without written permission from the employee, but they will give you dates of employment and often the area where the employee worked. That's all you really need for a job application."

Amazing. Not only was Karen Owenby not really Karen Owenby, she wasn't really a nurse. Molinaro was going to shit a brick when she found out.

"You know, there's something else we need to consider," I say, recalling my talk with Deborah the night before. I tell them what Deborah said about Karen's investment scheme involving doctors. "I have no idea what it might be," I tell them. "I wasn't aware of anything going on while I was working there, but I might not have been in the loop. Maybe we can find out more at the dedication tonight."

"We can certainly give it a shot," Izzy says.

"Which reminds me. Can I leave a little early today? I still have to find a dress to wear."

"Sure, if things stay quiet," Izzy says. "Just promise me you won't try to do anything textured and pouffy again. That dress you wore to the mayor's ball last fall made you look like a giant puffer fish."

Reload.

By the time I leave work I have just under three hours to find the perfect, non-pouffy dress and make myself presentable. Both of these tasks carry the threat of being overwhelming, if not impossible, although the latter is going to be less so thanks to Barbara's magical ministrations.

I hate shopping for clothes. Most women love it and treat me like a traitor to my gender simply because I loathe it. But then, most of those women are blessed with something close to a normal body whereas I am short-waisted, have arms like a baboon, and have thighs that rub together so tightly, I sound like a belt sander when I wear corduroy pants.

If I find a dress that's long enough for my body overall, the waist is usually somewhere around my hips. When I try to wear long sleeves, they often end up being three-quarter length instead. Tight-fitting or slim-line skirts bunch up at the thighs and make my ass look huge, whereas snug-fitting slacks tend to make me look like I'm heading out to the riding range in my jodhpurs. I have pretty decent cleavage with any bra but hesitate to wear the type of neckline that will show it off. The last time I did that, I was picking crumbs out of there most of the night.

I head for the only women's clothing store in town that has ever managed to provide me with passable stuff. Located just off Main Street, it is owned by a fifty-something German woman named Olga who is both tall and wide. Consequently, she carries a good assortment of clothing to fit women who possess either trait . . . or someone like me, who possesses both of them.

The first thing Olga digs up for me is a cocktail dress that fits snug to the waist and then flares out around the hips where the material is gathered in ruffled layers. It is sleeveless and has one halter type strap to hold it up. The color is a safe shade of beige and the flare of the skirt camouflages my thighs and hips—the same hips that David once told me were "obviously made for childbearing," a comment that led to a weeklong case of no-nookie disease.

The dress looks fabulous on the hanger and I am excited as I carry it into the dressing room and slip it on. A quick glance in the mirror doesn't make me gag, so I step out, my expression hopeful. I do a twirl as Olga casts her critical gaze upon me. Two seconds later she gives me a thumbs-down.

"What?" I whine. "What's wrong with it? *I* like it."

"Fine, wear it if you want," Olga says, her German accent turning every *w* into a *v*. "But it makes you look like a cauliflower."

I take off the beige dress and try on two pink ones, a hideous salmon-colored thing, and a teal-colored sheath that makes my skin itch. I'm getting cranky when Olga tosses yet another specimen over the dressing room door, this one in a shade of pale, silvery blue. I hold it up to my face and see that the color is very striking against my skin and hair, magnifying the blue of my eyes. I start to pull the dress on over my head when I notice the back of it.

"Olga, have you lost your mind?" I yell over the dressing room door.

"What's the matter? You don't like the dress?"

"It has a bow on the ass, Olga. A really big bow. I'm not wearing any dress that has a bow on the ass."

"Come out here and let me see," Olga says.

I pull the dress on, my jaw set in determination as I take a quick glance in the mirror at my profile. The bow makes my butt look bigger than Minnesota and it's a shame because, from the front the dress looks great—shapely, but not snug. The style is a good one that hides most of my natural flaws.

Disappointed, I step out of the dressing room and stand sideways in front of Olga with a What'd-I-tell-ya? look on my face.

Olga turns me around, fiddles with my butt for a second, and says, "You are right. No butt bow."

I sigh and glance at my watch. I've already used up nearly two hours of my time and I'm about to ask Olga what else she has when she snaps her fingers. "Gone, like that," she says. "I take the bow off."

"I'm pretty pushed for time, Olga. This thing starts at six."

"Give me five minutes. I just need to open the seam, take the bow off, and close it back up. You can't spare five minutes?"

I glance at my watch again, and then take another look in the mirror. Other than the bow, the dress is perfect. I glance at the price tag. High, but within range. "Okay," I say. "But hurry."

"You know, I have a nice shawl that would go great with that dress," Olga says. "Do you have a wrap of any sort?"

I don't and ten minutes later Olga has a big smile on her face, I am $278 poorer, and there are only forty minutes left before I am supposed to meet Izzy. When I realize I don't have any shoes to wear with the dress, Olga takes pity on me and loans me a pair of hers, which are half a size too small but look great. I hurry home, dress, and do a quick fix to my hair, all of it under the watchful eyes of Rubbish, who circles in and out between my feet, nuzzling my legs and mewing.

Izzy, who hates being late, shows up as I'm starting my makeup. "You about ready?" he asks.

"Not quite. I need a couple more minutes."

He sighs and stands in the bathroom doorway watching me, trying to be patient, but tapping his foot and glancing at his watch every few seconds. Rubbish, who is sitting at my feet, suddenly gets up and opens the bathroom cabinet with one paw. He climbs inside, letting the door shut behind him.

At the sound of the *thump-ump,* I laugh and say, "I see you've finally mastered it."

"Mastered what?" Izzy asks.

"I was talking to the cat. He likes to play in this cabinet. See?" I reach down, swing open the door, and apparently scare the hell out of Rubbish, who runs out of the cabinet and leaps for my arms. Unfortunately, he doesn't make it past my knees, where he sinks his claws in and starts to climb. By the time I pry him loose I have two flaming red scratches and several trickles of blood on my leg, as well as a pair of panty hose that resemble a railroad switching yard.

"Well, that's just great," Izzy says. "Hurry up and change, please."

I reach up under my dress and yank the panty hose down to my knees. "I don't have any other hose here, Izzy. We'll have to stop somewhere." I kick off my shoes and peel the hose the rest of the way off. Then I toss them to Rubbish, who immediately attacks and kills them.

"Can't you just go barelegged?" Izzy whines. "We're already ten minutes late. And none of the clothing stores are going to be open at this hour."

"I can't go to this thing barelegged. It's October. Not only would I freeze to death, it's an absolute fashion faux pas." The freezing part is a minor exaggeration. While it is true that my legs might feel a little cold, panty hose aren't likely to make a big difference. Besides, my tolerance for cold has always been pretty high. Having a layer of blubber does provide for a few advantages.

"A fashion faux pas?" Izzy echoes, his tone reeking with irony as he steers me out the door and to his car. "My, my. Aren't you a regular Martha Stewart."

"As if Martha Stewart knows anything about fashion," I sneer. "She has an entire closet filled with denim shirts."

"You're just jealous. I think she's an amazing woman," Izzy taunts.

"She's not a woman. She's an alien life form."

"Hey, just because you're not woman enough."

"Oh, puh-lease," I shoot back. "Just because I don't spend all day spray-painting pine cones or making hors d'oeuvres out of phyllo dough and cocktail weenies doesn't mean I'm not a woman. Hell, even Martha doesn't do that stuff. She has an entire corporation of employees who do it for her. I'm telling you, the woman's a total fraud. I'd suggest she hang herself, but I don't think I have the patience to wait for her to grow some hemp so she can make her own rope."

I realize we are already halfway to the hospital. "Hey, pull in to the Quik-E-Mart up here, would you?" I say. "I saw a rack of panty hose when I was in there the other day."

Izzy hits the brakes so hard that the vehicle behind us, a gray-and-burgundy van, has to swerve onto the shoulder to keep from rear-ending us.

All the Quik-E-Mart has for panty hose is a generic brand with the world's biggest lie stamped on the front of the package: ONE SIZE FITS ALL. I pay for them and dash back out to the car.

Izzy peels out as I kick off my shoes and go through an array of gymnastic contortions trying to get the panty hose on. By the time I'm done, I have an indentation in the middle of my forehead from the button on the glove box, a cramp in my thigh that makes me want to cut my leg off, and a panty hose waistband that is currently riding somewhere in the region of my pubic bone. I give Izzy a dirty look as he tries, unsuccessfully, to suppress his laughter.

"You're a misogynistic creep," I tell him.

"Au contraire," he protests. "I adore women. They are the most entertaining creatures I've ever encountered. Just because I don't want to sleep with them doesn't mean I don't like them."

When we arrive at the hospital, I manage to squeeze myself out of the car and do a quick tug-pull-wiggle maneuver to get my hose in the best possible position. I stretch the material as far as it will go but as we walk toward the entrance,

I can feel them slipping downward as the material contracts back to its normal size. I try minimizing my leg movement as I walk, hoping that might slow their descent.

Inside the hospital auditorium, a crowd of a hundred or more has already gathered. I hang my shawl on a nearby coat rack and then scan the room, marking my potential targets for the evening.

Sidney Carrigan and Arthur Henley—the other general surgeons in Sorenson besides David—are huddled in a corner with Joe Weegan, an internist. Cary Snyder, a plastics man who has sucked the thighs and bellies of at least half the women in the snooty neighborhood along Lakeside Drive, is chatting by the punch bowl with Mick Dunn, whose specialty is orthopedics. David is here, too, apparently none the worse from his overnight stay in a jail cell. He looks frighteningly handsome in his dark suit as he laughs at something he's just heard from Garrett Solange, a neurosurgeon and one of David's closest friends.

I recognize other faces, too, doctors whose specialties only occasionally involve surgery, like the OB/GYN and pediatric docs—a couple of whom are women—and the urology guys. I mentally add them to my list of targets, but put them at the bottom. If Karen Owenby had something going on with doctors who worked in the OR, I figure I'll have a better chance of finding out what it is if I question the "regulars."

I lean over to share my thoughts with Izzy only to discover that he has disappeared. I figure there's no sense wasting any time and zero in on the corner where Sidney, Arthur, and Joe are standing. But just as I take my first step, someone grabs my arm and yanks me back. I turn around and find myself face-to-face with David, and suddenly, looking at the expression on his face, it isn't hard to imagine him as a killer.

Chapter 17

David hauls me off toward an exit and I go along willingly for a few steps, mainly to avoid a scene. But when it looks like he is going to drag me outside, I put on the brakes and shake his hand loose of my arm.

"If you have something to say to me, David, say it here."

"Why the hell didn't you tell me? You deliberately sandbagged me!"

"What are you talking about?"

"That detective, Harley—"

"Hurley?"

"Whatever," he says irritably. "He said someone told him they'd seen me entering Karen's house on the night she was killed. And since I wasn't there, it's a boldfaced lie. Who else besides you would have a reason to say something like that?"

I stare at him, incredulous. "You really think I'd lie about something that serious? Why? Just to settle some imagined score or give myself some slight advantage over you in the divorce?"

"You said it, not me," David hisses through his teeth. "And being tried for murder isn't what I'd call a slight advantage. Christ, I know you're pissed, Mattie, but I never thought you'd stoop this low."

"I didn't."

"Bullshit," he says loudly, louder than he meant apparently because he flinches, takes a quick glance around, then leans in closer and drops his voice. "Why would someone make up a lie like that? I wasn't there, Mattie. So why would someone say I was? What could anyone possibly have to gain by doing that? Anyone other than you, that is," he adds with a sneer.

"Damn it, David. I didn't do it. I *wouldn't* do it. And frankly I'm surprised you think I would."

"Are you trying to tell me you aren't pissed as hell with me? That you wouldn't do anything to pay me back for the hurt I've caused you?"

I suck in a deep breath and try to calm myself before I speak. "Yes, David. I'm trying to tell you that I'm not pissed at you. Oh, I was. You're absolutely right about that. I was righteously pissed when I discovered you and Karen that night. But I'm over it. Way over it. Right now all I feel toward you is overwhelming indifference. With a little pity thrown in for good measure."

I can tell from his face that I've succeeded in wounding him, and for a brief moment I feel triumphant. Then I remember that I once loved this man and thought we would spend the rest of our lives together. God, how I want to believe him, to believe that he is innocent and that he still cares. But he's lied to me before and I just can't make myself believe in him now.

"Glad to see Lucien got you out of jail," I say with all sincerity, thinking it might lighten his mood.

"No thanks to you."

"I had to tell the truth, David."

"Is that all you told? Or did you throw in a few lies, too?"

"Actually, all I told Hurley was that I saw Karen and you together on the night she was killed. I didn't tell him you were fighting, or that Karen slapped your face."

"Well, you might as well have told him. How the hell was

I supposed to know what you did or didn't reveal? Once he made it clear that you'd told him Karen was there that night, I assumed you'd told him everything. So I admitted to the argument before I realized he didn't know about it. You love making me look like a fool, don't you?"

"You seem to be pretty good at that all by yourself." I am tired of bucking his accusations, defending myself when I haven't done anything wrong. So I decide to turn the tables on him. "Why didn't you tell me Karen was pregnant?"

His face falls and he looks away, scanning the room as a muscle twitches violently in his jaw.

"I wasn't sure if you knew," he says finally, killing my hope that he hadn't known. He turns and looks at me. "She told me about it that night, the night she died. That was the first I heard of it and, to be honest, I wasn't sure I believed her. And I figured that even if she was pregnant, I couldn't be sure it was mine. I always used protection. I didn't want to endanger my health. Or yours."

"How very considerate of you," I say snidely, not missing the fact that my safety was thrown in there as an afterthought. "You know as well as I do that nothing is 100 percent perfect, David."

"The point is, I think she was sleeping with someone else," David says feebly.

"Who?"

He shakes his head. "I'm not sure. But when I tried to get into one of the on-call sleep rooms one night, it was locked and I could hear . . . you know . . . sounds . . . heavy breathing and grunting coming from inside. Later, I saw Karen come out of that same room carrying a pile of sheets and the bed in the room had been stripped. But whoever she was with must have already left because there was no one else in there."

"When was this?"

David furrows his brow as he thinks and I feel a funny little ache as I remember how endearing that gesture used to be to me. "I'm not sure," he says, "but I believe it was after you moved out."

"Do you know who was on call that night?"

"Yep, it was Arthur Henley. But it couldn't have been him in the room because he was in an OR at the time along with Cary Snyder, working on a multiple trauma that came in through the ER."

"Regardless, it doesn't change the fact that the baby might have been yours, does it?" I say flatly.

David's shoulders sink and his whole body sags. He drops his gaze to the floor, no longer able to look me in the eye. "No," he says wearily. "It doesn't."

"I heard that Karen had some kind of investment scheme she was working on with some of the docs. Do you know what it was?"

"Investments? No idea." He looks away as he answers and I know he is lying.

"Right," I say, my voice dripping with sarcasm. "Now who's telling lies?"

I leave him standing there and work my way to the middle of the room, watching the crowd. There's another tap on my shoulder and I whirl around in anger thinking David is back for more, but instead I find myself face-to-face with Alison Miller, Sorenson's ace reporter. She is wearing a knee-length red dress made out of some shimmery material that looks great with her olive skin and dark hair. The effect is somewhat diminished, however, by the camera she has hanging around her neck. Alison never goes anywhere without a camera.

"Hello, Alison."

"Hey, Mattie. Saw you chatting with David. What's the scoop? I hear he spent the night in the lockup."

"He did."

"What was the charge?"

I give Alison a sardonic look. "Like you don't already know," I say.

She laughs. "One of the first things they teach you in any journalism class is to always verify your information. I just want to make sure all the facts jibe."

"I don't want to talk about David."

"Okay. How about that new detective, Steve Hurley?"

I can't help but notice the slightly breathless tone in her voice. "What about him?"

"Is he a hunk, or what?" she says, fanning herself. "I mean the guy is seriously cute! He's got great buns and those long, long legs. And the eyes! My God, those eyes! Bluer than my morning glories."

This isn't good at all. It looks as if Izzy was right—Alison is sniffing around Hurley for more than just news. "Hurley also has a full head of hair, Alison," I point out. "I thought you went for bald guys."

"That was last year. This year I'm into hair. And I wouldn't mind running my fingers through those locks of Hurley's. Yum, yum."

Fickle wench. "Try to control yourself, Alison. You're going to start drooling in a minute."

She laughs again. "I know but I just can't help it. That guy makes me crazy. Don't you think he's gorgeous?"

"He's okay, I suppose." I utter this with great nonchalance, trying to look bored. No way am I going to let Alison know that I want to rip her eyes out.

"Okay? Just okay? You must be in shock over this David thing, Mattie."

"Whatever." I let my gaze drift off into the crowd, the perfect image of indifference.

"Well, I've got a date with Mr. Gorgeous next Friday night," Alison says.

"A date?" I screech, my head whipping back around to her. So much for indifference. "With Hurley?"

"Yup. I can't wait."

Man, how I want to wipe that smug smile off her face. "Where is he taking you?"

"I don't know. Dinner somewhere. If I'm lucky, it will be at his place." She wiggles her eyebrows a few times and gives me a little nudge with her elbow. And suddenly I see it in my mind: an intimate little dinner for two with Alison and Hurley making goo-goo eyes at one another over a candlelit table. I feel like crying.

"Oh, look," Alison says, pointing across the room. "There's the mayor. Photo op! Gotta run."

She disappears into the crowd while I try to obliterate the image of her and Hurley from my mind. I remind myself that I am here for a reason. I have people to see, things to find out, doctors to talk to. I scan the room, searching out the faces I need as I tap into my knowledge of the surgeons.

Table talk, as OR chatter is sometimes called, can range from golf techniques and the latest film releases to last night's episode of *Grey's Anatomy.* It often invites the occasional personal revelation as well. Thus, I often knew who had a happy marriage and who didn't, who was sleeping with someone else and who was merely thinking about it . . . a fact that made the irony of not knowing these facts about my own husband much more bitter.

In the past, my insider knowledge has led to some awkward situations when I found myself sharing a social circle with the other wives. But I played my role well over the years, listening but never blabbing. This only strengthened the surgeons' trust in me, and with that trust came more knowledge.

Consequently, I am currently armed with enough ammunition to do some serious damage to several of them. It is ammunition I am holding in reserve, only to be used if I'm desperate to get them to talk to me. For I can't be sure how they'll treat me now that I'm no longer an insider.

I move three names to the top of my mental list, two of them, Mick Dunn and Arthur Henley, because I know they have slept with women other than their wives. The third name on my list is Sidney Carrigan's. While I'm not aware of any infidelities on Sidney's part, the mere fact that he has piles of money makes him a likely target for any investment scheme Karen might have cooked up. Plus, I feel that Sidney, more than any of the others, will still talk to me. We've always gotten along extremely well.

Sidney is in his early fifties, tall and slender, and has avoided the paunch some of his contemporaries have succumbed to. His hair is dark but graying at the temples, his features strong and patrician. His family money is evident in his impeccable manners, the expensive cut of his suits, and his air of confidence and privilege. He rubs elbows with the rich and famous on a regular basis and rumor has it he is even close friends with Steven Spielberg.

Yet despite all that inherited privilege, Sidney is a pretty down-to-earth guy. Down-to-earth for a surgeon, that is. There's a reason so many of them are thought to have a God complex. Slicing, dicing, or simply holding someone's heart or liver in your hands can seriously mess with your ego. It takes a certain amount of chutzpah, plus an unwavering and massive ego to cut open living, breathing people and muck around in their insides.

Sidney has all that and more. But there is this easygoing affability about him that seems to soften those traits. He hasn't always been that way; apparently he was something of a hellion during his twenties and thirties. But when Gina came onto the scene, Sidney settled down.

Despite her local fame, Gina remains something of a mystery, a fact that seems to only enhance her cachet. No one knows anything about her background or her family. She simply appeared at Sidney's side when he returned from a two-week trip to New York and, a month later, they were married. They have remained childless in the twelve years since then and I've never been sure if it's because they can't have kids or because they made a conscious decision not to.

I search the room for Sidney and spot him over by the bar schmoozing with the CEO of a large manufacturing company that is located just outside of Sorenson. I plaster a friendly smile on my face and move in. Halfway there I realize that I probably should have gone to the ladies' room first to make another adjustment on my panty hose; they are slipping lower with every step I take. But just as I am about to turn around to do that, Sidney sees me.

The CEO moves off and Sid quickly breaches the distance between us. "Mattie!" He gives me a quick hug and adds, "The prodigal nurse returns. It's really good to see you. How have you been?"

"Good, Sidney. Thanks for asking. You?"

"Doing just fine, thanks."

"You look a little tired," I note, observing the bluish circles under his eyes. I think I see something dark flit across his face, but it is there and gone so fast I can't be sure.

"Long night last night," he says with a smile. "I was on call. You know how that goes."

"Sure do." Knowing my time in the spotlight of Sidney's attention is likely to be short, I decide to plunge right in. "Damn shame about Karen Owenby, isn't it?"

"An awful thing," he says, shaking his head. "I hope they catch who did it soon."

"Me, too. I'll bet it's really disrupted things over at the hospital, eh?"

"It sure has. That and the fact that David's surgeries are subject to last-minute cancellations at the whim of the local cops. But then I guess you probably know all about that already, particularly since I hear your brother-in-law is defending him."

I nod. "Yes, Lucien's been keeping me informed. Hopefully, it will all work out soon."

"Will you? You and David, I mean."

"Will we what? Work out?"

Sid nods.

"I don't know, Sid. I don't think so. Things have gone too far."

"He made a dumb mistake, one I know he's come to regret. He's a good man, Mattie. I don't know why the cops are hassling him, because there is no way he did this. I'd stake my life on it."

A curious choice of words. And what does it say about the future potential for my marriage if Sid has more faith in David's innocence than I do?

"So," I say, deciding to fish, "were you in on that investment thing with Karen? I can't help but wonder what's going to happen with that now."

Sidney looks puzzled for a second, then a dawning awareness hits his face. "You mean that thing with the medical supply company? I didn't get in on that. It sounded a little too edgy to me and I don't really need the extra cash flow."

I have no idea what he means and am about to ask when a voice behind me interrupts.

"Hello, Sidney. Mattie."

It's Robert Calhoun, the hospital's CEO. Beside him is Gina. "I found your wife over in the corner charming the socks off a half dozen men," Robert says to Sid with a wink. "So I thought I'd return her to you."

Gina rolls her eyes at me and it is all I can do to choke back a laugh.

"There's something I need to discuss with you, Sidney," Robert goes on. "If you can spare me a moment."

"Certainly."

"Ahem," Gina says, leaning up and giving her husband a peck on the cheek. "While you guys talk business, we girls are going to have a little chat of our own. Try to stay out of trouble, you two."

With that, Gina links an arm through one of mine and steers me away. So much for my time with Sidney. Maybe I can try again later.

"That was a narrow escape," Gina says in a low voice. "Calhoun wants to talk to Sid about opening up a new women's suite at the hospital by converting the old nurses' quarters into an outpatient center. And trust me, when Calhoun gets to talking business, it's a real snore."

"I know," I say. "Been there, done that."

Gina laughs. "Sid knew Calhoun would approach him tonight. He got wind of it from one of the admin. secretaries. Every time Calhoun comes up with a new scheme, you can bet he's going to run it by Sidney first. The idiot thinks he has us fooled into believing that the only reason he comes to us is because he respects Sid's opinion and not because he wants Sid's money to back him up."

She pauses and flashes me a wicked smile. "You know what I told Sid last night when he mentioned this latest venture idea of Calhoun's? I told him he should suggest they open up a sleep studies center instead. Then, to help the patients nod off, they can bring Calhoun in and get him talking business."

We both snort a laugh and my spirits get an even bigger boost when I see that Gina has steered us to the bar, where she orders us each a glass of champagne.

"Cheers," Gina says, holding her glass aloft. We clink and drink. Then she shakes her head and smiles that megawatt smile of hers. "Mattie, I must say, you are looking fantastic tonight. That dress is beautiful."

"Thank you," I say. A few more compliments like that and my head will be so big I won't be able to fit through the doors.

"You've done something different with your hair, haven't you?"

"I have. I finally found a great stylist."

"Well, that *is* a coup!" she says. "Whatever you're doing, it's working. You've been turning heads since you got here."

"Really?"

"Yes, really."

I take a moment to relish the concept.

"Did David tell you I called?" Gina asks, interrupting my reverie.

"No, he didn't," I say, mildly surprised that she has.

"I was afraid he might not, but I didn't know how else to reach you. There's no phone number listed for you."

"I don't have a phone at the moment," I tell her. It's a lie, bit it's easier than admitting that I still don't know the number of my cell phone.

"Really? It doesn't bother you, not being able to call anyone?" She looks appalled and I imagine the thought of being disconnected from the rest of the world is tantamount to torture for someone like Gina.

"Not yet," I say with a smile.

"I'm sorry. I didn't mean to pry. It's just that I've been concerned about you ever since I saw you the other day. Wondering if you're doing okay with all the . . . changes in your life. It must be a very difficult time for you."

"I've had a few rough patches," I admit. "But I'm doing okay, Gina. Thanks for your concern."

"Hey, we girls have to stick together, you know. Keep the men from getting out of line." She gives me a warm smile, her eyes twinkling. "Though if this new look of yours is any indication, I'd say you're doing just fine."

"Thanks." My neck is starting to ache beneath the massive weight of my head.

"Don't mention it. And listen, if you ever want to talk, or just go out to lunch or something, don't hesitate to call me. Okay?"

"Okay."

"Promise?"

"I promise." A subtle shift of her gaze to the left gives me a second's warning before yet another hand clamps down on my shoulder.

"Well, if it isn't Mattie Winston!"

I turn and smile at Mick Dunn and his wife, Marjorie.

"Hello, Mick, Marjorie," Gina says, her voice noticeably cooler than it was a moment ago. She turns back to me. "Remember what I said, Mattie. Call anytime." With that, she slides away into the crowd, leaving me with Mick and Marjorie.

"It's good to see the both of you," I tell them, watching Marjorie glare after Gina. "How's the bone business, Mick?"

"The usual. A break here, a break there. Just steady enough that *I* never get a break." He laughs at his own joke and I manage a chuckle, even though I've heard that same line from him dozens of times before. "You really look great, Mattie! Ditching David seems to suit you," he says with a wink.

Marjorie's glare quickly shifts from Gina to me. Mick is a notorious flirt, a trait that has landed him in the beds of at least three other women I know about and who-knows-how-many that I don't. He has oodles of charm and is strikingly handsome with his sparkling blue eyes and cinnamon-colored hair. Because of his shameless womanizing, I want to dislike him. But I can't. He has a self-deprecating style that is not only irresistibly charming, it has the bonus effect of irritating the crap out of his wife, Marjorie, someone I've discovered I can dislike with ease.

Marjorie Dunn is one of the coldest, most snobbish women I've ever met. Her platinum-blond hair and steely blue eyes work to accentuate that icy impression. I have to give her one thing though; she looks pretty good for a woman of fifty-three. That is due in part to some help from Cary Snyder's scalpel. Marjorie has had a boob job, the tummy and thigh-sucker routine, and a nose job, presumably to make it easier for her to look down it at everyone else. Those are the surgeries I know about, and I suspect some other procedures have been done in Cary's office, because Marjorie's face has that tight, drawn look to it, giving her an expression of perpetual surprise. Her skin is stretched so taut over her cheekbones, she looks as if one good sneeze will split her face wide open.

I wonder if it is Mick's infidelities that drive Marjorie to surgically improve herself, or if it is simple vanity. Most of what I know about her leads me to believe she is far more interested in Mick's social position and earning capacity than his fidelity—or lack thereof. I figure that is why she stays with him even though she has to know about his many dalliances. What I don't understand is why Mick, who has a warm personality and an obvious zest for life, stays with a frigid little killjoy like Marjorie.

She finally acknowledges my greeting with a nod and the slightest hint of tedium in her voice. "Mattie. How nice to see you." I am instantly dismissed as she turns to Mick. "Darling," she says, her tone robbing the word of any hint of endearment, "you really should take advantage of the evening to talk with Ms. Molinaro about the nursing problems you mentioned. It's the perfect time, you know. What with the liquor flowing freely and the good PR this event will bring for the hospital, I'd wager her mood will be better than usual."

"You're right, of course," Mick says, his eyes roaming the room. Judging from the expression of anticipation I see on his face, I don't think it's Molinaro he's looking for.

"Let's try to find her before the dinner," Marjorie suggests, deftly steering Mick away and leaving me standing alone.

I watch them go and consider tagging along, thinking this could lead to some of the evening's best entertainment. Marjorie is a manipulative woman who hates to lose and Molinaro is as stubborn and mean as they come. I figure the two of them for even odds in a bitch-slap session but in the end I chicken out, fearful they might combine their considerable talents and use them on me.

Chapter 18

I flag Izzy down and meet him in a corner, where we compare notes.

"Find out anything?" I ask him.

"A little. Seems everyone is pretty shocked by the fact that Karen was killed, although so far not too many people seem to know about the fake identity thing."

I'm surprised by that. Normally, anything that newsworthy would move through the hospital grapevine like shit through a colon after a lower GI prep.

"I have no idea if anyone else was sleeping with the woman," Izzy continues. "I haven't quite figured out how to ask that question without being offensive. But Garrett did mention something about a medical supply company that Karen had some connection to and an ownership scheme that would allow the docs to refer to the place, share in the profits, and not get knocked for a conflict of interest."

"Sidney mentioned something about a medical supply company, too," I tell him. "Though he said he doesn't know much about it because he wasn't involved." And then a lightbulb goes on in my brain. "And there's something else. Something I forgot about." I tell him about my visit to David's office and the business card I found inside the tobacco pouch. "Maybe

I should check the place out," I suggest. "Poke around and see what turns up."

"Can't hurt," Izzy says.

A waiter comes by carrying a plate of hors d'oeuvres—little weenies wrapped in phyllo dough. That damned Stewart woman is everywhere these days, but while I harbor some philosophical differences with the woman, it isn't enough to overcome my incessant appetite. I grab a cocktail napkin and pile several of the hors d'oeuvres on top of it. As I pop one in my mouth, several others roll off my napkin onto the floor.

Izzy clucks his disapproval. "You are such a klutz."

"I am not."

"You are too. You're always dropping stuff, bumping into things, and stumbling about."

"I only stumble when I have to wear heels because I'm not used to them," I snap back. "And for your information, I didn't drop those wieners by accident. I was tossing them down so that bottom feeders like you won't go hungry."

"Very funny," Izzy says. "Short humor. Now I *know* I struck a nerve."

I bend down to pick up the wieners and feel something shift along my backside. Thinking it's the waistband of my panty hose slipping down the last few inches and that they will be pooled around my ankles soon if I don't act, I abandon the wiener grab, wrap the ones I already have in my napkin and shove them at Izzy. "I need to hit the ladies' room," I tell him. "Be right back."

Several steps later I hear Izzy call to me in a hoarse whisper. I ignore him, wanting to get to the ladies' room before my panty hose turn into knee-highs, but he calls again, louder this time. Irritated, I turn to look back at him and realize that most of the other heads in the room are doing the same. Then, as Izzy gestures for me to stop and wait, the heads all turn toward me.

I don't know what Izzy is up to but I'm not about to be deterred from my mission. I wave at him and continue toward the rest room. Seconds later I hear the first snigger and some sixth sense, some internal antenna, tells me I am the cause. Paranoid, I glance over my shoulder and see Izzy waving frantically now, moving toward me as fast as his stubby legs can carry him. Along the periphery of my vision I sense several people watching me with bemused expressions on their faces, but when I turn to look at them, they quickly turn away.

An instant later I become aware of a cool breeze on my cheeks—and not the ones on my face. I reach back tentatively with one hand and gasp when I realize that the seam in the back of my dress has pulled itself apart. I turn and slowly back into the nearest wall while everyone in the room giggles and pretends not to see what I'm doing.

Izzy finally catches up to me, breathless and red-faced from his exertion. "Your dress," he mutters. He squeezes his lips together hard.

"If you laugh, Izzy, so help me, I'll pummel you."

"I'm sorry." His mouth twitches and spasms as I stick my hand between me and the wall and examine the damage. At least eight inches of seam is open, maybe more. The waistband of my panty hose is halfway down my cheeks, cutting across them so that they bulge through the seam opening like a four-pack.

"Damn Olga and that stupid bow," I mutter.

"What bow?"

"There was a bow on the back of this dress and I made Olga take it off. I don't think she sewed things back up as well as she should have." I keep glancing around the room, seeing heads huddle, hearing whispers and giggles. I have a bad feeling I'm going to be the joke du jour come Monday and silently wish for a bolt of lightning to pop out of the sky and strike me dead. Then I nearly jump out of my skin when all the windows in the room light up bright for a second and a rumble of thunder shakes the building. Of all the times for God to finally start listening to me.

"Get me out of here, Izzy," I say, my voice low and thick. "Get behind me, stay close, and follow me out to the car."

"Yes, ma'am," he says, working to suppress a giggle. I want to pop him one but I need him to get me out of the room first and away from all these laughing, watching eyes. Thank goodness the rip is down low in the dress. Otherwise, Izzy wouldn't be tall enough to cover the damage.

He moves in and stands as close to me as possible, close enough that I can feel the heat of his breath through the sleeve of my dress. "Ready," he announces.

I turn slowly, Izzy following my every move as if we are practicing some sophisticated dance step. We walk out of the room together, moving our legs in synch, Izzy sticking so close to my backside he looks like a tumor on my ass.

When we reach the parking lot, I see that my hope for a lightning strike is becoming more viable with each passing minute. Streaks of it flit across the sky off in the distance and thunder booms all around us. It isn't raining here yet, but the air has that thick, ozone smell to it that says a deluge is on its way.

I hurry toward Izzy's car, no longer worried about him keeping up. I am still a good ten feet away when the sky opens up and releases sheets of icy cold rain that slake down my back into the dress. Belatedly I realize that I've left behind my shawl, which would have covered up my gaping seam nicely. Ah, the wisdom of hindsight, so to speak.

By the time I squeeze myself into the front seat of Izzy's car, I feel and figure I look like a drowned rat. Izzy climbs in, glances over at me, and snorts a laugh.

I give him my best glare. "A little heat would be nice," I say through clenched teeth. "And don't you dare say one word about the dress, or the rain, or anything else. Just take me home. And don't tell Dom about this either. Understand?"

"I understand." It's a token answer. We both know he'll tell Dom the entire story the minute he gets home. But for now, I need my delusions.

Izzy starts the car, pulls out, and, moments later, cold air is blowing in my face. The heater in the car takes forever to warm up and Izzy is convinced that running the blower on high helps to speed the process along. I start to complain but suddenly a horribly loud sound, like rocks hitting the car, make speech nearly impossible.

"Hail," Izzy yells over the noise. "Damn it. It will ruin my car."

I am less concerned about Izzy's car than I am the hail. Wisconsin is no stranger to killer tornadoes and, all too often, hail is the precursor. I stretch my neck out as far as I can and peer through the windshield at the dark sky. A streak of lightning flashes, blinding me, but my ears still work and I can hear the wind howling outside the car, screeching and screaming that it wants in.

"Izzy?" I holler. "Do you hear that wind?"

Izzy nods but he doesn't try to speak. He white-knuckles the steering wheel, his speed down to a crawl as the hail continues to pummel us. I don't know how he can see where the road is because no matter how hard I look, I can't see it at all. Finally, he makes a turn, eases the car over to one side, and stops.

"I can't see well enough to drive in this," he says. "Let's wait here a bit."

I nod, thinking it's a good idea, but then another flash of lightning streaks down from the sky and I see where Izzy has parked. Panic fills my throat.

"Izzy?"

"What?"

"You just pulled into Whispering Pines."

"So?"

"So what is Whispering Pines, Izzy? I'll tell you what it is," I say quickly, not giving him time to breathe, much less answer. "It's a freaking trailer park. You pulled into a trailer park in the middle of a thunderstorm. A thunderstorm that could easily be spawning a tornado as we speak."

I stare at him, waiting for him to shift the car back into

gear and hightail it out of there. Instead he stares back at me, a look of confusion on his face.

"For heaven's sake, Izzy. Don't you get it? This is a trailer park! You might as well hang a sign outside that says, TORNADOS WELCOME HERE. Everyone knows that trailer parks are the first to go in any tornado. Hell, they're tornado magnets."

He stares at me, his mouth hanging open. "You know, sometimes I think you are truly nuts," he says.

"Fine, be a skeptic," I tell him. "But think back on all the news footage you've ever seen of tornado damage. What's the one thing you always see? A trashed trailer park. Every time. Think about it."

He squints his eyes and gives me a look that says he is about to consign me to the nearest loony bin. But then he assumes a faraway expression and I know he is replaying those news reports in his mind. Another bolt of lightning zips across the sky and he looks out the window at the neat rows of trailers.

"Oh my God," he says finally. He reaches down and quickly shifts the car into gear. Then he creeps back out onto the main street and tries to stay on it as best he can. The hail stops almost as quickly as it started but driving rain and sleet come in its place, some of the drops splashing hard and thick, like overripe cherry tomatoes.

By the time we make it back to the house, the storm is still blowing furiously and the darkened windows everywhere tell us that the power is out. Since the automatic door opener won't work, Izzy parks just in front of the garage.

Dispensing with any niceties, I say, "See you tomorrow," pry myself out of the car, and run for the cottage. I can't move very fast as my feet are numb from both cold and a lack of circulation and the thick nylon in the panty portion of my support hose is like an iron band around my thighs, hobbling me. A flash of lightning momentarily blinds me, making me trip on the front steps. Cursing, I rub my bashed shinbone a moment before I struggle back to my feet and limp my way to the door.

Once inside, I kick off my shoes, hike up my dress and

peel off the hose, tossing them aside. I give the light switch a cursory try, but nothing happens. Feeling my way through the darkness, I head for the kitchen. I think of Rubbish in the split second before he decides to rub against my feet and I do an awkward little side hop to keep from stepping on him. I lose my balance and fall again, coming down hard on my left hip and elbow. Wincing with pain, I feel a warm wetness run down my arm that I am pretty sure is blood. I sit up, issuing forth with every cuss word I know. I call to Rubbish and as soon as I feel him at my feet again, I scoop him up and hold him close to my chest.

With the cat safely tucked away, I get off the floor and make it to the kitchen without further incident. I find a candle and some wood matches in a drawer and give myself a meager ring of light. Now that I can see, I put Rubbish back down and carry the candle toward the bathroom, setting it on a table just outside the door. I dig a towel out of the closet beside the toilet and plop down on the edge of the tub to dry off.

Beyond the flicker of the candle's light, I can see the window in the upper part of my front door as well as the two windows on either side of it. All of them are covered with thin, gauzy curtains and as I'm looking toward the window on the left, another brilliant bolt of lightning turns the night into day. And just outside the window, a shadow in the shape of a person appears.

At first I think it's just my imagination, but then I see that Rubbish is standing in the middle of the room staring at the front door with his back arched and his fur standing at rigid attention. The chill I feel in my marrow is from more than just the icy rain.

I know the shadow isn't Izzy or Dom—it is much too tall—but judging from the broadness of the shoulders and the overall physique, I am pretty certain it's a man. And I reason that anyone who is out in this sort of weather is either too stupid to live or up to no good. Images of Karen Owenby's dead body flash through my mind. The inquiries I've made into her life—and death—flash through as well. Have I gotten close to the truth without knowing it? Close enough to make someone think of me as a threat?

The shadow moves toward the door, which, I realize in a panic, isn't locked. I think of calling 911, but then remember that my cell phone is buried in my purse, which I dropped just inside the door as I entered the cottage. I could scream, but with the crazy weather outside, I am pretty certain no one will hear me.

Rubbish hisses, making my nerves jump, and I look around the bathroom for something to use to defend myself. An aerosol can of hair spray is the best I can find—I figure if I spray it in someone's face, it might disable them long enough for me to get away. At the last second I see the plunger with its thick wooden handle standing in the back corner beside the toilet and grab it, too.

When I look back toward the front door, the shadow is gone. Hair spray in one hand, plunger in the other, I stand in the bathroom, my gaze shifting back and forth between the windows. Outside, thunder crashes, wind howls, and rain pounds, but I can hardly hear any of it for the rapid *thump-thump* of my heart, which seems to have miraculously relocated itself in my ears. The branches of a nearby tree scrape along the roof as they are buffeted by the wind, and for a panicked second I think that whoever is outside is now on the roof. But then I see fleeting movement through the window in the door.

He is still on the porch. Rubbish tosses his bravado to the storm and hightails it into the bedroom, where I figure I will find him hiding under the bed. For a second I consider joining him, but it is a pretty narrow space and the thought of being trapped under there keeps me riveted where I stand.

I realize I have a slight advantage I might be able to exploit. With the power out and the house dark, I am able to navigate far more easily than someone who doesn't know the layout of the cottage. I suck in a deep breath to brace myself and stride across the room. I set the hair spray on a table by the door, and wield the plunger in one hand like a baseball bat. Then, with my free hand, I grab the front door and whip it open.

A horrific sight awaits me, a tall, hulking creature. And with a scream of mortal fear, I swing the plunger as hard as I can against its head.

Chapter 19

"Jesus Christ, Mattie!" David hollers, staggering under the weight of my blow. "What the hell are you doing?" He topples toward the door, nearly falling on me.

"What the hell are *you* doing lurking around out here? You scared the bejesus out of me, David!" Steady on his feet now, he rubs the side of his head where I can see a small trickle of blood running over his cheek.

"I wasn't *lurking*," he mumbles irritably.

"Get in here." I grab his arm and pull him inside, then steer him into the kitchen, stopping along the way to pick up the candle. I sit him down, put the candle in the middle of the table, and set the plunger, which I am still holding in one hand, on the floor by the kitchen doorway. Then I dig out two towels from a drawer and hand one to David so he can mop off his face while I use the other to clean and examine the wound on his head.

"It's not bad," I tell him. I dab and he winces. "It won't need stitches or anything."

"Christ, you probably gave me a concussion. What the hell has gotten into you?"

"I didn't know who you were," I tell him. "I'm a little spooked by all that's happened, okay? I mean, a woman in town was murdered a few days ago. Remember?"

David rolls his eyes. "How can I forget?"

"What were you doing out there on my porch?" I ask him. The lingering suspicion in my mind must have carried over into my voice because he turns to look at me and moans.

"You can't seriously still think I had anything to do with Karen's death," he says. "Christ, Mattie. What's it going to take to convince you?"

"What were you doing outside on my porch?" I ask again.

He sighs and leans forward, staring at his shoes. "Someone said you left the party in a big hurry and I was concerned. I've been wanting to talk to you but things got a bit nasty earlier tonight. So I came here to apologize for jumping all over you and to take another stab at talking things out. I wasn't sure you'd hear me knock given all the noise this storm is making so I was peeking through your windows to see if you were here or at Izzy's house. That's all. I was about to try a knock on the door when you whipped it open and bashed me on the head."

"Well, I'm sorry, but you scared the hell out of me," I tell him. "You looked a sight, all rain-drenched and hunkered down inside your coat like that. I couldn't tell it was you and figured it was safer to act first and ask questions later."

"I guess I should be grateful you weren't armed with a gun," he mutters.

The bleeding from his scalp wound has stopped and I set the towel aside. "I'd offer you a drink but I don't have any liquor here."

"I'm fine. Although I wouldn't mind some water."

I get him a glass of water from the tap and then settle into a chair across from him. His gaze rises from his shoes to my face and he studies me intently for a moment, as if he's trying to see inside me. I find it unnerving, particularly with the weird shadows the candlelight casts along his face.

"What is it you want to talk about, David?" I ask, hearing a hint of nervousness in my voice.

"Are you doing okay? Here, I mean," he says, making a

sweeping motion with his arm. "And here." He taps one finger on his temple.

"It's a little late to be asking, isn't it?"

He flops back in the chair with a sigh and folds his arms over his chest. "Man, you just never let up, do you? Are you ever going to forgive me for what I did? Or do you intend to hold it over me for the rest of my life?"

At first blush the life thing sounds pretty good to me, though it does seem a bit spiteful. For a brief second I think maybe he's right, maybe I *am* being unreasonable and too unforgiving. Then I realize he is up to his old games again, trying to shift the burden of guilt from his shoulders to mine.

"I don't see how it should matter one way or the other, David," I say coldly. "Because our lives aren't likely to be bound together much longer. I intend to file for divorce just as soon as we've been separated the required amount of time. And since I no longer work at the hospital, I have no reason to so much as look at you again. But to answer your question, no, I don't think I can forgive you. Nor can I ever trust you again. Does that help?"

He sits there for a second with a disbelieving expression on his face that quickly changes to anger. "It must be nice to feel so high and mighty and perfect," he sneers. "Did you ever stop to think that maybe this is partly your fault? That if you'd been a bit more willing in bed I never would have gone looking elsewhere?"

I narrow my eyes at him. "Don't you *dare* try to shift the blame of your sordid little affair off on me. Face it, David. You're a cheat and a liar. And frankly, I have too much respect for myself to spend one more minute married to the likes of you. In fact, I don't want to waste another minute speaking to you. Get the hell out of my house."

If I'm hoping for a reaction, judging from the look on his face, I am about to get one. His eyes narrow until they are little more than slits. A dark cloud of emotion seems to emanate from his every pore. I've seen him angry before, but this is different. There is something darker and far more unpleasant churning beneath the surface and I start to wonder if I've made a fatal error in judgment by believing him incapable of murder.

Wisdom tells me to leave things well enough alone, but I can't. I'm too pissed, too scared, and too emotionally volatile. "You seem awfully defensive, David. And it seems like every time I turn around I'm uncovering another one of your dirty little secrets. What else are you hiding? Did you kill her, David? *Did* you? Because based on everything I know, I'm beginning to think you did."

He pushes out of his chair and it tips over backward, crashing to the floor. He leans across the table until he is inches from my face. "You bitch," he hisses. "Are you really that bitter? Do you seriously think I'm capable of killing someone?" He pauses a moment and something alters his expression. "Wait," he says. "Of course. Why didn't I see it before?"

He moves even closer, getting right up in my face, and says, "Just how angry and bitter are you, Mattie? How do I know *you* didn't kill Karen out of some jealous rage? Hell, you already admitted you were stalking us, so it's—"

"I was not stalking you!" I yell, pushing back in my chair to get away from him. I stand and point a shaking finger toward the front door. "We are through with this discussion. I want you gone. Get out. Now."

He straightens, his face turning redder by the minute, his hands clenched into fists. This is not the carefully controlled anger I am familiar with. This is different . . . rawer . . . less controlled . . . more intense. It scares me. I sidle over to where I left the plunger and grab it, once again wielding it like a baseball bat.

David gawks at me, his eyes shifting back and forth between my face and the plunger. Then his expression changes from incredulity to rage. "You fucking bitch!" he seethes. He picks up his glass of water and heaves it toward the wall, where it shatters into a zillion pieces. Even though it lands a good six feet from where I stand, a sliver of glass ricochets off the wall and zips a gash in my forehead. I feel a tiny sting, like a mosquito bite, and seconds later, blood trickles into my right eye.

I swipe at it with my hand, stare at the blood in disbelief, and tighten my grip on the plunger handle. *"Get . . . out!"* I scream.

David blinks several times in rapid succession, then stares at my face with an expression of growing horror. "Mattie, oh, God, I'm sorry. Please . . ." He starts toward me but stops when I rear back with the plunger.

"Out! Now!" I scream at him.

"Let me look at your head."

He takes another tentative step toward me, but I stop him in his tracks by shouting, "Get away from me!"

"Come on, Mattie. Be reasonable. Let me look at that cut. I think you may need stitches."

Stitches? I feel woozy all of a sudden. I have no problem at all dealing with other people's blood and guts, but when it comes to my own, I'm a total wuss.

I loosen my grip on the plunger a tad and, sensing my momentary capitulation, David closes the distance between us in two steps, crunching bits of broken glass beneath his shoes. But instead of looking at my forehead, he reaches up and grabs the plunger instead. That action snaps me back to the real crisis at hand and I twist myself hard to the right, yanking the plunger free of his grip. The motion leaves us both a little off balance and David totters, trying not to fall on me. Scared, angry, and confused, I let loose with my best scream yet, an utterly primal yell born of months' worth of pent-up anger, frustration, and humiliation.

I hear a thunderous crash behind me and crane my neck to look. My front door is wide open, and standing in the middle of my living room is a dripping, dark figure, shadowy behind the radiant beam of a flashlight. I am momentarily blinded as the light washes over my eyes, but then the beam lowers, running down my backside and moving across the floor. It stops for a moment when it gets to my panty hose, which are still in a heap near the door.

I can finally make out a face in the backwash from the flashlight and am startled to realize it's Hurley. He glances at me, fixes his gaze on David for a second, and then lowers his head and charges across the room. I'm so stunned by the sight of this raging bull coming at me that I can't do a thing except step aside. He slams into David and a brief scuffle ensues, punctuated with several colorful cuss words. The flashlight beam bounces around the room for several seconds, before finally settling somewhere behind David's back.

I hear Hurley say, "You think you can force yourself on her just because you were married to her, asshole?" As my eyes adjust to the flashlight's glare, I can see Hurley standing behind David. He has David's right arm wrenched up behind his back and David's face is pinched with pain. Hurley looks at me and says, "You want to press charges against this asshole? Assault and battery? Attempted rape?"

"Rape?" I say, confused. "He didn't try to rape me."

David grits his teeth and speaks to Hurley in a low, dangerous-sounding voice. "Look, you cretin. I'm a surgeon and, as such, my hands and arms are very valuable to me. Now, I'm willing to be reasonable, but if you don't let up on my arm right now, I'm going to sue you and the city of Sorenson for every penny I can get."

Indecision flits across Hurley's face.

"Let him go, Hurley," I say. He hesitates, but does as I ask.

David steps away and massages his arm, glaring at Hurley. "And if you want to consider charges against someone," he snarls angrily, "look what she did to me." He raises his hand and points to the wound on his scalp.

Hurley glances at it, then at me. "Did you do that?"

I nod and set the plunger aside.

"Self-defense?" Hurley asks.

"Sort of," I tell him. "But I didn't know it was him. I saw

a shadow outside peeking in my windows and when I opened the door, there he was. He scared me. So I swung." I gesture toward the plunger.

"How did that happen?" Hurley asks, jutting his chin toward my forehead.

David answers before I can. "That was my fault. I got pissed and threw a glass. I didn't throw it *at* her but one of the pieces ricocheted and nicked her anyway." He looks at me, his expression apologetic. "I'm truly sorry, Mattie. I didn't mean to hurt you."

"What about your leg? And your arm?" Hurley asks me, his eyes narrowing.

I look down and see several scrapes covered with dried blood. "I fell and bashed my shin and elbow. But that happened before David ever showed up."

Hurley seems to weigh the facts for several seconds, then sighs heavily. "You got lucky this time, Doc," he says bitterly. "But I think you should leave."

"Why should I leave? Who the hell invited *you* here?" David snaps.

Hurley glowers at him and I'm afraid things are going to get messy soon if I don't do something. "David, please go," I say.

He stares at me in disbelief.

"You heard the lady," Hurley growls.

David hangs his head for a second, then moves toward the door, which is still open. Hurley steps in behind him and at that moment, I see Rubbish standing just inside the threshold, staring out at the rain. At the sound of the two men moving toward him, he startles, arches his back, and runs outside. Before I can react, the two men step out onto the porch and Hurley pulls the door closed behind him.

I rush over and look out through the window. I don't see Rubbish anywhere but the two men are standing on the porch, face to face, their fists clenched at their sides. I can hear Hurley's booming voice over the constant thrum of the rain but I can't make out any words. I watch the two of them, transfixed by this standoff at the Testosterone Corral, until David turns and stomps off into the night. Hurley watches him get in his car, start it up, and drive away before turning back toward the door.

His face looks as dark and thunderous as the weather outside but when he sees me peering out at him through the window, his expression softens, making my heart do a little flip-flop. I open the door and he comes in, gently pushing me to one side so he can shut the door behind him. He leans against the wall, his flashlight aimed at the floor, his eyes regarding me with an expression I can't quite decipher.

"A plunger?" he says finally, cocking one eyebrow. "You hit him with a toilet plunger? What were you trying to do, flush him out?"

Despite the tension I feel, I laugh. Hurley laughs, too, and I am amazed at how it transforms his face.

"Hey, any weapon in a pinch," I say stupidly.

He walks over, brushes aside the hair on my forehead, and shines his flashlight on my gash. He is so close to me, I can feel heat radiating off his body in a cloud of steam. I realize he is soaked to the bone, his jeans dripping wet as a puddle forms at his feet. And the idea of suggesting he get out of those jeans flashes through my mind.

The rest of me may be in shock, but my hormones are working just fine.

"I think you're going to need some stitches," he says. He walks into the bathroom and returns a moment later with a towel, which he uses to dab at the wound. "Want me to drive you to the ER?"

I nod. At the moment, I'd let him drive me pretty much anywhere. "What are you doing here?" I ask him. "Checking up on me?"

"Actually, it's your ex I'm checking up on. I followed him when he left the little hospital soirée and after a few blocks I guessed he was heading home. But then I saw him turn in here and got curious." He pauses and gives me a sheepish look. "I confess," he says, "I was trying to peek in through your windows but it was too dark to see anything. And then I heard you scream. When I opened the door I saw the two of you struggling and saw the torn stockings on the floor, the rip in your dress, your banged-up knees and that gash on your head . . ."

"And you thought he tried to rape me," I conclude. Now that I am seeing it from Hurley's perspective, it all makes sense. Inexplicably, I feel a bubble of laughter build deep in my stomach. I fight like hell to keep it there, but it bursts out of me anyway. It has a brittle, demented sound to it and seconds later I start to sob. Hurley's expression as he watches this little Dr. Jekyll/Mrs. Hyde routine goes from startled to horrified, and then to something solicitous and tender that makes my toes tingle and my blood flow hot.

I suspect that when it comes to Hurley, my hormones are like a cockroach. Even a nuclear holocaust won't keep them down.

Chapter 20

I change out of what's left of my dress and slip on jeans and a sweater. I towel-dry my hair, run a comb through it, and then pull it into a ponytail—even Barbara's magical ministrations can't rescue it now. I'm putting on my jacket when I remember Rubbish.

"Oh, no!"

"What?" Hurley looks instantly tense as I run to the front door and pull it open. He follows me, asking, "What?" about three more times before his finely honed detective mind figures it out after watching me yell, "Here, kitty, kitty," into the driving wind and rain. I'm heading into the woods when he grabs my arm.

"Come on," he says. "You need to get to the ER and have that cut looked at. It's bleeding again. I'm sure the cat will be okay."

"He will *not* be okay," I yell back, shaking my arm loose from his grip. "And he's not a cat, he's a kitten. He's tiny and he's too young to be out in something like this. Plus, he hasn't lived here very long. He doesn't know his way around."

I'm close to tears again, which apparently scares Hurley enough that he decides to help me look. But after half an hour of fruitless searching, I finally give in. Since I'm soaked, I change my clothes again, drying off as best I can. But even after donning a shirt and two sweaters, I still feel chilled to the bone. By the time I'm ready to leave, my teeth are chattering, partly from the damp cold and partly from the leftover adrenaline I have running around inside me. Hurley takes one look at me and disappears into my bedroom, reappearing a moment later with a blanket from my bed. He drapes it gently around my shoulders and then steers me out to his car.

The ride to the ER is a quiet one, at least in terms of conversation. The rain and thunder are too loud for normal talk, and given the way my teeth are chattering, I'll be hard-pressed to say anything that doesn't sound like a stutter from an evilly possessed typewriter.

At the hospital, Hurley pulls up by the ER entrance and escorts me inside, maintaining a light touch on my elbow. Halfway there I begin to feel a little woozy and I let my imagination go Victorian, imagining what would happen if I fainted. My eyes would flutter and I'd let forth with a dainty little whimper just before my knees give way. Hurley, warned by my delicate utterance, would catch me in his big, strong arms and hold me until . . .

Reality kicks in and my fantasy evaporates as I realize that my weight would likely be enough to break Hurley's arms or, at the very least, send us both crashing to the ground. That whole fainting scenario is the sole property of those genetically lucky women who shop at the five-seven-nine shops. It doesn't work well for someone like me, who makes sure to remove every stitch of clothing and jewelry, take in no food or water, and empty my bladder before getting on the scale each morning. Though actually, when I'm truly depressed, I'll spend a few days weighing with my clothes on, rationalizing in my mind that it isn't really *that* bad. Two socks, a pair of shorts, a T-shirt, and underwear must weigh at least . . . oh . . . eighteen pounds or so, right?

Fortunately I make it inside the ER without keeling over. The fact that I once worked here expedites my admission.

The registration clerk lets me go on back right away, asking only for my driver's license so she can make sure the information in the computer is correct. I look to see if Hurley is impressed by this VIP treatment, but all he does is wave me on, take a cell phone out of his pocket, and mumble something about needing to make a call.

Syph is on duty and after one sympathetic look from her, I burst into tears. She hauls me, sobbing and stuttering, into the ENT room, one of the few areas of the ER where you can get privacy behind a real door as opposed to a giant shower curtain.

She has me lie down and preps my wound while I try to tell her what happened. Lucky for me, the doc on duty is Walter Copeland, who has a delicate touch and a talented hand when it comes to suturing. While I'm not that vain, the idea of having a big scar running across my face doesn't exactly appeal to me. It's hard enough on my ego that I've been compared to Bigfoot in the past, simply because my shoes are large enough to carry a small family downriver. I don't need to add Frankenstein comparisons to my repertoire.

By the time Walter places the first stitch, I have calmed considerably and am happily numb. That's when Syph says, "Boy, that whole thing with Karen Owenby is so weird, isn't it? I mean, it's bad enough she was killed, but then to find out she was some kind of impostor."

"You heard about that?" I say. I'm surprised, remembering Izzy's earlier claim that no one seemed to know yet. I figure Molinaro is doing her best to keep the whole thing a secret for as long as possible.

"Celia," Syph says, and if not for the fact that I am lying under a needle and thread, I would have given myself a *duh* slap on the side of the head. "I can't believe no one suspected anything," Syph goes on. "Though I think her roommate knew something wasn't right. She kept saying she knew it was all going to fall apart sooner or later."

I almost sit bolt upright on the stretcher. "That's right!" I say excitedly. "I forgot that the cops brought her in here that night. Susan something, right?"

"McNally."

"Yeah, that's it. Larry said she was shocky."

"Not really. Mostly she was just nervous as hell. You can hardly blame her. It isn't every day you come home and find your roommate shot to death in the middle of the living room floor. We got her calmed down pretty quick, though. A little vitamin V and twenty minutes later she was floating."

"I'll bet she was." The one and only time I had Vitamin V, our code word for either Valium or another fun mind-bending relaxant known as Versed, was right before I was wheeled into surgery with a case of acute appendicitis. I not only felt really, *really* good, I was convinced I could do the surgery by myself. *On* myself.

"Did Susan say anything else about Karen?" I ask. "Anything that might shed some light on who killed her?"

"Not to me," Syph says. "Though I did hear her say something to one of the cops who was with her. Something about pushing things too far and how she knew it was all going to blow up in her face."

"Any idea what she meant by that?"

"Not a clue."

Walter finishes my stitches—three all together—and I sit up on the stretcher to make sure my dizziness has passed. I have Syph look up Susan McNally's ER record to see who she listed as next of kin. I figure the woman might not want to go back to the house she and Karen shared, assuming she even can since I'm guessing the cops have it locked up tighter than a drum at this point. So I want to know if she has any relatives living nearby she might stay with. Sure enough, there is a sister listed who lives in the nearby village of Parsons. I jot down the address and then go looking for Hurley.

The receptionist thrusts some forms at me and asks me to

sign them—permission to treat even though it's already been done, and a statement of responsibility that essentially promises my first-born child, most of my organs, and all my earthly possessions to the hospital in the event that my insurance doesn't pay. When I ask for my driver's license back, she tells me Hurley has it. The only problem is, no one seems to know where Hurley is. I'm frowning—not an easy task considering that most of my forehead is numb—and debating what to do next, when a uniformed policewoman comes up to me and says, "Are you Mattie Winston?"

"I am."

"I'm supposed to drive you back to your place," she says. "Whenever you're ready to go, just holler."

"Where is Hurley?"

She shrugs. "I have no idea. He said he couldn't stay here and wait on you and asked me to drive you home. Are you ready?"

I am crushed. Here I'd imagined Hurley sitting in the waiting area—actually I had him pacing—worried about whether or not I'd be all right. Instead, he has flown the coop and pawned me off on to someone else. And to think I was willing to faint into his arms just an hour before.

"Know what?" I say to the officer. "I'll just call my sister. There's no need for you to wait around or take me home. She can do it."

"Are you sure?"

"Positive. Thank you anyway."

"Well, if something happens and you can't get a ride, just call the station and tell them to contact me. Name's Brenda Joiner."

"Thanks, Brenda."

One phone call and ten minutes later, Desiree arrives with my niece and nephew in tow. No one would ever guess that Desi and I are sisters, though technically we're only half sisters since she has a different father. Desi's hair is raven colored, her brown eyes are so dark they look black, and she has an olive complexion and a short, wiry build. Erika inherited her mother's looks and coloring whereas Ethan, with his reddish-brown hair, fair skin, and freckles, favors Lucien.

"I didn't mean for you to make a family outing of this," I say as they all come trooping through the door. "Sorry to drag you out in this weather."

"Not a problem," Desi says, smiling. "The storm has abated for the most part anyway. Just some lingering drizzle now. And the kids wanted to come along. They haven't seen their aunt in ages and they haven't seen your new digs at all."

While I believe Ethan's motivation to tag along might be that he simply wanted to see me, I suspect it is something else altogether for Erika. As soon as she enters the ER, she scans the waiting room eagerly, no doubt hoping to see a severed limb or someone with an ax in their head. When the pickings prove to be utterly mundane, she tries hovering by the automatic doors that lead to the treatment area, peeking in when they open in hopes of catching a glimpse of something gory. When that fails to produce anything, she settles sullenly into a chair, gazing out the window with a wistful expression on her face.

Erika loves gore. She loves medical shows, horror movies, televised surgeries, and those medical forensic shows—the bloodier the better. Her fascination with blood and guts occasionally gives her mother pause, but it doesn't bother me at all. In fact, I think my niece has all the makings of a first-class trauma surgeon—as long as the patients don't mind having a doctor who looks like the Grim Reaper's kid sister.

Erika's current style of dress is a cross between Goth and Grunge. Tonight's outfit is typical: black leggings, black sweatshirt, and, beneath that, a man's black shirt with the tail hanging nearly to her knees. Her feet are encased in high-top black boots, and I have no doubt that beneath those is a pair of black socks. Desi recently gave Erika permission to wear makeup and her choices are kohl-black eyeliner, pale foundation, and black lipstick. Topping off this ensemble is her hair—jet black and poker straight—which hangs nearly to her waist.

Ethan is a stark contrast to his sister in more than just looks. He is oblivious to his surroundings. He follows his mother like a little robot, his eyes glued to the electronic game he has in his hands. He mutters the obligatory greeting but never once looks at me. In fact, he never looks at anything other than his game, apparently using some form of internal kid radar to keep from running into things. Not surprisingly, when I manage to sneak a peek at his game, I see some sort of multilegged bug thing racing around the screen.

After we're settled in the car on the way to my cottage, I give Desi a brief encapsulation of the night's events, though I gloss over a few items knowing that, despite their attempts to appear disinterested, the kids are hanging on my every word. They always do, something I've learned the hard way more than once. Tonight they give themselves away when I mention Rubbish.

"You have a cat?" Erika says.

"When did you get a cat?" Ethan asks at the same instant, though there is nary a pause in the bleeps and whistles coming from his game.

"I got him a few days ago. He's only a kitten. I think he's about twelve weeks old."

"Cool." Coming from Erika, this is high praise indeed.

"I found him in a Dumpster," I tell them.

"Way cool," Ethan judges. "Is that why you named him Rubbish?"

"Yep."

"And he ran away?" Erika says, suspicion lacing her voice.

"I hope not, but when I tried to find him, I couldn't. Will you guys help me look for him when we get home?" Both kids answer with an enthusiastic "Sure!" though I can't help but wonder how much help Ethan will be if he doesn't take his eyes off that game.

As Desi pulls into my driveway and parks in front of the cottage, I see that the power is still out. But the cottage isn't totally dark. The light from several candles glows through the front windows, making the hairs on the back of my neck rise since I know I only lit one and I distinctly remember extinguishing it before heading to the ER. I also remember that, once again, I didn't bother to lock the front door.

Then I see one of the candles move across the room as if it's floating on air, and I gasp. Either my cottage is haunted or someone is inside.

Chapter 21

I'm about to freak out and tell Desi to turn around and hightail it out of there when the floating candle approaches a window and I see Hurley's face behind it. Belatedly, I look around and see his car parked over near Izzy's garage.

The kids are out of the car in a flash, intrigued by the chance to peruse my new digs and eager to look for Rubbish. I climb out after them, not sure if I am glad to see Hurley or mad as hell that he is prowling around inside my cottage. Was that why he left me in the clutches of that police-woman? So he could come and search my house?

Feeling confused and betrayed, I stomp up the stairs to my porch and prepare for yet another confrontation. But as soon as I open the door my anger is gone. On the floor in front of the couch is a damp and bedraggled-looking Rubbish, contentedly lapping at a bowl of milk.

"Oh, thank God!" I say. I look over at Hurley. "He came home?"

"Hmph! Hardly. He was up in a tree about halfway between here and your ex's house. Wasn't too hard to find him; he was squalling like the storm itself. And he wouldn't come down either. I had to climb up there and get him."

Erika and Ethan surge toward the kitten, settling on the floor beside him, stroking, petting, oohing, and aahing. I, meanwhile, stand stunned as I consider what Hurley has just told me. Not two days earlier he was standing in my bedroom looking petrified at the thought of just being in the same room with the kitten. Now he's telling me he went out during one of the worst storms of the year and not only looked for the cat, but climbed a tree to rescue him and carried him back to my house.

"I thought you hated my cat."

"I don't hate it. I just don't like cats in general. And this one certainly hasn't given me any reason to think differently."

"Then why did you come back and look for him?"

Hurley shrugs. "I knew you were worried. So I thought I'd come back while you were at the ER to see if I could find him."

With this revelation I begin to think I might be totally, completely, head-over-heels in love with this man.

"Thank you so much," I tell him, giving him a warm smile. "You didn't have to do that but I'm certainly glad you did." I glance over at Desi, seeking confirmation that this is really happening, that I'm not simply dreaming. And then I realize that I haven't made any introductions.

"I'm sorry. Steve Hurley, this is my sister, Des—"

"Desiree Colter," Hurley says before I can finish. "Pleasure to meet you. And I assume those two are Erika and Ethan," he adds, nodding toward the kids.

"Have you met before?" I ask, looking at Desi, who shakes her head and shrugs.

Hurley says, "You know how small towns are. Everyone knows everyone else."

I narrow my eyes at him and he flashes me a cockeyed grin.

"I need to be going," he says then. "But I'd like a word with you first, if you don't mind." He gestures toward the porch and I understand that he wants to speak with me alone, though if I know Desi, she'll find a way to hear every word.

Despite the disparity in our looks, we do have a few things in common, nosiness being one of them.

I follow Hurley out to the porch, pulling the front door closed behind me.

"Here," he says, and he hands me back my driver's license.

"Oh, thanks. I'd forgotten about it." I shove it into the pocket of my jeans, a stalling move while I muster up the courage to say what's on my mind. "You didn't know who Desi was because this is a small town. You've been investigating me, haven't you?"

"It's my job," he says with no hesitation and no hint of apology. "I have a murder to solve. You are someone who knew the victim and you have a motive. Plus you have no alibi for when she was killed."

My hackles rear up immediately and now I know how David must feel whenever I question his innocence. Assuming, of course, that he is innocent.

"Am I still a suspect?"

"Technically, yes. At least until I can prove otherwise. But—"

"Oh, that's just great," I snap, not waiting to hear what his "but" might be. The realization that he considers me a potential killer not only pisses me off, it puts a definite damper on the romantic designs I have on him. "I guess my word carries no weight whatsoever with you."

"Pardon me, but your *word* has proven to be pretty suspect, wouldn't you say?"

"What's that supposed to mean? Are you calling me a liar?" I get up in his face, forcing him to look me in the eye when he answers.

"If the shoe fits," he comes back, not retreating an inch.

"What bullshit!"

"Oh, really? Did you not lie to me about what you did and what you saw the night of the murder?"

"I didn't lie, I just didn't tell you everything right away. I didn't think it was important."

"Oh, okay," he says, his voice dripping with sarcasm. "You didn't think it was important for me to know that you witnessed your ex and the dead woman together just hours before she was killed. And you didn't think it was important for me to know that they were fighting, or that you were spying on them at the time."

"I told you before, I wasn't spying. I was just trying to see who was there before I went inside."

"Then why didn't you go in? Were you afraid of Karen Owenby?"

"No, I wasn't afraid of her. What a ridiculous suggestion."

"Then it was your husband you were afraid of, perhaps?"

"No, not that either."

Hurley shakes his head in disgust. "Face it, Mattie. Honesty isn't your strongest suit."

"That's not true! I'm a very honest person."

"Oh, really? Then how come your driver's license says you weigh 130?" He steps back, eyeing me from head to toe. "Are you going to tell me *that's* not a lie? You're 150 if you're a pound."

I gasp with shock before I can stop myself. Actually, 150 is a gift, but I'm sure as hell not going to let him know that.

"That's a low blow, Hurley. There isn't a woman alive who has her real weight on her driver's license. And I can't believe you're wasting your time investigating me while the real killer is running around loose. If the rest of the police force is as swift as you are, heaven help the citizens of Sorenson."

"I didn't hear you complaining when I rescued you from your ex earlier."

"I didn't need rescuing, you Neanderthal. It wasn't what you thought. We were having an argument. That's all. Nothing else. I hate to strip you of your armor, white knight, but all you did was butt into a minor squabble and jump to a bunch of wrong conclusions."

"That's not how it looked to me. But then, maybe I did misinterpret things. Maybe you were just having a little fun, eh? Maybe you like it rough and you and your ex were just reliving old times. Was that it? Did I interrupt the grand reconciliation?"

"I was not . . . we were not . . . Christ! I give up!" I don't believe in physical violence, but I've never wanted to slap someone so badly in my life. Unless you count the time Desi told Greg Johnsen right before our first date that I never went on a second date unless the guy showed me his penis at the end of the evening.

"Damn it, Hurley. You've got it all wrong."

"Do I? Big fancy house. Handsome and talented husband. Must be hard to give all that up after seven years together. You wouldn't be the first woman to trade fidelity for some creature comforts and a cushy lifestyle."

I stutter with fury for a few seconds before I manage to spit out, "You're a pig, Hurley." I turn away from him to go back inside.

"Mattie, wait. Please."

Something in his voice makes me stop, but I don't turn back to look at him. I am afraid of what I might say, or of what I might see in his eyes.

"I'm sorry," he says finally. "I didn't mean all that. It's just that . . . I mean I . . . oh, hell." Suddenly he grabs my shoulder and spins me around to face him. Before I know what's happening, his lips descend on mine, crushing, urgent, and wonderfully needy. It takes all of a millisecond for my irritation to give way to total forgiveness and pure, unadulterated lust.

His tongue finds its way past my lips and I swear it reaches the bottom of my toes. One of my hands is pinned between us, the palm flat against his chest, the backside of it pushing against my breast. I can feel the rapid thrum of his heart and the incredible heat of his skin radiating through his shirt.

When he finally lifts his lips from mine, it is all I can do not to whine and whimper, to beg him for more, to throw him down on the porch and rip his pants off him to see what treasures lay beneath. Because judging from the feel of the humps and bumps that are pressed up against my nether regions, it is quite a treasure to behold.

He releases me so suddenly I almost fall over. "I gotta go," he says. And just like that, he is gone. I watch in stunned disbelief as he walks away.

"Well, well, well," Desi says behind me as Hurley climbs into his car and starts it up. "Isn't this interesting? A homicide detective with the hots for one of his suspects. A suspect who just happens to be barely married to his other suspect."

"What the hell was that?" I ask her, watching Hurley's taillights disappear down the drive. "I mean what the hell *was* that? Was it a test of some sort?" I lick my lips and can still taste him there. "Was he collecting evidence? What?"

Desi laughs. "Oh, man. You've got it bad. Mom isn't going to be happy about this, you know. It's bad enough you're giving up a doctor, but for a cop? She'll shit a brick."

"And then find some obscure reference to brick-shitting in one of her textbooks," I add with a laugh. "Some bizarre disorder like pica, but with it coming out instead of going in."

"What's pica?"

"It's a craving that makes people eat weird stuff, like dirt or clay."

"Then I'd say that detective is the one with the pica. 'Cause it sure looked to me like he wanted to eat you."

"Mmm," I murmur. "Kind of felt that way, too."

Take that, Alison Miller!

Chapter 22

My attendance at the hospital celebration was not only a sartorial disaster, it was only minimally successful in terms of getting any useful information about Karen. But Marjorie's comment to Mick—about how he should talk to Molinaro about some nursing problems he was having—gave me an idea. I realize that the wives, some of them anyway, might know a fair amount about the business end of their husbands' work. There is one wife in particular who I think will fit this bill, one who wasn't at last night's reception.

Arthur Henley's wife, Lauren, isn't like many of the other doctors' wives. Status and wealth seem to mean little to her. She attends most of the requisite social events and holds her own with the other wives, but she always seems apart from it all, never buying into the catty discussions or monetary pissing contests. She is tiny but strong, pretty, and well put together—one of those petite, graceful women I hate standing next to since it makes me look and feel like the abominable snowwoman.

David and I have shared dinners with the Henleys a number of times, both at their house and ours. As a result, I've come to know Lauren a little better than I do most of the other wives. What's more, I like her. She has an eager curiosity about her husband's work and a good knowledge of medical facts and terminology despite no formal training. She is clearly intelligent, generally confident, and occasionally, often amusingly, outspoken—at least in matters of general interest. Since she has an MBA, she is involved in the business end of her husband's practice and tends to it by going into the office a couple of days each week. The rest of the time, she busies herself making a comfortable home for Arthur and their two school-aged daughters.

It all looks great on the surface, but unfortunately, Arthur and Lauren Henley don't have the perfect marriage any more than David and I did. While Arthur isn't exactly a philanderer, he does have a mistress named Ruth he has kept on the side for nearly five years that I know of. And there lays the heart of my dilemma.

I've met Ruth a couple of times, and damn if I don't like her, too. She is an earthy, warm woman who is quick to laugh and seems totally at ease with herself. What's more, her interest in those around her seems utterly genuine—if it's merely an act, it's a damned good one. And she seems content to play second fiddle to Lauren whenever necessary.

For a straying husband, Ruth is the perfect mistress; to a wife, she is an utter nightmare. For me, she is a never-ending ethical debate. As a wife, I feel compelled to place her in the enemy camp. After all, wives know that mistresses are conniving, manipulative, money-grubbing whores who will perform any sex act at any time and pretend to love it even if they find it as appealing as scraping five-day-old roadkill up from the highway during an August heat wave. Even wives who were once mistresses believe that, ignoring their inherent hypocrisy.

But Ruth doesn't fit the typical mistress mold. Of course, I have no way of knowing what her and Arthur's sex life is like, but the rest of Ruth is as warm and personable as a woman can be. Which leaves me feeling like a traitor whenever I am around Lauren.

Perhaps that's why there is always a certain wall between

Lauren and me; even though we get along well enough, we aren't what I would call close. I know that if I'm to have any hope of getting personal information out of her, I'm going to have to strengthen the bond between us somehow. I need to find something that will tie us indelibly together as coconspirators.

And the answer is obvious: Ruth. Lauren and I are both women scorned. Women betrayed. We are members of an elite and exclusive club, one that requires a banding together. But while the answer may be clear, my willingness to use it is shaky at best. Arthur isn't obvious about his affair; in fact, he takes great pains to keep it under wraps. But in a town as small as Sorenson, secrets are hard to keep. Maybe Lauren already knows about Ruth, I surmise, but if she doesn't, do I want to be the one to tell her? Not only does it feel kind of mean, the whole thing could backfire and blow up in my face. Telling Lauren something as explosive as this might make her so angry that I'll lose whatever camaraderie we do have.

No matter how I look at it, it is a gamble, but one that offers the promise of worthwhile rewards. I figure I'll meet with Lauren and try to get the information out of her without playing the Ruth card, maybe by hinting around the idea of Arthur as a suspect in Karen's murder. If that doesn't work, I'll have to decide how far I want to push the issue—a decision I know I won't relish making.

Though I figure Lauren is my best chance at getting to some facts, I briefly consider adding some of the other doctors' wives to my mental interrogation list. I mull over and discard Marjorie Dunn; even if she does know something about Mick's business interests, getting it out of her will be damned near impossible. Then I consider Gina. She knew what Robert Calhoun was going to discuss with Sid last night and seems to be up to speed on Sid's business dealings in general. And she'd all but begged me to call her and do lunch, so why not take her up on it? I'm not sure if I'll get anything useful from her but I figure it's worth a try.

I get out of bed early on Saturday morning and plan my strategy over coffee and a half-dozen oatmeal cookies. First I call Lauren, explaining that I want to drop by to discuss something with her. She graciously extends an invitation, as I knew she would, and I arrange to come out around ten. I then place a call to Gina to set up a lunch date. Knowing how busy Gina's schedule is, I expect to have to wait several days before we can meet. But Gina surprises me by suggesting we get together that day. Sorenson only has a handful of restaurants and nothing that might be called fancy. So after a brief discussion, Gina and I agree to meet at noon at Carver's, a sit-in family restaurant that is one step above the typical fast-food outlet and serves the most wonderful turtle sundaes.

I head out for Lauren's house a short while later, my nervousness making me feel restless and fidgety. I arrive fifteen minutes early, and to kill time, I drive around the neighborhood, noticing as I make the first circuit that a burgundy-and-gray van seems to be following me. It stays far enough back that I can't see who is behind the wheel, but something about it strikes me as familiar. I watch it in my rearview mirror, trying to remember if I know someone who drives such a van.

On my third time around the block, just as I'm thinking about pulling over and waving the van past me, it hangs a left when I turn right and disappears. Then, as I pull my car into Lauren's driveway and think about the meeting ahead, my rising level of anxiety erases all thoughts of the van from my mind.

If Lauren suspects an ulterior motive or harbors any concern about the reason behind my visit, she hides it well. She greets me with a quick but warm embrace and a cheerful smile.

"You look great," I tell her. And she does. Her cheeks are rosy, her blue eyes sparkle, and her skin bears the remnants of a healthy summer tan. She's been working in the yard and even though the air has an autumn bite to it, she's managed to work up a bit of a sweat that makes the curls in her hair spring to life.

"Thanks. You look pretty good yourself, though perhaps a bit worse for wear," she says, eyeing the bandage on my head.

"Oh, this," I say, touching it. "No big deal. Just a freak accident, actually. I broke a glass and a piece of it ricocheted up and cut my forehead. Took three stitches."

"Ow," Lauren says, grimacing. "You're lucky it didn't hit your eye. It looks like it came close."

"It did."

"Well, come on in. I just put on some coffee and I have a sour cream coffee cake that's been calling to me all morning."

I follow her inside to the kitchen, where the smells of just-brewed coffee and cinnamon permeate the air. Lauren pours two mugs full, slices two generous helpings of the cake, and sets us up at the kitchen table. Her sleeves are rolled up to her elbows and I can see dirt beneath her fingernails. That's one of the reasons I like Lauren. There is no pretense, no sense of falseness about her. She is who she is and makes no apology for it. I taste the cake, which melts in my mouth, compliment her on it, and then set to devouring the rest of it.

"Thanks for inviting me over on such short notice," I say between bites. "As I mentioned on the phone, I have something I need to talk to you about, something related to my new job. I work at the medical examiner's office now."

"So I've heard. Arthur told me about it last night. It sounds exciting. Do you like it?"

"So far. Though I haven't been at it long enough to encounter anything too awful yet."

Lauren nods knowingly.

"What I want to discuss with you is . . . well . . . it's a bit . . . awkward."

Lauren smiles. "Don't worry about me. I've listened to Arthur talk about some of the stuff he's encountered in his work and I know it can get pretty gruesome at times. I'm used to it."

"Well, it isn't your tolerance for gruesome that I'm concerned about, Lauren. It's your privacy. I need to ask you about some very personal stuff."

That seems to give her pause but she recovers quickly. "Do what you need to do," she says brightly.

"You're aware of the Karen Owenby murder, aren't you?" It is more or less a rhetorical question, an icebreaker of sorts, since I have no doubt everyone in Sorenson knows of it by now.

"I am."

"Well, I spoke with a woman who knew Karen and she said that Karen mentioned some sort of business dealings—investments she called it—with some of the surgeons. It may have nothing to do with Karen's death, but it doesn't hurt to check everything out. I thought you might be able to tell me if you knew of anything like that, any business dealings that Karen might have had with Arthur or any of the other surgeons."

Now it is Lauren's turn to look hesitant. "Have you asked David about this?"

"I have. He won't tell me anything." I hesitate, then decide that a shared confidence from me might make Lauren more likely to reciprocate. "I don't know if you've heard or not but we're separated. He . . . um . . . had an affair."

Lauren nods and looks at me sympathetically. "I had heard. I'm sorry, Mattie."

I shrug it off, trying to pretend it's not a big deal. "Anyway, since David knows I intend to file for divorce, he refuses to discuss anything to do with money or business, fearing it may somehow affect the outcome."

"Divorce," Lauren says, making a face like she just tasted something disgusting. "Why does it always have to be so nasty?"

I wonder if Lauren's attitude toward divorce will be any

different by the time I leave. I also sense the merest hesitation, the barest flicker of doubt in her voice.

"People do some strange things when they're emotionally wrought," I say, watching her face closely. "Particularly when there's money involved. I don't know if David's reluctance to talk to me about business stuff means he's hiding something or not. But I'm going to try to find out."

"Well, I don't know about David, but Arthur wouldn't do anything like that," Lauren says, sounding as if she is trying to convince herself as much as me. "And since I do the books and financial reports for his office, I'm intimately familiar with all of his business dealings."

"So there's no unexplainable income you've noticed, or any expenses that seem odd."

"Of course not. And if there were, I'd be the first to know about them."

I make my first tentative foray into delicate territory. "Does Arthur have a checking account of his own?"

"He does. But I don't see how that figures into any of this."

"Where does the income for that account come from?"

"From his practice, of course. That, and a few investments. Why?" She frowns at me. "I mean, I really want to help you here, Mattie, but I'm not sure I see the relevance. Why are you asking me about this?"

I hesitate, carefully considering my response. "It's important that we investigate any aspect of Karen's life that might be significant, and there could be a connection between her murder and her business dealings."

Lauren pales. "You think . . . do the police think . . ." She tightens her arms even more and shakes her head vehemently. "No. No way. Arthur couldn't do anything like that."

"Arthur is a good man," I say.

"Yes," Lauren says quickly. "Yes he is."

"But even good men can stray," I add gently. I expect her to object but she says nothing, just eyes me with a wounded expression. A long silence stretches between us and then I make the decision to jump in with both feet. "Lauren, are you certain, absolutely certain you can trust Arthur?"

She flashes me an indignant look, opens her mouth, and then just as quickly snaps it shut again. Her whole body sags and her eyes dull just before she looks away from me. It is an awful, sad thing to watch.

"You know, don't you?" she says quietly. I don't answer, still reluctant to be the one to spill the beans in case I'm on the wrong wavelength here and Lauren is talking about something else. "About Ruth," she clarifies. "You know about her, don't you?"

My face flushes hot and I nod.

"I figured as much." She leans back and sighs, staring at the ceiling. "This damned town and all its gossiping biddies."

"Well, to be honest, I didn't find out through gossip, Lauren. Arthur is pretty . . . discreet here in town. But I bumped into him and Ruth at a medical conference a couple of years ago in Chicago. I don't think Arthur was expecting to run into anyone he knew there since he was the only one from Sorenson originally scheduled to attend. But David got called at the last minute to fill in for a speaker who canceled, and the two of us went on down.

"At first I thought Arthur was just having a one-time out-of-towner, and he seemed so embarrassed when he realized I'd seen the two of them together that I figured he'd drop what he was doing and straighten up. It wasn't until months later when Ruth came into the hospital as a patient that I realized she was local."

Lauren stares at me, tears welling in her eyes.

"I'm so sorry, Lauren. I know I should have said something to you, but it was awkward for me. I mean, I have to . . . well, *had* to . . . work with Arthur."

Lauren finally uncrosses her arms and waves away my apology. "I'd expect nothing less from you, Mattie. I know from our past dealings that you have a deep respect for people's privacy, and unlike some in this town, you can and will keep a secret. I knew it when you took care of me at the hospital a couple of years ago."

I nod.

"And then there's that whole patient confidentiality thing." She pauses, then says, "I'm guessing you have some kind of obligation along those lines with this new job as well?"

"Some," I tell her. "Obviously if I discover something relevant to a case I'm investigating, I have to share that information with certain people."

"But if it's not relevant?"

"Then my lips are sealed."

Lauren nods solemnly and takes a deep breath. She looks away for a moment, then turns back to me and says, "I've known about Ruth all along, Mattie. In fact, I knew before it ever happened."

I stare at her, confused. "*Before* it happened?"

I watch indecision, then resignation flit across her face. "What I'm about to tell you has no bearing on Karen Owenby or her case so if you breathe one word of it to anyone, I swear I will hunt you down and kill you," she says.

I laugh—a quick snort—then swallow it down. One look at her face and I know she isn't kidding. Having no desire to be laid out on Izzy's table, I nod my understanding.

She leans forward, folds her hands on the table in front of her and stares at them, picking at one thumb with the nail of the other. "When I was little, my father . . . he . . . abused me." She pauses and swallows hard. "Sexually. Beginning when I was about six and continuing until I left home at the age of seventeen."

"Oh shit, Lauren. I'm so sorry."

She shrugs. "It happens in the best of families. Or so my therapist says."

"Did you tell anyone? Try to get help?"

She gives me a wry smile and a quick, sad glance before looking back at her hands. "I told my mother when I was about twelve or so. She insisted I was making mountains out of molehills, that my father was merely an affectionate man and that such talk could ruin him and his reputation. The image of a happy, middle-class family was everything to her. It didn't matter what the reality was, all she cared about was what other people would think or believe. Protect the façade at all costs," she says bitterly.

I squeeze my eyes closed, blocking out the awful pain on her face.

"Once I left home I thought I'd be fine, but I was wrong. I love my husband very much, Mattie, and I believe that he loves me. But when it comes to sex . . . I . . . I . . . well, I can't. I tried during the early years of our marriage—that's how I came to be blessed with Jenny and Kelly. But I simply can't do it anymore. I become physically ill. And Arthur isn't the type to push himself on someone if he isn't wanted. Yet he has . . . needs. So I told him years ago that I would understand if he sought release elsewhere. The only thing I asked was that he not do anything to jeopardize our marriage or trigger gossip until the kids are grown." She lets out a sad little laugh. "Ironic in a way. I'm as much into the façade as my mother was."

I am utterly dumbfounded. I shudder to think of the mental and emotional effort it must have taken for this woman to keep it together and present a happy front all these years. "My God, Lauren. I had no idea. I'm so, so sorry."

She flashes me a weak smile. "Me too," she says. "It's not the life I dreamed of when I was a little girl, that's for sure. But I think it's as close as I'm going to get."

"Forgive me if I'm treading where I shouldn't here, Lauren, but are you still getting counseling?"

She shakes her head. "Can't see the point. I did it for nine years and it didn't change much of anything. To be honest, telling you gives me a huge sense of relief. I've been carrying this secret around so long . . . it feels good to finally share it with someone." She looks at me then and this time her smile is a warm one. "I've always liked you, Mattie. You've always seemed so strong to me and you're a good person. Honest. You have integrity."

She couldn't make me feel more ill at ease if she stripped me naked, painted BITCH on my back, and paraded me up and down Main Street.

"I trust you to keep what I've told you to yourself."

"I will," I tell her. "I swear. I'll take it to my grave."

She eyes me a moment and then says, "Yes, I believe you will. And since it's what you came for, I might as well tell you the rest. Arthur has some income that we don't keep on the books. It's his discretionary fund, money he uses for whatever . . . personal needs he has. Some of it comes from investments, some of it comes from side ventures we've dabbled in. One of those side ventures is an arrangement of sorts with a medical supply company that Karen Owenby had connections to, a place called Halverson Medical Supply. It's basically a convoluted ownership setup that allows the docs to invest in the place without any apparent conflict of interest problems. It's not strictly aboveboard, but it's not exactly illegal either."

As soon as I hear Lauren mention Halverson Medical Supply—the same name that was on the business card I found in David's tobacco pouch—I know I have to add a visit there to my day's agenda.

Lauren glances at the clock. "The girls will be home in half an hour."

I realize this is her way of signaling an end to our conversation and that she is asking me to leave. I rise from my chair and stand there a moment, wracked with indecision. Part of me wants to turn and run, another part of me wants to gather Lauren Henley into my arms and rock her like a child. But the expression on her face tells me she will tolerate neither cowardice nor pity. So I simply thank her, smile, and leave.

Chapter 23

I'm hungry and the coffee I had at Lauren's is churning away in my stomach, threatening to eat a hole in it. Consequently, I am looking forward to chowing down on one of Carver's cheeseburgers and topping it off with a turtle sundae. Gina arrives ten minutes late and, as usual, her entrance turns a few heads. Aside from being the closest thing to a famous person we have here in Sorenson, she is the sort of woman who attracts attention. She is dressed in black slacks and a simple pullover sweater. The only jewelry she is wearing is a pair of small gold hoops in her ears. Her short hair has a reckless, tousled look to it—loose blond curls that frame her face in a soft, golden glow—and the fact that her dark roots are beginning to show doesn't detract from her overall beauty. If anything, it simply adds to her air of casual self-assurance.

I wave to catch her eye and once she sees me, she heads to the booth where I'm seated.

"Hey there," she says, beaming me a huge smile as she slides in across from me. She eyes my forehead with a worried expression. "What's this?" she asks, touching her own forehead in the region where mine is bandaged.

"A small cut. Nothing serious."

"Ah, good. I'm so glad you called, Mattie. How are you?"

"I'm doing okay for the most part. But at times . . ."

She looks at me sympathetically. "You know Sid and I will always be there for you. Sometimes when couples split, their friends feel the need to take sides. But Sid and I won't do that. You and David are both our friends and we intend to keep it that way, no matter what happens."

"Even if he's guilty of murder?" I ask her.

She hesitates, then shakes her head. "I can't believe David killed that woman. What he *did* do with her was pretty damned stupid, but I just can't picture him as a murderer. It doesn't fit."

I'm glad to hear her echo my own thoughts. "I agree," I tell her. "But I realize now that I didn't know him as well as I thought I did. I don't think he's the type who would kill someone but I never thought he was the type to have an affair either."

"Men!" Gina says with disgust. "Sometimes you have to wonder what the hell they're thinking."

"I'm not sure there was much thinking involved with this."

"Or maybe he was just thinking with the wrong head," Gina says, a wicked gleam in her eye.

We both start to giggle, and it is all we can do to get ourselves under control when the waitress comes by. After placing our orders—a cheeseburger with all the trimmings for me and a healthy chicken salad for Gina—I get down to business.

"Thank you for your support, Gina. It means a lot to me."

"You're welcome. Like I said last night, we girls have to stick together."

"I'm glad you feel that way, because I could use some help on a particular matter."

"Great," she says. "Name it."

"I'm sure it will come as no surprise to you that I plan to file for a divorce from David. As soon as we've been separated long enough, I'll get the paperwork started. In the meantime, I'm struggling a bit with some financial stuff. I was out of work for two months and David controls all the purse strings in our household, so I'm a bit cash shy."

Gina pouts prettily. "A big mistake to let them have that much power," she says.

"I know that now."

"So do you need a loan? Is that it? Because I'd be happy to loan you whatever you need."

"No," I say, shaking my head. "Thanks for the offer, but that won't be necessary. I'm getting by and I do have income again. But when it comes time for the divorce, I want to make sure I get a fair share of the assets. I'm not out to take David for a bundle or anything, I just want enough to get by on."

Gina leans back and stares at me with an expression that is half frown, half smile. "That's a marvelous attitude, Mattie. And a rare one. Are you sure you want to be that understanding?"

I nod. Given Gina's declaration that she and Sid intend to keep both David and me as friends, I figure my best approach is one that will seem innocuous and equitable. "Actually, I think David will be more than fair," I tell her. "But given all that's happened, I just can't be sure."

"And you'd be foolish to trust your future to him at this point. You need to look after your own interests."

"And that's where you might be able to help. I think David may have some income sources that I don't know about, money that he's hiding away somewhere. I overheard bits and pieces of a conversation he was having about some sort of investment scheme. I don't know who he was talking to or what it was about, but I did get the impression that some of the other docs might be involved as well. Do you know if Sid is into anything like that?"

Gina thinks for a moment, then shakes her head. "I'm not aware of anything. We don't really need any extra income, you understand. So I'm not sure Sid would know if there was something like that going on anyway."

"Has David come to him for capital or a loan for any business ventures that you know of?"

"I really don't know, Mattie. Sorry. But I might not be privy to everything Sid's got going. Have you asked him directly?"

"I started to last night, but we got interrupted."

"Ah, yes. Calhoun."

"He did mention something about a medical supply company that some of the docs have invested in. Do you know anything about that?"

Gina frowns again, taking a moment to think. "You know," she says slowly. "I do remember hearing something along those lines." She pauses, seeming to give it more thought. Then she shrugs. "Sorry, I don't recall what it was."

"That's okay," I say. The simple fact that she's heard something is verification enough on the heels of what I learned from Lauren.

"I wish I could be more help," Gina says. She reaches over and lays a reassuring hand on my arm, her face again full of sympathy. "All of this must be so terribly hard on you."

"I'll get through it."

"Well, as I said, if there's anything I can do to help you along, don't hesitate to ask."

"Thanks."

"Now, then," she says, leaning back and smiling. "You must tell me about this new job you have. It sounds very exciting."

"I'm not sure *exciting* is the right word for it. Though it's certainly not dull."

"Do you help with the autopsies and such?" she asks, grimacing prettily.

"Yes, most of them anyway."

"And it doesn't bother you?"

"At times," I admit. "Death is always somewhat disturbing. But I'm getting used to it. It's really not that different from assisting with surgeries except that I don't have to worry about whether or not the patient is stable."

"No," Gina says with a chuckle. "I guess you wouldn't."

"I've only been doing it for a few days, but I've learned a lot. It's amazing how much science there is in death."

"How do you mean?"

"Well, there are several branches of forensic science, each one its own specialty. In addition to basic forensic pathology, which is what Izzy and I do, there are forensic odontologists who specialize in teeth, forensic anthropologists who specialize in bones, and forensic entomologists who specialize in bugs."

Gina shudders.

"It all sounds rather grim at first," I admit. "But there's a real science to it and that's the part of it I think I'm going to like the most. Biology, chemistry . . . even physics come into play. And the tiniest bits of evidence can prove to be significant—something as simple as a single hair or a bit of skin or even blood drops."

Gina swallows hard and I realize what I'm doing. "Oh, God, I'm sorry, Gina. What a great thing to talk about right before we eat, eh?"

"I'm okay," she assures me. But she doesn't look okay and I give myself a mental kick for being so stupid.

"Tell you what," I say. "Let's change the subject because there's something else you can do for me."

"What's that?"

"I've been out of the gossip mill for the past couple of months and I'm completely out of touch with all the latest scuttlebutt. Can you bring me up to speed?"

"Now you're talking," Gina says. "Have you heard that Myra Baldwin is pregnant with triplets?"

Chapter 24

Talking and eating at the same time is a bit of a challenge for me, and by the time I leave Carver's I have a mustard stain and a grease splotch on my blouse. I don't realize I'm wearing part of my lunch until after I am in the car, so I pull in to a gas station and spend ten minutes in the rest room trying to clean the worst of it off, though all I manage to do is make the blotches bigger and very wet. Resigned to looking like a slob, I get back in my car and turn the heater on, aiming the vents at my chest. After fanning and fluffing for a few minutes, I head for the small industrial park that serves as home to Halverson Medical Supply.

An annoying buzzer sounds as I open the front door and enter what is essentially a showroom. But there is no slick marketing here, just several artfully discreet displays of infirmity. Shelves along the wall hold things like bedpans, adult diapers, and bed pads. Set up in the middle of the room are various hospitallike tableaux composed of electric beds, portable commodes, wheelchairs, walkers, and other sundry signs of illness.

There is no one around but I notice a metal door at the back of the room and, given the size of the building, assume there is additional space beyond it, most likely a small warehouse of sorts. I guess that whoever is working the store is back there, so I kill a little time browsing amid the sickroom dioramas, waiting to see if the door buzzer has announced my presence.

After thoroughly checking out the merchandise without anyone coming forward to greet me, I think about opening the door to trigger the buzzer again. Then I notice there are two desks with accompanying file cabinets near the back wall and realize I might be missing out on a golden opportunity. While I'm not quite brave enough to open drawers and snoop, I figure anything out on top of the desks is fair game. I know the odds of finding anything useful are slim, but I figure it's still worth a shot. Maybe I'll get lucky.

I move toward one of the desks and am close enough to just make out the writing on an invoice when the door to the back opens. I jump and flash a guilty smile at the tall, bald, gaunt-looking man who steps into the showroom. For a split second I think I know him, but on closer scrutiny I realize I am mistaken. Before the door closes all the way, I catch a quick glimpse of the room behind it. As I guessed, it is a warehouse area filled with more equipment and supplies.

"May I help you?" the man asks.

"Hi there," I say, extending a hand. His handshake is quick but firm, the hand itself uncomfortably clammy. Now that I am here, I realize I haven't thought things through very well. I have no idea how to approach the matter and, after a quick mental two-step, I decide to take the most direct approach. I lie.

"My name is Mattie and I'm a nurse in a doctor's office. I heard through the grapevine that you are offering special deals for some of the docs so I thought I'd come by and check it out."

His eyes narrow and he takes a step back. "Deals? I'm not sure what you mean by that." He looks over his shoulder with a tense, wary expression, as if he thinks someone might be trying to sneak up on him.

"One of the surgeons told us about it. Dr. Arthur Henley?"

I watch closely for a reaction, but all he does is look over his shoulder again. As he does so, I notice a dark, bluish colored blotch on his neck and recognize it immediately—Kaposi's sarcoma, an opportunistic form of cancer commonly found in AIDS patients. That explains his gaunt appearance. As I study his profile, I am again struck by the thought that something about him seems familiar and I wonder if he might have been a patient of mine in the past. This feeling of déjà vu is strong enough that I finally ask, "Have we met before?"

He looks back at me with an expression of surprise, then shakes his head. "No, I don't think so. And I'm afraid I can't help you." He turns and disappears back through the metal door, letting it close behind him. I stand there, stunned by his abrupt dismissal and wondering if I should follow him into the back to pursue the matter. Then I think that maybe instead I should take advantage of his departure by having another look at the stuff on the desk. I shift nervously from one foot to the other, wondering if he might return and debating how brave I am.

I can hear muffled voices emanating from the back, letting me know the man isn't alone. While I can't hear any specific words or even tell for sure what gender the voices are, the overall tone is one of strident discord, suggesting an argument of some sort. Curious, I move closer to the big metal door, craning my ear toward it as if that will somehow help the sound waves come through it better. I keep an eye on the front door; if someone comes strolling in, I don't want to get caught eavesdropping. Doing it is one thing. Getting caught doing it is something else altogether.

As soon as I reach the door, everything in the back grows quiet. I wait several minutes and when nothing happens, I turn my attention back to the desks. I scan a pile of papers on top of the closest one and see that it is a stack of invoices, though there appear to be some different papers beneath them. Giving the front door another cursory glance, I reach over and push the invoices to one side. Just as I touch them, the phone on the desk rings with a harsh, shrill sound—not one of those modern, cricket-chirping rings—and between it and my guilt-edged nerves, I nearly jump out of my skin.

I back away from the desk quickly and stand a safe distance away, trying to make my heart settle down. A button on the phone flashes on and off as the thing rings and rings and rings. Somewhere around the fifth ring I start to count, making it to fifteen before the phone turns quiet and the flashing button goes dark.

It strikes me as odd that no one answered the call. . . . Odd and a bit spooky. I start to get a feeling that something isn't right and cautiously make my way back to the metal door. I put my ear to the surface but can't hear a thing. After a moment of debate, I grab the handle, depress the thumb latch, and slowly push the door open.

The room extends back about a hundred feet or so, the walls lined with shelves that hold every conceivable type of medical or personal care supply. In the middle of the room are groupings of hospital beds, wheelchairs, oxygen tanks, and other pieces of large equipment. At the back of the room is another metal door, this one with a push-bar handle and a red EXIT sign overhead. Directly to my right, nestled in the corner, is a small glass-enclosed office. The lights are on and one of the drawers to a big metal filing cabinet is standing open, but there is no one in there. In fact, there is no one anywhere that I can see.

"Hello?" I try. "Is anyone here?" Not so much as a whisper. Goose bumps raise along my arms.

On the far side of the room I see another closed door located midway down the wall. There is a piece of paper taped to it and I move closer until I can make out what is written on it: REST ROOM. I breathe a sigh of relief as I realize the gaunt man is probably in the john. Knowing what I do about the effects of AIDS and its treatments, it isn't a stretch to think he might have some physical problems that require a lot of bathroom time. I decide to wait a little longer but after another few minutes of the eerie silence, I can't take any more. I move toward the bathroom door, intending to knock on it—courtesy be damned—but slow when something beneath it catches my eye.

I gasp when I realize it is a pool of dark red blood that has oozed under the door from inside the bathroom and is now spreading its way across the floor. My nursing instincts kick in and I rush toward the door, trying to sidestep the gruesome puddle. I grab the doorknob and discover the door is locked.

I knock loudly. "Hello? Sir? Are you okay in there?" I holler. I lean close and listen but hear nothing. I try again, this time pounding on the door with my fist. "Hello? Are you okay in there?" Still nothing. And the circle of red at my feet is growing. I study the doorknob, see one of those little holes you find on interior doors and realize I can get the thing unlocked if I can find something small enough to poke in there.

I head to the corner office, search around and spy a container of paper clips. Grabbing one, I bend it out as straight as I can and hurry back to the bathroom, where I jam it into the hole in the doorknob. After groping around for several seconds I finally hear a click and turn the knob. The door opens only a few inches before meeting some sort of resistance. Pushing harder, I feel the tiniest bit of give and strengthen my efforts, eventually getting a wide enough space to stick my head into the room.

And then wish I hadn't.

The gaunt fellow I saw earlier is, indeed, in the bathroom. Though to be honest, I can't be 100 percent sure it is him since his face is badly misshapen and part of his head is missing. But the clothes, the overall physique, and the Kaposi's sarcoma I can see on his neck suggest it is the same man. He is wedged between the toilet and the door, his head—or what's left of it—is turned to one side and one leg is crunched up between the toilet and the wall. On the floor, in his right hand, is a gun. His index finger is loosely curled around the trigger.

Aided by adrenaline, I push the door as hard as I can, shoving the man's prostrate body through the slick pool of red that surrounds him until I can squeeze myself into the room. I kneel down and instinctively start to place my fingers along the carotid artery in his neck, but then I stop myself. There is no doubt this man is dead. His skin is dark and dusky and there is brain matter splattered on the floor and walls. And I suspect he might have AIDS.

While I've seen some pretty gross things in my nursing career, and there aren't many things that bother me anymore, something about this scene makes my stomach churn threateningly. Maybe it's the close quarters, which seem to concentrate that awful, charnel smell. Or maybe it's the sudden awareness that I am alone with this corpse, isolated and far from help. I stand, turning my head away from the body and toward the sink, feeling like I might throw up. Eventually the feeling passes and the clinical side of my brain takes over again.

Reluctantly, I look back toward the body, trying to recall some of the things I have read in the office library or been told by Izzy regarding the assessment of a death scene. Too late, I realize I have already contaminated a fair amount of the evidence simply by entering the room and moving the body as much as I did to get through the door. Still, given what I can see, it seems pretty obvious that the man has committed suicide—stuck a gun to his head and blown a good part of it away.

Carefully, hoping not to contaminate the scene any further, I work my way out of the room and head back to the small office, where I grab the phone off the desk and punch in 911.

"9-1-1 operator. Do you have an emergency?"

"Well, it's not exactly an emergency," I tell the woman. "But I have a dead man here."

"You have a dead man there?" she repeats, her voice shrill.

"That's right. He shot himself."

"Is this 2104 Callaway Road?"

"Yes, I believe so. I'm at Halverson Medical Supply."

"Um . . . may I have your name, please?"

"Mattie. Mattie Winston."

"Okay, Mattie. Um . . . I will . . . I *am* dispatching police and emergency rescue to the scene and they should be there shortly. Um, let's stay calm. Panic is our enemy."

So far, the only person who seems to be panicking is the operator. "I'm okay," I tell her.

"Okay . . . um . . . can you tell me the victim's name?"

"I don't know who he is."

"Okay. Okay. Um . . . are you near the victim?"

"Not really. He's in a bathroom a little ways from here."

"Are you using a portable phone?"

I am, and say so.

"Okay. Good. Um . . . I want you to go back to the victim and listen carefully to what I'm going to tell you. We're going to render some first aid until the rescue team arrives, okay?" Her voice wavers as if she is about to burst into tears.

"I really don't think first aid will help at this point," I tell her as I make my way back to the bathroom. I wince when I see the bloody footprints I've tracked across the floor. "He's dead."

"Please," she says. "Stay calm and listen to me. What you and I do in the next few minutes may save this man's life."

I can hear the frantic rustling of papers in the background and figure it is her step-by-step CPR instructions. I sigh. "Pardon my bluntness, ma'am, but nothing you or I can do will save this man's life. He is dead. Very dead."

"We can't be sure of that," she says quickly, her voice high and squeaky. "Sometimes people only look dead."

"No, I'm certain he's dead. Totally and completely dead." Some dark corner of my mind urges me to sing out in a Munchkin voice: "He's really most sincerely dead."

"Now, please, don't panic. Just do what I say. I want you to go to the man and look to see if he is breathing."

"Look, I'm a nurse. I know what I'm looking at here and this man—"

"If he isn't breathing, then you will need to give him artificial respiration, or mouth-to-mouth breathing. To do that, you first need to open his airway by tipping his head back. Place one hand beneath his chin and the other one on his forehead."

There is a rote quality to her voice that tells me she is reading what she's saying. "You don't understand," I interrupt. "He—"

"Then you need to tip his head back by lifting up under the chin and exerting downward pressure on the forehead. Then—"

"Lady, he doesn't have a forehead!" I say it a bit more abruptly than I mean to, but it is the only way I can think of to break through this woman's automaton frame of mind.

There is a moment of startled silence. Then, in a high, squeaky voice, "What did you say?"

"I said he doesn't have a forehead. Not much of one anyway."

"He doesn't have a forehead?"

I hear more papers rustling and stifle a bizarre urge to laugh. "I don't think your instructions will tell you what to do if someone is missing a forehead," I say calmly. I hear her swallow—a big, echoing gulp—followed by a little cough. "You're kind of new at this, aren't you?" I say.

"Um, yeah. Is it that obvious?"

"Probably not to everyone. But I spent several years working as a nurse in the ER, so I'm kind of jaded."

I hear a noise and turn to find a uniformed police officer standing in the doorway to the showroom. It is Brian Childs, one of the cops I know from working in the ER, and he looks wired and ready to jump. As soon as he sees me he relaxes a little, though his hand hovers close to the gun strapped to his side.

"Mattie, hi," he says. "Are you okay?"

I nod. He looks around the room warily.

"Are you alone?"

"Far as I know," I tell him, to which the 911 operator says, "Pardon me?"

"Sorry, I was talking to an officer here."

"An officer is there?" She sounds greatly relieved.

"Yes. Brian Childs."

"Okay. That's good."

"What's your name?"

"My name?" She sounds shocked that I would ask such a thing. "It's Jeannie. Why?"

"I just wanted to know. Thanks for your help, Jeannie."

"I wasn't very good, was I?"

I realize then that she probably thinks I want her name so I can file a complaint about her. "You did fine, Jeannie. Honest. The first few times are always rough."

"I guess."

"Hey, someday I'll tell you about a few things I bungled back when I first started working in the ER. It will make you look like a pro."

She lets forth with a nervous little laugh but I can tell her tension has eased some.

"Look," I say, seeing Brian signaling to me, "I need to talk to Officer Childs, so I'm going to hang up."

"Okay."

"And, Jeannie?"

"Yeah?"

"Hang in there. It gets easier."

"I'm not sure that's a good thing," she says. "But thanks."

Brian speaks to me as soon as I disconnect the call. "Dispatch said there was a shooting here?"

I point to the bathroom door and say, "In here," though I could have saved my breath since he is already heading in my direction, his nose wrinkling at the acrid smell of blood.

"Whoa!" he says, sticking his head through the opening in the door and looking inside. "Guy did a number on himself, didn't he?"

"He did that," I agree, peering over his shoulder to see if it is as awful as I remember. It is.

Brian lifts a walkie-talkie to his mouth and hits the button. "All clear in here, Junior."

Junior, I know, is Jonathan Feller, another cop about my age.

"Shit, Mattie. This is a mess, ain't it?" Brian says.

It certainly is, enough of a mess that my lunch begins to churn menacingly in my stomach. I gulp in a breath of air and not only smell the thickening blood that suddenly seems everywhere, I swear I can taste it. My stomach lurches, tossing a burning dose of acid up my throat, and I swallow hard several times, hoping to convince my GI tract that down is the only way to go. I get a brief reprieve when I hear the door to the front showroom open. I turn, grateful for the distraction and expecting to greet Junior.

But it isn't Junior; it's Steve Hurley. He sees me and frowns, not quite the response a girl hopes for from the man who kissed her silly just the night before. He walks toward me, and I can't help but wonder if he is remembering the kiss, too.

The mere sight of him gets my pulse racing, and when he stops and looks at me with those gorgeous blue eyes, my legs begin to shake. My stomach gets this odd, squishy, butterfly feeling and his closeness seems to rob me of all self-control, leaving me stunned and senseless.

All thought escapes me. As does my cheeseburger, the remnants of which splatter all over his shoes.

Chapter 25

As Hurley reveals his impressive knowledge of profanity, my mind clicks back into detached clinical mode as I eye the mess I've just barfed all over his shoes. A pickle slice, whole and intact, rests on his laces and I make a mental note to try to chew my food more thoroughly in the future.

"Jesus Christ, Winston!" he says, shaking his foot. "Couldn't you have tried to make it to the bathroom?"

"Well, I suppose I could have," I say crossly. "But there's the little matter of a dead body in the only bathroom I see here, which is what made me lose my lunch in the first place."

"Oh, that's just great," Hurley mutters. "How the hell am I supposed to clean this off my shoes if I can't use the bathroom?"

"Try this," I offer, grabbing a bottle of sterile water and a package of waterproof bed pads from a nearby shelf. I notice some bottles of mouthwash nearby and grab one of those, too, stuffing it in my pocket. I don't normally condone theft or shoplifting, but I figure in this case it is for the greater good, a benefit to mankind . . . well, at least the mankind who have to share breathing space with me.

Hurley is working at cleaning the vomit off his shoes when Junior comes in through the back door. As soon as Junior joins Brian in the bathroom and I'm certain Hurley is well distracted, I head for the door Junior just came through. Behind the store is a narrow alleyway that backs up to a hill. Checking to make sure the door is unlocked, I let it close and open my bottle of mouthwash. I gulp a mouthful, swish it around, then spit it out onto the pavement. Twice more and I almost feel human again. Shoving the bottle in my pocket, I reach for the handle to head back inside, only to have the door meet me halfway, colliding painfully with my hand as Hurley pushes through it from the other side.

"Ouch, damn it!" I yell, shaking my hand and hopping around as if that might somehow lessen the pain.

"Sorry," Hurley mumbles. "Didn't know you were there."

I suck at the base of my thumb where the worst of the pain seems to be concentrated while Hurley stares at my mouth with an expression of unadulterated hunger that makes me ache in a whole different way.

"What are you doing here already?" he asks, dragging his gaze up to my eyes and shaking free of whatever fantasy he's created.

"Already?" I repeat, puzzled.

"Where's Izzy? Don't tell me he's got you out on your own already. You're hardly ready."

"I'm not here in any official capacity," I explain. "And how do you know I'm not ready?"

"If you aren't here in an official capacity, then why *are* you here?"

It's a good question, one I'm not too keen on answering since I don't want Hurley to know I am conducting my own investigation into the death of Karen Owenby. "Personal business," I say, thrusting my chin out in a way that dares him to call me a liar.

"And you just happened to find this dead guy here in the back?"

"Actually, he was alive when I got here."

"What?" Hurley barks. "You were here when he killed himself?"

"Apparently. Like I said, he was alive when I got here."

"Are you sure?"

I roll my eyes. "Yeah, I'm pretty sure," I say with no small amount of sarcasm. "I talked to him up front in the showroom area. Then he disappeared into the back. When he didn't show up again for a long time, I got curious and poked my head into the back. I saw blood coming from under the bathroom door and that's how I found him."

Hurley pauses thoughtfully a moment and I see his gaze drift toward my shirtfront.

"Um, hellooo," I say, snapping my fingers high above my head. "Did someone tell you about the nipple incident or are you just admiring my assets?"

"Neither," Hurley says, looking away. He clears his throat and then asks, "Didn't you hear the gunshot?"

I think about that for a second and realize I didn't. "No," I tell him. "In fact, it was a little too quiet in there once the yelling stopped."

"Yelling? What yelling?"

I tell Hurley about the muffled voices I heard. "Then it got eerily silent, except for one time when the phone rang. It was pretty loud," I tell him, remembering how it made me jump. "I guess it could have drowned out the sound of a gunshot, though to be honest, I'm really not sure what a gunshot sounds like. Besides, the bathroom door was closed. Between that and the metal door to the showroom being closed, I'm not sure how much I would have heard anyway."

"Who opened the bathroom door? You?" The tone of Hurley's voice suggests he isn't going to be pleased with my answer.

"Yes. After I unlocked it."

"You unlocked it," he says with a tone of barely contained patience, shaking his head. "That's just great, Mattie. What else did you do to mess up the scene?"

His smart-assed tone strikes a nerve and I decide I've had enough of his bullying attitude. "Screw you, Hurley. There was blood oozing under the door. I'm a nurse, or at least I used to be. And I thought someone might be hurt and in need of help in there. I knocked first and when I got no answer I went in. What was I supposed to do, just let whoever was in there die? I had no way of knowing what was behind that door."

I pause long enough to catch a breath, expecting Hurley to jump in with an angry rebuttal. But to my surprise, he bursts out laughing instead.

"You got spunk, Winston. I'll give you that."

"And I did what any concerned person would have done under the circumstances."

"Okay, fair enough. Did you disturb anything else in the bathroom?"

"No. I looked the guy over for any signs of life and then I left him."

"Okay." He shoves a hand into his pocket and fishes out a handful of change. "Izzy should be here soon and then the two of you can process the scene. In the meantime, there's a soda machine out front. Let me buy you a Coke or something to settle your stomach. Have a preference?"

"Something clear. Like a 7-Up or ginger ale," I tell him. "Thank you."

Hurley walks around the side of the building toward the front of the store, leaving me standing alone and unwatched. I pull the mouthwash from my pocket, chug another mouthful, swish and spit. I take a few moments to collect myself and when I head back inside, I see that Izzy has arrived. He and Hurley are standing just inside the door to the showroom area, talking. As soon as Izzy sees me, he hurries toward me, Hurley close on his tail. I see Izzy glance at the bandage on my forehead.

"Are you okay?" he asks.

"I'm fine. Did Hurley fill you in on the details?"

"More or less. But he didn't say anything about you being injured."

"I wasn't. This"—I touch the bandage—"is from last night. A little accident."

"I've been calling and paging you but I got no answer. I was starting to worry."

Belatedly I realize that both my beeper and my cell phone are in my purse, locked inside my car. "Sorry. I'm not used to carrying the cell phone around yet," I say feebly.

"Are you sure you're all right?" he asks again, eyeing me worriedly.

"Yes, I'm fine," I assure him. "I had a little touch of the ickies, but it's gone now."

"It happens to the best of us," says Hurley. He hands me a ginger ale and says, "Easy does it with the drink. Feeling better?"

"I am, yes. Thanks."

Hurley's kindness toward me is exciting and I bask beneath his attention. As I sip my ginger ale, I briefly consider taking advantage of his solicitous mood to flirt with him a little. But then I realize that the lingering dregs of my vomit on his shoes might not set the best stage for a seduction.

"Well, let's get to it," Izzy says. He turns to head toward the bathroom, then stops and looks back at Hurley. "Is it okay for Mattie to assist me, given that she was the one who found him?" he asks.

Hurley nods and waves us on, saying, "Judging from the mess in that bathroom and the fact that the only splatter I can see on the front of Winston's blouse is a big mustard stain, I'm pretty certain she wasn't anywhere near the guy when he did it."

I give Hurley a dirty look, pissed at both his cavalier attitude and the realization that when he was staring at my chest, he wasn't admiring my boobs, he was checking me for blood splatter.

I follow Izzy back to the bathroom, unsure of how well I will handle being near the body again. Normally I have a cast-iron stomach; after years of dealing with the nastier bodily secretions we humans produce, most nurses become pretty stalwart about such things. But despite my usual fortitude, the right set of circumstances can occasionally get to me. I fear this is one of those.

But as Izzy and I don the gloves, paper booties, and waterproof paper gowns he removes from his black suitcase, I sense that my cast-iron stomach is back in place. There is a subtle shift in my mind, a mental distancing that is almost automatic to me now. And with that shift comes the clinical detachment I need. Plus, the cops have removed the bathroom door by taking it right off its hinges, opening up the room a little more.

The first thing Izzy does is take several pictures of the overall scene, including close-ups of the wounds and the hand that holds the gun. Once that is done, we begin our exam at the man's head.

"Tell me what you see, Mattie," Izzy says.

This isn't the first time I've seen how much damage a bullet can do to a head. We had three victims from a drug deal turned sour in the ER one night several years ago and one of them had incurred a similar wound. Plus, I've been reading up on gunshot wounds at the office, familiarizing myself with such details as ballistics, calibers, gunpowder residue, tattooing, and the geometry of entry and exit wounds. I pull from what I've learned and try to describe what I see before me. My task is made easier by the fact that this man is bald.

"It looks as if he held the gun to his right temple with his right hand. This hole here in his right temple is the entry wound. The larger damage on the other side of his head is caused by the bullet exiting and taking a good portion of the skull and brain with it."

"Good so far," Izzy says. He looks up at the wall to the man's left and points toward a hole near the top of the blood splatter. "My guess is the bullet entered the wall there."

He stares at it for a few seconds, then turns back to the victim's head. "Tell me more about the entry wound, Mattie."

"Okay. It's a round hole about a centimeter in diameter with some signs of hemorrhaging around the periphery."

"What does that tell you? Anything?"

I think back to what I've read. "Well, the fact that the entry wound is round suggests that the muzzle of the gun wasn't in tight contact with his temple. If it had been, the skin around the entry site would have burst because of the pressure of gases that are released from the end of a muzzle during firing. That leaves a sort of star-shaped injury, right?"

"Right. And other than the bruising you mentioned, what other markings or discoloration is there in the skin surrounding the entry wound?"

"There are these dark specks scattered around the circumference of the entry hole," I tell him, pointing to a narrow band of spots extending out an inch or so beyond the wound perimeter. I make a quick swipe at them with a piece of gauze. "They don't wipe off so it's not soot. Is it gunpowder tattooing?"

"It is." Izzy beams at me like a proud parent. "What does that tell you?"

"That the gun was not in direct contact, or even very close to the skin when it was fired. It had to have been anywhere from six inches to two feet away."

"Good. Now how about the exit wound?"

"Well, given the extent of the damage, I'd suspect that either a large caliber bullet was used or that it was a hollow-point bullet of some type."

Izzy nods toward the gun near the man's right hand. "That's a .357 Magnum. Big enough to cause this much damage?"

I think about it but I'm not sure. Sensing my hesitation, Izzy says, "Yes, it can, and often does. It's a popular revolver among hunters and law enforcement officers because it's designed to bring a target down in one shot. Now tell me what you can see about the angle of the bullet as it was fired."

I describe what I see, beginning with the entry wound, which is on the man's right temple about even with the lower margin of his eye socket but set back from it an inch or so. I then move to the exit wound, which encompasses most of the left side of his forehead and temple area. "It looks as if the bullet traveled slightly forward toward the front of his head and slightly upward as well," I say. Izzy says nothing, but he smiles.

We continue our exam, working our way down the body. When we reach his neck, I point out the Kaposi's sarcoma, explaining to Izzy how I noticed it when talking with the man earlier. When Izzy gets to the man's right hand he takes several pictures of it before carefully removing the gun. He examines the skin of the hand with his naked eye and then again with a magnifying glass. When he finally sets the hand back down, he looks at me with a worried expression.

"Tell me again the sequence of events that led up to this man's death," he says. "As carefully as you can and with as much detail as you can remember."

I reiterate the whole thing for him, and when I get to the part where the dead man disappeared into the back and I thought I heard voices, Izzy slows me down.

"Who was the source of the other voice?" he asks.

I shrug. "I have no idea. I assumed it was an employee of some sort who left through the back door. But I really don't know. I never saw anyone but this guy."

Izzy picks up the dead man's hand again and holds it out for my inspection. "The gun used here was a revolver and they are notorious for leaving soot on the hand that fires it because of the gap between the chamber and the muzzle. Do you see any gunpowder residue here?" he asks.

I look carefully, using the magnifying glass Izzy used, then I shake my head. I feel a tiny chill snake its way down my spine.

"Okay. That's not definitive, but highly suggestive. We'll have to do a test on his hand when we get him back to the lab to see if there might be microscopic particles of residue. Now, let's try something else. This finger"—he wiggles the man's index finger—"was curled inside the trigger guard when you found him, right?"

I nod. He sets the man's hand back on the floor, then forms his own hand into the shape of a gun, his index finger serving as the muzzle, his thumb folding the other three fingers back. "Pretend this is a gun and you're going to shoot yourself with it in the head like this man did." He held his "gun" near my right temple, about six inches away. "Now I want you to hold this gun and pull the trigger. Pretend my thumb is the trigger."

I reach up, take a hold of his "gun" in my right hand, and try to fire it, but I have to contort my hand so much, I can barely get my index finger to touch the trigger, much less pull it. I try holding the gun with my left hand instead and then triggering it with my right index finger, but it's still almost impossible. "It would be easier if I could use my thumb to pull the trigger," I say finally.

"Exactly!" Izzy says.

I put it all together and feel my blood run cold.

"What are you saying, Izzy?" asks a voice behind me. I've been so caught up in what Izzy and I are doing that I failed to notice Hurley hovering in the doorway, eavesdropping on our every word.

"I'm saying that someone tried very hard to make it look like this man committed suicide," Izzy says gravely. "But he didn't. He was murdered."

Chapter 26

As the meaning of Izzy's declaration sinks in, my body begins to tremble.

Murdered. While I was standing out front in the showroom area, someone in the back of the store murdered a man in cold blood and then set the scene to make it look like a suicide. Had the killer known I was in the store? Was I left alive intentionally or merely as an oversight? Could I have done anything to prevent this poor man's murder?

Upon hearing Izzy's verdict, Hurley's attitude changes dramatically. He perks up like a hunting dog on point, rigid and attentive. Then he starts barking out commands. Several other police officers have arrived on the scene and they are scouring through the place, searching the file cabinets, sorting through stacks of papers, rifling through desk drawers, and brushing surfaces for fingerprints.

Izzy and I continue our examination of the man's body, wrapping him in the requisite white sheet when we are done and zipping him into a body bag. From paperwork the cops find in the office, we assume that the man's name is Mike Halverson, though we will have to find something far more conclusive before officially establishing his ID. Other documents the cops find suggest that Halverson owned the business as a sole proprietor, with no obvious partners or corporation to share in the proceeds. But I have my doubts as to the authenticity of those papers and want desperately to get a peek at some of the financial statements.

Izzy says he wants to autopsy Halverson as soon as the body reaches the morgue since he has to leave town that evening for a medical conference. Hurley asks if he can observe and leaves another detective in charge of the scene so he can accompany us to the morgue.

We strip off our protective gear and bag it, then follow the body outside. We are watching the ambulance crew load it inside their vehicle when a red Toyota pulls up beside us and screeches to a halt. Alison Miller climbs out, her camera slung around her neck, her eyes wide with curiosity. She grabs the camera and tries to sneak a shot of the body bag inside the ambulance, but the techs are too fast for her and have the doors closed before she can focus.

She frowns briefly, then sidles up to Hurley with a big smile on her face. "Hello, Steve. Something going on?" she asks in a sexy, seductive voice I find utterly inappropriate.

"Hello, Alison," Hurley says, smiling much broader than I like. "I can't give you anything yet. You'll just have to wait."

Alison pouts and moves in a little closer, stroking her hand along Hurley's upper arm. "Oh, come on, Stevie. Just a hint? Please?"

Stevie? I roll my eyes, half expecting Alison to rub up against him next, or start humping his leg.

"I can't, Alison." Hurley repeats.

Her pout deepens and she looks around, her gaze settling on me. With a smug little smile, she says, "Okay, Stevie. If you insist. But promise me you'll tell me as soon as you can. Otherwise, I may not be in a very good mood for our date on Friday."

Hurley casts a quick glance my way, then blushes six different shades of red as he pries Alison's hand off his arm. Without another word he hurries off to his car and peels out of the parking lot.

I give Alison a smug smile of my own and saunter off to

my own car. Thirty seconds later, I leave her behind in a cloud of parking lot dust. *Bitch.*

Izzy and I start suiting up again as soon as we get to the morgue: gown, gloves, booties, and face shields. The ambulance crew has already unloaded Halverson's body, switching it from their stretcher to one of ours. Hurley is there already, too, and after donning gloves and a gown himself, he stands against the wall, watching.

As soon as I am suited up, I push the stretcher that holds Halverson's body onto a giant scale built into the floor. The scale is calibrated and computerized so that it will take the total weight of the stretcher and the body combined, subtract the known weight of the stretcher, and then display the remainder, which is the body weight. After noting the result, which is a rather pathetic 135 pounds, Izzy and I wheel Halverson into an X-ray room where we shoot several films of his head and upper torso through the body bag. We then wheel the stretcher into the main autopsy room, positioning it beside one of the tables. Hurley is waiting for us there, and as I wheel the stretcher past him I can't resist saying, "Excuse me, *Stevie.*"

I unzip the body bag and Izzy runs a small vacuum device along the inside of it to collect any trace evidence that might have come along with the body. We then unwrap the sheet and Izzy vacuums it as well, while I use needles and syringes to collect blood, urine, and vitreous samples from the body the way Izzy taught me.

Izzy carefully examines the front of Halverson's body using a fiber optic light and special goggles that make it easier to detect hairs, threads, and other near-microscopic bits of evidence. Then we turn Halverson up on one side and do the same thing on his back. There is a wallet in his back pants pocket, which Izzy removes and hands to Hurley. Inside the wallet is a driver's license with the name Mike Halverson on it and a picture that bears a vague resemblance to the man on the table—more evidence but still not conclusive enough for establishing an identification.

We carefully remove Halverson's blood-soaked clothing, laying the individual pieces out flat so they can dry. Once the body is naked, we position it on a pad of rollers and move it from the stretcher onto the autopsy table. After photographing and swabbing both of the hands, we use ink and a card to record all ten fingerprints.

Using the light again to scan Halverson's skin, we hose the body off and Izzy makes the usual Y-incision in the man's torso. I am aware of Hurley standing off to the side, watching us and scowling as he chews at the inside of his cheek. I sense something is bothering him but figure it will be a waste of my time to ask him what it is. Hurley is definitely one of those close-to-the-vest, reticent types, a trait I find frustrating but, oddly enough, wildly attractive.

I soon forget about Hurley as I become engrossed in what Izzy and I are doing. We dissect the neck and chest cavity first, finding nothing of interest other than some minor lung scarring that is most likely the result of past bouts with pneumonia. We are about to start on the abdominal cavity when a woman with red, frizzy hair, pop-bottle-bottom glasses, and a face full of freckles appears in the doorway.

"Hey, Izzy," she says.

"Hey, Cass. What's up?"

Cass? I stare at the woman, then look over at Izzy, my eyes questioning. He smiles back at me over the top of his mask.

"Dom called," the woman says, "He wants to know if you'll have time for supper before you leave for Chicago tonight, or if he should fix you something to go."

I gape at the woman in the doorway, unable to believe it is the same one I saw yesterday. Not only does she look completely different, her voice doesn't sound the same. This woman speaks with a pronounced Southern accent.

"Tell him I'll be home for dinner," Izzy says. "Thanks, Cass."

"You're welcome."

As soon as the woman is gone, I say, "No way is that the same woman I saw yesterday."

"It is."

"No."

"Yes."

"I don't get it."

Izzy chuckles. "Cass belongs to a local theater group—the same one Dom's in, in fact. That's how I met her. As part of her actor's training, she likes to try on a different persona each day. So she makes up characters, gets into the proper clothing, wig, and makeup, and then adopts whatever personality she thinks the character should have. The only thing that doesn't change is her name. No matter what character she is, her name is always Cass. Even when she's a man for a day."

"She does men, too?"

"Yep, and quite convincingly, I might add."

Hurley, who is standing off to the side listening to our exchange, says, "It sounds like one of those multiple-personality things to me."

Izzy shakes his head. "Trust me, Cass is as sane as you and I and maybe saner than Mattie here." He pauses and looks over at Hurley. "You have heard about the nipple incident, haven't you?"

"Hey!" I grumble.

"Hey is right," Izzy echoes. "Look at this." He has just cut through the fibrous layer of tissue covering the abdominal cavity, thereby exposing the organs. "What do you see, Mattie?"

My eyes are immediately drawn to the liver, which is grossly misshapen, its surface covered with rounded bumps that look like fluid-filled blisters. "Bad liver," I say. "Cysts?"

"That's exactly what they are." Izzy severs the necessary connections and hands me the organ so I can weigh it. While I do, he pushes aside the man's intestines to expose a kidney. "Aha," he says with an unmistakable grin, even though it is hidden behind his mask. "More of the same."

I look at the kidney, and something clicks in my brain.

My mind instantly makes the connection but then discards it almost as quickly. Surely it can't be. But I remember my discussion with Arnie about Karen Owenby and her polycystic kidney disease. Her *congenital* polycystic kidney disease. What are the odds of these two people having the same rare inherited disease?

And then I remember how Mike Halverson seemed vaguely familiar to me when I first saw him. Now I know why. It isn't because I'd met him before, it's because I'd met a relative of his: Karen Owenby.

"We can't know for sure," Izzy cautions, sensing my excitement. "Not until we do a DNA test or find some other evidence to link the two."

Hurley, who doesn't catch the significance of the liver and kidney at all, looks at us with a puzzled expression. "What are you two talking about?" he asks. "Link *who* two?"

"Karen Owenby and Mr. Halverson here," Izzy says. "They both have the same rare congenital disorder. There's a possibility they may be related."

"There's a physical resemblance," I tell them. "I noticed it when I first met Halverson. He seemed familiar to me yet I couldn't place him. Now I realize that the reason he seemed familiar was because he looks so much like Karen."

"Okay," Hurley says. "So we're talking possibilities here, right? What kind of possibilities? Likely? Remote? What?"

"Hard to say with any certainty," Izzy offers. "A rare congenital disorder like this *could* occur in two random, nonrelated people who just happen to live in a town the size of Sorenson, but I'd have to say that the odds are overwhelmingly against it. Statistically speaking, you'd stand a better chance of winning the lottery. And while I can't vouch for the physical resemblance that Mattie noted, I'm inclined to trust her judgment on the matter. So I wouldn't be at all surprised to discover that the two are brother and sister, given the closeness in their ages."

"And both were killed with a .357," Hurley muses. "Want

to bet ballistics proves that both bullets came from the same gun? What a nice little package, eh?"

I have no idea what Hurley means and hesitate to ask since I don't want to look stupid. For a brief second, vanity struggles with curiosity, my inherent nosiness emerging a clear winner seconds later. "What do you mean by 'a nice little package'?" I ask.

Hurley's baby blues take on the cold depth of glacial ice. "It means that someone wants us to think that Halverson here first killed Owenby and then killed himself, supposedly out of guilt or some need for self-punishment. The gun was left at the scene with the assumption that we'd make the connection."

"Well, it does seem like a good motive for suicide," I say. "A murder on the conscience plus a full-blown case of AIDS."

"How do you know he had AIDS?" Hurley asks.

"We don't," Izzy says, giving me a cautioning look. "We're running a test to be sure. But given that he has some of the classic physical signs of the disease, my —" He pauses, looks at me and smiles before continuing. "*Our* educated guess is that the test will be positive."

"Okay," Hurley says thoughtfully. "So how did he contract the disease? Blood transfusion? Dirty needle?" He pauses and looks at his shoes. "High-risk sex?"

Izzy chuckles. "It's okay, Steve. You can say 'gay' in front of me. As a gay man, I'm keenly aware of the high prevalence of AIDS among gay men. All of us are, though unfortunately not all of us are careful enough to avoid high-risk activities."

"Is there any way for you to know how this guy got it?" Hurley asks.

Izzy shakes his head. "Not with any certainty. But I *can* tell you that he doesn't have any tracks or needle marks that would indicate either a past or a current drug problem. I can requisition his medical records to see if he's had any blood transfusions in the past. He has no scars of any sort to indicate surgery or trauma, but those aren't the only circumstances that might call for a transfusion. As for determining his lifestyle, you probably know best how to go about that."

Hurley nods, a thoughtful look on his face.

The rest of the autopsy proves uneventful, the examination of the head wound providing nothing new. When we examine the contents of the vacuum bag, we find two hairs that—given Halverson's baldness—are likely from someone else. But given where Halverson was lying—on a bathroom floor where stray hairs of all kinds are likely to be found—their significance as evidence is questionable. We have Arnie look at them anyway and he comes back with his report just as we are placing Halverson into a fresh body bag.

"We've got a match," he announces. "Those hairs are identical to the ones that were taken from David Winston's hairbrush a few days ago as well as one of the ones we found on Karen Owenby."

I feel the stares of all three men in the room but avoid them and keep my eyes focused on Halverson's body bag. My heart sinks as I realize this latest revelation further seals David's fate. It isn't definitive evidence, but it certainly strengthens the case against him.

Then my mind zeroes in on an alternate explanation and I raise my eyes to the others in the room. "Is it possible the hairs could have come from me?" I ask. "David was at my cottage with me for a while last night. Some of his hairs might have transferred to me, and then from me to the crime site."

No one says anything but after a few seconds, Izzy shrugs. I take that as acknowledgment of the possibility. I expect to feel relief but it doesn't come.

Nothing is resolved. A DNA test will prove whether or not Halverson is related to Karen, but those results could take a week or longer. In the meantime, all I have are suspicions, doubts, and speculations. But I also have some ideas on how to turn my speculations into cold, hard facts.

But first, I need an accomplice.

Chapter 27

Before leaving the office, I remove my bandage and clean the stitches on my forehead. I think about leaving them uncovered, but they look too much like a hairy mole, so I trade in the big white bandage for a smaller, skin-toned Band-Aid.

I leave the office and drive over to Karen Owenby's house. As I park at the end of the cul-de-sac in front of her house, I happen to glance out my side window and see a burgundy-and-gray van stopped in the middle of the street. In a flash I remember how a gray-and-burgundy van almost rear-ended Izzy and I on the night of the hospital shindig. And how there was one this morning at Lauren's house, too. Now here is another one. It seems like too much of a coincidence to me. Or am I just being paranoid? I am considering walking up to it to see who is driving when it backs up several feet, makes a U-turn, and disappears back the way it came.

I turn my mind back to the task at hand, although I keep glancing up the street from time to time, half expecting the van to return. I study the other houses in the neighborhood, wondering which of them harbors the mystery caller who claimed to have seen David on the night of the murders. Given that Karen's house is at the end of a cul-de-sac, it doesn't make sense that the witness was simply driving by.

And while I suppose it is possible the witness was merely a visitor to one of the other houses on the street, I figure it is far more likely to be someone who lives here.

According to Larry Johnson, my police-officer friend, the eyewitness said she recognized David because she was a patient of his. I jot down the numbers of all the houses, knowing there must be a way to find out who lives where. I'm thinking that if I compare those names to David's patient roster, I might be able to find a connection.

With that done, I head out of town toward the village of Parsons and find the address Susan McNally listed on her ER record for her sister. It is a cozy little home in an older neighborhood: two-story, clapboard, with a small patch of lawn out front and another in back. I pull up to the curb and climb out of the car just in time to see a burgundy-and-gray van turning down a side street about a block behind me.

I freeze, my heart thumping so hard I fear it will leap from my chest. I wait, watching the surrounding streets for another five minutes, but I don't see the van again. I realize I might be acting silly, but that doesn't stop me from looking over my shoulder several times as I walk up to ring the doorbell.

The woman who answers is a freckle-faced, fiery-haired nymph, a tiny woman with a waist about as big around as a pencil. Her hair is a wild mass of curls, her eyes a color of green so vivid it has to come from contacts.

"Hi, can I help you?" she asks.

I have my badge out and show it to her, trying to adopt an official pose. "My name is Mattie Winston and I work in the Medical Examiner's office. I'm looking for Susan McNally and was wondering if she might be staying here. I need to ask her some questions about the death of her roommate, Karen Owenby."

The smile on the woman's face evaporates. "The police have already questioned her several times. Can't you get your information from them? Susan's pretty upset by all of this. As I'm sure you can imagine."

"I won't be long, but I really do need to speak with her," I push. "The focus of our investigation is a bit different from that of the police. They don't always ask the right questions for what we need to know."

If anything, the woman's expression only grows more determined. "Susan is sleeping right now. Why don't you call and make an appointment to meet with her?"

The implication—that I am rude to show up without calling first—is unmistakable. And hard to argue with. Tiny though she is, the woman before me looks to have a spine of steel and a determination to match. I am about to give in when a figure materializes like a poltergeist behind her. Actually, doppelganger would be a better term, since the two women are virtually identical. Twins.

"It's okay, Shannon," says the second woman. "I'll talk to her."

Shannon gives me a disgusted look that makes her opinion of the situation crystal-clear. I ignore her and focus on Susan instead.

"Did you say your name was Winston?" Susan asks me.

"Yes. Mattie Winston. I work with—"

"Yes, I heard you tell Shannon. But your interest in this is more than just professional, I'd wager. David Winston is your husband, isn't he?"

Busted.

"Yes. Almost ex-husband, though."

Susan flashes me an ironic smile. "I would imagine so." She steps around her sister and onto the porch. "Let's walk," she says. "Shannon's kids have big ears and I don't want them to hear what I have to say."

I can feel Shannon's eyes burning little holes into my back as I step off the porch with Susan. Since I'm not sure just how much Susan knows about Karen at this point, I decide to start with a general question and see what she offers before getting specific. “How long were you and Karen roommates?”

“Not long. Six months. There was someone else before me but I gather that she and Karen didn’t get along too well.”

“How did you know Karen?”

“I didn’t. I answered an ad she placed in the paper. We met, seemed to hit it off, and I moved in a week later. Frankly, I was desperate. I had to move out of my old apartment because the owner had sold the building and I had nowhere to go. What Karen proposed was the perfect solution, one I could afford. I sensed early on that something wasn’t quite right with the woman, but I wasn’t in any position to be picky.”

“What do you mean?”

“Well, that whole impostor thing.”

So she did know.

“I don’t get it,” she goes on. “I mean, I always thought Karen was a bit strange, but I never suspected anything like that.”

“I’m not sure anyone did. Do you know if she owned the house?”

Susan shakes her head. “I assumed so at first, but it turns out she was just renting the place. The owner is willing to let me stay there, though I’m not sure I want to at this point. And I don’t know how long it will be closed off for the police investigation.”

“You work at a bank, right?”

She nods, shooting me a wary glance before looking away again. I notice that her eyes are a more natural shade of green than her sister’s.

“Did you have a feel for Karen’s financial situation at all? Was there anything unusual you were aware of?”

She hesitates, as if unsure of her answer. “Funny you should ask that,” she says finally. “Money was a subject Karen didn’t like to discuss. There were times when I saw her counting wads of it—tens, twenties, even hundreds. Yet she always seemed broke and the balance in her checkbook was always low."

She pauses, giving me a sidelong glance. "I'm not usually a nosy person. I try to respect other people's privacy," she says. "But I knew something was going on with Karen and was worried that she might be dealing drugs or something like that. I work at Community Bank and Karen is a customer there. So I sort of peeked at her account activity one day while I was at work."

"And?"

"And all she ever deposited were her paychecks. Every two weeks. No unexpected withdrawals, no savings, no investments that I know of. So where did all that cash come from? And where did it go?"

"You have an idea, don't you?"

We have reached a corner and stop there by some unspoken agreement. Susan looks at me and nods, then drops her gaze to her feet. "I think she was blackmailing someone."

"Any idea who?"

"I thought at one time that it might have been your husband," she says, giving me a quick, guilty look. "I overheard her on the phone one night threatening to squeal to the wife of whoever she was talking to about his fooling around."

"Did you tell all of this to the cops?"

"Not all of it. I told them that she'd been seeing your hus–David. But I didn't think of the money thing until recently, the past day or so. I've been so . . . upset by the murder that I haven't been thinking straight. Besides, I knew they'd look at her financial stuff as a matter of course anyway, and if anyone found out I'd looked at Karen's account the way I did, I could get fired." She gives me a fearful, pleading look.

"I won't tell anyone," I assure her. "In fact, our entire conversation is just between the two of us."

"Thanks."

"The police said there was an anonymous caller, a woman,

who claims to have seen David at your and Karen's house the night of the murder. Was that you by any chance?"

She frowns and shakes her head. "No. I was gone all night. I wasn't even in town. My boyfriend lives in Madison. I went there to stay with him for a few days. I had Monday and Tuesday off but I was scheduled to return to work on Wednesday. Rather than fight the rush hour traffic in the morning, I decided to come home Tuesday night. I'd just gotten home when I found Karen."

If Susan isn't the eyewitness, I feel certain it must be one of Karen's neighbors.

"You said you thought at one time that it might have been David she was blackmailing. Does that mean you don't think that now?"

"I haven't thought that for a while, though that's based on a hunch rather than any facts," she says. "Thing is, I think she genuinely cared for David. I don't think she would have done that to him. To anyone else? Yeah. But not to him."

How sweet, I think with no small amount of sarcasm. If what Susan is telling me is true, Karen and David were probably an item much longer than I originally suspected. The realization that the two of them were meeting and conspiring behind my back while they smiled and talked directly to my face every day is galling. Right now I hate them both passionately, particularly Karen. And hating a dead person is a wholly unsatisfactory state of being. It's hard to imagine what sort of revenge you can wreak on someone who's already dead.

Susan reaches over and touches my arm, letting her hand rest lightly near my elbow. "There's something else I should tell you, and I can't think of a way to broach the subject delicately so I'm just going to ask. Besides, if you work in the coroner's office, you must know already."

"That Karen was pregnant?"

"Yes." She breathes a sigh of relief, closing her eyes. When she opens them again, she studies me closely for a few seconds and then pulls her hand back. I guess she figures it is safe to let go since I'm not about to launch myself into the stratosphere. As if a featherweight like her could hold down a heavyweight like me if I did.

"Did she tell you who the father was?" It pains me to ask and I fear the answer will hurt even more.

"Hell, she didn't even tell me she was pregnant. I found out when I emptied the trash. I saw the home pregnancy test in her bathroom garbage. Later that night I asked her about it. I expected her to be mad at me for finding out, but she seemed quite happy and unbothered by it all."

She pauses and gives me an apologetic look that tells me something more is coming. "I overheard her telling someone about the baby on the phone. She said she hoped it would be a boy and that he would grow up to be a doctor as talented as his father."

I swallow hard, then grasp at a straw. "That still leaves the list of suspects pretty wide open."

"Perhaps," Susan says, grimacing now. And then she gives the knife she's unwittingly plunged in my back a wicked twist. "But it gets pretty narrow when you consider that I also heard her say she wanted to name the baby David. After his father."

Chapter 28

I drive home in a deep funk, mourning the death of my marriage. At first I simply feel depressed, but by the time I pull into the driveway, my emotions have transformed themselves into a quiet but intense rage. Dead or not, I hate Karen more than ever and I am determined to get to the truth about her, whatever it takes. I sense that Halverson is tied to it all somehow and target him as the next focus of my attention.

I get home just in time to see Izzy off on his trip to Chicago. He won't be back until late Sunday night, which works just fine with my plans since I sense he might not approve of what I am about to do. Dom and I wave as Izzy drives away, and as soon as the car is out of sight, I turn to Dom and link my arm through his.

"Want to do the town tonight?" I ask him.

"Do the town?"

"Well, how about if we do The Cellar?" The Cellar is a small, nicely kept bar owned by two gay men. Located just beyond the town limits, it has a reputation for good music, affordable drinks that aren't watered down, and a liberal atmosphere that generally attracts like-minded people.

"The Cellar," Dom says. "Man, it's been a long time since I've been there. Izzy doesn't much care for the place."

"I know. It's not the sort of place he wants to be seen in,

given his job. Though ironically, the job is precisely why I want to go there tonight." I then tell Dom what we know about Mike Halverson and what I want to try to find out. "The Cellar seems like the logical place to start," I conclude, and Dom agrees. But he still looks pensive and hesitant.

"Don't worry about Izzy," I tell him. "I'll say that I made you come along and that it was strictly business. Besides, you'll have me along as a chaperone to keep you out of trouble."

"Keep *me* out of trouble? What's that cliché about the pot and the kettle?"

"You game or not? I'm going regardless. I just thought you might be able to make things a little easier for me, pave the way, and save me some time, being that you know folks there."

"I used to, but it's been several years since the last time I was in the place. Who knows if any of them are still there?"

"Where else would they be?"

He considers that, shrugs, and says, "You have a point."

The bars in Wisconsin are kind of like the cheese—there are lots of them and most of them smell funny. Many towns have more bars than gas stations, and even in the tiniest villages, where the life expectancy of the average retail business is about six months due to a lack of customers, disposable income, or both, half a dozen bars will coexist in relative harmony and financial comfort.

In every town there is always one place designated as the official football bar. It's typically decorated in classic Packer colors—green and gold—and whenever the Packers play, every square inch of the place will be occupied by rabid fans, some of whom don't think twice about wearing a giant foam cheddar cheese wedge on their heads.

In Sorenson, the official Packer bar is The End Zone, the closest thing to a men's club the town has ever had. It's a hotbed of out-of-control testosterone located on Main Street between a deli and a pet store. Consequently, it is pretty much guaranteed that talk at the bar will include an assortment of pussy jokes, a remark or two about doing it doggy-style, and the ever-ubiquitous salami comments. Most of the women who dare to venture inside The End Zone generally come back out rather quickly looking pale, appalled, and frightened.

Given the crowd that typically holds down the bar stools in The End Zone, it is hardly surprising that the gay clientele—at least those who are out of the closet—went elsewhere and established a bar of their own. That this bar is located outside of town doesn't hurt any. Homophobia is alive and well in Sorenson, and while tolerance reigns most of the time, it is often maintained only because most of the gays keep a low profile.

While I don't want to be presumptuous, I am pretty certain Mike Halverson was gay. It isn't just the fact that he had AIDS, which, as Izzy has been so careful to remind me, he could have gotten several other ways. There is something about the way he carried himself and the way he spoke that makes me certain. It's a gut instinct, nothing more, but it is a strong enough instinct for me to act on. If Mike Halverson was indeed gay, chances are he would have found his way to The Cellar. Maybe someone there will recognize him and be able to clue me in as to his friends, lifestyle, or anything else that might be of help.

Dom and I arrive at The Cellar a little after eight and the place is already hopping. It's Disco Night, one of the many theme nights the bar periodically holds. There is one of those hideous, spinning light balls in the ceiling, lots of Bee Gees music, and a dozen or so John Travolta look-alikes on the dance floor, not all of whom are guys. In fact, I suddenly realize just how effeminate Travolta is when I see that most of the women imitators look more like the real thing than the men do.

On the flip side, most of the Travolta knockoffs have dancing partners who are decked out in flared skirts, tight blouses, bright red lipstick, and lots of mascara . . . and not all of them are women. Half the fun of going to The Cellar is trying to figure out the gender of the patrons, a task made even more challenging because the hip atmosphere of the place attracts a fair number of heterosexual patrons as well.

We find a table where two women are paying their tab and hover nearby, swooping down on their seats the second they are vacated. Once we are settled, Dom signals to one of the bartenders, a guy named George who is an old friend.

Dom introduces me, and after shaking George's hand, I get right down to business by showing him a picture of Mike Halverson. It's a blowup of the shot from his driver's license, which unlike most such photos, is actually a good picture, though it bears only a vague resemblance to the man I saw earlier today. Although the license was renewed last September—a little over a year ago—the Mike Halverson pictured on it is far healthier-looking and more robust than the man I met.

"Have you seen this guy in here before?" I ask George.

George barely glances at the picture before nodding. "Oh, yeah. Plenty of times. Not recently, though. Not for about . . . oh . . . two, maybe three months. Name is Mike something, I think."

"Mike Halverson," I offer.

"Sounds right," George muses. "Heard he picked himself up a sugar daddy and that's why he doesn't come around here anymore."

"Well, he won't be in again," I say. "Somebody killed him."

George looks appropriately shocked. "Killed him? How?"

"Shot him. In the head. Very messy."

George swallows hard a couple of times and winces. "Any idea who did it?"

"Not yet. That's why I'm here. I was hoping you might be able to give me a lead on the guy—who he saw, who he knew, if he had any enemies, that sort of thing."

George seems to consider this for a few minutes. "I don't

think it was anyone from here he hooked up with. But there were some folks he talked to pretty regularly. Maybe one of them knows something." He points to a tall, attractive blond woman with a knockout figure who is out on the dance floor. "Chris used to talk to Mike a lot. You might start with him."

Him?

The pronoun makes me whip my head back around toward the dance floor so fast I feel like Linda Blair in *The Exorcist.* I stare at the person in question, looking for a clue, but all I see are long, shapely legs, gorgeous hair, great-looking skin, and perky little breasts—all in all, one fine-looking woman. If she is actually a man, you couldn't prove it by me. The one reliable characteristic (other than the obvious ones that nurses may get to see but the average public doesn't) is the presence of an Adam's apple. But Chris is wearing a wide choker of some sort that hides that part of his neck.

As far as my eyes can tell, Chris is all woman, and a hellacious-looking one at that, so much so that I sink down a little lower in my chair. There's nothing quite as humbling as realizing that a man in drag makes a better-looking woman than you do.

George walks up to the dance floor and whispers in Chris's ear, pointing toward our table. Chris nods, gives his dance partner a quick buss on the cheek, and sashays his way toward us.

"Hi there," he says, and I notice that though his voice is deep, it is not distinctly masculine. He settles into an empty chair, crosses his shapely legs, leans back, and lights a cigarette. He gives Dom a thorough once-over that should be intimidating, maybe even insulting. Yet instead it seems strongly sensual, enough so that Dom begins to squirm. Smiling at Dom's obvious discomfort, Chris then turns that sensuous gaze toward me, giving me the same deep perusal.

"Love that lipstick you're wearing," he says, his gaze settling on my lips. "Sort of a cross between mocha and coral."

"It's called Sandy Sunset," I tell him. "Part of a new color scheme my stylist turned me on to."

He eyes my face and hair for a moment, then gives a nod of approval. "The colors are interesting. Darker than I might have guessed for your complexion, yet it works. And your hair! It's to dye for. Get it? To d-y-e for?" He laughs and tosses his own blond locks before taking another drag on his cigarette.

"Your stylist is obviously talented," he says through a haze of exhaled smoke. "Who is it? Will you share? Or is it a big secret?" He sighs and takes another drag. "It's so hard to find anyone good these days."

"I'll share. But you might not like her. She's a bit . . . different."

"Oh, I don't care about that," he says with a wave of his hand. "I mean, come on. Look at me."

He has a point.

"Her name is Barbara Moyer. She works at the Keller Funeral Home in Sorenson. I don't know the number but you can reach her if you call the funeral home. That's where her, um, salon is."

"A funeral home? How twisted," Chris says with a wicked grin. "I like it. I'll definitely have to check it out. Thanks, girlfriend."

"Sure. Tell Barbara I sent you."

"I will. Now, let me return the favor. I understand from Georgie Porgie that you want to know something about Mike Halverson."

I nod and wait as Chris takes another drag off his cigarette and surveys the room. I sense he is someone who won't be rushed, who will dish on his own time and on his own terms. So I wait. In the interim, I watch him closely, enthralled with the way he oozes sensuality without being blatantly sexual. I study his mannerisms, his gestures, the subtle shifts of his legs, and his overall body language. I try to memorize it all, figuring if I can learn to be half as seductive as he is, my social life will improve by leaps and bounds.

"Well, Mikey was a character, I'll tell ya that," Chris says finally, exhaling a long, curling plume of smoke that spirals lazily toward the ceiling. "He was a real sucker for the GQs."

"GQs?"

"Yeah, you know the type. Three-piece suit, Yuppie airs, money to burn. Problem is, a lot of those guys spend their lives in the closet."

"George said he thought Mike had hooked up with someone a few months back. And that's why he stopped coming in here."

"He did meet someone," Chris says, looking off across the room again and taking another drag on his cigarette. "I don't think they ever came in here together, though. Mike generally came in alone. But he sure did talk about the guy. Let me think. . . ." His eyes squint with the effort. "I can't remember Mikey ever mentioning a name, but he said the guy was a big shot of some sort. Lots of money, very handsome."

"Any idea how long they were seeing one another?" I ask.

Chris shrugs. "Last time I saw Mikey was probably two months ago or more. And I think he'd been seeing this GQ for a while at that point."

"Did you know that Mike had AIDS?"

Chris makes a cute little pout. "Ooh, no, I didn't. Not sure anyone else did either." He shakes his pretty head and I again find myself amazed that there is a man somewhere inside that body. "Usually word of something like that gets out rather quickly. So I suspect Mikey wasn't telling. That's bad. Very bad." He pauses a second, cocking his head to one side and staring off into space. Then he looks at me and says, "Do you think that's why he was killed?"

"I don't know," I tell him. "Right now I'm just trying to get a handle on who he was and who he knew."

"Well, I'll tell you this," Chris says, stabbing out his cigarette and leaning across the table to speak in a conspiratorial whisper. "I've never seen Mikey like he was the last few times he was in here. He was all goggle-eyed and couldn't stop blabbering on about this new boyfriend and their future together. He had that look—you know the one—the look that says this one is different. I think Mikey was genuinely in love. And if what he said was true, the two of them were meeting several times a week at the Grizzly."

"The Grizzly?"

"That's a little motel over near Fond du Lac. It's a popular stopping-off point, if you know what I mean," he says, wiggling his perfectly tweezed eyebrows suggestively. "It's owned by a brother and sister who have set up one whole section to cater to the"—he pauses and makes little quote marks in the air—"fast-food crowd. It might be worth asking them if they know who Mikey was seeing. They're generally pretty tight-lipped about who their customers are, but Calvin's here tonight and I do believe he has a bit of an in with the owners. They might tell you something if you were to take Cal along."

He pauses and fans his face with one hand. "Calvin," he says with a tone of reverence. "Don't you think that sounds terribly masculine?" He says the name again, more breathily this time, as he glances around the room. Finally his gaze settles on the dance floor.

"That's him out there," he says. "The bald guy in the leather jacket." I look and see a well-built man of medium height dressed from head to toe in leather. He is dancing—quite well, I notice—with a thin, freckle-faced guy who has an unruly mop of curly red hair.

"Would you like me to see if Calvin's willing to help you out?"

"Yes, please," I say. "Thanks, Chris."

He removes a compact from the small purse he has slung over his shoulder. Flipping it open, he checks his face in the mirror, primping his hair a bit before he snaps it closed. "How do I look?"

"Stunning," I say with all honesty.

His smile broadens as he hoists himself up and straightens out the wrinkles in his skintight skirt. He sashays his way to the dance floor and I watch in amusement as he expertly corrals Calvin and steers him away.

"Damn," Dom says, his tone respectful. "He's good."

Chris brings Calvin to our table and introduces him. Up close I see that Calvin has huge, soulful brown eyes that seem to twinkle with some hidden source of humor. His voice is deep but softly sensual and whenever he speaks or smiles, the ends of his moustache tease dimples in both cheeks. And speaking of cheeks, the physique is quite nice too—muscular, tight, and tanned.

And gay. Damn it.

As soon as the introductions are out of the way, I explain the story all over again to Calvin, including the fact that Halverson had AIDS and was brutally murdered by someone. "I understand the need for discretion at the Grizzly," I tell him. "But we need to know why Mike Halverson was murdered. It could be we have some sort of homophobic vigilante on our hands."

I don't actually believe that, but I figure it can't hurt to make Calvin feel as if he is doing something righteous and in favor of the overall gay good by helping us talk to the motel owners. I take Calvin's slight nod as evidence he agrees and push a little more.

"Any chance you might be willing to introduce us to the owners?"

"Sure," he says. "I can't promise they'll help, but I'm happy to give it a shot. When do you want to go?"

I look at Dom, my eyebrows raised in question. He gives me back a shrug of indifference. "Can we do it tonight?" I ask, turning back to Calvin.

He considers this, then smiles. "Why not? Just give me about fifteen minutes to tie up some loose ends here." With that, he rises from his chair and disappears into the crowd. I thank Chris for his help and watch as he stands, smoothes the lines of his skirt, and scans the room for his next target. Then he, too, disappears into the crowd.

While we are waiting for Calvin, Dom and I order a couple of beers and spend some time rating the moves of the Travolta imitators on the dance floor. After the promised fifteen minutes have passed, I start searching for Calvin but spot another familiar face instead.

"Oh, hell," I say, giving Dom a nudge with my leg. "Looks like we aren't the only ones to zero in on The Cellar. Lookie there." I nod toward the main entrance. "That tall, dark, and handsome fella over there by the door is Steve Hurley, the homicide detective on the Owenby case."

Hurley sees me, waves, and heads toward our table. "Well, hello there," he says when he reaches us. Grinning smugly, he grabs a chair, spins it around backward and straddles it. For the first time in my life, I am envious of a chair.

"Detective Hurley. What brings you out here on a night like this?" I ask.

"I might ask you the same thing."

I ignore his rebuttal and gesture toward Dom. "Have you two met?"

Hurley glances at Dom, nods, and mumbles a greeting. Dom mumbles something back and quickly looks away, his arms folded tight across his chest. I'm dying to know why it is that Dom dislikes cops so much, but every time I try to ask him about it, he changes the subject.

"So, what *are* you doing here?" Hurley asks me.

"Just enjoying a night out," I tell him. "Izzy's away at his medical conference so Dom and I thought we'd go out and have a little R&R."

"R&R," Hurley repeats, his tone rich with skepticism. "When will Izzy be back?"

"Tomorrow night."

"Don't tell me he left you in charge while he's gone."

His tone of disbelief pricks my ego. "Why wouldn't he?"

"Well, for one thing, you haven't been at this very long. I would think he'd want someone with a bit more experience."

"I'm a quick learner."

"Are you now?" he says, flashing me a crooked grin.

The truth is, Izzy has a couple of forensic pathologists who fill in for him from time to time. If any autopsies need to be done, they will do them and either Arnie or I will assist. But that is the extent of my duties while Izzy is away. As for the day-to-day office stuff, some of that is done by Arnie, but most of it falls to Cass.

Dom is starting to squirm, and as much as I am enjoying my repartee with Hurley, I fear he might start asking questions I don't want to answer. Withholding facts from him is one thing. Lying directly to those blue eyes is something else again. I can't trust my hormones not to betray me. And I don't want Hurley along when Calvin takes us to the Grizzly.

"Well, it's great seeing you, Hurley, but we were just about to leave." I drain the last of my beer and stand. Dom takes the cue enthusiastically and is halfway to the door seconds after I'm on my feet.

"Heading home?" Hurley asks, his tone suspicious.

"I'm tired. It's been a long day." It's the truth, and if Hurley assumes from that statement that I have answered his question in the affirmative, so be it.

"Yes, I imagine it has been," he says, studying me intently. "In fact, I'm surprised to see you out and about at all tonight."

"Hey, a girl is entitled to a little fun, isn't she?"

"Fun? Is that what you came here for?"

"Sure. This is a pretty happening place." I look about the room as if to confirm all the "happenings" but I really just need to look away from Hurley while I lie to him.

"Really?" The skepticism in his tone is thick enough to slice.

"Yes, really." I see Dom over by the exit, standing next to Calvin.

"I'm surprised you're not staying longer then," Hurley challenges. "You got all dolled up and drove all this way and you've only been here . . . what"—he glances at his watch—"twenty, maybe thirty minutes."

Now how did he know that? Has he been here all along? Did he follow me here? That might explain the burgundy-and-gray van—maybe it is one of Hurley's cohorts tailing me. I wonder if Hurley or his goon squad will try to follow me when I leave. That simply won't do. Calvin and the Grizzly are my finds. Besides, I suspect the presence of an overbearing police detective might put a damper on Calvin's willingness to help, not to mention the motel owners' willingness to share. Somehow, I have to find a way to keep Hurley here long enough for us to get a head start. And as my gaze wanders over the dance floor, I get an idea.

"I guess I underestimated just how much the day took out of me," I tell Hurley. "I really need to head home, but hey, it was good seeing you. Have fun and I'll catch you later."

With that, I turn away and head onto the dance floor, where I grab Chris, whisper, "I need your help," and escort him toward the opposite side of the room, as far away from Hurley as possible.

I look back quickly to see if Hurley is watching me and, seeing that he is, I turn Chris around so he can see Hurley over my shoulder. "Act as if we're just two buddies saying good-bye. Smile, laugh, look casual," I say.

Chris instantly complies. "But of course," he says, smiling broadly. "What's up, girlfriend?"

"See that real tall fellow over there at the table where we were sitting?"

Chris glances quickly, licks his lips, then turns his gaze back to me. "How could I miss him, honey? That is one *fine* specimen of manhood."

He is that, and I take a second to ponder the irony of discussing Hurley's sexual appeal with another man. "Yes, he is," I agree. "But he's also a cop and I think he's following me. And I don't want him tagging along when Calvin takes us out to the Grizzly."

"Hmm, yes. I can see where that might be a problem," Chris says.

"So here's what I want you to do. . . ."

Chapter 29

Ten minutes later, Dom and I are following Calvin's motorcycle down a two-lane highway and there are no headlights we can see anywhere behind us. Thirty minutes after that, we pull into the parking lot of the Grizzly Motel.

There are probably plenty of places that are tackier than the Grizzly but it is hard for me to imagine any. Out by the road, a giant grizzly bear rises up in green and pink neon, his arm pointing the way to the main office, which is sandwiched between two long wings of rooms. Below the bear is another splash of neon that says VACAN_Y, the *Y* blinking on and off as it threatens to join its darkened neighbor. Another sign, this one in simple white light with black lettering, advertises seventy-five cable channels.

The parking lot is surprisingly full. We follow Calvin around to the back of the place and I see that each wing has rooms both in front and in back. We pull into an empty spot near the middle of the two wings and Dom turns off the engine.

Calvin parks his motorcycle and we are about to get out of the car and meet him when he signals for us to stay put. He walks over to our car and I roll down my window.

"Wait here," he says, leaning down close enough for me catch a whiff of something spicy and tantalizing. "I want to approach them alone first. I don't want it to seem as if I'm making any assumptions or putting them on the spot. I'll come out and get you if things look good."

We sit and wait, watching the activity around us. And the Grizzly is plenty active. Within a few minutes, the door to one of the rooms opens and two men emerge, climb into separate cars, and drive away. Minutes after that, a maid enters the just-vacated room with a cart loaded with towels, sheets, and cleaning supplies. Speedy nighttime maid service isn't the hallmark of your typical roadside motel. It doesn't take a rocket scientist to figure out that the Grizzly is renting rooms by the hour.

"Interesting place," I mutter.

"It's clean and the owners are discreet," Dom says.

I shoot him a look. "You know this place?"

"A little. I came here myself a time or two, years ago. Before Izzy."

I ponder that.

"And before you get all high and mighty," Dom continues, "you might want to know that the owners aren't particular about who they rent to. Yes, it's a popular spot for us homos because the place is clean and quiet and the owners are willing to look the other way. But we're not the only ones who find that appealing. There's a brisk hourly trade among the breeders here, too."

Sure enough, another door opens a few minutes later and a man and woman step outside. The man escorts the woman to her car, leans in through the window to give her a kiss, and then watches her pull away before climbing into his own car. A few minutes later, yet another maid appears, wheeling her cart into the room the couple just left.

"Good Lord," I say, shaking my head. "What if some family showed up here to spend the night?"

"The entire left wing is reserved for regular overnight business," Dom explains. "Only the right wing rooms are available to the hourly crowd."

Calvin reappears then and I fear bad news when I see the grim expression on his face.

"Randall isn't here right now but his sister is," he says, leaning in through my window. "She isn't real pleased with me for bringing you here and she won't commit to anything. But when I told her why you needed the information, she said she'd hear you out as long as you promise her the Grizzly won't get caught up in some official investigation. It wouldn't be real good for business . . . if you get my drift."

"I understand," I tell him. "I can't guarantee that the cops won't show up here on their own, but I can promise that I won't bring them here."

"Tell her that, not me," Calvin says. "Come on and I'll introduce you."

Dom waits in the car while I follow Calvin into the office. A thick fog of cigarette smoke hovers in the air and the tiny room has a dull, dingy look to it as if everything is covered with a fine layer of dust and ash. Behind a small, yellowed countertop stands the biggest woman I've ever seen. She has to be close to seven feet tall and has the broad, thick shoulders typical of swimmers. Her hair is cut short in a Joan-of-Arc-type fringe and she is wearing a blue plaid flannel shirt and blue jeans. I can't see her feet but mentally outfit them in a pair of heavy work boots. I nickname her Babe, like the blue ox.

"This is Mattie Winston," Calvin says, gesturing toward me.

"Winston, eh?" Babe says, her brows knitting together.

"Yes."

"And this," Calvin says, giving Babe a nod, "is Cinder."

"Cindy?" I say, not sure if I've heard right.

"No, Cin-der," the woman says, enunciating each syllable in a voice that I'm sure could rattle windows.

"Oh, okay. Like Cinderella," I say, smiling. The smile doesn't last long, and if looks could kill, Calvin will soon be hauling me out of here in a body bag. Cinder's face looks like a major storm front, the kind that spawns giant hailstones and F5 tornados.

"It ain't Cindy," she growls. "And it sure as hell ain't Cinderella. Got that?"

I nod so vigorously I give myself a mild case of whiplash and decide that Cinder is obviously short for cinderblock.

"Calvin here says Mikey got kilt by someone," she says. "And that you think maybe the friend he usta bring here might know sumpin 'bout it."

"Yes." I say nothing more. It is hard enough getting that out; my mouth is so dry, my tongue keeps sticking to my palate.

I hear the door open behind me but don't look. In fact, I instantly drop my gaze to the floor, resisting the urge to squeeze my eyes closed. I feel like a witness to a killing, knowing that if I dare to look at the murderer, I'll become the next victim.

Cinder reaches beneath the counter and I half expect her to come back up with a gun. Instead she is holding several sheets of paper, stapled together. She hands them to me and says, "These are the titles we have in stock. VCR rents for ten bucks an hour." Then she dismisses me and turns to whoever came through the door. "Help you?" she grunts.

I get the hint, but just in case I didn't, Calvin tugs at my arm, pulling me off to one side. I look at the papers Cinder handed me and realize it's a list of videos available for rent. And not just any videos. I scan the titles, finding such gems as *Ass Ventura: The Crack Detective, The Blow Bitch Project,* and *Bonfire of the Panties*.

I am vaguely aware of a man checking in for a room, but keep my eyes on the list. *Ferris Bueller Gets Off, Forrest Hump, Good Will Humping.*

The man checking in pays and Cinder gives him a key. I keep reading. *The Madam's Family, Muffy the Vampire Layer, Position: Impossible.*

The man finally leaves and I hear Cinder clear her throat.

I scan a few more titles as quickly as I can—*The Sperminator, Saving Ryan's Privates, Snatch Adams*—before reluctantly handing the pages back to her.

"Calvin says you work with Izzy Rybarceski," Cinder says.

"I do," I say, raising Cinder up a notch for pronouncing Izzy's name correctly and without hesitation.

"He here?"

"He's out of town."

"You're not a cop, right?"

"No way, Jose." I giggle then, a stupid-sounding nervous giggle that I fear might be grounds for murder. Cinder narrows her eyes and it is enough to scare the giggle right out of me. I try to swallow and can't.

"We have a lot of respect for our clients' privacy here, ya know."

"I'm sure you do."

"We figure what they do on their own time is their business. Long as they're adults, pay for the room and don't bust nothing up, we don't care what they do."

I nod.

"We don't even pay attention to who comes with who or who leaves with who."

My hopes sink like a two-bit criminal tossed into the East River wearing a pair of cement overshoes.

"But I don't cotton to people killing one another. That's wrong."

I barely dare to breathe. What is she saying? Does she or doesn't she know anything? And if she does, is she going to tell me?

"So happens I did see who it was came to meet Mikey one time," Cinder says. "Just a few days ago, in fact. I guess there was a mix-up cause he didn't know what room to go to. So he came here first. I don't usually ask for names or nothing but I seen this guy before someplace else. Knew him from there."

"Where?"

"From the hospital over in Sorenson. He yanked out my brother's appendix two years ago."

"He's a surgeon?" I say, feeling suddenly faint.

"I sure as hell hope so since he cut my brother's belly open."

"And you know his name?"

"Of course. You think I'd let somebody carve Randall up without knowing his name?"

I feel as if I am leaning over a high ledge, petrified of the drop before me yet fighting a strange compulsion to throw myself off. And before I can think twice, I leap.

"Who was it?" It comes out as little more than a whisper. For one fleeting second, I hope she won't tell me. I pray that some lingering vestige of her strict confidentiality rule will take over at the last minute.

But she does tell me and my life falls apart.

"Funny thing," she says, not knowing that what she is about to say is the most unfunny thing she could possibly tell me. "His last name is the same as yours. Winston. Dr. David Winston."

Chapter 30

Dom pulls his car around behind the house and into the garage. The drive home was a silent one once Dom gave up on his attempts to get me to talk. I can't talk. I am too stunned, too confused, and too heartbroken.

I notice the car parked beside the garage—a dark sedan I recognize immediately—with a sense of resignation. The car itself is empty, but when I crane around to look back at the cottage, I can make out a dark shadow sitting on the steps of my porch.

"You can come into the house and hide out if you want," Dom offers as he turns off the engine and hits the button on the garage door opener.

I give him a wan smile. "Thanks, but I can handle Hurley."

"He's gonna be pissed after the way you ditched him at The Cellar."

"He'll get over it."

I open my door and start to get out but Dom reaches over and stops me with a hand on my arm. "Are you going to be okay?" he says, concern marking his face.

I nod, though we both know I might never be okay again. I spent the ride home trying to make the facts add up to something other than the inevitable conclusion, but it was like trying to prove that two plus two equals five, an exercise I failed in my high school algebra class and can't seem to master any better now. Still I keep trying, unable—or maybe unwilling—to accept the obvious.

I can't even harbor any last hopes that Cinder might have mistaken someone else for David. She described him to a tee and when I showed her a picture from my wallet that was a group shot of David and me with Desi, Lucien, and two other couples, Cinder picked David out without hesitation.

I am struggling to accept the fact that the man I married, the man I thought I knew, is involved in all of this. I find it hard to believe that I've been so blind, so utterly clueless all this time.

I am appalled, confused, and furious. I want to scream, hit someone, kick someone, or *break* something. Which is why I feel prepared to take on Hurley. Right now, any man that ticks me off even the slightest bit will be putting his life—and a few precious anatomical parts—at great risk.

I lean over and give Dom a quick buss on the cheek. "I'll holler really loud if I need anything, okay?"

"Okay, I'll be listening. Hey, why don't you come over and have breakfast with me in the morning?"

"Thanks, but I don't think I'll be very good company."

"Since when does that stop you?"

Despite the vicious storm roiling inside me, I smile. "Thanks for the offer, but I think I'll be better off alone for now, Dom."

"I'll make Belgian waffles."

Dom's Belgian waffles are legendary, the stuff culinary wet dreams are made of. The fact that his offer doesn't make me instantly start to salivate proves just how upset I am.

"Please, Mattie? I'm kind of lonely with Izzy gone and I'd really enjoy your company, bitchy or not. Besides, I want to know what happens with Mr. Gold Star over there," he says, nodding toward Hurley.

I know Dom is no more lonely than he is straight, but I

am touched by his efforts nonetheless. "Okay, fine. You win. I'll see you in the morning."

As I step out of the garage and walk toward Hurley, I concentrate on keeping my face impassive. My breath clouds before me as I sigh, and I wonder why Hurley is sitting outside on my steps rather than in his car, given that the temperature is hovering somewhere in the midforties.

"Aren't you cold?" I ask him when I am a few feet away.

"I seem to be rather hot at the moment," he says, his voice tight. "I get that way whenever someone tries to make me for a fool."

"Who did that?" Pure innocence.

"Give it up, Mattie. You sicced that . . . creature on me on purpose, didn't you?"

"Whatever are you talking about? You've lost me, Hurley."

"No, I'd say it was you who lost me. And nicely done at that. Distract me by having some she-male try to rape me in public and then sneak out the back door. Very clever."

"I left out the front door."

"It's a figure of speech," he says irritably. "And you know what I mean. Where'd you go?"

"Dom and I stopped at another bar for a nightcap."

"Bullshit."

"Are you calling me a liar?"

"Gee, I don't know. Have you ever lied to me?" he snaps back.

Score one for his side.

I don't want to play any longer. Generally I enjoy Hurley's presence, not to mention the opportunity to just look at him. And that kiss we shared is still hot on my mind. But discovering that the man I've been married to for the last seven years had a romantic liaison with not only another woman, but with an HIV-infected man, doesn't exactly put me in the mood for romance. I need to be alone.

"Go away, Hurley. I don't want to play your games tonight."

I storm past him and onto the porch. I unlock the door, push it open, reach in, and flip the light switch. I am about to look back to make sure Hurley is leaving when I see what awaits me in the living room.

"What the—"

Hurley comes up behind me and leans in over my shoulder. The two of us stand there, staring, trying to make sense of what we are seeing.

My living room floor is covered with dozens of white fluffy tufts, like some sort of cotton batting. It looks as if someone murdered a small mattress by blowing it to smithereens. Except most of these chunks of stuffing have strings attached. Scattered amidst the tufts are tiny pieces of shredded paper, some with blue writing on them. I tilt my head to read a fairly large piece near my foot, making out the letters *t-a-m*. And then Rubbish struts out from under the couch proudly carrying his latest kill in his mouth—more of the white cottony stuff. But this piece is as yet unchewed and unclawed and in its original form, the string trailing along the floor.

Hurley reaches down and picks up one of the malformed tufts by its string. He holds it aloft, staring at it. "What the hell is this?" he asks.

"It's a tampon, Hurley. Don't tell me you've never seen one before."

He drops it as if it burned him and takes a quick step back.

"Geez, Hurley, relax. They haven't been used or anything."

His face turns a bright shade of crimson and suddenly I know how to get him to leave. I lean over and pick up the mutilated tampon he just dropped.

"Want me to explain how it works?" I say, swinging it by the string like a hypnotist's watch. I step closer.

He backs up another step. "No, really. That's not necessary. I . . . um . . . I just wanted to make sure you got home okay. Everything looks fine here so I guess I'll be on my way. Good night."

He spins around and is gone so fast I start to wonder if he was ever really here. Seconds later his car engine fires up and I listen to the sound of it fading as he goes down the drive-way. When he reaches the road, I hear him lay down rubber as he peels out.

Oddly, the sound brings tears to my eyes. I brush them away and begin rationalizing to myself. *It's good that he left. I need to be alone. I need to think. The last thing I need around me tonight is some damned man.*

I hear a mew followed by a *thump-ump.* I laugh and then, as I start to pick up the mess on my living room floor, I cry.

After tossing and turning most of the night, I give up on trying to sleep once the sun comes up. I feel edgy and hung-over, so I make a pot of coffee and sit on the couch, trying to figure out what to do next. I realize I'm going to have to con-front David, and the thought of doing so fills me with both sadness and dread.

A little after eight, I head over to the main house, know-ing Dom will be up and about by now. Half an hour later we are seated at the kitchen table, our plates heaped with fluffy waffles smothered with fat strawberries and mounds of whipped cream. Bright morning sunshine streams in through the window in stark contrast to the darkness inhabiting my soul.

"Thank you for insisting I come over here this morning, Dom. Being alone wasn't as good for me as I thought it would be."

"Did you get any sleep?"

I answer him with a weak smile.

"Didn't think you would."

"I just can't believe it," I say, shaking my head. "I mean,

forget the risk to me. David is a surgeon, for God's sake. He's routinely messing with other people's bodily fluids and delicate organs. Doesn't he realize what could happen? What the hell was he thinking?"

"Sounds like he wasn't thinking," Dom says. There is a period of silence and then he adds, "Assuming he did what you think he did."

I look up at him, my mouth hanging open in disbelief. "Don't tell me you're going to defend the bastard."

"Not defend necessarily, just give him the benefit of the doubt."

"Doubt? What doubt? There is no doubt, Dom. Cinder clearly identified him as the man who met Mike Halverson at the Grizzly. So what's to doubt?"

He shrugs. "I just think you might be jumping to conclusions. David never struck me as the type."

"You mean the type to screw around? Because I can assure you he *is* that type. I saw that with my own eyes."

"That's not what I meant. Obviously he did the nasty with Karen. I meant I don't think David is gay. My gaydar may not be infallible, but it's pretty good. And David just doesn't fit."

"Oh, yeah," I scoff. "*There's* solid evidence."

"Come on, Mattie. You're usually more open-minded than this."

"Excuse me if having my life blow up before my eyes doesn't do much to enhance my objectivity."

"Look, I know I'm acting on nothing more than a gut feeling. But I think you should try to talk to David, hear what he has to say before you jump to any conclusions."

"Oh, I intend to talk with him all right."

"Mattie."

"Oh, all right," I say, tossing my fork down in frustration. "I'll try to give him the benefit of the doubt."

There is no conviction in my voice and Dom is too smart not to notice. "You should take someone with you," he says.

"That will help you stay calm. I'll be happy to go along."

"I think I'd rather do it alone."

"You're too emotional. Too close to it all. All you'll end up doing is pissing him off. Besides, if you truly have doubts as to what David is capable of, it just makes sense not to confront him alone."

He is probably right, but I know that with him or anyone else there, David will never open up like he would to me alone. Besides, this is so very personal. Yet if I know Dom, he'll insist on coming along and will badger me about it until I give in. I think fast, knowing what I have to do but not sure how to pull it off. Then I remember that it is Sunday and, being a creature of habit, Dom always does his grocery shopping before noon on Sundays. He swears it's the best time to go if you want to avoid long lines because so many people spend the morning in church.

I don't want to make my capitulation look too easy, so I spend a few moments playing with different facial expressions, going from stubborn to conflicted, and finally, resigned. "You're right," I say with a sigh. "How about if I call David and see if he'll be home this afternoon. We can go over there then."

"Great. That will give me time to get my grocery shopping done."

Bingo!

We finish eating and after helping with the cleanup I head back to the cottage. Within the hour I hear the rumble of the garage door and watch as Dom backs out and heads down the driveway. As soon as he turns onto the road, I throw on a jacket and head off through the woods.

The one flaw in my little scheme is that I no longer know anything about David's on-call schedule and I'm not sure he'll be home, so I'm relieved when I see his car in the drive. As I cross the yard I notice that the wheelbarrow is gone, though there is a small pile of mulch beneath the window, serving as a testament to my stupidity. I climb the porch steps and, out of habit, reach for the doorknob. Then I remember that I don't live here anymore. Feeling awkward and oddly conspicuous, I ring the doorbell instead.

David answers wearing shorts and a T-shirt. A fine sheen of sweat covers his body and a small towel is draped around his neck. I know from past experience that he's just finished his morning workout on the treadmill. In the past, David's obsession with fitness struck me as appropriate, considering that he is a surgeon and presumably, somewhat health-conscious. Now, it seems merely obsessive, one more fault in the ramshackle construction of his personality.

"Hi," he says, his face registering surprise at finding me here. "Is this a social call?"

"Not exactly. I need to get some clothes. The weather is getting cooler and I need warmer stuff."

"No problem." He steps aside and waves me in with a magnanimous gesture that pisses me off. After all, this is my house, too. At least it used to be.

While the clothes thing serves as a delaying tactic, it is also a legitimate need. Worried that we might end up at one another's throats before my visit is done, though hopefully only in the metaphorical sense, I opt to gather the clothes first before saying anything. David tails me the entire time, indulging in inane chatter about the hospital, the OR, and a recent case he did. His incessant yammering annoys me and the way he follows me around everywhere I go, watching my every move, makes me wonder if he thinks I'll try to take something I shouldn't.

After sorting through the closet and dresser, I pack a suitcase full of sweaters, slacks, and flannel jammies and haul it downstairs, parking it by the front door. Then I go to the foyer closet and dig out gloves, a scarf, a sweater jacket, and my best winter coat, tossing them atop the suitcase. Nervous and anxious to be done with it all, I turn to David and, with no segue or warning, launch my first missile.

"I take it you know about Mike Halverson's death," I say.

He nods. "Tragic thing."

I stare at him for several seconds, appalled. "That's it?" I say. "That's all you have to say? 'Tragic thing?'"

His brow furrows and he looks confused. "What were you expecting me to say?"

"Oh, I don't know. Maybe something a bit more emotional. I mean, you were sleeping with the guy, weren't you?"

He staggers back a step and all the blood drains from his face. *"What?"* he says, the word coming out like a gunshot.

"Don't try to deny it, David. I have a witness who saw you at the Grizzly Motel. You met Mike Halverson there. It doesn't take a rocket scientist to figure it all out."

"The Grizzly?" Then dawning spreads across his face. "Oh."

"Yes, *oh.*"

"It's not what you think," he says quietly. "You don't understand."

"Damn right I don't. You did know Mike Halverson was HIV positive, didn't you?"

"Yes, I knew." He crosses his arms over his chest and tightens his lips. His calm complacency infuriates me.

"Jesus Christ, David. Wasn't screwing around with Karen enough for you? Didn't that pose enough of a risk to me? Not to mention your patients? My God, don't you realize what you've done?"

"Mattie, you've got it all wrong."

"Oh, really? Then pray tell, David. What's the story? Did you kill Mike Halverson, too?"

"What the hell are you talking about?" he says. "Mike Halverson committed suicide." He pauses a second, looking at me. "Didn't he?" he adds.

"No. It was staged to look like a suicide, but he was murdered."

"Christ," David says, raking his fingers through his hair and staring at the floor. I watch the muscles in his cheeks twitch and leap. When he looks back up again, I see resignation in his face. But I have no idea what he's resigned to do. "I think you better come and sit down," he says.

The look in his eyes frightens me and suddenly I remember Dom's cautionary advice. Have I just made a fatal error in judgment? "If you have something to say to me, say it here," I tell him. I want to stay close to the door, just in case.

"Fine. Have it your way." He shifts uncomfortably and stares off into space for a second, seeming to gather his thoughts. "Yes, I knew Mike Halverson," he says finally. "And yes, I did meet him at the Grizzly one evening. Just once, and he didn't know I was coming. And it wasn't for what you think. All I did was talk to them."

"Them?"

I see a montage of emotion flash across his face: doubt, indecision, fear, and sadness. "Yes, *them.* Mike and his lover."

"His lover," I repeat, thoughts racing through my mind. "His lover? What, were you jealous? Is that it? You wanted him for yourself?"

He groans in frustration, his hands clenched into fists. "Christ, Mattie. Do you seriously think I'm gay? Or a murderer?"

"I don't know, David. I don't know what to think anymore." Hearing the shrill tone in my voice, I take a deep breath and try to calm down. "Everything is so confusing. People are getting killed and I have no idea why or who's doing it. But it's hard for me to ignore the facts, David. And an awful lot of the facts point to you."

"Well, I'm not a killer," he says, calmer now. "Nor am I gay." He sucks in a breath and squeezes his eyes closed. "But," he adds, "Sidney Carrigan is."

Chapter 31

At first I'm not sure if David means Sidney is gay, a killer, or both. As it turns out, David isn't sure either about the killer part. That Sidney is gay, he is certain of. That Sidney is a killer, he doesn't want to believe. Nor do I. *No way,* I think. But one look at David's face and I know he has spoken the truth. The tragedy of it is written there, plain to see.

I finally take the seat David offered earlier and sit in stunned silence as he tells me everything he knows. It is a puzzling, sad, and sordid tale, one that makes me wish I'd kept my damnably curious nose out of things.

David explains how he first became aware of something going on when he overheard Sidney and Karen having a heated argument in an on-call room one night a couple of weeks ago. "I couldn't hear everything they said, but certain words came out quite clearly," David says. "I understood that Karen was asking Sid for money and threatening to reveal something about him if he didn't. The next day I confronted Karen and, after first trying to deny it all, she just broke down and sobbed. That was when she told me about Mike, that he was her brother, that he was gay, and that he had AIDS.

"She told me how they were orphaned when Karen was nineteen and Mike was still in high school. She assumed responsibility for him then and has felt she has had it ever since. Apparently, it's been quite a struggle, emotionally and financially. When Mike was diagnosed with AIDS, things really got bad. They had no health insurance and the cost of the drugs he needed to take to keep the disease under control was astronomical."

Something clicks into place in my mind. "How long ago was he diagnosed?" I ask.

"I'm not sure. But I gather it was a number of years ago. Karen said he came close to dying once before. That was before the current protease inhibitor treatments became available."

"That might explain why she took on that nurse's identity," I muse. "If she was hurting for money, the difference in pay between an OR nurse and an assistant could have made a significant difference. Plus, it might have given her access to supplies she would have otherwise had to buy for him."

"I don't know," David says. "I suppose it's possible. I didn't know Karen wasn't who she said she was until after she was killed. All I knew was what she told me, that she'd been trying to care for Mike for the last twenty years. She was buying his drugs, paying his rent, and she also set him up in his business."

"You mean the medical supply company? Karen set that up?"

"So she said. Apparently it's organized under a fairly convoluted corporate structure that hides the real owners' names behind a series of dummy companies, with the main one looking like a sole proprietorship owned by Mike Halverson. In truth, the place is owned by Karen. That's why she was trying to talk some of the docs into investing in the place. She had it set up so that they could become blind owners, their names never appearing anywhere in any official capacity. Then the docs could refer business there and convince their associates to do so, too, profiting from the revenues their referrals generated."

"Did anyone buy into it?"

"I'm not sure. I know she was upset when I declined to participate, but she seemed to take it in stride. Though to be honest, in retrospect I think my refusal was why she turned her attentions toward me in another way."

"Meaning?"

"Meaning her seduction."

I give him my best skeptic's look. "I suppose you're going to tell me it was all her fault."

"Of course not. I let myself get caught up in it all. I felt sorry for her at first and simply wanted to help her. Then one thing led to another and . . ." He shrugs, as if it is no big deal. "Maybe she was hoping to blackmail me. I'm pretty sure that's what she was doing to Sidney. But your untimely arrival in the OR that night sort of eliminated any hold she had over me."

"How convenient."

David lets out a mirthless laugh. "Go ahead. I deserve whatever nastiness you want to dish out. What I did was stupid and thoughtless. I never meant to hurt you, Mattie. You don't know how many times I've come to regret what I did."

"Did you kill Karen?"

"What do you think?"

I study him a moment, gathering my thoughts. "I think," I say finally, "that you're not the man I thought you were. I think that you have betrayed my trust. I think your supposed love for me, or for anyone else for that matter, isn't nearly as deep as your love for yourself."

I pause, seeing the misery my words have triggered in him and trying to take pleasure from the fact. But for some reason, all it does is make me feel worse.

"But no," I conclude somewhat anticlimactically. "I don't think you are a killer."

"Thank you for that, anyway." His smile is grim.

"I'm curious, David. What were you and Karen fighting about the night she was killed?"

"I confronted her about Sidney. I could tell something was bothering him; he just hasn't been himself lately. And because of the argument I overheard, I couldn't help but think that Karen had something to do with it. She tried to tell me that the argument was just her getting upset with Sid because she asked him for a loan and he refused her." He pauses, his expression growing sad. He turns away from me and looks out a window.

"But I didn't believe her. I've heard things about Karen over the past few weeks that are rather disturbing. Arthur Henley told me about a conversation he had with her where she kept mentioning Ruth and making suggestive comments that made it sound as if she might let something slip to Lauren."

"That wouldn't have gotten her very far," I tell him. "Lauren knows all about Ruth."

"She does?"

I nod. "She and Arthur have . . . well, I guess you could call it an understanding."

"Guess that explains why Arthur didn't seem too bothered by Karen's hints. Anyway, then I heard a similar story from Mick Dunn. Seems Karen made some suggestive comments to him, too, after he'd slept with her several times. She was threatening to let it slip to Marjorie."

I laugh. I can't help it. "Like Marjorie doesn't know about Mick." I shake my head. "Man, poor Karen. She kept picking all the wrong people to try to blackmail."

"Until Sid," David says. "Sid never did come right out and admit anything, but there were things he said that made me think Karen might be trying to blackmail him, too. I just couldn't figure out what she had over him. I didn't know then that Sidney was seeing Karen's brother, or that Sidney was gay. But when I confronted Karen and told her I wasn't going to allow her to get away with blackmailing Sid, she told me everything, not only that Sid was gay, a fact he was desperate to hide, but that he was HIV positive. She cried and pleaded with me, saying that Sid's money was the only way she could keep Mike on the drugs he needed, that he'd already developed an intolerance for one protease inhibitor and had to be switched to another one that was even more expensive."

He pauses, lost in memory for a moment. "I thought about

what she was saying and tried to see things from her point of view, to understand her situation. But I kept coming back to the fact that Sidney was HIV positive and operating on patients."

He leans forward, burying his face in his hands for a moment. When he straightens up and looks at me, I see the raw emotion, the exhaustion and misery of it all reflected in his eyes. He looks haggard and bereft, and I fight an urge to go to him, to hold and comfort him. When he continues, his voice is flat and impassive.

"While I don't condone Sid's lifestyle, I've always liked and respected him. His family is highly regarded here in Sorenson and I have a great deal of respect for Gina and her work, as well. I know that a scandal like this will be devastating to them. Not to mention what it will do to the hospital if word gets out. But while I'm not eager to expose Sid, I still feel morally obligated to do something.

"I told Karen I was going to talk to Sid and try to convince him that he should retire and move away somewhere. Try to start over. I suppose in a way what I was planning was a form of blackmail as well. For I'd pretty much decided that unless Sid left voluntarily, I was going to report him. I hoped that by doing that I might be able to control the fallout and minimize the damage somehow.

"But when I told Karen what I intended to do, she went berserk. Then she told me about her pregnancy. I suspected it might be a last-ditch effort on her part to get me to side with her, to have enough sympathy for her plight that I wouldn't expose her or Sid. But I wasn't convinced she really was pregnant. Or if she was, that it was mine."

He looks at me then, a pleading question in his eyes.

"I can't tell you, David. The DNA results haven't come back yet."

He sighs, his face rigid.

"Did you go to Karen's house that night? Hurley said he had a witness who saw you there."

"That's total bullshit. According to Lucien, this purported

eyewitness was just some anonymous woman who called from a pay phone at the Quik-E-Mart. Lucien thinks it was a crank looking to get a cheap thrill. I never went to Karen's house that night. In fact, I never saw her again after she left here. But I don't have an alibi for the period of time in question. Actually, I do have one, but I haven't been willing to share it yet."

"What do you mean?"

"After Karen left that night, I put in a page to Sidney, found out he was over at the hospital trying to catch up on his back charts, and went over there hoping to talk to him when he was finished. I got there just as he was coming out of the hospital and we spoke in the parking lot. I confronted him with what I knew and he didn't deny any of it."

He shakes his head. "You should have seen him when he talked about this Halverson guy. He kept saying he was truly in love for the first time in his life and that, faced with a considerably shortened lifespan, he no longer felt the need to hide who he was, to be so circumspect about his sex life.

"I told him that was all fine and good, but that I couldn't ethically allow him to continue to operate on patients if he was HIV positive."

"What was his reaction?"

"He was obviously upset. . . . Devastated might be a better word. I don't know. I think he was so caught up in the euphoria of his relationship with Halverson that he hadn't really thought through all the consequences. Then he got pissed at me. He got in his car and left, refusing to hear me out.

"I didn't know what to do at first. But I knew I couldn't let things go on the way they were. So I headed out to his house hoping to talk to him some more. Except when I got there, no one was home. I knew from Karen that Mike frequented the Grizzly Motel and I guessed that was the most likely place to find Sid. So I headed out there, and when I saw his car, I bluffed my way into finding out what room he was in. Then I laid down the law to him and Mike."

"And how did you leave it?"

"I told Sid I'd give him a week to make up his mind. Either he leaves voluntarily or I report him. And the week will be up the day after tomorrow. That's why I didn't tell that detective where I was the night Karen was killed. I knew Sid would just deny it all and then I'd only end up looking worse."

"If Sid doesn't withdraw from operating voluntarily, are you going to go ahead and report him?"

"Yes." His sigh carries the weight of the world with it. "But I have to tell you, Mattie, I don't like being in this position. Sid is not only a respected colleague of mine, he's a friend. I'm trying to do what's right, but for some reason it feels all wrong."

He buries his head in his hands and again I am struck by an urge to reach out to him, to pull him to my breast and comfort him. I still hate him for what he did, for his betrayal of me, of us. But I loved him deeply once and I suppose that on some level, I still do. It's not an emotion I can just turn on and off with a switch. And seeing how utterly dejected and tormented he is by all that has happened, I can't help but feel some empathy for him, a softening of my anger.

"What about Gina?" I ask him. "Do you think she knows any of this?"

"I have no idea."

Then I ask the question that hangs between us, the one neither of us wants to verbalize. "Do you think Sid killed Mike Halverson?"

"I don't know," David says. "God, I hope not." He gets up and walks over to a window—the same one I peered into on that fateful night—and stares out at the world, his expression troubled. "Why would he kill the guy if he loved him?"

I've already asked myself this same question. "Maybe Sid has some other problems. Maybe his touch with reality isn't too strong right now."

David says nothing.

"Or maybe he discovered that Mike wasn't as enamored of him as he was of Mike. Maybe Mike was only using him, the same way Karen tried to use everyone. Maybe Mike took over his sister's blackmailing scheme and Sid finally killed him in a brokenhearted rage."

David stays quiet, but the very lack of any denial from him tells me all I need to know.

"David, you know we can't keep this to ourselves. I like Sid, too, and I certainly don't want to think of him as a killer. But we can't pretend all of this hasn't happened."

"I told him I'd give him a week," David says.

"Look, it doesn't have to come from you. I can call Steve Hurley, tell him what we know, and let him handle it from here. Sid doesn't have to know that any of it came from you."

David turns from the window and looks at me, his face stricken. "You're going to just sic the police on him? Christ. Isn't there an easier way? Can't we give him a chance to turn himself in?"

"What if he doesn't? What if he runs, David?"

"He's not going to run, Mattie. Besides, he's on call this weekend."

Oh, yeah, like that will stop him. If nothing else convinces me how deeply disturbed David is by all this, the inanity of that comment does.

"Can't you just wait until tomorrow?" David pleads. "Sid won't go anywhere. I'm sure of it. And in the meantime, maybe I can figure out a way to talk him into turning himself in."

My mind churns, trying to think it all through. I nod absently, knowing it's what David wants. But the more I think about it, the more I want to talk to Sid for myself. Some part of my mind realizes that confronting a possible killer alone might not be the wisest thing to do. But another part of me, the part that worked side by side with Sid for nearly seven years sharing tension, laughter, and surgical instruments, refuses to believe the man will harm me.

"Okay, I won't talk to Hurley until tomorrow," I tell David, wincing a bit on the inside. After all, it isn't a lie exactly, it just isn't the whole truth.

Chapter 32

When I return to the cottage I'm relieved to see that Dom isn't back yet. He pulls in ten minutes later and I go out to help him unload the groceries. I need to waylay our planned visit to David but I don't want Dom to know I've already been there, so I tell him I want to wait to give myself more time to think things through. He seems relieved by my apparent capitulation and I feel a tiny twinge of guilt for deceiving him. I know he has my best interests at heart, but I also know that no matter how well-intentioned his motives are, his idea never would have worked.

Once the groceries are unpacked, he invites me to stay and watch a video he's rented, bribing me with promises of a lunch that includes Sara Lee cheesecake for dessert. The offer is tempting but the issue with Sid is far more pressing, so I thank him and decline, telling him I am going to spend the afternoon at my sister's—lie number two. I'm going to hell for sure.

Since the hospital is closer, I drive there first, cruising through the parking lot in search of Sid's car. I don't see it, but as I turn the corner from one row of cars to the next, I glimpse the top of a van several rows over—burgundy-and-gray. I hit the gas and go after it, but by the time I get to where it was, it has disappeared. Annoyed, I leave and head out to Sid's house, keeping one eye on the rearview mirror the entire time.

The Carrigan home is a stately but tasteful place that sits on a hill about five miles outside of town. It isn't overly large, but clearly shows the wealth of its owners. It has been in Sid's family for four generations, and as the sole heir to the family fortunes, Sid took it over when he married Gina. Sid's parents, tired of winter weather that made their arthritic bones throb and ache, moved to Arizona.

The house is over a hundred years old, and while improvements have been made on it over the years, it still retains much of its original charm and character. The front of it is done in stone, as is the circular drive and the retaining walls that grace the hills behind it. I know from prior visits that the lawn is plush, green, and amazingly soft but, at the moment, most of it is buried beneath a blanket of red and yellow leaves that have dropped from the many stately trees peppering the grounds.

Overall, the house has a mellow but dignified country look—peaceful and comfy—the exact opposite of how I feel. There is no peace, no comfort for me here today.

The garage door is closed so I have no way of knowing if Sid is home or not. I consider using my cell phone to call him first but quickly rule out that idea since I don't want to give him a chance to decline a visit or let him know I'm coming. I want to catch him unprepared, hoping that will make it easier for me to get the truth out of him.

The truth. It's what I want, but it scares me to death.

I park in front of the house, slip my cell phone into my jacket pocket, and walk up to ring the doorbell. I half expect one of the house staff to answer; whenever I've been here for parties and such, that is what usually happens. But to my surprise, Sid himself answers the door.

"Mattie! What a pleasant surprise." His smile is warm and genuine, but he looks tired and sad despite it. "Come on in."

He seems relaxed. If my unexpected arrival has disconcerted him in any way, it doesn't show. At first I think this is a good sign. I mean if Sid is guilty of murder, he would look more nervous and edgy, wouldn't he? But then it occurs to me that he might be a sociopath, a serial killer like Ted Bundy—an emotionless creature with no sense of remorse or guilt, a social charlatan who hides his true nature beneath a veneer of well-practiced charm. After all, Wisconsin has served as home to more than its fair share of serial killers, with Jeffrey Dahmer, Ed Gein, and John Wayne Gacy all conducting business within or just outside its borders. Maybe there's something in our water.

All this flashes through my mind in the time it takes me to smile back at Sid and accept his invitation to come inside.

"What brings you out here?" he asks as he closes the door behind me.

Too late to turn back now. I'm trapped. It makes me glad I have the cell phone tucked inside my pocket. Sid gestures toward the living room, indicating I should go in and have a seat, but I stand where I am in the foyer.

"I want to talk with you, Sid. It's about Mike Halverson."

His expression falters, but only briefly. A split second later, that complacent smile is back in place. Then I hear a female voice that makes my heart race with panic.

"Mattie? Is that you?"

Gina. I completely forgot about her. How could I be so stupid? On the drive out here, I tried to imagine how this visit might go, playing out several different scenarios in my mind. None of them included Gina.

I turn and see her standing down the hall in the doorway to the kitchen. As usual, she looks perfectly put together, right down to the apron she is wearing over her tailored, camel-colored slacks and yellow angora sweater.

"Hello, Gina."

"Hi there. I didn't know you were dropping by. Forgive

me," she says, gesturing with a wooden spoon she has in her hand. "I have something simmering on the stove and can't leave it for long. But I'll be done in a few minutes."

"That's quite all right. Take your time. I'm sorry to drop by unannounced like this but something came up and I need to talk to Sid for a few minutes. I won't be staying long."

"Okay then," she says, flashing me her TV smile. "I'll just finish up out here while you two talk. Holler at me if you need anything." She disappears back into the kitchen and I look at Sid.

"Why don't we step into my den," he suggests. I notice his smile is gone, replaced by a furrowed brow of concern.

Sid's den is my favorite room in the house. It fits him perfectly, possessing many of the same characteristics that drew me to Sid himself. It has a relaxed and unpretentious air, a sense of warm welcome that makes one want to settle in and never leave.

Whenever I came out to the house for parties or dinners, I would always find an excuse to slip into the den and spend a few peaceful moments on the old leather couch or its matching leather chair, their surfaces so perfectly aged and worn, they are as smooth and soft as a baby's bottom. A beautiful Persian rug in shades of cranberry, teal, and ochre covers much of the hardwood floor and it, like the furniture, looks lovingly worn. The walls are paneled and Sid's desk, which sits catty-corner beside a window, is an old, sturdy oak piece that probably weighs a ton.

Today, however, the room fails to comfort me, even as I sink down into the cushiony softness of the couch. I watch Sid close the door, and the minute he turns toward me and I see the sad, resigned expression on his face, I know everything David told me is true.

"I take it you've spoken to David," he says, wasting no time.

"Yes."

"And do you hate me as a result?"

"Hate you?" I ponder the question. "No, Sid. I don't hate you," I say honestly. "But I think it's time you were straight with me." It is a notably poor choice of words, but since Sid doesn't seem to catch the pun, I quickly push ahead. "Right now I have good reason to think that you are involved somehow in the murders of two people—Karen Owenby and Mike Halverson."

Sid opens his mouth to say something but then he freezes without uttering a sound. He stares at me for several moments, looking first confused, then stricken. "Murder?" he says finally, swallowing hard. "Mike was murdered?"

I nod.

"But I heard it was deemed a suicide." He looks frighteningly pale and I start to entertain a new scenario, one in which he drops dead of a heart attack.

"Someone tried to make it look that way," I tell him. "But they didn't do a good enough job. There's no doubt he was murdered."

He staggers and grabs at a bookshelf to steady himself. This is no act—that he is surprised by my revelation is obvious. But what I'm not sure of is the reason for his surprise. Did he truly not know that Mike was murdered? Or is he simply shocked to learn that someone figured out the truth?

Slowly he makes his way to the chair and collapses into it. He leans forward and buries his face in his hands. He stays that way for several moments, and when he finally straightens up and looks at me, his expression is horribly sad.

"I never thought I could be as happy as I was with Mike," he says. "I wasn't even looking for a relationship. I was trying to put that whole lifestyle behind me. But then Karen Owenby approached me a year or so ago about this medical equipment company she said she'd invested in. I got curious and went by the place to check it out and that's when I met Mike."

"Sid, I—"

"We kept it very hush-hush at first, of course," Sid goes on, ignoring me as he loses himself in his memories. He has this beatific little smile on his face that is both touching and pathetic. "We never met here in town at all. We only went to the Grizzly or to other towns where no one knew either of us. When I found out that Karen was actually Mike's sister, I knew then that our secret wouldn't last forever. But by the time she found out about us, I'd already decided I didn't care anymore. I was tired of living a lie."

"Did Mike tell you he was HIV positive?"

Sid nods. "He was very honest with me, and I with him. In my younger years I wasn't always as careful as I should have been. And then a little over a year ago I started noticing some changes in my health: weight loss, muscle wasting, weakness, frequent colds . . . all the signs were there. I told Mike when I met him that I suspected I was not only HIV positive but might have AIDS." He pauses a moment and tears well in his eyes.

"Have you been tested?"

He shakes his head. "I know I should have been but I didn't want to give up operating yet. I've always been very, very careful. I double glove and I've never had any nicks or punctures during a procedure so I'm certain I haven't exposed any patients."

"But you didn't tell them, either, did you? The patients you worked on have a right to know, Sid."

"I didn't tell them because I wasn't sure there was anything to tell. That's why I didn't want to get tested, plausible deniability in case everything came out somewhere down the road. Maybe it was wrong but I thought I could. . . ." His voice breaks and it takes him a moment to collect himself.

"Anyway," he continues after clearing his throat, "once David confronted us at the Grizzly, I told Mike we might have to move, to start over somewhere else. But Mike knew how much I loved my work and didn't believe me when I told him I could walk away from it. He broke it off, said he never wanted to see me again."

He buries his face in his hands. "Oh, God," he mumbles.

"I didn't mean for it to turn out this way, Mattie. I loved Mike. I didn't want to hurt him. I didn't want to hurt anyone."

Oh my God. He did *do it.* I want to cry. "Sid—"

He turns his back to me. "Please, Mattie. I need some time alone. I need to think."

I don't know what to say, so I say nothing. A surge of compassion makes me get up and walk over to him. "I'm sorry, Sid," I whisper, settling my hand on his shoulder. My apology is an all-encompassing one that covers the way I feel about what he has done as well as what I will now have to do.

"So am I," he says. "God, so am I." He looks up at me, his expression pleading, his eyes bright with the sheen of tears. "Tell me you believe me, Mattie. Tell me you believe that I never meant to hurt anyone."

"I believe you, Sid," I say through a sheen of my own tears. My heart feels as if it is being minced into tiny pieces.

"I never thought it would come to this," Sid whispers. Then he holds his hand up as if he is warding off an evil spirit and turns away from me. "Please leave, Mattie. Go. I need to be alone. Please just go."

I don't see as how I have any choice, but I can't just leave. I realize, too late, that coming here alone was a mistake. I should have called Hurley and let him handle it. Feeling helpless, I look around the room, unsure of what to do next. Will Sid try to run? Have I blown the whole case because of my own stupid naïveté and some misguided notion about my friendship with Sid—a man I thought I'd known but who has proven to be as unpredictable and secretive as David? Maybe more so?

Then I remember my cell phone. I can step out of the house and call Hurley from my car, then drive out to the end of Sid's drive and wait there until Hurley arrives. That way, if Sid tries to run, he won't get far. Concern for my own safety never enters my mind. Despite what Sid has done, I can't make myself believe he would ever hurt me.

I step out into the hallway, quietly closing the door to the den. The aromas of garlic and basil waft toward me and I remember that Gina is in the kitchen. I briefly debate going to her to talk about all that has happened but I'm not sure how much she knows, and if she is unaware of Sid's alternate lifestyle, I sure as hell don't want to be the one to tell her. Watching Sid start to self-destruct has been torture enough for one day. I can only imagine how Gina is going to react. And given her popularity, I know that if the media gets wind of the story, they'll have a heyday. Gina and Sid will both be publicly crucified.

I hear Gina moving about in the kitchen and duck toward the front door, suddenly afraid of having to face her. I ease the door open, step through, and am about to ease it closed again when I hear a loud *bang* from within the house. I pause and look back down the hallway, my hand on the doorknob, my mind already screaming in denial.

Gina appears at the other end of the hall, sees me, and cocks her head to one side, her face wearing a puzzled expression. I watch as her eyes flit toward the door to Sid's den, then back to me. It seems like an eternity that we stand there just staring at one another, yet I know it is mere seconds, a meager breath of time wherein we both cling desperately to our doubts and denial, feeble as they are. For I know what that sound was. I don't want to know, but I do.

And judging from the look on Gina's face, she knows, too. As she stares at me, I think I see something else there as well: accusation and blame. Much as I would like to shrug it off, I can't. She is right. I try to offer her an apology with my eyes but all I can feel coming through is the terrible weight of my guilt.

Gina shifts her gaze back to the den door and slowly walks toward it. She looks like a zombie operating off of some ancient instinct that is pulling her toward a fate she neither wants nor understands. I don't want it either; I don't want her to go there, to look in the den and make it all real. For a brief moment I seriously consider running down the hall and tackling her to the floor. Anything to stop her. But she keeps on going and I keep on watching. As she opens the door and looks inside, I hold my breath.

She rushes into the room and my hope surges. When nothing happens for several seconds, I slowly start moving back toward the den, still clinging to my denial even as an all-too-familiar scent reaches my nostrils. I hear a faint *thump* and something about it makes my nurse's training kick in. Shaking off my daze, I hurry the last few steps toward the room, thinking, hoping, it might not be too late.

Chapter 33

It is definitely too late. Sid's body sits on that lovely butter-soft couch, his head hanging forward, a growing pool of blood gathering in his lap. The back of the couch and part of the wall behind it is painted in red gore. Sid's right hand lays open, palm up. Beside it is a revolver.

Gina is sitting in the chair where Sid was moments before, staring at her husband, her face curiously blank. I move closer to Sid and see that while the wound in his head isn't nearly as severe as Mike Halverson's was, his situation is no less grave. I can see bits of gray matter clinging to both his skull and the wall behind him.

I stare at Sid's chest and see he isn't breathing. I don't bother to check for a pulse because I know that surviving a head wound such as this is nigh onto impossible.

I turn back to Gina and find her staring at me, her eyes searching mine with begging appeal. I shake my head and feel my heart clench as the light of hope in her eyes extinguishes itself.

"I'm sorry, Gina. So sorry."

She says nothing, does nothing. Her lifeless expression frightens me.

"We need to call the police," I say gently.

She nods then, mechanically.

I look over at the phone on Sid's desk and start to reach for it. But then I remember what I've learned about crime scene preservation and how I managed to mess up the two I've been to so far.

"Come on, Gina," I say, urging her gently. "Let's wait somewhere else."

I take her elbow and she rises from her chair like a robot. As she shuffles forward, one foot catches itself along the edge of the rug and she nearly falls. I hold her arm tight as she disentangles her foot and lets the rug fall back down against the chair legs. Then I steer her gently out into the hall and we enter the living room, where she sinks into a chair.

I move back out into the hallway, pull my cell phone out of my jacket pocket, flip it open, and punch in 9-1-1. Gina does nothing. She just sits there, not crying, not moving, staring empty-eyed off into space. I fear she is in shock and worry that she might try to do something desperate herself.

My anxiety isn't relieved any when my call goes through and I recognize the voice on the other end. It is Jeannie, the same woman who answered when I called about Mike Halverson.

"9-1-1 operator. Do you have an emergency?"

"Jeannie?"

"Yes, this is Jeannie. Do you have an emergency?"

"Kind of," I say, realizing that this sort of call is getting uncomfortably close to becoming a habit. I move away from Gina and lower my voice. "I have a death here. A suicide. He shot himself in the head."

There is the briefest of pauses, then, "Mattie? Is that you?"

"It is."

"And you really have another dead man?"

"I'm afraid so."

"Do you know who this one is?"

"Yes, it's Sidney Carrigan. Dr. Sidney Carrigan."

I hear Jeannie gasp, which isn't surprising. Pretty much

everyone in the county knows the Carrigans. But she recovers quickly. "Give me the address."

I do so.

"Okay, I'm dispatching police and rescue now. They should be there in five minutes or less."

"Thank you."

"Are you okay, Mattie?"

"I'm pretty shook up, but I'll be fine."

"Okay. We'll keep talking until someone arrives."

"Okay. Thank you." I am impressed. Jeannie is getting better at this pretty fast.

"Um, how dead is this one?" she asks me.

"Very."

"No point in making any rescue attempts?"

"Nope."

"For my records, can you describe the extent of the wounds?"

I do so, trying to be as sterile as I can when describing the grimmer parts, keeping a wary eye on Gina the whole time. She still hasn't moved.

"Is anyone else there?" Jeannie asks.

"Yes, Sid's wife, Gina."

"Is she okay?"

"As okay as you might expect, I guess. She may be a bit shocky." Off in the distance, I hear a siren.

"Officer Childs should be pulling up any second now, Mattie," Jeannie says.

Ah, Brian again. That is good, I suppose. "Thanks, Jeannie. You did really good this time."

"Thank you. I've been practicing."

Out the front door, which is still open, I see a squad car pull up. "Brian just arrived," I inform Jeannie. "So I'll let you go."

"Okay. Take care of yourself, you hear?"

"I will, Jeannie. You, too."

I meet Brian at the front door so Gina won't be able to hear me and quickly fill him in on the highlights: Sid's affair with Mike Halverson, their HIV status, David's ultimatum to Sidney, and then finally, my visit, ending with the sound of the gunshot. I also let him know that I am unsure how much of this Gina knows. Brian asks me to wait and heads inside. After a quick look around the den, he steps across the hall to the living room and focuses on Gina.

A rescue squad pulls up and after assuring the techs that I am okay, I direct them inside. Then I collapse on the front stoop, wanting to cry, but too tired and drained to summon up any tears. Instead, I just sit there listening to the wind and welcoming the fading warmth of the sun on my face. Moments later another squad car arrives and right behind it comes Hurley.

He parks and stares at me through his window for a moment. Then he shakes his head and gets out. "Are you all right?" he asks, stopping in front of me.

I nod without looking up at him.

"Okay. Wait here. I'll be right back." He disappears into the house and I hear the low murmur of voices. A few minutes later, Hurley comes back outside and settles down beside me on the porch.

"What a damned mess," he mumbles. "Can you tell me what the hell is going on here, because Gina doesn't seem to have a clue. She said you dropped by unannounced and she's been in the kitchen cooking. Next thing she knows, her husband is lying dead from a self-inflicted gunshot wound to the head."

"It's my fault," I mumble. "I should have known he'd do something stupid like that."

Hurley reaches over and cups my chin in his hand, turning my face to look at him. His eyes probe mine for a few seconds, then he brushes my hair back from my face with a touch so gentle, so sweetly tender, that it finally breaks the dam. The tears come and they keep on coming. And coming.

And coming. I try to talk, but can't. Hurley gets up and disappears into the house again, then returns and hands me a wad of tissues. This final act of kindness only makes me cry harder. Finally, he puts an arm over my shoulders and pulls me to him.

There, cuddled against the solid warmth of his chest with his arms holding me tight and protected, I cry out all my guilt and grief.

It is several hours before the investigation at the Carrigan residence is finished and Sidney's body is removed. One of the backup pathologists covering for Izzy comes out to process the scene, and the body is taken to our morgue, where tomorrow, Izzy will do an autopsy. I'll get Arnie to help him because I don't think I can bring myself to participate in an autopsy on Sid.

I am surprised we are even going to bother with an autopsy, since both the cause and the circumstances of death are pretty obvious. But then Hurley reminds me that suicide is a crime and as such is a coroner's case. I nod automatically, but then spend several minutes trying to figure out why suicide is a crime. Who can you possibly prosecute?

I eventually tell Hurley everything I know, filling in those details he is missing, like my trip to the Grizzly. I conclude by relaying the conversation I had with David and my decision to come out and see Sid. Then I recall, as closely as I can, Sid's comments before he killed himself. I can tell Hurley is pissed at me, but he holds his tongue and keeps his thoughts to himself. Probably because he can see how much my guilt is eating away at me.

He spends about ten minutes gently questioning Gina about Sid. I listen as she tells him that she has no idea why he would want to kill himself and that she still can't believe he's actually done it. I imagine that once she learns the truth, she'll be devastated.

When Hurley asks her about the gun Sid used, Gina tells him that Sid always kept a pistol in his lower right desk drawer—according to Sid it was for protection. I start to interrupt at that point because I am certain that Gina is confused. I recall a night several months back when David and I attended a soirée here and ended up in Sid's den with Sid and two other doctors. Sid collapsed on the couch, half-drunk, laughing, and obviously enjoying himself. He played the dutiful host by asking us if we wanted to sample the thirty-year-old scotch he had in his desk drawer.

I passed on the offer, since the taste of scotch is about as appealing to me as the idea of drinking antifreeze. But the others accepted and Sid asked me to fetch the bottle for him from the drawer . . . his bottom right desk drawer, though he was initially confused and said left. When I pulled open the left drawer, all it had in it were dozens of hanging files. I finally found the scotch in the right drawer and I'm certain there wasn't any gun in there. But then I realize that it doesn't matter much where the gun was. The simple fact that Sid had it is enough.

When Hurley finishes questioning Gina, he offers to have one of the officers drive her somewhere. She protests at first, saying she wants to stay in her own home. But when Hurley explains to her that the house will need to be closed up until it is cleared as a crime scene, she gives in and decides to stay with a friend for a few days, until she can figure out what to do.

The press has already sniffed out the story, most likely by picking up the dispatch on a police scanner, and an officer posted at the entrance to the Carrigan driveway has been working steadily to keep the reporters at bay. Of course, that doesn't stop Alison Miller, who takes off on foot and hikes up to the house through the neighboring woods.

"Yoo-hoo! Stevie!" she hollers as she approaches the front of the house. Hurley and I are sitting side by side on the front stoop and Alison stops in front of us, sparing a spiteful glance at me before she turns her smile back on for Hurley. "This is just awful," she says. "Is it true that Sid Carrigan is dead? That he shot himself?"

Hurley stands and takes Alison's arm, dragging her off to one side. I look away, trying to act indifferent though I keep sneaking peeks at them from the corner of my eye as I struggle to overhear what they are saying.

"Look, Alison. This is a delicate situation just now," Hurley tells her. "I'm still processing the scene and trying to figure out exactly what happened. If you'll be patient and let me finish here, I promise you I'll give you the whole story."

"When?" Alison asks. "The Monday edition gets put to bed at eleven tonight and this should really be in there. This is hot news."

"I'll try to get it to you tonight, Alison. But no promises. Give me a couple of hours, okay?"

"Okay," she says, flashing him a coquettish smile. "Thanks, Stevie." She stands on tiptoe and plants a kiss on his cheek. Then, after shooting a smug glance at me, she struts down the driveway.

Hurley walks over to me while I do my best impression of someone who hasn't seen or heard a thing. I keep my eyes diverted, afraid to look at him. "When was the last time you ate anything?" he asks.

"I'm not sure. Breakfast I think. But I'm not hungry." An historic moment.

"You should eat something anyway."

"Maybe later." I am pouting and determined to disagree with whatever he says, angry over the cutesy little exchange I observed between him and Alison.

"Okay," he says with a sigh. "Come on. I'll drive you home."

"Thanks, but I can drive myself. Besides, I don't want to leave my car here."

"I can have one of the uniforms drive it for you."

"That won't be necessary. I'm fine. Really."

"Then I'm going to follow you home."

Obviously he doesn't realize that I've already made the burgundy-and-gray van and know he's been having me tailed for the past several days. Still, when I think about him following me home tonight, I find I kind of like the idea. "Okay," I say, giving him a tired smile.

The sight of Hurley's headlights in my rearview mirror makes me feel warm and tingly all over. I imagine what might happen when we get to the cottage. I'll invite him inside, of course. Good manners dictate as much. After that, who knows what might happen. And if he wants to call and talk to Alison Miller, I'll find a way to let her know where he is. In fact, maybe I'll encourage him to call her from my place so I can hear every word he says.

But my fantasy blows to pieces as I pull into my driveway and watch Hurley drive on by, honking once as he passes. He's probably on his way to meet Alison, I think, and the idea crushes me.

Once inside, I decide a nice, hot, soothing bath sounds wonderful, so I strip out of my clothes and put on my robe. The pile of dirty clothes in the corner of the bedroom is getting pretty high, so I throw a load into the washer. Then, rationalizing that I need something cold to balance out the heat from the bath, I dig a new carton of Cherry Garcia out of the freezer and settle in on the couch with it and a spoon.

Inevitably my mind wanders back to the afternoon's events and the image of Sid sitting in that chair, his head in his hands, his posture slumped and defeated. That image is in stark contrast to the man I knew, the man whose vivacious humor and gentle manner have charmed me for years.

Then I flash on the empty, dull-eyed expression I saw on Gina's face as she sat in the same chair and, oddly, this disturbs me even more. Something about the way she was sitting there seems wrong. I can't put a finger on anything specific, but it keeps nagging at me.

I try to shake it off by focusing on Rubbish instead, who is playing with a mangled tampon he most likely fished out of the bathroom garbage. I laugh as he bats the tampon across the rug and hunkers down, his pupils huge and dark, his little ass wiggling. Then he springs in for the kill, grabbing the tampon between his feet and rolling with it. He tosses it away, hunkers down again, and repeats the attack. At one point he manages to push the tampon under the corner of the rug, where he then spends several minutes trying to get at it from above. Finally he gets wise and burrows his way under, creating a tiny, wriggling hump in the rug.

And that's when it hits me. It's not the way Gina was sitting in the chair that bothers me, it's what happened when she got out of it.

I have to go back to the house. I run into the bedroom to dress, only to realize all of my bras are in the washing machine. After digging around in the few clean clothes I have left, I choose the loosest-fitting top I can find, not wanting to advertise the fact that I am braless. Minutes later, I am headed out of town, stopping briefly at the Quik-E-Mart to buy a disposable camera.

The Carrigan house is dark when I pull up out front but there is a police car parked in the drive. Sitting inside it is Brian Childs. The front door to the house is sealed shut with crime scene tape. Brian gets out and walks over to me as I climb out of my car.

"What are you doing back here?" he asks.

I show him my camera. "I need to get some shots of the den," I tell him. "For Izzy."

"We already took a bunch," he says. "Can't you use those?"

"I suppose we can, but Izzy likes to have his own. And this way, we don't have to wait for you guys to make copies," I explain. I hold my breath, hoping Brian will go for it.

"Okay," he says with a shrug, and I breathe a sigh of relief. I follow him onto the porch, where he slices through the tape and peels it away. "I'll replace this when you're done," he says. "And I'll have to record that you were here," he adds. "Scene preservation, you know."

"No problem," I tell him. If my suspicions are right, by the time anyone else learns I was here, it will be a moot point. As soon as he has the door unlocked, I scurry down the hall and enter the den. I grimace at the lingering scent of dried blood that hangs in the air, and when I flip on the light switch, I see that the room doesn't look any different than the last time I saw it.

I turn back to Brian, who has followed me. "I need to close the door so I can take a shot of this end of the room," I tell him, and as I hoped, he backs up. "It'll only take me a minute," I promise, closing the door before he has a chance to come inside.

Immediately, I move over to the chair, standing in front of it and digging into my memory. Just as I thought, the edge of the Persian rug is up against the front legs of the chair. But I'm certain that when Sid was sitting there, the chair had been angled toward the desk, the two back feet resting on the hardwood floor, the two front ones resting on top of the rug. I remember how Gina nearly fell when I helped her up because her foot became entangled in the rug's edge. And I remember how the curled-edge fell back down, stopping in the position it's in now.

Obviously, the chair had been moved between the time I saw Sid in it and the time I saw Gina in it. I recall the noise I heard not long after Gina entered the room, the faint *thump* sound that spurred me to action. I suppose the noise could have come from Gina collapsing into the chair, but that would have moved the chair backward, away from the rug. How had it ended up closer?

I reach down and pull back the edge of the carpet, peeking underneath. There, about a foot and a half from the edge, is a small defect in the hardwood, a metal ring set into a hollow in the floor. I kneel down and study the ring more closely, realizing it's a handle. When I grab it and pull, a six-board section of the floor opens up, revealing a large, velvet-lined space beneath. Molded into the velvet are three imprints, each one bearing the recognizable shape of a gun. Next to the empty imprints is the real thing: a cold, deadly-looking pistol.

A loud noise out in the hallway startles me and I jump, letting the section of floor fall back into place. I hear the door to the den open and start to turn, but I'm not quick enough. From the periphery of my vision I see something coming toward me just before I feel a crashing pain on my head. For an instant I see a flash of bright, blinding light, but after that, there is nothing but darkness.

Chapter 34

I can't remember ever feeling so cold. My teeth are rattling and every muscle in my body is trembling as I try to shiver my way to warmth. I am curled into a fetal position and I try to tighten it, to pull all my parts closer together so they can warm one another. But the movement sends shock waves of pain from my head down my neck and back, making me moan.

"Ah, good. You're awake."

Slowly, carefully, I open my eyes, wincing as the room's light pierces its way through to my brain. Fuzzy shapes come into view, familiar shapes. Sid's den. I place one hand on the floor and, bracing myself against the pain, I push myself into a sitting position. Gina is standing in front of me, a gun in one hand. It doesn't take me long to figure out where she found it or what she intends to do with it.

Seeing the direction of my gaze, Gina holds the pistol up for a moment, eyeing it appreciatively. "Is this what you were looking for?" she asks.

"Apparently," I mumble.

"Too smart for your own good, aren't you?" she sneers. "I knew you would figure it out sooner or later. That's why I came back here to watch the house. I thought you might show up."

"Brian . . ." I mutter, my head pounding in pain.

"Oh, he's out there in the hallway," she says. "But if you think he's going to help you, you're sadly mistaken. I've taken care of him."

I take a moment to mourn Brian and to allow my head to clear. "It was you," I say, all the pieces finally clicking into place. "You killed Karen and Mike."

"I had to. That Owenby bitch just refused to listen to me. Kept insisting she was going to milk Sid and me for every penny she could get. So I had no choice. I shot her."

The cold indifference in her voice makes me shiver even harder.

"The next morning," she continues, "when Sid told me how he'd run into David the night before, I realized what a perfect setup it was. I figured David was probably somewhere between here and that sleazy motel around the time of Karen's death, so he wouldn't have any alibi. And I knew all about him and Karen—hell, half the town knew. They were together all the time at the hospital until David broke things off with her. Then she started getting desperate and stupid, chasing after him, making threats, picking fights. Several people at the hospital witnessed it. It made him the perfect fall guy. All it took was one anonymous witness to get the cops sniffing at his door."

"It was you who made that call."

Gina smiles broadly.

"Pretty coldhearted."

"Hey, a girl's gotta do what a girl's gotta do."

"But why? Why did you have to kill Karen?"

"Because she was blackmailing Sid, and he, the dumb sonofabitch, was paying her. She discovered him one night at the hospital in an on-call room with Mike. I don't think she knew about Sid's little secret before then. No one did. Even I didn't. I didn't find out until Karen came to me, hoping to wring even more money out of us with her little blackmail scheme."

I realize then that Sid must have figured it all out. He may have only guessed at the truth with regard to Karen's murder, but this afternoon, when I told him Mike's death was a murder and not a suicide, he had to have made the final connection. It wasn't guilt over his own actions that drove him to desperation, it was his grief over Mike and the knowledge of what his wife had done.

"So you killed Mike thinking that would put an end to it?" I say.

"Well, it did, didn't it?" She smirks. "I realized that if I used the same gun on Mike that I used on Karen and tried to make it look like a suicide, everyone would think Mike was the one who killed her. The gun, which came from our stash here"—she gestures toward the floor—"can't be traced back to me. I've had it for years, something my mother picked up from a street junkie.

"So it seemed like the perfect setup. And if someone managed to figure out that Mike's death wasn't a suicide, the finger of guilt would still be pointing at David for Karen's death, and the cops would likely try to pin Mike's death on him, as well. Just to be sure, I got a couple of hairs from the brush David keeps in his locker at the hospital and left them on Mike's body. I have you to thank for that idea," she says with a wry smile. "All that talk about trace evidence the other day at lunch."

"I was there," I say, horror dawning in my mind. "I was there in the front of the store when you killed Mike."

"That was you?" Gina laughs. "If I'd known that, I could have killed you then and saved myself a whole lot of trouble. I thought it was just some customer. I told Mike to get rid of whoever it was or I'd kill everyone in the store. He didn't know that I intended to kill him anyway and just wanted to be sure there weren't any witnesses."

"I suppose you would have killed Sid, too, if he hadn't gone ahead and done it for you."

"Kill Sid? Are you crazy?"

Somehow I don't think the irony of that question will register with her.

"Keeping Sid alive has been my whole purpose, you stupid bitch. Sid is . . . was my meal ticket. That's why I had to kill Mike. Sid was in too deep. He was getting ready to throw it all away over some misguided notion that he was in love with that diseased little freak."

"Did you know that Sid was likely HIV positive, also?"

She shrugs. "It doesn't matter. We've never slept together. Our marriage was purely for show. Sid needed someone to make him look legit and I wanted the money and the prestige. His parents were the ones who arranged it all. They basically delivered an ultimatum to Sid: either keep your dirty little secret in the closet or lose the family millions. Though to be honest, I don't think the money mattered all that much to Sid, the fool. It was the thought of losing his job that convinced him to go along. He loved being a surgeon; it meant everything to him."

"He loved Mike Halverson, too."

"That wasn't love," Gina spat out angrily. "It was just some stupid middle-aged crisis. He would have gotten over it eventually. If that Owenby bitch hadn't messed things up, everything would have been fine. Then you had to go poking your nose around."

"You can't seriously believe you'll get away with this, Gina. As it stands now, the cops think Sid killed both Karen and Mike. If you kill me, the cops will know Sid was innocent."

"It doesn't matter if the cops know it was me," she says, making my blood run cold. "I won't be around anyway. There's no point in staying. Everything I had, everything I worked for, it's gone. All of it."

"It doesn't have to be," I say, thinking fast. "Surely you'll inherit some money with Sid's death. I mean, legally you were his wife, right?"

"Is that what you think this is all about? Money?"

"It's not?" My head feels like it's about to explode, and the room keeps spinning. I feel myself growing more impatient and irritable with each passing minute.

"Of course not!" Gina fairly yells, making me wince. "The money was nothing more than a means to an end. Don't you understand? People here looked up to me. They respected me. They admired me. I was Gina fucking *Carrigan.* I was a someone. My face was on TV and in the papers; my voice was on the radio. I was invited to all the major social events and rubbed elbows with some of the richest, most famous people in this country. Did you know I was being considered for a part in a Spielberg movie?"

"Really? Spielberg is putting insane, coldhearted killers in his movies now?"

She flashes me a sardonic grin. "Very funny," she says. "You're a real smart-assed little bitch, aren't you?"

At least she called me a little bitch instead of a big one.

"Go ahead and act smug," she taunts. "They can carve that into your headstone. 'Here lies Mattie, smug and catty.' "

She cackles at that and I sense that what little self-control she has left is fading fast. My legs feel a little stronger but my head keeps swimming dangerously and I have serious doubts about my ability to stand. Yet I know that if I don't do something soon, she'll simply shoot me where I sit.

"You just don't understand what it was like for me before I met Sid," she explains. "My father died when I was a baby and my mother was a drug addict. I was living on the streets by the time I was sixteen, surviving as best I could on my wits and my looks."

She starts pacing and I take advantage of her inattention to shift my position and get my legs beneath me. I lean forward, putting my weight on my arms. She pauses then and stares at me, a frown on her face. "What are you doing?" she asks, her voice shrill.

"I feel sick. I think I'm going to throw up." I make a couple of retching sounds and act like I am about to heave.

"Oh, for Christ's sake!"

I retch again, shifting forward just enough to rise onto the balls of my feet. I am positioned for launch and hope that, with one good push, I can reach her. Maybe I can knock her down. And maybe, if luck and God are with me, I can avoid getting shot in the process.

"I've wasted far too much time on you already," she says.

The tone of finality in her voice tells me it is now or never. I retch once more, transforming it into a primal scream. Summoning up all the strength I can, I push off and lunge at her. As soon as Gina sees me coming at her, she raises the gun and pulls the trigger, but my foot snags in the edge of the folded rug and I fall flat on my face inches from her feet, probably saving my life. Had I continued my headlong run toward her, the bullet most likely would have slammed into my head. Instead, it sails by harmlessly above me and hits Sid's desk instead.

In desperation, I reach forward and wrap my arms around Gina's feet, pulling as hard as I can. She falls backward with a loud *whoomph* and I hear the gun clatter as it skitters across the floor and hits the wall. I quickly climb up her body and put all my weight on her legs, pinning her to the floor.

Shrieking like some crazed harridan, she reaches down and grabs handfuls of my hair, yanking as hard as she can. I yelp and try to pry her hands loose as her feet squirm beneath me, trying to wriggle free. Unable to loosen her grip on my hair, I reach up and grope around until I feel some skin. Then I pinch it up and twist as hard as I can.

Gina screeches and lets go of my hair. I roll to one side, closer to the gun, but that gives Gina enough leverage to squirm loose. The gun is mere inches away when she grabs my shirt and yanks as hard as she can, trying to pull me back. I feel my collar tighten around my neck, her pull so strong it bends me backward off the floor. Then the pressure eases suddenly with a loud ripping sound. A second later, I realize I am bare-chested.

The site of my bare bosom stuns me for a moment, allowing Gina to reach for the gun. But before she can pick it up, I lunge forward again, crashing into her arm and throwing all my weight on top of it.

"Get off me, damn you," Gina mutters, writhing beneath me. There is a tremendous crash behind us and I feel Gina grow still, then stiffen. "What the hell is *that?*" she screeches.

I roll slightly to the side and glance up. There, standing in the doorway, is a huge monolith of flesh encased in red spandex, replete with boots, gloves, and a long red cape. On the chest is a huge yellow letter *H.* The face of this mind-boggling apparition is partially hidden behind a red, Lone Ranger-type mask, but I know who it is.

"Joey, help me!" I shout. But he just stands there, his gaze transfixed on my bare chest.

"Damn it, Joey. She's got a gun!"

Joey shakes off his reverie and springs to action, leaping toward us and falling on top of me, squishing all the air from my lungs. I hear a *snap* from somewhere beneath me and Gina screams out, "My arm! You broke my fucking arm, you bitch!"

I want to tell Joey to move, but I can't suck in enough breath with his weight on top of me. So I reach up and hit him on his shoulder instead, hoping I can communicate my need to him some other way.

"What the hell is this?" says a different voice.

Hurley? I can't believe what I'm hearing. I crane my head around to peer over Joey's shoulder and sure enough, Hurley is standing in the doorway.

Joey finally rolls off of me, reaches over, and picks up the gun.

"Hey!" Hurley yells, pulling his own weapon and aiming it right at Joey. "Drop it!"

"It's okay, Hurley," I say quickly, grateful I can finally breathe. "He's one of the good guys. This one's the one you want," I tell him, gesturing toward Gina. Gina moans and I roll off of her, sitting up and exposing my naked torso to the world. "She's the one who killed Karen and Mike. It wasn't Sid, it was Gina."

Joey carefully sets the gun he is holding on the desk. Then he gawks at my chest again, his eyes huge.

Hurley sheathes his own gun, then unbuttons his shirt and takes it off, tossing it to me on the floor. "For heaven's sake," he mutters. "Cover yourself up."

Just as I pick up the shirt, Alison Miller appears in the doorway, her ubiquitous camera hanging from her neck. She looks at Hurley and his bare chest, then at me and mine. For a fleeting second, she allows herself to pout. Then the reporter in her takes over and in one swift motion, she raises the camera, aims it at me, and snaps a picture. "Does this have something to do with this nipple incident thing I heard about?" she asks, snapping a second shot. She moves deeper into the room and aims once more. "Ooh," she says as the camera clicks. "I wonder if the paper will print these."

Chapter 35

It's seven o'clock on Friday evening and Izzy, Dom, and I are sitting in the Peking House looking over our menus. Actually *I* am looking over my menu, since Izzy and Dom knew what they were going to order before we ever got here. I can't keep my eyes on the menu for long though. I keep watching the door instead.

"Are you sure this is where he said they were coming?" I ask Izzy.

"I'm just as sure now as I was when you asked me five minutes ago. And five minutes before that. Can we please order before I die of starvation?"

"Sorry." I force myself to focus and choose a beef and broccoli dish, fried dumplings, and pork fried rice. When the waitress comes over to take our order, my eyes once again stray toward the door.

"Would you just relax?" Izzy says as soon as the waitress is gone. "They'll either show or they won't. Not much you can do about it now."

"But you're sure this is where he said—"

"Yes, I'm sure." Izzy sighs.

"Okay, I'm sorry." I pry my eyes away from the door and look at Izzy. "You're right. I'm being stupid. Talk to me about something. Distract me."

"Okay, you asked for it."

"Uh-oh."

"I got a call about the DNA results this afternoon right after you left."

"Which ones?"

"All of them."

"Oh." I feel panicky all of a sudden. My worst fears are about to be either confirmed or laid to rest and I'm not sure which outcome I want. "Tell me about the test on Karen and Mike first."

"Okay. Karen Owenby, or should I say Sharon Carver, and Mike Halverson were definitely brother and sister, just as we suspected."

"Not a big surprise given what we know," I say.

"Why the different names?" Dom asks.

"Sharon Carver was once Sharon Halverson," I explain. "Arnie uncovered a Kentucky marriage license issued to a Sharon Halverson and a Nathaniel Carver. Apparently they divorced less than a year later but Sharon kept the name."

Dom nods. "And do you know for sure that the woman you knew as Karen Owenby was Sharon Carver?"

"We do," says Izzy. "We finally tracked down a dentist in Kentucky who treated Sharon Carver and got some dental films for comparison. It's definitely the same woman."

There is a moment of silence, during which I stare at the tablecloth, afraid to meet Izzy's gaze. Finally he says, "Do you want to know about the DNA test regarding the baby or would you rather I keep that one to myself?"

I take in a deep breath and brace myself. "Tell me."

"David was the father."

I don't know what to say. I expect to feel something—anger, disappointment, righteous indignation . . . something. But I don't. Izzy watches me with a wary expression on his face. "Aren't you going to say anything?"

"What's to say? It happened. It's done. It's time to move on."

"You make it sound awfully simple."

"It is," I tell him with a shrug. "It took me a while to get past the emotional aspects of David's betrayal. I'm still not completely over it, but at least I'm to the point where I can look at everything with a bit of objectivity. And I realize that by sleeping with someone else, David showed a total disregard not only for our marriage, but for my health, hell, for my *life.* I can't forgive him for that. Nor can I ever trust him again."

Izzy leans close and drops his voice to just above a whisper. "I do have one other bit of news for you," he says. "But you can't let it go beyond this table because I violated some rules to get it."

"Okay."

"You already know that the HIV test we ran on Karen came back negative," he says, and I nod. "But I had Arnie run one on the blood sample from David, as well. It was also negative, so you don't need to worry."

I squeeze my eyes closed with relief. "Thank you, Izzy. I definitely owe you for this one."

"You're very welcome."

Dom says, "What a mess this has been."

"You've got that right," I agree. "Though there is at least one person who benefited from it all. Alison Miller."

Because Sid and Gina were both prominent figures and the sordid details of their secretive lives made for sensational coverage, reporters from all over the country have descended on Sorenson in the past week, hounding anyone and everyone they think might be able to give them any information. Izzy and I have kept our lips zipped, refusing to give a statement. But Alison Miller has been basking in her newfound celebrity, doling out tidbits as she sees fit, wielding her power with utter joy. Rumor has it she's been negotiating with several sources for the rights to the pictures she snapped of me, so I called Lucien and had him threaten both Alison and the paper with a major lawsuit should the pictures appear in any form, anywhere.

Lucien informed me this morning that Alison has since withdrawn the pictures from the market, but I am only partially relieved. The knowledge that Lucien insisted on copies of the pictures, purportedly for his case file, makes me shudder.

"And speaking of Alison Miller," Izzy says, "guess who just came through the door?"

I start to turn and look but stop myself. "I don't want them to think I knew they were coming," I say. "Or that I care at all that they're together. So you have to tell me what's going on."

"Well, they're hanging up their coats now and—"

"Did Hurley help her take off her coat?" I ask.

"He did," Izzy says, giving me an apologetic look.

"Damn."

"Now they're talking to the hostess and . . . here they come, heading for a table."

"Does he have his arm around her?"

"Nope, no physical contact of any kind."

"Good," I say with a wicked smile. "Are they coming by us?"

"Yes, they are." I expect Izzy to divert his gaze but instead he perks up and waves. "Hello there," he says loudly.

I sense Hurley's presence behind me before I turn to look at him. There he is, in all his long-legged, blue-eyed glory. And standing right beside him is Alison, looking much better than I like in a snug-fitting slacks-and-sweater outfit. Not surprisingly, her choice of jewelry includes a camera, which is hanging around her neck.

"Good evening, folks," Hurley says, nodding at Izzy and Dom before turning those baby blues on me. "Fancy meeting you here." There is a twinkle in his eye and I know he suspects our presence here isn't mere coincidence. Particularly since Izzy, at my behest, pumped him for information earlier in the week about where he was taking Alison on their date.

"Hello," I say, giving the two of them my best smile and noting that Alison looks infuriatingly smug.

"Would you care to join us?" Izzy offers. "There's plenty of room."

"No, thank you," Alison says quickly.

"We'd love to," says Hurley at the same time.

I want to grab Izzy's face and give him a huge kiss.

"I meant to call you today anyway, Izzy," Hurley says. "To clear up some final details on the Owenby and Halverson cases."

"Well, if Alison won't mind us talking business over dinner," Izzy says. "I'll try not to touch on anything too unappetizing."

I arch my brows at Alison but keep my smile in place. I can tell she is warring with herself over her desire to keep Hurley away from me and her desire to hear what Hurley and Izzy are going to discuss, knowing they might provide a few juicy new details that can further augment her position as the quintessential news source in town.

"Okay," Alison says finally, the professional side of her ego winning out. "We'll be happy to join you. And I'm sure I can take whatever you two fellas want to dish out."

We are seated at a corner booth with me on one end and Dom on the other, Izzy positioned between us. Alison quickly sizes up the situation and slides in next to me, no doubt to keep Hurley from sitting there. That leaves the spot next to Dom for Hurley, putting him across the table from me and Alison.

"I got the results back on the DNA test for Owenby and Halverson," Izzy says. And with that, my joy at having Hurley at the table is replaced by a fear that the other DNA test will be discussed in Alison's presence. "They were definitely related," Izzy tells him. "Brother and sister."

"So that's confirmed?" Alison asks. "I can print that?"

"Yes, you can print it," Izzy says.

Alison looks mightily pleased. This latest tidbit is just what she needs to support the speculations she's already written up for the paper regarding Karen Owenby's fake identity. As a result, the hospital is facing a PR nightmare, trying to explain how one of their surgical nurses not only lied about who she was, but also about being a nurse. I am pretty certain Alison's name has to be at the top of Molinaro's Fecal Roster right about now. In fact, they are running a pool down at the bakery as to how long it will be before Alison disappears. It can't be soon enough for me.

Molinaro does get one break, however. The blood tests on Sidney Carrigan failed to reveal any sign of the HIV virus. He did, however, have colon cancer. It was discovered during the autopsy and it was so widespread that Sid's life expectancy couldn't have been much more than a year. While we can only guess at the truth, it seems to make sense that Sid took his overall loss of health—the muscle wasting, loss of appetite, and all the other physical symptoms brought on by the cancer—as a sign that he had developed AIDS. Given his lifestyle, Mike Halverson's status, and the degree of intimacy the two men shared, it's easy to see how Sid came to that conclusion. He had probably shared his suspicions with Mike, who then passed them on to his sister, giving her the ammunition she needed for her blackmail scheme.

Sid's misfortune is serendipitous luck for the hospital. One minute they were facing the ordeal of trying to explain to hundreds of patients how they might have been contaminated with the HIV virus by their surgeon, a prospect that had lawyers from thousands of miles away sniffing around every Sorenson resident who had been operated on during the past five years. Now the hospital is in the clear in that regard, though it will probably be years before they can breathe easy over the whole mess, if ever.

"Well, it's nice to know we had a few of the facts right," Hurley says. "I swear, I've never seen such a jumbled-up mess of evidence."

"Is it true that you actually suspected Mattie at one point?" Alison asks. She follows the question with a little laugh, no doubt intending to make it appear as if her interest is purely conversational.

"Not really," Hurley says, smiling at me and winking. "I was pretty certain that the shock she expressed at the scene of the Owenby murder, when she first realized who the victim was, was genuine. Someone with a real acting talent might have been able to fool me, but the more I got to know Mattie, the more certain I became that acting isn't one of her fortes."

I scowl at that, but let it go. I am too pleased with the fact that Hurley winked at me in Alison's presence to let such a petty criticism get me down.

"There's one thing I still don't understand," Alison says. "How did this Joey Dewhurst guy happen to get involved?"

Izzy jumps in to answer that one. "He was following Mattie around. According to Arnie, the guy's got a huge crush on her."

"Had," I corrected.

"You're right," Izzy says. "Your little matchmaking scheme worked like a charm. Arnie said Joey and Cinder have had lunch together twice already and have plans this weekend for dinner and a movie."

"This Dewhurst guy was stalking you?" Alison says, looking over at me.

"Not stalking, exactly," I explain. "He's basically harmless, just a bit eccentric. He's got the mentality of a twelve-year-old and has this superhero fantasy. So he would drive around in his van wearing his superhero outfit, pretending to save me from all sorts of imagined perils, until he finally saved me from a real one."

I shift my attention to Hurley. "I thought that burgundy-and-gray van I kept seeing was someone you had tailing me. It never occurred to me that it might be Joey."

"I probably should have had someone tailing you," Hurley says, making Alison frown. "As it was, you're lucky Joey was there."

"Damn right," Izzy says. He looks at Alison and continues his story. "So Joey was driving by Mattie's house that night when he saw her pull out of her driveway. He followed her, and when she pulled in at the Carrigans', he drove by, parked a ways down the road, and walked back. He saw Mattie and Brian go into the house and then he saw Gina show up. He heard a shot and moved in closer, saw that the front door was open, and saw Brian bleeding and unconscious in the hallway."

"How is Brian?" I ask.

"He's okay," Hurley says. "The bullet didn't hit any major organs. It will be a while before he's back to work, but he's damned lucky to be alive."

Alison scowls again and looks at Hurley. "So how did *you* end up at the Carrigan house?" she asks, her voice tinged with suspicion.

"Well, after following Mattie home, I came here and ordered some stuff to go. I was worried that Mattie hadn't eaten anything." Alison's scowl deepens and I can't resist a smile. "But by the time I got back to Mattie's place, she was gone. Then Brian called me on his cell phone to tell me that Mattie was out at the Carrigans', so I headed out there to see what kind of trouble she was getting into."

"I was just doing my job," I say defensively.

"Almost getting yourself killed in the process," Hurley grumbles. "Going back out there was a stupid thing to do. We would have found that gun cache soon enough."

"But Mattie figured it out first," Dom says proudly.

"It was the rug that did it," I tell them. "That and Rubbish." I explain how watching the cat play with the rug tipped me to the changed position of both the rug and the chair in Sid's den. "I didn't know why the chair had been moved," I told them, "but I felt certain it had been and that Gina was trying to hide something. And then I remembered that the second hair we found on Karen Owenby's body was short and bleached blond—just like Gina's hair. That's when I knew I had to get back out to the house and look under that rug."

"You should have called me," Hurley grumbles.

"I realize that now. Sorry."

"Apology accepted."

"I want to know how *you* came to be at the house, Alison," I say, shifting to face her.

She looks a little embarrassed. "I was, um, hoping to get some pictures. For the paper."

I don't believe her for a second. I suspect she was following Hurley, possibly in hopes of getting a news scoop, but more likely because she was worried about Hurley's interest in me.

"There's still one other matter I'd like to clear up," Hurley says.

"What's that?" Alison says, looking relieved that the subject matter has shifted from her own escapades.

A wicked smile flits across Hurley's face and he leans across the table, locking eyes with me. "What's this nipple incident I keep hearing about?"

Izzy snorts and says, "You don't want to know."

I stare at Hurley, hesitating, and he stares right back, waiting. The energy between us sparks and snaps. Alison glares at us both for a second and then leans toward me, trying to get in the way of our eye contact.

A chirping sound breaks the tension and Hurley reaches into his pocket for his cell phone. He flips it open, listens a minute, and then says, "Be right there."

I smile sweetly at Hurley. "Darn," I say. "No time to explain now."

"There's time," Hurley says, snapping his phone closed and looking smug. "You and Izzy are coming with me. Better get your food to go because we have an appointment with another dead body."

Halloween night in Sorenson, Wisconsin, usually resembles any other small town: trick-or-treaters, costume parties, and lots of cheerfully scary decorations. But Deputy Coroner Mattie Winston is finding this year a little different, because among all the fake carnage is a very real, very dead body . . .

When Mattie and her boss/best friend, Izzy, are called to the home of waitress and part-time model Shannon Tolliver, they find the ghoulish decorations just a bit too authentic. For among the fake blood and skeletons is the corpse of Shannon herself—and the evidence screams murder.

Since the whole town knows Shannon recently had a very public argument with her estranged husband, Erik, he's suspect #1 for homicide detective Steve Hurley. Tall, dark, and blissfully blue-eyed detective Steve Hurley, that is. . . . But Mattie happens to know Erik truly loved his wife, and is simply incapable of the brutal act—even though he owns the exact same caliber handgun as the murder weapon . . .

Determined to unearth the truth—and maybe spend a little quality time with Detective Hunky—Mattie puts her scalpel-sharp medical skills to work, and digs a little deeper. What she uncovers is stranger than anyone could have imagined . . .

It seems Shannon's murder is just the tip of a very fatal iceberg. Now, in order to solve a case that's getting more dangerous by the minute—and to save Erik from the slammer—Mattie will have to risk everything to catch a killer who's capable of doing anything once he's cornered. And this time, it's not just Mattie's life that's on the line . . .

Turn the page for an exclusive sneak peek at *Scared Stiff*,
the new Mattie Winston mystery by Annelise Ryan.
Available in hardcover in September 2010.

Chapter 1

Despite the fact that I hang around dead bodies a lot these days, I find the scene before me very disturbing. The backdrop is ordinary enough: a well-maintained, ranch-style suburban home set on a generous plot of land near the edge of town. But any sense of normalcy ends with the front yard, which is littered with dead bodies. Fortunately, only one of the bodies is real, though I suppose it's not so fortunate for the victim in question, who I've been told has been murdered.

As if the body farm isn't surreal enough, my clothing adds to the absurdity: I'm wearing a full-skirted, white ballroom dress with puffy sleeves that make my shoulders look wider than a linebacker's. Clipped to the bodice is my ID badge, which bears my name, Mattie Winston, and my title, deputy coroner. Though I'm still kind of new at this dead body stuff, I'm pretty sure my outfit isn't the sort of couture one would normally wear to a crime scene. But then, who knows? I don't think there's a designer who has tackled this particular niche. I can see possibilities though: shirts and pants with chalk outlines drawn on them, sexy, peek-a-boo blouses with strategically placed bullet holes and knife tears, and, of course, lots of blood-red colored material.

In spite of the macabre scene and thoughts, in a perverse sort of way I'm happy to be here. Five minutes ago I was at a

Halloween costume party being bored to tears by "William-not-Bill," an obsessive-compulsive accountant in a Dracula costume. He is a date my friend, Izzy, fixed me up with, making me wonder what horrible thing I've done to Izzy to earn such retribution. After less than an hour in William-not-Bill's company, I was trying desperately to come up with a plausible plan of escape when my beeper chirped and saved me. My relief was countered by a smidgen of guilt when I remembered that work for me meant someone else was dead, but probably not as dead as the date I was on. It was stone-cold, bones-only, well-beyond-the-putrid-stage dead.

I tried not to look too relieved at my reprieve as I snatched my beeper up from the table and gave William-not-Bill an apologetic smile. "Duty calls," I said, feigning disappointment. "I'm afraid we'll have to make it an early night."

William-not-Bill frowned and said, "Darn it. Are you sure you need to go?"

I'd never been so sure of anything in my entire life. "I'm afraid so," I told him.

"I'd really like to see you again. Can I give you a call sometime?"

I would have rather stabbed myself blind with a dull fork and was tempted to say so when Izzy, who is only five feet tall and dressed tonight as the Keebler Elf, tapped me on the shoulder.

Aside from being my date rescue, Izzy is my neighbor, my landlord, and my boss. He is also the anti-me: dark where I'm light, short where I'm tall, and male to my female. We do have three things in common however: fat-hoarding metabolisms, fondness for men, and jobs that require the removal of human organs. Izzy removes organs because he's the county's Medical Examiner. I used to remove organs, or at least assist in the process, inside a hospital operating room, which is where my soon-to-be-ex-husband, David, works as a surgeon. But after catching a coworker named Karen Owenby playing with a certain private organ on David, I ditched both him and the job. Now I work with Izzy in the M. E.'s office and while I still assist with organ removal, the goods aren't as fresh as they used to be.

"Mattie? You ready?" Izzy asked as William-not-Bill pouted like a child.

"Absolutely." I got up from the table and beat a hasty exit—not an easy task given the wide girth of my gown, the two-foot wand I was carrying, and the crown that kept sliding off my head. I left Izzy, whose legs are only a third the length of mine, behind in my wake, along with several broken drink glasses my skirt knocked from tables as I passed. By the time Izzy caught up to me I was standing next to his car in the parking lot, tapping my foot impatiently.

"What's the rush?" he asked. "Afraid a house might drop on you?"

"I'm Glinda, the *good* witch," I reminded him. "Houses don't fall on Glinda."

"Then why the big hurry? I haven't seen you run that fast for anything other than ice cream in a long time."

"Very funny," I said, giving him a dirty look. "I didn't want to give Dracula a chance to ask for my number again. Though I have to admit his costume was perfect. He spent the last two hours sucking the life out of me." I shook my head woefully. "I can't believe I let you talk me into dating that bozo. He has a comb-over for Christ's sake. His only saving grace is that he's tall." This is actually an important asset for me. I hit the six-foot mark at the age of sixteen, which made me a good foot taller than all of the boys for most of my high school years. That, combined with my ample bosom, made me very popular during the slow songs at school dances.

Izzy opened his door, got in the car, and reached over to unlock my side. The car is a fully restored Impala from the sixties. No such thing as automatic locks. Unfortunately, there are no bucket seats either, which means I have to pretzel six feet of me into the same amount of space Izzy uses.

I ripped the crown from my head and threw it and my

wand into the back seat. Then I tried unsuccessfully to stuff the skirt of my gown down around me. As we pulled out of the parking lot, I imagined it must look like a giant puff ball was sitting in the passenger seat.

"Give William a break," Izzy said as I spat taffeta. "So he's got a touch of Obsessive-Compulsive Disorder. What's the big deal? It's his attention to detail that makes him such an ace accountant."

"A *touch* of OCD? I'll have you know he shot his cuffs at least fifty times, straightened the tablecloth a dozen times, and counted how many people were at the party every ten minutes. I can't guess how many times he cleaned all the silverware at the table. And don't even get me started on the fangs."

Izzy conceded with a sigh. "Okay, maybe he's a little anal retentive."

"Doubt it," I snapped back. "He's got his head so far up his ass there isn't room there for anything else. And just how old is he, anyway?"

"Late forties, maybe early fifties."

"That's a bit of a spread, don't you think? He's got to be at least fifteen years older than me."

"I'm twelve years older than Dom."

"That's different. You're gay."

"What's that got to do with it?" Izzy laughed. "Besides, it's not like you were looking for a serious date. You just wanted someone to tote along to make Hurley jealous."

This was true. Steve Hurley is a tall, dark, and blissfully blue-eyed homicide detective that I've known for all of three weeks, ever since I became Izzy's assistant. For me it was lust at first sight, which unfortunately occurred over Karen Owenby's freshly murdered body. Things kind of went downhill from there, particularly after I became a suspect in the case.

"Clearly it was a wasted effort," I pouted.

"Hey, it's not my fault Hurley didn't show up at the party."

With that one sentence, Izzy shot straight to the heart of my misery. I sulked for the remainder of the journey, which was all of three minutes since Sorenson isn't a very big town. When we arrived at our destination, I unfolded myself from Izzy's car like a performer in Cirque du Soleil and stood a moment to let the blood flow back into my legs. Then I reached into the back seat and took out my processing kit.

That's how I ended up here on the edges of suburbia, surrounded by bodies on a Saturday night, dressed like a white witch carrying a large tackle box.

Chapter 2

Izzy and I pause long enough to don gloves and shoe covers. With that done, he grabs his camera while I take out the digital recorder he gave me a couple of weeks ago for documenting scene observations. I turn the recorder on and put it in voice activation mode. After trying to find a place on my outfit to clip it, I settle for sticking it down inside my cleavage, or what a boy in my high school geography class once dubbed the "hot-and-gentle divide."

Despite the darkness outside, the yard is brightly lit thanks to Halloween spotlights and the flashing bars atop the cop cars parked in the driveway. At the foot of a huge oak tree off to my right, a man sits strapped into a large wooden chair. On his head is something that looks like an old-fashioned electrocution helmet. Nailed to the tree a foot above his head is a large board that has the words ON and OFF painted on it with a fork-shaped lever clearly placed in the ON position. Wires are running from the lever to the helmet and the clothes on the man appear to be singed.

On closer inspection I see that the helmet is actually a metal mixing bowl turned upside down and the handle on the board is made out of tin foil, but the effect is realistic enough to make me shiver.

On the opposite side of the tree is another body, this one

hanging from a thick rope, its face painted a ghastly blue color, the body swinging slightly in the night breeze. A third body is half buried in a makeshift grave, its hands and feet protruding from the freshly-turned soil. At its head is a gravestone that bears the inscription: *Who turned out the lights?*

Four more bodies are strewn about, all of them wearing blood-soaked clothes: one has a large butcher knife protruding from its chest; another has its head lying a conspicuous distance from its body. The third one is missing its arms and legs, though they are lying nearby, and the fourth one is splayed halfway down the steps of the front porch, a glistening trail of blood marking its journey from the front door.

This last body is the one I zero in on since there is a trio of police officers—two in uniform, one in plainclothes—grouped around it. I know most of the cops in town either because they're Sorenson lifers like me, or because we became acquainted years ago when I worked in the ER. I even dated one of them briefly, a sweet guy named Larry Johnson who is the plainclothes officer in tonight's group. I never felt any reciprocal attraction to Larry, but if I had it would have died some time ago when he came into the hospital for hemorrhoid surgery. I was the scrub nurse on the case and the sight of Larry's jingleberries hanging above his dingleberries would have put a definite damper on future intimacies.

One of the uniforms in tonight's group is a guy named Al who I've known for a decade or so, but the second uniform is new to me, and he looks like he's twelve. The one face conspicuously absent from the group is Steve Hurley's.

"Hey, where are Sleepy, Sneezy, and Dopey?" Larry yells as Izzy and I approach. Al and the new guy snigger. I realize they have misinterpreted our costumes, mistaking me for Snow White and Izzy for one of my dwarfs.

"I don't know," I say, setting down my scene kit and glancing around the yard. "Where are the real cops?"

"Ouch," says Larry as the other two groan. "Okay, truce."

I turn my attention to the body on the stairs and wrinkle my nose. There is a faint odor in the air, one that tells me this body has been here a while. The weather over the past week or so has been uncharacteristically warm for late October in Wisconsin, with temperatures in the high seventies during the day and the low sixties at night. Normally we'd expect highs in the fifties with frost or snow warnings at night, but this year October decided to go out on a high note. This last gasp of summer proved a delightful treat here in a state where snow blowers are considered a necessity five months out of the year, but it also allowed putrefaction to set in a little sooner than it otherwise would have.

"Do you know who she is?" Izzy asks, using his camera to shoot pictures and video of both the body and our immediate surroundings.

"We're pretty certain it's Shannon Tolliver," Larry says.

One of the advantages of living in a small town is that eventually you get to know almost everyone, if not by name, than at least by face. Here the six degrees of separation are often narrowed down to one or two. I'm at a slight disadvantage because of my last job. Even though working as a nurse in the operating room of the town's hospital allowed me to cross paths with a lot of people, most of them were draped, gowned, bonneted, and drugged into oblivion. As a result, I'm quicker to recognize some people by their navels or knees as opposed to their faces.

Tonight's victim is someone I do know by face, though it's hard to be sure it's her. The body is lying on its back with the feet at the top of the stairs and the head at the bottom. Gravity has done its job. What little blood is left in the body has settled in the head and face, causing gross discoloration and swelling.

"Who found her?" I ask.

Al says, "A couple of trick-or-treaters who got the scare

of their lives when their parents drove them to this house. The parents rounded the kids up and then called it in on a cell phone."

I grimace. Kids traipsing near our corpse and running hell-bent through the yard means contamination of our scene.

I note two holes in Shannon's torso that appear to be bullet entry wounds, both of them surrounded by the blood-soaked cloth of her blouse. Years of working as a nurse have gifted me with the rather dubious talent of being able to estimate blood loss with a reasonable degree of accuracy. A quick estimate of the dried pool beneath Shannon's body and the trail leading back from it to the house tells me there's a good chance she bled to death.

Squealing wheels sound behind us and, as I turn to see a familiar black car pull up, my heart quickens and a different kind of shiver goes through me.

Hurley.

He parks right behind one of the spotlights, forcing me to squint as I search eagerly for his long-legged stride. But something is wrong. The silhouette I see has two heads and way too many arms. For a second I think it must be Hurley's Halloween costume but it turns out to be something much scarier. It's Hurley walking side by side with Alison Miller.

I feel a pang of jealousy and mutter a curse under my breath. Alison Miller, a photographer and reporter for the bi-weekly *Sorenson Journal*, used to be my friend. We went to high school together and while we never hung out much, we maintained a cordial, if distant, relationship. Our current status is a bit more strained, thanks to her attempts to print a picture of me bare-chested on the front page of the paper a few weeks ago, and the fact that she has suddenly become the main obstacle between me and Detective Hurley, assuming, of course, that Hurley has forgotten about that unfortunate incident when I barfed on his shoes.

It isn't just the sight of them together that bothers me. I

knew they had plans to attend a Halloween party tonight—the same party Izzy and I just left—because I was there a week ago when Alison all but threw herself at Hurley and demanded that he take her. What bothers me is the fact that they never made it to the party but are still together. What have they been doing for the past two hours while I sat letting Dracula turn me into one of the undead?

Both of them are in costume: Alison looks disturbingly cute dressed as a genie, and Hurley, rather unimaginatively, is dressed like an Elliott Ness era FBI agent, though the hat does give him a sexy, debonair, I-want-to-bite-your-lip quality. I give their outfits a quick once-over searching for signs of disarray or a fresh-out-of-the-sack look, but don't find any. It's a mild reassurance at best and any relief I might feel vanishes when I see the smug expression on Alison's face.

Her camera is slung around her neck and she is holding it with one hand, prepared to take a quick snap if something worthy should present itself. Even in high school Alison always had her camera close by and ready. It earned her the nickname Snapper, a moniker that always made all the boys snigger. Nowadays she's a freelance reporter/photographer and the primary photo source for our local paper, so a camera is still as ubiquitous an accessory as ever for her. I briefly wonder if she sleeps with it but as soon as the thought hits my mind, I flash on an image of Hurley naked in bed with her, and my face grows uncomfortably hot.

"Hi, everyone," Alison says with a perky little wave of her hand. She eyes me and Izzy and says, "How cute, Snow White and Doc. What a clever idea."

Before I can correct her she has raised her camera, snapped a shot, and blinded me with her flash.

"No pictures unless I say so," Hurley grumbles and I am instantly grateful for his reprimand. I smile in his general direction and blink hard several times, trying to get my vision back. Then I realize I probably look like I'm batting my eyes at him and stop.

"Not to worry," Alison says. "That was just a fun picture for Mattie and Izzy, nothing official."

I can see the vague outlines of everyone as my eyes struggle to adjust to the dark, and it seems they are all looking at Shannon again. So I focus my own gaze in the same direction.

"What do we have?" Hurley asks.

Izzy says, "Mattie, do you want to take this one?"

Oh goody, a chance to impress Hurley! I nod solemnly to hide my delight. Since I can't see very clearly, I try to remember what I'd noted earlier as I start to speak.

"The victim's tentative ID is Shannon Tolliver, a thirty-something female and the resident of this house. It appears she was shot at least twice, once in the chest and once in the upper abdominal area. Given the location of the wounds and the amount of blood beneath the body, I'd guess one or both of the bullets pierced the liver or aorta and she quickly bled out."

"Any guess as to time of death?" Hurley asks.

I'm still half blind so as I move closer to the body to check for the presence of livor mortis and rigor mortis, I fail to see the bottommost step to the porch. My toe rams into the riser and my upper body continues its forward motion as my feet stop dead in their tracks. I feel myself falling and pinwheel my arms in a desperate effort to regain some balance, but the laws of physics are against me. I'm bracing for a collision with the hard wooden stairs when a strong arm wraps around my waist and pulls me back.

"Careful there," Hurley says, his breath warm in my ear.

I'm momentarily in heaven as I feel the length of my backside come into contact with Hurley's front side, but my rapture evaporates with his next words.

"Christ, you're like a bull in a china shop."

Hurley's arm uncoils itself from my waist and I miss its warmth immediately even though my face is burning hot enough to start a fire. My vision is almost back to normal and I can see Izzy shaking his head. He steps up and takes over the examination, leaving me to stand where I am, trying not to look as stupid as I feel.

A few seconds later I step forward more carefully and kneel on the other side of the body, taking care to shove the bulk of my gown between my legs so I don't contaminate the blood pools.

Together we begin our examination, looking for any gross trace evidence on the surface of the body before we touch or move anything. There are several stray hairs stuck in the congealed blood surrounding her wounds but their long length and blonde color makes me suspect they are Shannon's own. I pick them up one at a time and place each in its own evidence envelope, sealing and labeling the specimens as I go.

Shannon's left arm is beneath her body, hiding that hand from view, so examination of that will have to wait until we move her. But on her right hand, which is flung out in front of her, I notice that the knuckles appear raw and abraded. I wonder if she incurred this injury in her crawl and fall down the stairs, or if she managed to deliver a blow to her attacker during a struggle. If the latter, I know there might be valuable evidence there so I carefully place a paper bag over the hand, securing it with evidence tape. In doing so, I notice her arm is stiff. Izzy notes the same thing in both of her legs.

"None of the lividity blanches and it appears she is in full rigor," he announces.

Eager to redeem myself in front of everybody, I jump in and say, "Given the outside temperatures we've had, that means she's likely been dead for somewhere between twelve and thirty-six hours."

Izzy nods approvingly and says, "That is correct."

I hear Alison mutter a little *hmph* behind me and can't help but smile. But then she says, "Twelve to thirty-six? Is that the best you can do? That's a twenty-four-hour window of time."

My initial impulse is to leap across Shannon's body, grab Alison by the throat, and throttle her. But before I can, Izzy jumps in.

"It appears there is the start of some putrefaction here," he says, pointing to a faint greenish patch of skin on the lower right side of Shannon's swollen abdomen, just above the waistband of her pants. "That helps us narrow things down a little more. Odds are she's been dead for around twenty-four hours, give or take a few. Here in the field, that's the closest prediction I can make but once we get the body to the morgue and do some further analyses, we might be able to pinpoint the time of death more precisely."

I glance at my watch, see that it's just past eight-thirty in the evening, and do a quick mental calculation. "So time of death for now is likely sometime yesterday evening." I pause and glance around, suppressing a shiver when I realize Shannon's body lay out here all day long with no one noticing. It saddens me to think how hard she worked to decorate her lawn for Halloween, not knowing she would soon become a part of her own gruesome diorama.

After unfolding a white plastic sheet and carefully placing it over the body to preserve any surface evidence we might have missed, Izzy and I turn Shannon's body on its side to examine her back. There is a slight sucking sound as her body separates from the large pool of congealed blood beneath her and that, combined with the wafting scent of rot and decay, makes my stomach lurch.

Izzy examines Shannon's back and announces, "It's hard to be sure with all the blood but I don't see any exit wounds. So hopefully we'll have some ballistic evidence once I do her post."

Hurley is scratching down notes in a small spiral-bound notebook as we ease the body back into its original position, first making sure to tuck the plastic wrap sheet in place. With that done, Izzy and I secure the wrap, completely enclosing the body. Then we stand, remove our bloodied gloves, don new ones, and start taking in the rest of the murder scene.

I study the blood trail leading from the body to the porch and from there into the house. "It doesn't make much sense for the killer to have dragged her outside where she might be found sooner," I surmise. "And the amount of blood in this trail suggests she was alive until she got to the stairs. So I'm guessing she was shot somewhere inside the house and managed to drag herself out here."

Izzy says, "I agree."

"But why?" I pose. "Why come out here rather than phone for help from the house?"

Hurley rewards me with a smile that makes Alison's pout deepen. "Excellent question," he says. "Let's go inside and find out."